To Bruce,
"last of the real grumpy men"!

ABBADON'S HANDMAN

by James Caton

PublishAmerica
Baltimore

© 2006 by James Caton.
All rights reserved. No part of this book may be reproduced, stored in a retrieval system or transmitted in any form or by any means without the prior written permission of the publishers, except by a reviewer who may quote brief passages in a review to be printed in a newspaper, magazine or journal.

First printing

All characters appearing in this work are fictitious. Any resemblance to real persons, living or dead, is purely coincidental.

ISBN: 1-4137-9468-8
PUBLISHED BY PUBLISHAMERICA, LLLP
www.publishamerica.com
Baltimore

Printed in the United States of America

To Vi.

To Mac, who never flinched in the face of the appalling and unrelenting ignorance of the writer with the word processor. Thanks.

Prelude

The island lay sprawled in the vast sea, fifty miles long and twenty-seven wide. It was dominated by a huge mountain, that reared from the sea at the southern tip and thrust out into the sky like a huge arm, before falling sheer down to the sea five thousand feet below.

The island was ringed almost all the way by jagged rocks, where the sea met the land, with only a small patch of sand where the men laid up the boats. The black earth of the island was more dust than soil and yielded up a sparse harvest of crops every year, forcing the people to take their food from the sea.

The islanders had fished the unforgiving waters for centuries and accepted the death that rode with them on the little boats. The island and those that lived on it existed in a universe dominated by the sea and the inferno of the sun.

Chapter One

The small boats came sliding up through the surf, finally stopping and tilting over onto the sand. The men scrambled over the sides and started up the beach, exhausted by the sea that had fought them through the long night. Now there was wine, food and sleep ahead of them before they would be back, casting the nets, and struggling to live in the great waters. They left the fish heaped on the decks. Others would come down to clear the catch when the sun rose higher in the sky.

Slowly they began to walk across the shelving beach to begin the long climb up the narrow path to the village. Suddenly the man in front stopped and turned round. He held up his hand and motioned them to silence.

"Listen," he said.

They looked around. The pale fingers of light were just flickering through the rough grasses on the dunes.

"What is it?" asked one of them.

The first man pointed down to the beach. "Something there."

The man at the end of the line stumbled and cursed. "There is nothing." He gestured upwards. "Move on!"

It was then that they heard it. A long soft cry of pain. They looked at each other. The sound came again.

"Down there. Behind the high ground." The one who had spoken first stepped off the path and began scrambling over the rough ground down to the dunes. When the sound came again, more urgent this time, they all began to follow him. They came to the dunes and started to climb up through the soft sand, falling back and recovering until they were over the top. They stopped and stood still, listening. This time the sound was a sharp-edged scream.

"There," one of them said, "behind the boat."

Long ago the wrecked boat had slipped from the shore and been smashed against the rocks. It had been pulled up and dragged round to the valley between the dunes and left there. As they rounded the broken timbers they came to a sudden halt.

"Mother of God!" The words hung clear in the morning air.

A woman lay on her back on the sand with her legs drawn up and thighs open. When she saw them she rose up and cried out in a language they did not understand. Then she fell back, her body jerking spasmodically.

They looked at one another.

"She bears a child," said one of them. "Run to the village. Fetch a woman."

She arched her back and screamed shrilly. They gathered round her and knelt down on the sand.

One of the men took off his coat and placed it under the woman's head. "There is no time," he said. "Look at her."

The woman reared up and screamed again, then fell back, her arms spreading wide. Her eyes began to glaze over and her mouth fell open.

"She is dying!" one of them said.

The man who had given the woman his coat looked at the rest of them. "We can save the child."

"How? She is dying…"

"We can cut it from her body," he said.

There was a silence broken only by the sea surging against the rocks at the far end of the beach.

"You would do this?" asked one of them.

The man bent over and put his fingers on the woman's throat. He waited then looked at them and shook his head. "If we wait the child will die."

He pushed the mane of hair back from his eyes and fumbled at his waist and drew out a broad-bladed knife. The others drew close and formed a ring around the woman's body. They were all men who lived with the sea and life and death in its most sudden and extreme forms so they were not deterred by the task before them.

The man with the knife reached down and slit the dress from the woman's body. The men on either side of her pulled it away from the swollen flesh. The knife gleamed in the man's hand as he held it upright above the abdomen. Working quickly, he pierced the distended belly and cut a long channel in the body.

"There is no blood… where is the blood?" he said wonderingly. "She is dry." He laid the knife aside and carefully drew out the tiny body. "Take the blade… cut the cord… quickly."

When the cord was severed they knotted it and the man stood up holding the child. He peered at it.

"It is perfect," he said. "Look!" He held it out for them to see. "It is a man child."

They gathered closer and gently touched the little body. "He does not cry… my own always cried when they came into this world."

The man with the knife gave the child to one of the others and took off his shirt and wrapped it gently round the infant. "We must hurry. He will need milk and a warm place."

"There is a woman who brought a stillborn child four days ago. She will have milk to spare for him," said the man who had first heard the cries of the woman.

Someone pointed at the still figure on the ground. "What of her?"

They looked at one another. Then one of them bent down and took hold of the woman's arms.

"Help me to lift her." He pulled her upright. "We must put her in the dark water."

He nodded. "It will take her far out from the land. We will not see her again."

It was true. The riptide at that point was awesome in its power and rolled out to sea for miles. Anything caught in its path was lost.

Two of the men took her legs and the three of them lifted her and started back along the beach to where the mountain loomed immense against the sky. The others hurried back to the path and began the ascent to the village. The sun was on their backs as they reached it and news of the child had gone before them.

People came out to look at the boy and wondered how he was so peaceful. He made no noise and when the men took him to the woman that had brought her own child a few days before, he settled to her and suckled contentedly.

Everyone came through the narrow streets and gathered at the inn. It was the hub of the village and all discussions of any importance were held within its walls. The men told the rest of the people what had happened on the beach and what they had done with the child's mother.

No one questioned their action. They never wanted intrusions from the outside world and to have told the story to anyone on the boats that came to the islands to buy fish would have certainly brought officials from one of the mainlands with their questions that were not worthy of answers. The woman was gone and they did not speak of her again.

Once a month a police officer from Turkey would come over to the island in a small launch and scramble ashore. He would spend the day sitting in the inn drinking coffee and trying to talk to people that refused to speak to him. His notebook remained empty of the crimes he had come to report. The islanders dealt with their affairs without written laws and did not recognise the ruling of the outside world.

Stealing, assault and adultery were punished by beatings carried out by the relatives of the aggrieved parties. A few murders had been committed throughout the years, and if the guilty ones were found and judged to have acted wrongly they were taken to the high ground and flung into the riptide. There had never been a survivor. It was a harsh system, but they were people with a powerful sense of natural justice and they acted according to their instincts.

The boy remained with the woman that had given him her milk. The villagers gave what food they could spare and he was raised with her four other children as if he were of her own blood. He worked in the fields and took his place in the boats when they put to sea and was part of the life of the village.

It was when he had grown to almost twelve years that the people realised he had powers beyond their understanding.

It had been the time of the great storm that had raged for thirteen days, pounding the island with seas that roared up the beaches and flung the little boats far up into the dunes. The people remained in their homes up on the hillside and watched from the windows at the fury below.

On the fourteenth day, the men struggled through the slashing rain to meet at the inn. Their food was almost gone and they knew the seas were too huge for boats from the mainland to bring help, even if they had known of their plight.

They stood, drinking the bitter wine from the stone mugs and listening to the booming of the surf pounding the shore.

Yola Mora, the innkeeper, shifted his vast bulk on his stool and broke the silence. "A man would be looking for death to put out in that," he said.

Farl, who had four children and was waiting for his fifth to enter the world, shook his head. "My woman is almost at her time. We must have food." He turned to the tall bearded man with the scarred face standing at the window. "What do you say, Lendos? We must do something."

Lendos shrugged. "My children have not eaten for two days. I cannot stay and look at them."

"Better a hungry child than a dead father," said the innkeeper.

"My children will die soon enough if they do not eat," replied Lendos. He moved away from the window and slammed his mug on the rough-hewn wooden counter. "This bastard sea," he said savagely. "I have never seen it like this for so long. Why does it not end?"

Farl shrugged. "It has no reason. It is just the sea."

It was then that they saw the boy in the doorway. The rain had soaked him and the water ran down from his clothes on to the floor. He stood silent, watching them.

Mora moved ponderously out from behind the counter and walked over to him. "What do want here, boy?" he asked.

The boy looked up at him, then round the room. "I have to speak to you... all of you," he said.

Mora gestured impatiently. "Go home. Do you not see there is trouble here? This is no place for you." He took the boy by the shoulder and turned him to the door.

The boy put his hand on Mora's arm. "Please," he said softly.

Mora looked at him for a moment, frowned, then released the boy's shoulder. "What is it?" he asked.

The boy walked to the centre of the room and halted. He wiped his hand over his face and shook his head sending the raindrops flying. "You have to go to the sea tomorrow." His voice was low, but heard by all of them.

Farl laughed harshly. "The storm has made him mad."

The boy held out his hand to them. He spoke slowly, "There will be no danger. All that go will return."

"That is because no one will go," said Farl bitterly. He gestured to the window. "Can you not see? Do you not hear? There is a hell out there. Would you ask men to go into that?"

The boy reached out and took hold of Farl's arm and gently pulled him closer. He looked into his face for a long moment. Then he released him and turned to face the rest of them. "You have to believe me... you will all be held safe," he said.

"Why would they do as you say?" asked Mora contemptuously. "Farl is right. To take a boat into that is to die." He turned to Farl. "Tell him you will not go."

Farl was silent, staring at the boy. "How do you know that I would not die?" he asked slowly.

"Because it is given for me to know," the boy replied.

The room had gone very quiet with all of them intent on the boy. There was no wisdom in the words he spoke, but they were people who understood that sometimes things had no shape or form to put a name to. They watched and listened now.

"Who has given you this to tell us?" asked Lendos.

The boy was silent and then shook his head slowly. "I do not know. But I know that I could never harm you. You brought me into the world and gave me life."

One of the others started to speak but fell silent as Lendos raised his hand. "I have not finished," he said. "Would you come with us?" he asked the boy. He gestured out of the window. "Into that?"

The boy spoke very softly. "No. I must wait on the shore until you return."

"Hah!" the innkeeper sneered. "He will not go with you." He looked round at the men. "He is not as mad as he sounds."

Lendos turned and looked at him, his eyes hard with anger. "Enough!" he said harshly. He stabbed his finger at Mora, the scars on his face white against the dark skin. "You stay here and sell your wine while we fight the sea. You have no words in this." He looked at the rest of them. "We decide."

He turned back to the boy. Despite the roaring outside his words were heard clearly by them all. "If I go and do not return my people will take you to the high ground and give you to the dark water." He looked round the room at them all again, then back to the boy. "Do you hear what I have told you? It will be your life for mine."

The boy stood silent for a moment and then nodded his head once. "Yes."

Lendos went over to the window and stood staring out. Then he turned to them. "I will go."

Mora shook his head disgustedly, but said nothing. The others looked at Lendos and waited. "I will go because to stay here is to starve," he said. "If he is right then we have a chance to live." He gestured at the boy. "If the sea takes me then it takes him."

What he said had truth in it. Their choice was simple. They were all men of the sea and go to it they must even if it took them down into its enormity.

The boy's words had struck into them. Everyone knew how he had been taken from the dead woman's body a long time ago. It had always been felt that he was set apart from them and now they had heard his words they knew it was true. And he had agreed to give up his life if Lendos did not return. Who would do such a thing unless his eyes could see past today?

In the morning the seas were still as high. The men took leave of their families and fought their way onto the beach. The boats had to be dragged down from the dunes and pulled to the shore. The men fell, stumbling and cursing, the ropes burning their hands. The boy watched them until they were all grouped and ready to leave. Then he went to each of the boats and placed his hand on them and said something that the roar of the sea took from their ears. When he had finished he stepped back and nodded to Lendos.

When they had gone five lengths of a boat from the shore the sea fell around them and they vanished from sight.

The boy stayed on the beach all day huddled by a rock and soaked by the spray. No one came near him. The women had wept and begged their men not to go and said the boy was mad. Now they shunned him. Some even made curses in his name. Lendos had told his people what had passed between him and the boy and now they came down to the shore to watch and wait.

As the day died into night and the sea still broke with shattering force against the land, the fragile hopes they had tried to hold onto were lost. They knew that nothing could live in those monstrous waters. More of them came to the beach now and stood bent against the tearing wind. They held onto one another and spoke, pointing at the boy and nodding. The people of Lendos began to move towards him. They had waited long enough. It was time for the boy to match the sacrifice that Lendos had made.

They had almost reached him when one of the women standing higher up the beach cried out and pointed to the sea. They turned from the boy just as the first boat crashed through the surf and ground to a halt on the shore. The people stood transfixed for a moment, then raced down to the men clambering down from it. They embraced them and gazed at them with wonder. Then a second boat and a third came in. Then all of them returned. The people from up in the village who had been watching from their homes came running to the beach. Some wept and were unable to speak at the sight of the men that had come through the hell.

Then Lendos walked slowly over to the boy and held him in his arms. He did not speak and they stood for a moment in silence. Then the tall man turned to the rest of them and shouted above the wind.

"There is enough for all." He pointed at the boats. "They are full. Take what you need and feed yourselves."

Everyone came and helped to unload the fish. In one hour the smoke from the cooking fires was being snatched from the chimneys by the wind. People sat in their homes and ate and praised the boy who had known that the sea would not harm them.

That night they gathered at the inn to hear the men tell of what had happened. Mora had laid a huge log on the fire and the red-glow heat warmed the room.

When the men had mugs of wine in their hands Lendos stood up and looked round at them all. "I did not think I would ever be in this place again," he said. There were murmurs of assent from the men that had gone with him.

He took a pull at his wine while they waited for him to continue. "When we left it was to die." They nodded in agreement. "The sea was too strong for us," he went on. "We did not use the sails… they would have gone before we put a rope to them." He stopped, searching for the words to tell it. "We just moved through the water… as if something was drawing us on…"

Farl broke in eagerly. "Then the miracle… the wind died… the sea was calm… but the sky was like night." He shook his head amazed. "We did not believe it… it was as if we were held in a safe place while all outside was madness."

"And the fish," said Lendos, "the fish were everywhere around us." He spread his hands wide. "A man could pick them out of the sea… the boats were too small to take them all." He stopped, his eyes gleaming with excitement at what they had seen. "We could have filled them again and again!"

One of the old men that had sat and watched for them leaned forward. "Were you not afraid to leave such a place to bring the boat back through the storm?" he asked.

Amas, the youngest to have gone, shook his head. "I was afraid when we went out. But then we came to the still water and I knew that we would live to come back."

The old man spat into the glowing fire and shrugged his shoulders. "I gave you to the dead."

They stayed long into the night telling it over and over, hardly believing what had happened to them. The children finally fell asleep and the men carried them through the narrow streets to their homes. The people were sure now that they had enough food to last until the sea ran at peace again.

After that the boy began to hold a special place among them. He sought nothing that he did not earn in the fields or at sea. But they would go to him when something happened that needed a judgement beyond their wisdom. As he grew older they spoke among themselves, and said that he should take a woman to live with and bear his children. When it was put to him he said that his life would not be lived like that. They asked him what he meant. He shook his head and did not answer. They did not ask him again.

One year a sickness came to them, a death that took only the young. Some thought it came in with rats off the boats that came from the mainland to buy their fish. Others said it was carried on the winds from other lands. Whatever journey it made it began to attack the children under the years of five. They would lose their strength and fall into a sleep that had no awaking.

The people tried to halt it with herbs and potions used by them for centuries—powerful remedies that had fought off the ills from the outside world. But this time the death had its way. Four of the little ones died and their bodies were burned to stop the evil spreading.

But seven more children began to drift silently into the deadly sleep. Their mothers were frantic, sitting with them, weeping and praying for a miracle. Then the boy came to them and said the children must be moved to one place. They did not question him and lifted the still bodies from their beds and carried them to the inn and laid them on the floor. The boy told them that they must all leave. He had to be alone with the children.

Mora said he would not be turned out. The children could stay, but it was his place and he would remain. The boy said no. Only he could be with them. Mora began to protest, but then one of the fathers put his hand to the knife in his belt and looked at him. The innkeeper fell silent, then turned and lumbered out. The child's father said that he would sit outside the door. The inn remained closed for three days. The people came and gathered before it and listened. But no sound came from within. The man with the knife said he would kill anyone that tried to enter.

At the end of the third day the door opened and one of the children came out and asked for food. Then all of them appeared. Their parents snatched them up, weeping with joy. When the people looked inside the boy was sat on the floor, his head resting on the wall, his eyes closed.

One of the women went to him and touched his face. She snatched her hand back. "He has the coldness of death!" she said.

A man came forward and bending down lifted the boy up. "I will take him to my home. He can rest and when he wakes there will be food for him."

He pushed gently through the crowd as they thronged round him, touching the boy tenderly, saying how had it happened, what he had done to heal the little ones and that it was a miracle.

They put him on a bed and covered him with rugs. The boy lay in a great sleep. It was as if he had died in place of the children. The room was crowded with people who had come to see him. They sat and spoke to one another in whispers.

Then, on the following day, he opened his eyes and sat up. When they spoke to him he did not see them. His face contorted with pain and he wept for a long time, his body wracked with grief.

"What ails him?" asked one of the women. "Why does he suffer so?"

"I do not know," said the man who had brought him to the house. "I can see no wounds on him."

The woman took the boy's hand and stroked it. "His pain must be hidden inside. He suffers from something we cannot know."

The man looked at the boy's agony. "Better not to," he said softly. He shook his head. "The pain of each day is enough for me."

Suddenly the boy relaxed and fell back on the bed. After a moment he looked up at them, his eyes clear. "The children," he said slowly. "What of the children?"

The woman squeezed his hand tenderly. "They are well. The sickness has left them."

The boy smiled and nodded. "The evil has gone." He sat up and looked round the room at them all. "It will not return," he said.

The people never spoke of the boy to anyone from the outside world. His mother had not been a woman of the island, but the birth had taken place on the dunes and they considered that made him one of them.

Chapter Two

Fidel Bardi turned over in the bed and slowly opened his eyes. The woman beside him groaned softly in her sleep and stretched her body before relaxing back into the mattress. Bardi looked at her tangled mass of streaked blonde hair cut close to her head. Then he checked his watch. Six-thirty. The room was already hot and the sun made bars of bright dusty light through the slats on the shutters. He threw back the thin sheet and lay for a moment looking at the woman's body.

She was smooth-skinned and powerfully built, with heavy breasts and a full stomach creased with faint stretch lines. *In her early fifties and struggling to hold the years back*, he thought. *They're all the same. They come to a different country and they have no shame. When they are at home they hide their lust. They go to their clubs and their meetings and make respectable talk to each other. But here they open their legs and pay strangers to fuck them.*

He wondered where she had left her husband. *Probably at home making money. So she can spend it like this.* He got up and went into the bathroom and looked at the bottles of perfume and toilet water on the glass shelf over the basin. *Enough money there to keep me for half a year*, he thought.

He looked at his face in the mirror, seeing the thick black hair cut close to his head like a pelt. The eyes were so dark that they seemed to have no other colour. His mouth was wide with full lips drawn over large teeth that glistened when he smiled.

He lifted the lid on the toilet and urinated into the pan. His cock felt sore and he remembered how hard she had gripped it whilst they were fucking. He stroked it gently and felt it begin to stiffen under his fingers. When he finished he wiped it with a tissue and threw the tissue into the pan.

The woman was sat up in bed when he came back. She had not bothered to cover herself with the sheet and was naked. Her face was streaked with make-up from the night before; her lipstick smeared over the fleshy mouth.

"Throw me the cigarettes," she said. "They're on the dressing table."

He picked up the pack and the gold lighter and tossed them on the bed beside her. She took one, lit it and punched the pillows up behind her shoulders. Then she put her hands behind her head and leaned back.

Bardi looked at the big breasts hanging down, touching her belly. She had a deep all-over tan, except for a faint white line round her hips where she had worn a thong.

As he watched she drew up her legs exposing her shaven crotch, and he felt a slow stirring in his groin.

She looked at him with knowing eyes and smiled. "Christ, it's hot!" she said.

She took a long pull at the cigarette and ran her hand over her breasts and down her belly and looked at it. "I'm sweating already."

"It's August," he said. "It's always like this." He opened the glazed doors and then pushed the shutters open. Light flooded into the room and he looked out at the bay.

The sea was moving very gently and the rising sun cast a slanting light over the encircling mountains. A few fishing boats were returning, lying low in the water with their loads.

He stepped out onto the small balcony and leaned on the rail. A concrete jetty jutted out from the beach and a man dressed in a white tee shirt and blue shorts was standing at the far end looking all round the bay through a pair of binoculars.

Some of them get up at dawn, he thought. *They want to get as much for their money as they can.* He heard the woman moving and looked round as she went into the bathroom. He wondered how much money she would give him. Some of them were not so generous in the morning light as they had seemed in the heat of the night before. He thought the American women were more generous than the Germans, although the Germans were usually better in bed.

Not that he cared how good they were. He could give them more than they ever got with their husbands. The woman came out and stood beside him. She was still naked and she stretched, putting her arms above her head, then leaned forward on the balcony rail.

She took a deep breath and then let it out in a long sigh. "I think I'll go back to bed some more," she said. "Are you coming?"

She's not asking me, he thought. *She's telling me.* He shook his head. "I'm not tired."

She looked at him, then reached down and took hold of his cock and squeezed it hard. He began to erect immediately. She laughed and pumped it harder. He felt his buttocks contract.

"Who said anything about sleep?" she said. She looked down at him. "God! You should be in a freak show with that thing."

It was true. He was of muscular build, but only of medium height and there was no indication of the size he possessed. When slack it was of average length, but when he fully erected it was huge. Right now it was hard and throbbing in her hand.

She turned from the rail. "Come on. I want it now." Then she stopped and looked out past Bardi. "Will you look at that guy?" she said. "Out there… on the jetty… with the glasses!"

Bardi turned his head and saw the man in the tee shirt and shorts that he had seen earlier. He was still at the end of the jetty. Now he had the glasses trained on them.

"He's watching us," she shrilled. "The guy's watching us!"

Bardi began to turn round but she caught him by the arm. "No… don't let him know we've seen him."

She turned back and leaned over the rail beside him again. Then she smiled at Bardi, her lips pulled back over the expensively cared-for teeth. "Let's give him something to see."

She turned him round so that they both faced out to the jetty and then kissed him, her tongue flicking in and out of his mouth.

She opened her legs slightly. "Touch me!"

He ran his hand down over her belly and into her crotch. She murmured softly as his fingers entered her.

"Is he still there?" she asked.

He glanced up. "Yes."

She rubbed his cock gently, her fingers teasing along its length. He pushed against her hand wanting more.

She shook her head. "Not yet." Letting go of him she put her hands under her heavy breasts and lifted them. "Kiss."

Bardi put his mouth over one of her nipples and ran his tongue across it and then bit it. She put her hand behind his head and tried to force more of the breast into his mouth, thrusting her hips tight against his hand. "Touch me harder."

He slid his fingers deeper inside her and increased the pressure. She moaned and squirmed. "Oh, Christ, that's good!" Suddenly she broke away from him and fell to her knees. Reaching out she took his cock and closed her lips over it. Bardi put his hands each side of her head as she slid his cock in and out of her mouth.

She looked up at him. "Is he still there... still watching?"

He put his head back. "Yes. He hasn't moved."

"He's still got the glasses on us?"

"Yes."

Just as Bardi thought he couldn't hold back any longer she stood up. Sweat ran down her face and her lips were swollen. She looked out to the jetty again then back to Bardi. When she spoke her words sounded deep in her throat. "Come on... let's do it." She bent over the rail and looked round at him.

He touched her anus. "You want it here?"

She nodded. "Yes. I want him to see us."

She reached round and pulled her big buttocks wide apart as he eased his cock gently into her anus. He pulled back, then slid in deeper. She grunted softly and writhed as they worked to a rhythm. "That's good... but slowly," she warned. She took her hands away and gripped the rail hard.

He looked over her shoulder and saw the man on the jetty was still there, glasses up, totally still. Bardi felt the blood pounding in his head and began to go harder. She struggled, but he held her tighter.

"No! That hurts...! Stop now!" she said shrilly.

He thrust in, feeling her helplessness and pain. Then he withdrew completely, and cupping her breasts in his hands kissed the nape of her neck, tasting the salty sweat on her skin.

"You bastard!" she said angrily. "You hurt me!" But even as she spoke her body was pressing back against him and he knew she was ready.

"He's still there," Bardi said. "Let's give him what he wants." He rubbed her nipples hard, then ran his hands down to her hips and gripped the plump flesh.

She looked round at him. Her eyes were bright and hot. "Do it to me," she said harshly. "Let him see everything!" She bent back over the rail and opened her legs again.

Bardi eased his cock up into her wet cunt and she grunted softly as he filled her. They went into the rhythm immediately, she pushing back as he lifted his hips to crush against her buttocks. She threw her head back and pressed her body harder to the rail. "I'm close," she gasped.

He held her tighter. "Tell me," he said.

"Nearly... I'm nearly there!" she began to moan deep in her throat in time to the action and he felt her movements quicken as her orgasm started. "Oh, Christ!" she gasped, "Yes...! Yes...! Do it... oh! yes!"

Her body shuddered violently as it swept into its climax and Bardi struggled to hold her as she bucked and jerked in her frenzy. He waited until she was almost finished before he let go and spurted into her, jamming her up tight to the rail and holding her there until he was spent. Then he stepped back, his cock sliding wetly out of her, still semi-hard as she slumped to the balcony floor.

She looked up at him, her face slack and her eyes glazed. Then she slowly turned her head and looked out to the jetty. The man was in the same place, the glasses still on them.

She laughed, a short explosive sound, and stood up. Then she waved her hand to the man who lowered the glasses and turned away looking out to sea

"The show's over," she said. She gestured at the jetty. "I guess he won't be getting anything like that."

Bardi nodded and wondered when he could get away. "Not with a woman like you," he said.

She stared at him for a moment then wiped her hand over her face. "You made me all sweaty. I'll have to take a bath." She smiled at him tightly. "Will you be here when I finish?"

Bitch, he thought. *After you put on a show you want me ask for my pay*. "I ought to be going," he said coolly.

She smiled again, a satisfied smile that spoke of money and control. "Suit yourself." She went back into the bedroom and Bardi felt a slow anger begin to burn through him. He went in after her.

She was sat at the dressing table looking at herself in the mirror. "Christ, what a mess," she said disgustedly.

He began to dress, slowly pulling on his shirt and pants. When he had finished he stood and looked at her silently.

"You're going?" she asked.

He nodded.

"I'll say goodbye, then." She smiled and he felt the anger again, stronger this time. *Be calm*, he thought. *Just wait.*

"Oh God! I nearly forgot." She laughed shortly. "You want money. Right?"

You cunt, he thought, *You rich American cunt with your money and your good style of living. You treat people like shit and they take it because they don't have money. So you think your some kind of a special class that can do whatever you want. Have anything or anybody. Just pay for it. That's all you do. Put your hand in the money bag that has no bottom and pull out whatever it costs.*

"That's right," he said evenly. She nodded and picked up the crocodile skin bag from the bed. Snapping it open she pulled out a tan leather wallet. "How much?" she asked, her eyes intent on him.

It's like she's asking a taxi driver for the fare, he thought.

He shrugged. "Whatever."

She opened the wallet and drew out some notes. She looked at him, evaluating, then took out more money. "You were really good," she said. "I did so appreciate it."

Bardi took the money from her outstretched hand. "Thank you," he said.

She stared at him, her eyes suddenly cold. "Now if you'll leave I want to take a bath."

He picked up his bag from the corner and moved to the bedroom door. He looked back at her. "Goodbye," he said.

She ignored him. He went into the small hall and let himself out into the corridor. As he closed the door he gently clicked the lock catch up. He leaned against the wall and lit a cigarette and waited.

After a few minutes he heard a door shut and then the sound of running water. He checked his watch and waited another five minutes. He looked up and down the corridor and then slowly opened the door. He waited and listened. Then he stepped silently into the room and stood very still. He could hear her splashing in the bathroom, and he went into the bedroom; crossing to the dressing table, quickly picking up the diamond set watch and the gold lighter. He opened the bag, took out the wallet and put the banknotes in his pocket. Then he left the room, went swiftly down the back stairs and out past the kitchens and into the street.

He lit a cigarette with the gold lighter and thought how she would react when she found out what had happened. He was sure she wouldn't call the police. They never did. If she tried to blame it on a casual thief there was no point. If she gave him away to the police she faced the scandal of admitting that she had picked up a stranger for sex. Anyway, they always had more money. All she had to do was contact her husband, or whoever kept her, or just go to her bank and money would be hers instantly.

Chapter Three

He moved on down to the town centre where it would be safer in the crowds. He would sell the watch and lighter in a bar. He knew he wouldn't get a tenth of its real value but he didn't care. It would be money to keep him in food and drink until the next time.

It was the way he had lived for a long time, satisfying the desires of the wealthy people who liked to keep their pleasures secret. When he had left home as a young boy and come to the big cities to escape the toil of staying alive by wrenching a living from the land, he had quickly come to understand that some people had strange tastes in human behaviour. He had also discovered that he did not care. Nothing that they asked offended him. When he realised that they were prepared to pay to gratify their needs he saw that here was a way to survive.

As time passed he also understood that his nature suited what he did and he came to enjoy his part in the fulfilment of their wishes. Best of all, apart from the money, was the control over them. Having some rich woman, naked and entreating him to use her body, or a man of great wealth, weeping and begging for punishment, filled him with a sense of power. As time passed, he began to need the feeling more and more. Sometimes, alone with one of them, or perhaps even two or three, he would feel like a god, understanding their cravings and giving pleasure and pain to them as they desired. He also knew that afterwards they often hated him.

He had come to understand the unspoken language of the eyes glancing across a cafe or bar and the subtle nuances of unspoken suggestion and invitation. He knew how to indicate that he was aware of the hungers they carried hidden inside and that he was ready to satisfy them.

Once he had been asked back to one of the big yachts that cruised the islands. The man that owned it had wanted to be bound tightly while Bardi had sex with his wife. The woman had to resist as strongly as she could. Bardi had tied the man securely, then the woman had stripped off her clothing and launched herself frenziedly at him, shrieking rapist and fighting him with all her strength.

He had struggled with her whilst her husband had begged him to stop. Finally, Bardi had hit her hard in the face and she had fallen to the floor. He had stopped and looked at the husband who had nodded for him to continue. Bardi had picked her up and laid her on the bed and ran his hands all over her body. She had stared up at him, her eyes glowing in the dim light of the cabin. He had climbed on top of her and tried to insert his cock in her cunt, but she kept her thighs tightly closed. It was not until he had raised his hand and threatened to strike her again that she opened her legs. He went in slowly, letting her feel all of his size.

She had taken it without pain, just opening her legs wider to accept him. He had ridden her slowly at first, sliding in and out, bracing himself on his arms and looking down into her face. She had thrown her head from side to side and pleaded with him to stop but Bardi had continued, gradually quickening as he felt her hips begin to rise and fall to meet his thrusts.

The husband had noticed and began to curse, calling her a whore and a slut. She had laughed at him and said he could never do it to her like this. Then she clamped her legs round Bardi and raising her hips had lifted him off the bed with the force of her frenzy. He drove into her as hard as he could and the bed rocked, the husband wept and his wife poured a stream of filth from her mouth as she rode with Bardi to a shuddering climax that left them stretched out exhausted, still locked flesh to flesh.

Finally, she had pushed Bardi off and gone to her husband, untied him and cradled him in her arms like a small child as he sobbed, and she comforted him and said he was the best boy in the world and that she would never love anyone as she did him.

Then she had rounded on Bardi and said that he had raped her and that she was going to ring for the police. The husband stopped weeping and said that the night was finished and Bardi should go before he got into trouble. Bardi had asked for money and the husband paid him. Then the wife said he could get back to the shore on his own, because they were staying out in the bay all night. Bardi had tied his clothes in a bundle and slung them round his chest, then lowered himself over the side and made the long swim back to the harbour.

The money the husband had given him was soaked and he sat up in a room over a taverna with it spread out on the bed to dry. That had been an interesting night even by his experience. He sometimes thought how simple it was. You just had to know them when you saw them. They might be in the lounge of a hotel, or drinking at a taverna. People that had money had it stamped on them.

Then you could exchange a few remarks and wait to see if they gave out the signals that he had learnt to recognise. If they did he would stay in their company during the day, then go with them into the night to whatever fantasy they desired. He was thirty-two years old and had lived for the past fifteen years on his ability to satisfy the unspoken cravings of the people that came for a different kind of pleasure.

During that time he had moved around most of the islands, sometimes working in hotels as a waiter or kitchen hand, anywhere that gave him the opportunity to be close to the people that he needed.

Now he sat in a taverna on the harbour and counted the money he had taken from the American woman. It was much more than he had anticipated and he ordered another brandy, lit a cigarette and looked out over the harbour. The ferries were busy now in the full flow of the season and he watched as the crowds streamed off one that had just docked.

They come from their cold lands to the heat, he thought, *and for a few days or weeks they want to change how they live, to be part of a way of life they had only read of and could not endure for a day. They think we're all drinking the wine, dancing and smashing plates in the cafes. They see the old women in the black dresses working in the fields and the men sitting in the villages drinking coffee and talking together and they marvel at our wonderful way of life, so easy and so good.* He laughed silently. *Nobody tells them of the poverty and the hunger that was here before the tourists came, how we threw away the old tradition of living on the edge of nothing and welcomed them all in.*

He took a long pull at the brandy, tasting the fire as it went down. He signalled to the waiter for a coffee and thought how good it would be to sit in the warmth of the sun and let the day slide slowly by. He had used the rich five times on this island already and only a fool tempted fate. It would not be wise to stay longer. He wondered about Crete. It was a big island, and he had not been back for almost four years. There were big towns on the north shore with good hotels and wealthy clients. After working those he could always go south. The very rich would come across from Africa on their luxury yachts and sometimes he would get work on them. It was a good way to travel and eat free and when he got tired of it he would leave, taking whatever jewellery and cash that he could steal.

A police car drove past and Bardi watched it until it was out of sight. The police had no record of him and Bardi intended to keep it that way. He decided to see if there were any boats, fishing or cargo heading down to Crete. He finished the coffee and drank what was left of the brandy and paid the bill. As he walked along the harbour front, he thought if he did well in Crete he might go to Athens. A man could really enjoy himself there if he knew where to go. There were people in the city he hadn't seen for a couple of years and he could look them up and renew old vices.

He walked along the dock looking at the battered fishing boats and rusting ships that moved cargo to and fro between the islands. Just before the end of the harbour he stopped at a small boat with packing cases piled up on the deck. There were two men sitting at the stern and he asked them where they were headed.

They told him the cargo was for two ports, the first for Monemvasia at the southern end of the Peloponnese and then on to Crete with the rest of it. They were leaving the next day. Bardi asked them if he could sail with them to Crete. He would pay them and also help to unload the cargo. They looked at each other for a moment, then agreed. He was asked no questions.

He took a taxi to the outskirts of the town and booked a room in a small hotel. He was sure the American woman wouldn't make a fuss, but if she did the police would look down by the beach area where all the action went on. Even then he knew they wouldn't bother much. They would know that she had bought him for sex and lost more than she paid for. A slow drive in the patrol car with the windows down and the cops looking out would satisfy them.

He bought a bottle of ouzo and cigarettes from the store next to the hotel, went back to his room and sat in a chair by the window. He wondered if he could find a woman for the afternoon but decided against it. It might attract unwanted attention out here. He drank a glass of ouzo straight and clear without adding water. The sun streamed in the window and he lay back in the chair feeling the slow power of the drink working gently through him.

The next day he was up at the first sunlight and walking back to the town. The driver would have remembered a taxi at that hour in case the police asked questions. He got a ride in a truck that dropped him off at the edge of town and he made his way down to the harbour and sat on the wall and waited for the crew to arrive. They showed up at seven-thirty and were under way by eight. Bardi sat and talked with them as the old boat wallowed steadily through the calm water.

When they pulled in to Monemvasia they shifted some of the cases onto the dock and he waited while they collected their money for the work. Then they went to a taverna and ate sardines and drank the rough wine.

When they fired the engine and got under way again the sun was high and they hoisted a sheet to shelter from it. They played cards to pass the time on the long haul. Bardi had learned a trick that required a cool head and a strong nerve. It could only be used once because the chance of it happening twice in the same game was not possible without serious questions being asked. It also helped to have an exit close by. He had worked it a few times in dock bars where the other players had drunk deeply of the wine. Twice he had taken big sums away from the table with him. He made it a rule never to go back to the same place. Now he played just to please them, losing a little and winning it back so casually that they never knew he controlled the game. He played so that they all broke even. He would not risk winning from them. The water was too deep and the boat too far from land for that.

Finally, they sighted Crete and the boat ploughed on into the harbour at Chania and he helped them unload the boxes. When he asked how much he owed them they shrugged and waved him away, saying that he had shared the work.

Chapter Four

Bardi thanked them and walked up the road into the town thinking how stupid they were. They worked under the fire of the sun, hauling loads, just making enough to live and they were too proud to take his money. He shook his head in contempt and thought of the island where he had lived as a child; the relentless labour in the fields and on the sea, the grinding struggle that took you into old age with only death to bring rest to it all. He had endured it until he was almost seventeen and then told his father that he would not live like an animal any longer and that he was leaving.

His father, Frado Bardi, had asked him not to go, saying that the world outside the island was no good and the people were not like them. Fidel had laughed at him and thought how could he know. His father had lived all his life on the land where he had been born and had never left it. There had been a great bitterness between them and his father had turned his face from him. They shared the same house in total silence until the day Bardi had put his few belongings in a cloth bag and left. His father had stood in the doorway and watched him walk down the track that led to the beach until he was out of sight.

The boats were over from the mainland to buy fish and Bardi had sailed away from the island on one. That had been fifteen years ago. He had never gone back. The old man had found it hard to stay alive. He was in his sixty-fifth year and a lifetime of toil had worn him down. Two years before that he had wrenched his back when he had been flung from the deck of a boat as it crashed up onto the beach. Time had done nothing to mend the injury and he needed the strength of his son to survive. He had no other family alive. Two sons had been taken by the sea many years ago and his wife had died bringing the youngest child, Fidel Bardi, into the world.

The way of her death had been so strange and shocking that it had been woven into the lore of the island. There had never been anything like it. She had carried the child for nine months and prepared for his coming into the world as she had for the other two sons before him. She had gone into labour attended by two of the village women. They had delivered many children in the small community and were always sent for when the time was reached. Her water had broken as the sun went down and Bardi's father had gone to the inn to sit with the men as was usual at this time.

After four hours had passed one of the women had called to fetch him. She would not say why, only that he must come quickly. When he arrived at the house he found his wife crouched over at the end of the bed, her face and body running with sweat and her hands outstretched as if warding off some unseen horror. Bardi's father had tried to calm her, taking hold of her by the shoulders and pushing her back down. She had stared up at him, her eyes wild with terror, then screamed and flung him across the room. The women called to her to be calm and let the child come. she had cried out, "No... no... no!"

They stayed with her for three days as she went in and out of madness. She had torn off her clothes and stayed in the crouching position as if to block the birth. The stench of her body wastes was overpowering in the tiny room, but she would allow no one to clean her. When she was in her senses she wept and repeated the one word "No!" over and over. Then she would go back into the great fear that possessed her completely.

At the end of the third day she became calm and fell back on the bed as if all her strength was gone. Then the birth began. The women took hold of her and began to ease the child out. As it appeared she sat up and asked what it was. They held it up for her to see.

"It is a boy," one of them said, "a man-child with hair as black as night."

They cut the cord and washed the infant and tried to give it to her to hold. She had cried out, telling them to take it away. They had reasoned with her, saying her breasts were heavy with milk and she must feed her child. She had screamed at them, her face contorted with fear, saying that the thing must not suck from her body.

Bardi's father had attempted to soothe her, but she would not be still, throwing herself so violently from him that she fell from the bed and sprawled on the floor. She crawled to a corner of the room and pressed herself against the wall, staring at the child, her mouth working soundlessly and her arms pressed tightly across her body. Frado told the women to take the child from the house. They took it to a girl that had given birth three days earlier to a stillborn infant. Bardi's father sat in the room with his wife and watched the life driven from her body by a terror that she could not speak of and that he could not understand. She died in the morning as the first rays of the sun reflected off the sea and struck into the darkness of the room.

He put her into the hard ground at the end of the island where all the dead lay. He carved a flower in a chunk of stone and placed it on her grave. She had been a good woman to him and the sons that had gone before her, and he would try to remember her that way. The child had thrived with the girl, sucking strongly from her breasts and growing quickly. Bardi had brought food to her while the boy lived in her house and had waited till five years passed before he saw fit to bring him back to his rightful home.

Chapter Five

When he reached ten years he was put to work on the land and sea.

The people shared the food that came from their labour and all were expected to turn their hands to the toil. The boy did not shirk from his tasks but he was sullen and withdrawn, only speaking when spoken to and never joining in when they played their music in the evening after a day of work.

Bardi would shake his head when the others said his son was not like the other children. "How could he be?" he would say. "The world had not welcomed him; he had to fight to enter it."

He tried hard to be the father to the child that he had been with his other two sons but age and the daily struggle wore him down, until it was easier to accept the silence between them than try to overcome it.

When he was fourteen the boy was as tall as his father and had inherited the old man's strength of body. He never entered the harsh games the rest of the children shared and he would permit none of them to put their hands on him in play. If they tried his eyes would glow, black and hard, as he retaliated swiftly and powerfully, inflicting such pain on those that sought to engage him that they learnt to leave him to himself.

There were no formal marriages on the island. No service was read to man and woman. They said to all the people that they wished to live together and did so. Children were born and the family created. There was no divorce. To leave a partner was considered a betrayal and could bring about a beating from the relatives, which usually sent the offending person back to the home. Young girls were watched closely for signs of sexual misbehaviour and swiftly punished if found offending. Young men had to live without the pleasure of a woman's body until they entered a lasting relationship.

Fidel had felt the urgent belly-clenching desire for a woman and had fought to control it. He knew the savage retribution that would fall on him if he failed. Sometimes he would seek relief with his hand, but he knew it could never be like the total experience that a woman could give him.

Then he had noticed the girl that walked the shore line collecting the shells that her parents sold to the men that came to the island to buy fish. The people had no name for her trouble. She had been a normal child in every way. Then one day a wave had crashed over a rock where she had been standing and lifted her off her feet, flinging her to the ground. Her parents had taken her home and covered the bruise on the side of her head with a mixture of ground herb leaves. When she woke she had not known them, and her mind had been empty. They had struggled to reach her for a long time but finally accepted that she would never know the fullness of life. Her hold on reality was fragile but they had taught her to dress and feed herself and carry out other simple tasks.

At fourteen she was strong with the full body of a woman and the awakening that came with it. Her people were troubled by this and did not know how they would contain her hunger. Then the islanders had a meeting and it was agreed that if a man touched her he would bring death to himself. They spoke of it as a law and there would be no other punishment.

Now Fidel watched her, with her basket, making her daily journey along the rocks, stooping down now and then to pick up a shell, sometimes putting it in the basket, sometimes throwing it away. He watched her all the summer, while the fire burned in his loins and his throat tightened. He watched until he knew where she would be at every step of her walk. He walked the cliff top path as she walked far below him on the shore, matching his steps to hers, until she came to the place where the rocks jutted out above the sea and she was lost to his view. He knew that she would sit under the rocks for a while before starting again. He made his plan, driven by the relentless pounding in his blood, knowing that if it failed he faced a swift and brutal death.

Finally, on a day when the sun made a glittering mirror of the sea and the land lay gasping under the scorching heat, he took the first step into the darkness of his nature. He began to walk the cliff top path, slowly picking his way among the scrub. When he reached the first rise in the trail he stopped and peered carefully over the edge. Far below, down where the sea met the land, he saw the girl walking. He stood for a moment, like an animal watching prey, then stepped back and continued along the path. His breathing quickened and he felt fearful, yet desperately alive.

After a while he looked up at the sun and knew that she would be at the place where she rested. He looked over again and saw her just as she went under the huge flat rocks. There was no path from the cliff to the sea and he had to scramble down, sometimes falling and saving himself by catching hold of the spiky branches that grew out of the cliff face. It was a long climb, and he leaned back against the rocks when he reached the bottom and waited till his breathing eased.

He looked all around. There was no one in sight. Picking his way over the rocks he came to where the cliffs soared out over the sea. As he stepped out of the sunlight and went into the cool shade under the ceiling of rock he saw the girl sitting on a boulder a little way along, arranging her shells in small piles. She looked up at him as he stood before her. Although she had seen him before there was no recognition in her eyes.

Fidel saw the full thighs exposed where her shift had slid up as she sat and the heavy breasts outlined under the thin material. He felt the taste of his lust thick in his throat and his groin begin to stir. As he stared into the vacant eyes he slowly reached down and touched her shoulder slipping his fingers under the cloth of the shift and sliding it down her arm.

She turned her head and watched as he undid the three buttons on the front and exposed her breasts. He crouched down and touched them, feeling the ripe flesh and brown circular nipples. The girl was quite still, watching intently, as he bent his head and began to suck at her breasts.

Suddenly he stopped and stood up and looked all round. Then he put the shells back in the basket, picked it up and took hold of her arm and drew her to her feet pushing her back into the cave. As they moved closer to the rock wall she stumbled and he caught hold of her round the hips, feeling the soft flesh of her body as she fell against him. He steadied her as she regained her feet, and then in two paces they were at the rock face. His fingers trembling, he undid her shift and let it fall to the ground, stepped back and stared at the mature woman's body before him. She was everything he had wanted and now she was here.

Fidel pushed her to the ground. He wrenched his rigid cock free from his clothing and fell on her, forcing her thighs apart and entered her brutally in a few quick lunges. She struggled briefly as he tore into her, then spread her arms wide, palms down on the rocks and remained still. When he had spent he raised up and looked down at her face. Her eyes were glazed over and she seemed to have gone into a trance. He slapped her hard, and she blinked, then shook her head and tried to sit up.

He pushed her back and said, "No."

When she began to struggle he hit her again, harder this time. She raised her arm across her face in fear and lay back down. He raped her twice more as the blazing sun moved through the shimmering sky. The third time he was slower with her and she had an orgasm. She whimpered and grunted, thrashing wildly beneath him, her thighs opening and closing on his heaving body as he drove into her. During her orgasm she kicked out with her legs and began to scream. He rammed his fist into her mouth to stifle her cries until she had finished.

When he was finally done he stood up and leaned against the rock and looked down at her. She lay hunched over in a foetal attitude, weeping softly. There were raw scratches on her back where she had writhed against the rocky floor and livid streaks of blood ran down her thighs.

As he looked at her Fidel felt a great sense of ecstasy soaring through his body. He had never imagined it would feel like this, to have a human being totally in his power. He reached out and pushed her with his foot so that she fell over onto her back. After a while she sat up and crawled slowly over to the wall and slumped trembling against it.

Fidel looked at the shadows on the rocks outside the overhang. It was good. The sun was still climbing in the sky and he knew he would have time to get back and be seen by enough people so that he would not be under suspicion when the girl returned home.

He began to walk away from her and was almost out from the overhang when he heard a choking sound. He turned and saw the girl rising to her feet, her arm outstretched and pointing at him. Her mouth worked convulsively and her head rolled on her neck as she fought to speak.

He watched in horrified fascination as the emptiness left her eyes and her lips found one word at last. "Fi... del."

The word was his name! He stared at her as she nodded her head at him and repeated her word. "Fi... del.... Fi... del." She said it over and over again like a litany of accusation.

Suddenly, like a lightning flash, he had a blindingly clear picture of what would happen to him before the sun set. He would be found wherever he hid and beaten until his body was broken, then taken to the high point where the water thundered out for miles destroying anything in its path. There he would be cursed by the girl's family and then flung down for the sea to take.

The girl was stumbling towards him, still pointing and mouthing his name. His mind cleared and he began to think. Everything had changed now. He couldn't leave her to be found, or for her to make her way back to the village. He knew that if the women saw her they would know what had happened. He had to put her where she would not be found. He felt the great sense of power that he had experienced when she lay before him. It would be her life for his. There was no other way.

She stood trembling before him, her pointing hand almost touching his chest. The side of her face was swelling where he had struck her and tears were streaking through the dirt on her cheeks.

Fidel took hold of her arm and began to drag her towards the sea. She struggled violently and fell to her knees. He pulled her along the ground until they were at the edge. Then he struck her several hard blows across the face until she lay still. He looked all round. There was nothing, only the sound of the sea rising and falling against the rocks. He bent over and reached through the clear water to pick up a stone, then swung it high in the air and brought it smashing down on her head. Her body heaved up in the air and then slumped back to the ground. A long moan came from her and then she relaxed.

Fidel pushed her into the sea, gripped her head and held it under. Her hands reached up and clawed at the air, flailing wildly for a few moments, then fell back into the water. A stream of bubbles poured out of her mouth and rose to the surface. Then her body arched in one final spasm and went slack under his hands. He looked into the eyes that, for a few horrific moments, had known the world clearly for the first time since her childhood, as the life went out of them.

He knew now what must be done. She had to be put into the sea under the high cliffs where she would be taken out in the great passage of water that nothing could stand against. He would have to carry her the short distance from where she lay, then go into the sea with her until he could feel the pull of the force and let her go.

He went back to the wall and picked up her dress, put it in the basket and rammed a stone on top of it and hurled it into the sea and watched as it sank. Then he went to the end of the overhang and looked up at the cliff top. It was deserted. His mouth was dry with fear and he knew this was the time of great danger.

He picked up the girl's body, slung it over his shoulder and started to walk as fast as he could along the shore to where the rock reared far up out of the water, all the way up to the high point.

His fear drove him into a staggering, scrambling run over the broken ground, his legs flailing as he fought to remain upright. Finally, he reached the end of the shore. The rocks fell sheer into the sea and he could go no further. He fell down and crawled into the scrub, exhausted, and dragged the body in behind him. He lay, gasping, drawing air into his heaving lungs.

When he had recovered he looked out at the sea to where the water changed from the translucent green to a dark mass, that smashed in against the rocks high overhead, then boiled back under and went down to the huge trench, which had opened up in the ocean floor when the earth's plates had moved millions of years ago. As the water went under it was crushed down by the fresh mass moving in to the shore, and channelled into the trench under enormous pressure. It poured along the seabed for miles, moving with ferocious power.

Many years ago the people that made maps of the sea had sent a boat and a crew to examine the area. They had gotten too close to where the sea ran wild and the boat had been taken down. Only two of their team that had been out in a small dinghy away from the boat had survived.

There had been no other attempts to survey after that and, as it was not on any major shipping lanes, the mapmakers had simply shown it as a danger area to be avoided.

Now Fidel saw that he could not just put the girl into the sea as he had planned. He was not near enough to the dark water and he could not reach it from the land. If he threw her in she might just float until she was found. The fear rose in him as he realised that he was going to take her in the sea with him until they were close enough so that he could let her go.

He forced himself to be calm and waited until he felt in control. Then he took off his clothes, bundled them up and pushed them under a bush. Standing up he took one last look up at the cliff top then took hold of the body by the arm and dragged it to the sea.

There was no gradual slope in here, he just slid into the water and pulled her in after him. He was a strong swimmer, as almost all the island people were and he struck out easily, pulling the body along beside him.

As he swam on he felt the sea begin to resist him and he knew he was moving into the stretch of water that was the fringe of the dark mass. The fear rose in him again, but he fought it and swam on. Then, suddenly, the water picked him up and threw him out to sea.

He went under, choking and kicking his way frantically to the surface just as the girl's body hurtled past him and vanished into the dark water. The sea took him again and he felt the power pulling him down and knew that he was going to die. He could hear the dull roaring of the great water as it moved through the trench as he turned over and over as the current took him deeper.

As his lungs were about to burst in his chest the water carrying him struck the tip of a huge rock formation jutting up from the sea bed and soared high into the air. He was lifted with the motion and slung out of the sea, then plunged back down again.

When he came up he lay on the surface and looked up at the sky; then realised that he was moving very gently, and realised that he had been thrown clear of the great water. He sucked down air and began to swim slowly back to the land.

When he reached the shore he crawled into the shelter of the bush and lay trembling until his body dried and his strength returned. Then he dressed and started to climb slowly back up the cliff, moving carefully until he reached the top where he looked out to sea.

There was no sign of the body and he knew that he was safe. She had gone into the dark water and would never be found now. He made his way back to village, gathering wood for the fire as he walked.

It was not until the sun was on the other side of the island that the girl's parents began to search and, not finding her, ran to the village and called the people to help them. Soon everyone was out on the mountain and along the shore.

When night brought the darkness flaming torches were carried from the village so that the hunt could continue.

Fidel joined in with them—to have refused might have caused suspicion to fall on him. He stayed out all night, tracking back and forth over the island. Finally, with the sun's first light, everyone came back to the village to rest. Wine was drunk and bread eaten, and people spoke of the places that they had searched. After some discussion it was agreed that the girl must have slipped into the sea and drowned. It was known that she could not swim, and if she had fallen in over the steep rocks that almost surrounded the island she would not have been able to struggle back to land before the sea took her.

Fidel joined the rest of them as they filed past the girl's parents and offered words of comfort for their grief. He felt a keen sense of something completed. An action of great danger and pleasure that he had controlled totally. His one regret was that the girl was gone. Had she lived and her mind remained in the empty land he might have pleasured himself with her again.

The next three years he had simply existed as a beast of burden, working beside the men of the village, but never part of them, always alone and content to be so. When he went from the island he was never spoken of again.

Now he walked slowly through Ghania amid the crowds thronging the narrow streets and the busy waterfront. He felt the same sense of anticipation that he always experienced when he came to a fresh place. There would be new people to meet; people that had money and who might be willing to part with it to someone that understood their needs.

Chapter Six

Fidel sat in the corner of the crowded taverna watching the noisy group of American sailors at the bar. He knew they were off the two big ships in the water outside the harbour and that they were taking part in some combined naval exercise out at sea. He thought they probably hadn't had shore leave for a while. They had that air of reckless belligerency that servicemen get when they have been away from drink and women for a long time. He knew they would get drunk first, then look for the women.

He watched as they called for more drinks, pushing their way in front of other people and looking around them with the aggression born of the safety of a pack. He waited until they finally moved away from the bar and sat, sprawling, at two tables; legs stretched out in front of them, bottles raised and lowered, faces becoming slacker and flushed, the talk... *Always the endless talk*, he thought. *Filling the place with their noise*.

He waited patiently until they were totally into the mood they had created, the heat, the sound, the drink and their being all together in this place. He smoked a cigarette slowly and drank his beer, savouring the sharp taste as it slid smoothly down his throat.

Then he drew the pack of cards from his shirt pocket and placed it on the wooden beer-stained table in front of him. As he pulled the cards from their case he caught the eye of one of the two men sat at the next table. He smiled and held up one of the cards in invitation.

The men spoke together briefly and then the first man nodded at Fidel. They both stood up and moved across to his table and sat down.

"What do you play?" asked the larger of them. He was a man in his early fifties; stocky-bodied and grey-haired with the weather-beaten skin that told of a life lived outdoors. His clothes were worn, the blue shirt faded with a tear at the elbow and hanging loose outside the patched trousers.

Fidel smiled gently. "Nothing too serious. A little poker… to pass the time."

They looked at each other for a moment.

The first man spoke. "As long as the money is small I will play." He spoke quickly with an accent that Fidel did not recognise, but thought was probably from far inland, maybe back up in the mountain country.

Fidel shook his head. "Just to pass the time," he said again.

When the game began the two men played cautiously, not wholly trusting him and waiting to see how good he was and if they would lose the small amounts they backed their hands with.

He let them win a couple of games, then he won one and they relaxed as the cards were played and re-shuffled and played and re-shuffled and the beer was drunk and the cigarette smoke hung in a slowly drifting haze above the table.

As he played he watched the sailors. *Just a little longer*, he thought. *If I do it, it has to be right.*

He felt a cold knot of anticipation hardening in his stomach. There could be no certainty to it. If he got it wrong….

They played three more hands and he knew the time was now. He got up from the table. "I need some cigarettes," he said.

They nodded and watched as he made his way through the tables until he stood beside two of the sailors who were leaning on the bar.

They looked at him as he ordered cigarettes from the barman. He nodded to them and smiled. "Good evening, gentlemen."

They stared at him silently. He smiled again, his lips peeling back over the large teeth that gleamed wetly in the harsh light. "My luck is good," he said. He rubbed his thumb and forefinger together. "The cards are running well for me."

One of the sailors, a big heavy-set man with cropped red hair, straightened up off the bar and pushed his face close to Fidel's. "You some kind of hotshot card player?" he asked sneeringly.

He nudged his friend. "Hey, Charlie; guy here's a regular gambler."

The other sailor swivelled his head round to look at Fidel. His eyes swam through the drink in his head and slowly focused on Fidel. "Yeah." He frowned. "He don't look like much to me, Stan."

Stan nodded, "That's right." His face moved even closer to Fidel's. He spoke slowly. "I never knew a wop that could play cards." He raised his voice so that everyone could hear. "Not real cards." He looked Fidel over from head to foot. "For real money, I mean."

Fidel knew then with absolute certainty that he would be the one. Even if he did not play he would be the one that would make it begin.

He smiled at Stan, the wet-toothed smile, holding it just long enough to make the sailor's eyes tighten with anger.

"You think money makes a good player?" he asked the suddenly hostile face before him. "You do not think a man should have a good brain to play well," he said gently.

Stan picked up his glass and took a long pull at it. He banged it down on the bar. "Hey, you, fill this again!" he shouted. He turned back to Fidel. "You still here?"

Fidel picked up his cigarettes. "I am just going...." He spread his hands and shrugged. "I am sorry if I gave you offence. It was not intended." He turned to go, then turned back and stared for a moment at the sailor, nodded, then went back to his table.

The two men looked at him as he sat down and asked what the Americans had said to him.

Fidel laughed and said that they were just sailors on leave who had a little too much to drink, nothing to worry about.

They resumed playing again and Fidel signalled the waiter to bring more drinks. He watched the sailors at the bar. They seemed to be arguing, with Stan banging his fist on the bar and the other man shaking his head at him.

Suddenly, Stan lunged away from the bar and made his way through the tables until he stood in front of Fidel. He swayed to one side, and then pulled himself upright and glared down at the seated men.

"You wanna play cards?" he said, his face red with anger. "I mean really play...." He gestured at the two men with Fidel. "Not with these bums." He swept his arm out in a flailing gesture that almost unbalanced him. "With real players... like these guys." He indicated the sailors sat at the nearby tables. The two men with Fidel stiffened at the sailor's words and looked at each other.

Fidel put his hand on the shoulder of the nearest one and said, "It is nothing... do not be offended." He looked up at Stan. "Do you wish to join us?" he asked.

Stan leaned forward and slapped his hand on the table. "You don't listen good. I'm askin' if you got the guts to play with real card players?" He turned and held out his arms to his comrades. "These guys here… play these guys.…"

The two men with Fidel stood up. One of them shook his head at Fidel. "This is enough," he said quietly. "Thank you for the game."

He watched them thread their way through the room and out of the door. Then he stood up and gathered the cards and slid them into their case.

"What the hell you doin'?" asked Stan.

"I am leaving," Fidel said evenly. "I have had enough cards for tonight."

Stan stepped closer to him. "No you ain't." He shook his head emphatically and stabbed his finger hard into Fidel's chest. "No you ain't," he repeated. "What you're gonna do is stay here and show us all what a great card player you are." He looked round at the others. "You guys wanna see a really great player in action?"

He looked back at Fidel and smiled drunkenly. "You shot your mouth off tellin' us what a good brain you got. Now you can show us," he said triumphantly.

One of the other sailors stood up. "You tell him, Stan." He motioned to the others. "Come on. Let's show this guy some American style card play."

Fidel thought how stupid they were as they sat down round his table, shouting for more drinks and for the action to begin. How easy it had been to manipulate one man who had lost his control so much that he had brought all the others in with him.

He also thought suddenly, with a sliver of fear, that there were many of them, seven in all, and that if it went wrong he would be in very bad trouble. Then the coldness came upon him and his mind settled into a calm pattern of action.

Amid much shouting and arguing they decided who would actually play. Fidel saw that Stan insisted on being included in the game. When they were ready to begin Fidel produced his cards and placed them on the table amidst the beer cans and glasses.

Stan held up his hand for silence and leaned forward to pick up the cards. He held them aloft and shouted to the bartender. "Hey! You got cards back there?"

The bartender looked behind him and picked a pack off a shelf. He nodded. "Here."

Stan threw Fidel's cards high into the air. "Okay!" he crowed, "We ain't usin' no marked stuff now." He glared at Fidel, who was silent.

"This game goin' to be played straight… no fuckin' funny business," he went on. The rest of the sailors cheered wildly, and one of them fell off his chair onto the floor, where he sat hooting with laughter.

Some of the other customers began to get up and leave, slipping quietly out through the double doors. The bartender watched them go and frowned, but his face changed back into a broad bland smile as the sailors called for more drink, and he worked as fast as he could move his hands, opening and passing out cans and bottles from the cooler.

Before the play began Stan dug a wad out of his pocket and threw it on the table. "That's real money," he sneered at Fidel. "American money." He looked round the table at the rest of them. "Am I right?" he demanded. "Ain't that the best fuckin' dough in the goddammed world?"

They roared their agreement and pounded the table with their fists. Stan leaned over to Fidel, his face charged with blood and gleaming with sweat. "I s'pose you're gonna expect us to take that Greek shit money when you lose," he asked. "That dumb mickey mouse stuff." He sat back in his chair and brayed with laughter. "You guys see that crap? You gotta get a mountain of it to stand up beside a dollar!"

Fidel smiled easily. "It's all I have."

One of the sailors leaned forward. "That's not a problem. We just work out the exchange rate and he can settle up after the game." He looked at Stan who nodded and winked.

"That's right. We can take all his dough when we beat the shit out of him." He threw back his head and gave his braying laugh. "Won't need no workin' out then."

The game began and he played carefully, testing the strength of them. When he purposefully lost the first hand there was a concerted roar of delight from round the table.

The next got under way and he went right up to the few last calls before throwing down his cards.

"Too much for me," he said evenly.

The sailors exchanged glances and Stan looked at him. "You ain't thinkin' of quittin'?" he said threateningly.

Fidel smiled. "No. Are you?"

Stan's face was as red as his hair. "No I ain't," he snorted. He reached into his pocket and pulled out a creased brown leather wallet and pulled another wad of bills out and threw them down in front of him. "Come on, you guys, let's see some dough on the goddammed table."

The game went on, and Fidel lost and won just enough to hold their interest in what they hoped would be his impending downfall. Not one of them could really play well, they simply went through the motions, keeping to the rules, without the inspired skill to make a run and risk everything on their nerve and wits.

So he waited, and watched, and stayed smoothly in the game. Several times he faded to Stan to keep the big man alive. When this happened Stan would rise from the table and punch his hands together over his head like a victorious fighter.

"See! See!" he would crow. "They ain't got the fuckin' brains to stay with real players!"

After an hour he knew this was the time. Barring Stan they had all drunk enough to be on the edge of sliding all the way down into oblivion. He just had to keep them on that edge while he created the situation where he walked away with everything on the table. Stan was the last obstacle. The big man had drunk as much as the rest of them but it seemed that his desire to see Fidel beaten was so powerful that it had channelled his mind into a place where the liquor couldn't overwhelm it. He knew that while Stan had control there was a chance that he would see what was happening. He had to find a way to take him out of the game. He stood up and stretched.

"Where the fuck you goin'?" Stan rasped truculently, half rising out of his chair.

Fidel smiled the gently irritating smile and motioned to the bar. "To get a drink."

"Sit down, Stan," one of the sailors said. "He ain't goin' nowhere."

Fidel looked round the table. "May I buy anyone a drink?" he asked. They all shouted together for more beer and Fidel caught the bartender's eye who nodded at him.

"I will fetch the drinks," he said. As he walked to the bar he knew Stan was watching him and he wondered how anyone could succumb to such a totally irrational hate. A man he had met just over an hour ago was desperate to see him publicly humiliated.

The barman opened the bottles and grouped them all on a round tray. "Anything else?" he asked.

"You have whisky?" Fidel asked.

The barman nodded and gestured behind him at the gleaming row of up-ended bottles hanging from the rack on the wall. "What would you like?"

"Jack Daniels, if you have it."

The barman picked up a shot glass and held it up to one of the bottles, nudged the tap up and began to fill the glass.

"Half full, please," said Fidel.

The barman nodded again and shut off the tap. He set the glass down carefully on the tray with the rest of the drinks.

Fidel drew out his wallet and placed it on the bar. "You have ouzo?" he asked quietly.

The barman picked up a bottle of the clear liquid and reached for a glass.

Fidel held up a restraining hand. "Wait." He leaned across the counter and spoke softly to the man. "You have the real stuff?"

The barman stared at him, his face as blank as every good barman knows how to be. Fidel took a ten thousand drachma note from his wallet and slid it over the counter. The barman's hand closed on it and he reached under the bar and came up with a dark bottle. He held up his other hand and closed his fingers into a clenched fist and nodded at the bottle. "This," he said tightly.

"Good," said Fidel. He picked up the dark bottle and filled the whisky glass to the brim. He gave the bottle back to the barman who put it back under the counter.

"Now a small glass of water," he said. The barman brought it and Fidel paid him for all the drinks. He turned and made his way back to the table. The sailors passed the bottles round and started drinking right away.

Fidel held up the whisky glass and held it out to Stan. "American whisky," he smiled. "They say it is very strong."

Stan stared at him for a moment, then took the glass from his hand. "Sure it's fuckin' strong," he sneered. "It's genuine stuff." He looked at the glass of water that Fidel had picked up.

"What's that goddam crap? Your national drink?" He gave a rasping laugh. "Look at it… looks like piss!"

The rest of them roared at this and Stan beamed. He held up his glass and turned it in his hand watching as the light glanced gold off it. He nodded. "Real drink," he intoned. Then he looked at Fidel and snorted contemptuously. "Here's to this stinkin' third world craphole you live in." He drained the glass, shook his head and blew out his breath in one explosive gasp. "That's real drinkin'," he said hoarsely. He punched his fist hard up into the air. "Come on, drink that stuff you're holdin' and let's get the playin' on."

Fidel smiled at them and lifted his glass. "Your health," he said, and drank the water down.

Stan grunted. "See, like I said. Pisswater."

The game resumed and Fidel watched Stan. For five hands he showed no change in his attitude and Fidel began to wonder if he were impervious to drink. Then, halfway through the sixth, he began to fumble his cards and twice dropped them, the second time for them all to see. In the ninth he sat staring at his cards for so long that the others became exasperated and told him to put up or close. He looked all round the table very slowly, then slumped back in his chair and closed his eyes.

"Christ, he's smashed!" one of them said.

They shook him and shouted his name in his ear. He simply sat lower in the chair and began to breathe heavily.

"Leave the bum. He don't hold his drink that's his tough luck," said the sailor that had stood with him earlier in the evening.

"Sure, come on. We got this guy's ass to whip."

He knew this would be the last game. Without the big man they had no leader, no one to incite them into violence. He closed his mind down into total concentration.

The hand began and he played steadily and coldly, taking them further and further along until the money was spread all over the table. He knew that there would be enough to keep him for a long time. And dollars were always easy to sell.

He drove the bids up, keeping their hopes alive all the time.

As the game progressed he realised that there would be no need for him to use the trick. The sailors were not only too drunk, they were also not good enough to beat him. He watched them peering at their cards, lips moving silently as they tried to work out their chances of winning or losing. Some of them even craned over and looked at their neighbour's hand. Nothing worked for them. They had simply got themselves in a situation where everything they did made it worse. So he raised and called them and relentlessly destroyed each one so that they flung their cards down in disgust, cursing futilely and blaming each other for their mistakes.

When the last of them was done Fidel sat back and looked at the big pile of money spread out before him. He reached out and gathered in his winnings, folding the notes into a wad and put them into his hip pocket.

Then he stood up and looked at them. If they were going to make trouble this would be the time but they only stared at him, eyes trying to focus properly and unable to comprehend what had happened, blaming each other for the way they had lost their money. Stan remained in the same position he had slumped into when the drink hit him, impervious to everything.

Fidel walked across the room to the door. There was no sound other than the sailors confusedly arguing. The few people that had remained while the game had been in progress were silent as he left. Just as he got to the door he glanced at the bartender who looked back at him and raised his hand in a half salute, his face expressionless. Fidel nodded.

It was only when he was in the street that the elation hit him. He had done it. He walked steadily, moving down to the dock area where he had rented a room in a small hotel. He needed to get off the streets with all the money he was carrying. He quickened his steps, then had to pull up short as a man stepped out of the darkness of an alley and stood in front of him.

Fidel went to go round him, but the man caught him by the arm. "I saw what you did," he said.

Fidel looked at him. His mind registered the face as one of the people that had been in the taverna. The man was tall and thin with prominent cheekbones and narrow eyes that stared down at Fidel. "I saw what you did," he repeated. "You fixed the sailor's drink."

Fidel pulled his arm away and stepped back. He shook his head. "You are wrong," he said tightly.

The man stepped close to him. "I want half the money." He nodded at Fidel. "Give me it or I'll tell them what you did." He gripped Fidel's arm again. "If I do they'll come after you and break your legs."

"No!" Fidel said harshly. He pushed the man aside and went to walk away. The man lunged at him and sent him sprawling into the alley.

As he scrambled to his feet the man was on him, throwing him hard against the wall where they both fell to the ground. The tall man was on his feet first and kicked out at Fidel catching him in the chest. Fidel rolled over, feeling the pain flare up through his ribs. The man was at him instantly, hitting him with clubbing punches to his head and shoulders. Fidel tried to stand up and clutched at him round the waist and they stood locked together until the man whirled him round and slammed him back against the wall.

"Give it to me!" the man snarled, holding him by the front of his shirt. He shook Fidel back and forth. "Give me the money!"

Fidel put his hand in his shirt and felt for the knife that hung in its sheath from a cord that was slung round his neck and down under one arm. It was a weapon that he had made himself from a broken sword that he had found when working with a builder renovating an old house. The builder had told him that the place had been owned many years ago by a sailing man and they had supposed that the sword had been one of the things that he had brought back from his travels.

The metal of the sword had cleaned to a dull bluish glow, and he had worked very patiently on it, cutting a long thin sliver away from the main piece, then cutting out a thinner strip for the handle which he'd bound round with copper wire very tightly for a solid grip. He had honed the blade on both sides with a flat grinding stone.

It had taken many hours to put an edge on it, first with a few drops of thin oil on the coarse side of the stone, then oil on the fine side and gently stroking the metal one way, then turning it over and bringing it back up the stone. The steel had gradually taken on an edge so fine that he could hold a thin sheet of paper in one hand and slash it in half with almost no pressure at all, simply letting the weight of the blade carry it through. Fidel had honed both sides of the knife so that it was like a stiletto with razor sharp edges.

Because of the keenness of the blade it would have cut through a leather sheath so he made a metal one out of a copper tube, and bound it with velvet, so that it would not chafe his skin when it rested against his side.

Now his fingers gripped the copper wire handle and he wrenched the blade out of the sheath. He twisted his body to one side and lunged upwards with the knife, punching it into the man's chest. There was a frozen moment to the action when the man gave a soft gasp and they both stood quite still. Fidel felt the steel hit the bone of the ribcage, stop momentarily, then glance off and slide on in, right up to the hilt.

Suddenly, the man stood up on his toes as if to escape the agonizing thing in his chest, then gave a long sigh, and slowly collapsed forward onto Fidel, who, as he felt him going down, let the body hang off the blade, until it slid smoothly free of the steel and slumped very gently to the ground.

Fidel stepped back and looked down at him. The man lay on his back with his arms spread out wide. He looked up at Fidel with an expression of shocked surprise on his face as if he had no idea why this had happened to him. Then he stiffened and turned partly over on his side and relaxed as if sleeping.

Fidel bent down and peered at him. His eyes were open but totally empty and Fidel knew that he was dead. He wiped the blade clean of blood on the man's shirt and put it back in its sheath. He turned to walk out of the alley knowing that he had to get far away from this place.

As he emerged into the light of the street he collided with a bulky figure and almost fell. A hand grasped his arm and steadied him. "Are you all right, my son?" asked a deep voice.

Fidel looked up with a shock of recognition at the tall black-robed figure standing in front of him.

Before he could speak the priest peered round him and gasped. "My God!"

He took a couple of steps into the alley. Then turned and looked at Fidel in horror. "What is this... what have you done...?"

He went further into the darkness and knelt down to the still figure and touched his face. Then he turned his head and stretched out an accusing hand at Fidel. "Did you do this...? Did you kill this man?"

Fidel stood as if rooted to the ground. His mind raced furiously. The man was dead and the priest had seen his face. Not just a quick glimpse, but a proper look under the street lights. He would not only know Fidel again, he could give the police a full description of him, one that could be all over the island in a matter of hours.

He looked up and down the street. A car drove slowly past and he averted his head, then looked again. Nothing. He stood motionless for a moment thinking desperately. There was nowhere he could hide if he was known. His mind locked on to a decision.

He walked back into the alley and the priest stood up to meet him, pointing down at the man. "What happened... was there a fight... how did this happen?"

Fidel went right up to him and lunged with the knife, striking him in the neck. The priest recoiled, crying out with a thin scream of terror as the blood flooded down the front of his coat. Fidel struck him again, this time in the chest, and, as the blade went in, he ripped it savagely to the side, tearing the flesh open.

The priest slumped down, holding his arms over his head in a futile attempt to protect himself. Fidel moved behind him and, reaching over, took hold of his chin and forced his head back and up. Then he plunged the blade down in to his throat. As he did the blood welled up and gushed out and he let go and pushed the priest forward onto the ground where he crawled forward a few paces, then stopped and slumped onto his face.

Fidel bent down beside him and lifted his head. The priest stared at him in anguished horror as death came for him. His lips moved as he desperately tried to speak. Then the death was upon him. Fidel let go of his head and it thumped gently back to the ground. He stood up and looked at the two bodies as they lay, sprawled together in the total indifference of death.

As he left the alley and walked down the street he tried not to run. He knew he had to get off the island as soon as he could. There was nothing to link him with the killings, but the police would be spurred on by the enormous outcry at the killing of a priest. And someone might tell them of the card game with the American sailors in the taverna. It was close enough to the alley to make a possible link if anyone remembered that the thin man had been in the bar and left after Fidel.

He tried to think where he could find a hiding place. The police on all the islands would be alerted about the murders, maybe with descriptions of possible suspects. Places flashed up in his head and were discarded just as quickly.

Then it hit him suddenly with such a jolt that he almost stopped walking.

He would go home. Back to the island, the beyond of nowhere, the place where he would not stand out because he was one of the people. He laughed bitterly at the thought of going back to that stinking hellhole and being one of the people because it was the only place that could give him sanctuary.

He wondered if his father was still alive. If the old man had died and no relatives came forward to claim the house, then it would stand empty for one year before any couple wishing to live together could occupy it. His mind was racing with the events and he forced himself to concentrate on one thing—to get clear of Crete as quickly as he could.

He reached his hotel and went in through the tiny entrance hall and up the stairs to his room. Stripping off his clothes he went over them, carefully checking for bloodstains. When he was sure there were none he put them in his grip and changed into a fresh pair of jeans and a clean sweatshirt. At least if anyone had given a description of him he wouldn't be wearing the same clothes.

He knew he couldn't remain in the hotel. When the bodies were found and it was known that a priest had been killed, not only the police would be searching for the killer, people everywhere would join the hunt. There was no way that he could risk waiting till morning to get off the island. The ferries would have police checking everyone trying to board. If he didn't move now he had no chance. He placed the money in a small plastic bag and stuffed it at the bottom of the grip. Then he folded his clothes and spare shoes and put them on top of the money.

He opened the bedroom door slowly and checked the hall. Moving quickly he went down the stairs and out into the street. When he reached the main thoroughfare he saw that everything was as usual. People were still strolling in the warm night air and the cafes and tavernas were full of holidaymakers eating and drinking. There seemed to be no sign of any police activity at all and Fidel wondered if the bodies might lay undiscovered in the darkness until morning. That would give him a chance to get on one of the little boats plying their trade between the islands.

He thought the police would be watching the big ferries first. They just wouldn't have the manpower to check everything that floated. All he had to do was stay hidden until the sun rose.

Once he was out of the teeming area on the waterfront he quickened his pace until the bright lights of the harbour were left behind. He moved into the ground where the boats were laid up for repair or overhauls. Soon he was down at the shoreline and he kept moving, keeping away from the road and always almost in darkness. In a couple of hours he was far enough from the town to feel secure that even if the bodies were found the police would limit their search to the harbour area.

He found a rocky part of the beach and curled up amongst the huge boulders and spent the rest of the night drifting in and out of a fitful sleep. In the morning he woke early and looked for a boat to anywhere off the island. He found one heading for Karpathos and the captain agreed to take him. Money changed hands and he settled down on the deck as they chugged out into the open sea.

Fidel felt a sense of relief as he watched the land slowly disappear behind them. He knew that at Karpathos he could find another boat to make the final part of the journey to the island—the place, that after fifteen years away, he would once more call home.

Chapter Seven

A week later he jumped down from the deck of one of the little boats that had come over to buy fish and stood in the water looking up at the huge mass of rock with the cluster of stone houses sprawling down beneath it that he had never wanted to see again. He turned and reached into the boat for his grip.

"You live in this place?" asked one of the men on board staring up at the bleak landscape.

Fidel did not answer and started up the long path to the village.

The man who had spoken looked after him and shook his head. "God go with you."

As he climbed higher Fidel felt the heat burning on his shoulders. *It has not changed*, he thought, *still an anvil for the sun.*

The black dust from the track kicked up beneath his feet and he remembered all the times he had walked this path. Down to the boats to fish and at the end of the trip the long exhausted trudge back. Now the houses loomed larger and people began to appear in doorways, staring at him. No one from the mainlands ever came this far up from the shore and he knew he was the object of their curiosity. When he drew level with the first house he stopped and looked at the old woman standing outside.

He dropped the grip in the dust and wiped the sweat from his face with his hand. "Tell me," he said, "does the old man, Bardi, still live in his house?"

The woman did not answer but simply stared at him. Then she stepped forward and came close, peering into his face, her eyes sharp in the seamed skin. She frowned for a moment, then stepped back and pointed her finger at him. "You… you are Fidel… the son of Bardi… the one who went away!"

She turned and called to two women on the other side of the track. "It is the son of old Bardi," she shrilled. "He has come back."

Fidel shook his head impatiently. "Is my father still alive…? Is he still in his house?"

The two women had joined them and they were all chattering together in the language that he could hardly remember.

One of them turned to him. "Your father still lives." She shook her head. "His life is not good… he is old and sick… maybe now you are here…." She shrugged and grimaced.

He picked up the grip and started up the hill again. He heard one of them call after him. "Why have you come back?"

He did not answer. *There will be much for them to cackle over now*, he thought. *It will be all over the island by nightfall that the son of Bardi has returned.* He smiled bleakly, a sudden flattening of the full lips over the strong teeth. *If they knew why*, he thought, *if they knew why….*

Now he was into the main part of the village walking through the choking heat that rebounded off the walls of the little houses. Most of them had the shutters drawn against the midday sun and the streets were empty. He knew that the men would be out fishing, or in the fields on the other side of the island.

He passed the big stone well in the main square, with the wooden bucket hanging from the beam with its iron handle and he remembered the times he had struggled to draw the water and carry it home. *I was right*, he thought. *They still live like animals. And they will never change.*

He turned off the square and went on up the sloping street until he was almost at the top of the village. He stopped then and turned to look down on the irregular spread of stone roofs, all of different angles and sizes that lay under the merciless sun.

Suddenly a cat leapt down from a low wall, and on seeing him flattened its emaciated body into the dust, slitted eyes watching, whip-thin tail lashing from side to side. As he walked past it crouched even lower, then exploded into movement and vanished down the street.

Fidel finally stopped at the end of the track and looked at the house where he had been born. It was low, with three rooms, two small windows and built of the stone the people hacked out of the rock face and fashioned into workable sized slabs. Now the roof had fallen in at one end of the building and the broken timbers stuck out through the slabs like giant fingers. The door hung on one hinge and was open.

He looked inside and, as his eyes grew accustomed to the gloom, he saw the figure of the old man sat slumped in a chair by the window. He hesitated a moment. "Father," he said.

There was no answer and he walked over and stood looking down. Time and toil had exacted a harsh toll on his father. The once powerful stocky body had shrunk to half the size that Fidel remembered and he had to strain forward to hear the faint irregular breath rustling in and out of the sunken chest.

He touched the old man on the shoulder, feeling the bones under his hand. "Father," he said again, louder this time.

His father stirred ever so slightly, then relaxed back into the chair.

Fidel shook his head impatiently and this time gripped the shoulder hard. "Wake up, old man."

He continued shaking until his father sat up with a gasping snort and tried to focus his clouded eyes upon him. He looked at Fidel for a very long time.

Finally, he stretched out his arm and touched him on the chest. "You…" he said uncertainly. His voice was cracked and very weak. He tried to rise, but fell back in the chair.

Fidel watched him silently, feeling nothing.

"Is it… you… Fidel?" the voice quavered, the hand pressing harder now into Fidel's chest.

Fidel nodded and pushed the enquiring hand away. "Yes… I have come back." He stepped away from his father and watched as the old man struggled out of the chair and finally stood up.

He took an uncertain step forward and peered up into Fidel's face. Then he nodded his head.

"You are Fidel," he said wonderingly. "Fidel." He looked all round the room and nodded again. "You went away… a long time ago… you did not stay…."

"No, I did not stay," said Fidel, "but now I have come back. Is there food? I have not eaten since yesterday."

"Food." The old man's brow furrowed as he tried to think. "Food… yes… there is bread."

He went to the small table and picked up a loaf that had been half eaten and held it out to Fidel.

"There," he said. "Take it."

"Is there no meat?" Fidel asked, looking at the bread.

"Meat…" repeated his father bewilderedly. "No meat…."

"Never mind," said Fidel disgustedly. He tore a chunk off the bread and ate it hungrily. "Have you wine?"

His father sat down again. "Wine…"

"Yes… wine… to drink," Fidel said impatiently.

The old man shook his slowly. "No… no wine." He pointed to a pitcher on the table. "There is water…."

"Never mind," said Fidel. "Is the inn still in the village?"

"Yes." He frowned. "But I have not been down there for a long time…." His voice trailed away into silence and he sat staring at Fidel unblinkingly.

Fidel finished the bread and reached for the pitcher. He took a long drink of the water and shuddered at the rank taste. He wondered who looked after the old man. Probably someone who knew him from long ago. He suddenly realised that now he would be expected to care for him and felt a sense of disgust at the thought.

"Where can I sleep?" he asked.

His father craned his head towards him and frowned. Fidel repeated the question, louder this time.

The old man nodded and pointed to the other room. Fidel picked up his grip and went in. The room contained a wooden bed, a chair and a small table with a candle holder on it. On the floor lay a dirty blue worn rug. Other than that the room was bare.

Animals, he thought, *no better than animals*. He walked back out to his father who was dozing in the chair. "I'll sleep out here," said Fidel.

The old man looked up and nodded slowly, then drifted back into the half sleep. Fidel walked down through the village until he came to the inn. There were a couple of tables outside in the street and a dog lay panting in the heat under one of them.

Fidel went inside. It was almost as he had remembered it. The few tables and the big stone fireplace at the end and the wooden counter, wine-stained and worn smooth. There was a man standing at a window, looking down to the shore. He turned as he heard Fidel and nodded then stared hard at him for a long moment.

"Are you…?" He stopped and frowned and shook his head. "I thought I knew you," he said slowly.

Fidel smiled. "I am Fidel Bardi. I was born here."

The man clapped his hands together. "I knew I had seen you before." He was a small man, slightly built, with a heavy dark beard and hesitant eyes. He moved behind the counter and picked up a flagon of wine and looked at Fidel expectantly. Fidel nodded and the man poured the wine into a stone mug and pushed it across the counter to him. Then he leaned back and looked at Fidel, who picked up the mug and drank deeply of the harsh dark wine which came from the grapes that were grown in the black earth; on the slopes behind the mountain.

When he had drained the mug he put it back on the counter and wiped his hand across his mouth.

He nodded to the man. "That is good on a hot day," he said.

The man smiled as his eyes slid over Fidel's face, never meeting his eyes for more than a moment. "Another?"

Fidel nodded and the man refilled the mug for him. "Have you seen your father?" the man asked, wiping a cloth along the counter.

Fidel nodded again. "Yes." He shook his head. "Time has not been good to him." He took another long pull at the wine as the man nodded.

"Some of the old women go in to him." He shrugged. "They do what they can."

"I will look after him now," said Fidel firmly. "It is right." He set the mug down and looked at the man. "What happened to Mora—he was the innkeeper here when I lived on the island?" he asked.

"He was my father," said the man. "I am Yole Mora."

Fidel remembered the huge bulk of the innkeeper and wondered how he could ever have sired a son as small as this. Yole Mora smiled thinly, his eyes fixed on a spot above Fidel's head. "You are wondering how a man of my father's size...." He did not finish his words, but shrugged again.

Fidel nodded. "It happens."

"I am the living proof of it," said Yole Mora.

Just then the door opened behind the counter and a woman came through carrying a stone flagon. Fidel caught his breath at the sight of her. She was tall and strongly built with long black hair that fell in a wild tangle down over her shoulders. Her skin was darker than that of the people of the island and had a soft sheen to it. She put the flagon on the floor and straightened up and looked at Fidel.

"Who are you?" she asked. Her voice was deep, almost harsh.

Fidel smiled. "I am Fidel Bardi."

The innkeeper broke in. "His father lives up at the top of the village... old Freda Bardi."

The woman nodded. "I have heard them speak of you." She stared at him, then smiled, a long drawing back of the full lips flattening against the white teeth. "You are the one that escaped."

Yole Mora frowned. "You have no respect to speak in that way, Lyra," he said reprovingly.

Fidel laughed. "It is true. I did escape." He opened his hands expressively. "And now I am a prisoner again."

The woman stared at him. He thought what amazing eyes she had, like the paintings of the Egyptian women that he had seen in museums. They were long and full, slanting at the corners and the deepest shade of green that caught and reflected the light as she moved her head.

She shook her head, the dark gleaming hair swinging out. "I would not have come back." She looked at her husband and smiled coldly. "Ever."

Mora tightened his lips and shook his head. "Take the empty flagons outside," he said harshly. "Do not waste your time here."

She looked at him for a moment, then nodded. Fidel watched her as she walked across the room to the row of empty flagons stacked by the door. She moved with the unconscious grace of an animal, the rounded hips swaying at each stride and the dress tight across her buttocks. She stooped down and picked up two of the flagons holding them to her body, then reached for a third. He watched her again, the flagons crushed against the lushness of her breasts, and he felt the flare of desire in his groin. She straightened up and saw him staring at her. Fidel turned back and picked up his mug and drank, savouring the power of the wine.

As she went through the door she turned her head and looked at him. Her face was empty of expression, but the huge green eyes burned into him. Then, she was gone.

The innkeeper came back and stood behind the counter. He looked at Fidel, his face closed. "Your father is old... he needs help... will you stay now?" he asked.

Fidel nodded slowly. "I will stay. As you say he is old. And I have been away a long time." He shrugged. "The age comes to us all." He smiled bleakly. "If we do not go before we run our time."

Yole Mora nodded and gestured out at the sea. "That has taken many who did not."

Fidel looked around the inn. "Better to stay here than go to the sea."

Mora frowned. "I had no choice. My father put me to this life." He looked down at the counter. "Maybe if I...." He stopped, but not before Fidel had heard the bitterness in his voice. Mora looked at him, his eyes sliding away from Fidel's. "I have never been away from this island," he said. "Is the outside so different from here?"

Fidel nodded slowly. "Yes... it is different." He gestured at the island through the windows. "You look at this rock we stand on, then you leave it and go to the mainland and you are on another world."

He took a pack of the small cigars from his shirt and offered them to Mora who shook his head. Fidel took one and lit it, drawing on it and looking at Mora through the smoke. *The man is like a too tightly wound spring*, he thought. *There is trouble in him.* He wondered if it were his wife. She looked too much woman for the man whose eyes were never still and who had scarcely contained his anger when she had spoken to a stranger.

"You have never been away from this place?" he asked.

Mora shook his head. "No." His jaw tightened. "No," he repeated, "I have all that I need here."

Fidel drained the mug and set it down. "That is good," he said evenly. "It is a good thing to be content with life." He watched the cigar smoke sliding through the still air in the room and easing its way round the open window shutter. "It is not a thing that comes to all men."

Mora stared at him closely for a second, then looked away. "I do not say I am content," he said quietly. "If a man could go back to the beginning of his life..." he paused, "and have some words in what is decided for him..." he shrugged, "who knows how his life might have gone."

Fidel smiled gently. "You are a philosopher, Mora," he laughed. "Be careful. A man that thinks too much is not always a happy man."

"I did not say I was unhappy," said the innkeeper. "It is only that sometimes a man wonders on these things."

"Of course," Fidel agreed. "And if he has never seen any other place, but where he was born, then he has nothing to compare to."

Mora nodded. "That is it." He smoothed the counter with the palm of his hand. "You are right. I have not travelled as you have... you have been to many places?"

"Enough," said Fidel. "Enough to know that there is more to the world than where a man is born."

"But you have come back to this place," the innkeeper said. "You said you have come back to take care of your father but he has been weak for many years. He needed you a long time ago."

He gave a small smile of triumph that vanished from his face instantly. "I ask you not to be offended by my words, it is only that it was not thought to see you ever again."

Fidel shrugged. "What you say is true," he said. "I should not have returned." He looked at the innkeeper thoughtfully. "Sometimes there are other people who decide which way we go. When a man would go one way sometimes he is stopped, because someone else wishes him to go the other way. Maybe he is married...." Mora stiffened. "Then he has to listen to what his woman wants, which may not be the same as he wants...."

"I am the master in my house," said Mora coldly. "When I decide a thing it is done."

"Of course," said Fidel easily. "A man could see that by how you were with her just now." He drew on the cigar and looked at Mora who looked back at him, searching for the insult in Fidel's words, his eyes almost, but not quite, holding contact with Fidel's, as he struggled to control himself. Finally he spoke, his voice low and strained.

"You were right when you said you have been away a long time, Fidel Bardi. Your ways are different now."

Fidel nodded. "Then it is a good thing that I have come back." He smiled the teeth glistening smile at the innkeeper. "Now I will have time to know them again."

He drained the mug and set it down in front of Mora. "Thank you, Mora, for your company. It is good that there is still a welcome here." He picked up the pack of cigars and threw some coins onto the counter. "I will see you again."

He walked slowly down the hill that lead to the shore. He thought about the innkeeper. Mora had shown the same weak spite that his father had. There was no difference in them, save that the son was smaller. But the woman; she was different. He wondered how she had come to be with Yole Mora. He tried to remember her from amongst the people that had been on the island before he left, but could not. He thought she might have come over from one of the smaller islands and stayed.

She was certainly something for a man to think on. Then he remembered the punishment for a woman taken in sin and how sometimes the beatings had ended in a man being killed. *Still*, he thought, *she might be worth taking the risk for.*

He came to the end of the track and began to walk along the shore. As he picked his way among the huge rocks he was aware that some of the old women outside of the houses closest to the sea were pointing down at him and jabbering among themselves. *They all know now*, he thought, *Fidel Bardi has come back.*

He was suddenly filled with the desire to get on the next boat and leave. It was only now that he was really here that he knew just how much he hated the place. Already the great cliffs, standing stark and sheer out of the sea, seemed to close off the outside world. Then he thought bitterly how right he had been to come to this place to hide. This was perfect for him. All he needed was the patience to wait until the time was right to go.

Chapter Eight

He stopped as the rocky shore line plunged into the sea and he could walk no further. Instead, he began to climb through the scrubby grass up to the top of the cliff. As he moved higher he could feel the sun beating into him; the harsh unyielding fireball that always seemed so much more powerful on this hellish rock than anywhere else that he had ever been.

Halfway up he stopped to rest, and looked out at the vast glittering mirror of water that seemed to stretch on forever. He lit a cigar and sitting down on the dusty earth leaned back against a rock. He inhaled deeply, enjoying the taste of the tobacco.

He remembered how time here never seemed to have the same importance as on the mainland. Here they just existed.

Almost like living in a dream, he thought. *They eat, sleep, make children with their women, become as the animals and die. Sometimes the sea takes them and sometimes they are like the dribbling ruin that is in the house up on the hill. And now his good son has returned to look after the old father*, he thought. *And I am here because some fool decided to be greedy over a game of cards he didn't even play. And don't forget the priest who died because he was a bigger fool.*

He got to his feet, crushed out the cigar, threw it down and carried on up to the top where he stood and looked out over the broken-backed crouching beast that was the island. The sea was too calm for a breeze, even this high, and he thought the only place where the water would be running with power would be round at the high point where it was never still. He began to walk along the cliff path looking down at where the sea touched the rocky shore line.

As he drew nearer to where the path began to descend through the scrub he saw the figure of a young boy sitting alone on a huge slab of rock jutting up out of the earth.

As he drew closer the boy turned his head and looked at him. Fidel saw that he was about fourteen or fifteen years old, slightly built, with long fair hair bleached almost white by the sun, and gentle eyes that were the colour of a tranquil-blue sea. His shirt and cotton trousers were old and faded. Fidel stopped and raised his hand in greeting.

The boy looked at him for a long moment. "You are Fidel Bardi," he said softly. His face was closed, but his eyes were intent on Fidel. "I knew you were coming."

Fidel frowned. "What?" he asked. "What did you say?"

When the boy spoke again his voice was stronger. "I knew that you would come to this place."

Fidel shook his head. "I don't know what you are saying to me." He stared hard at the boy. "Who are you and why do you speak to me like this?"

The boy had sat on the rock and waited for Fidel Bardi all day. He had not known the exact time when he would see Bardi, only that this would be the place, high above the village and away from the people. Now he looked into Fidel's eyes that were without light and he felt a fear that had no name, only as if a shadow had passed across the sun.

"I know why you came back," he said.

Fidel felt a jolt of fear at the boy's words. How could he know any of what had happened on Crete? Then he relaxed. The boy knew nothing. Maybe he was mad... one of the island's inbred secrets. "What do you know, then?" he smiled coldly.

The boy looked at him, the calm eyes searching. "You must leave," he said softly.

Fidel leaned forward. "What are you saying... leave?" He shook his head. "I am here less than a day and you say I am to go?" He laughed harshly. "I have a father that is old and sick. He needs me. That is why I am here."

The boy put his head down and was silent for a long moment. When he looked up again he spoke slowly and clearly.

"You did not come back for your father."

Fidel felt the knife press against his side as he leaned forward again, the swift anger rising. "You make no reason with your talk," he said. "You are a stranger to me, yet you tell me I must leave my home." He swept his arm out in a half circle. "I belong here. I have a right to be in this place. Where do you belong?"

"I was born on this island," the boy said slowly. He shook his head. "I never knew the woman that gave me life… the people here cared for me…." He paused. "Now I care for them."

Fidel gave a short explosive laugh. "You," he sneered. "*You* care for them? You are a boy. You cannot care for anyone!"

Once again the boy felt the fear, stronger this time and closer to him. Fidel's eyes were even darker now and hot with rage. The boy stood up, so close he could feel the anger in Fidel's body. He spoke directly into Fidel's face. "If you stay here you will bring great evil to this place."

There was a long moment's silence as Fidel looked all round at the empty landscape. Then he reached out and took hold of the boy's arm. He drew him close, seeing the pain in his face as he tightened his fingers into the soft flesh.

"Listen to me," he said, his eyes slitted into two dark lines. "Do not tell me what I must do."

He made a movement across his chest with his other arm as if reaching for something, then stopped and released the boy, pushing him away hard so that he staggered and almost fell.

Fidel took a long deep breath and stood quite still. When he spoke again his voice was calm. "I have come back to care for my father." He nodded twice. "That is all." Then he turned and carried on down the path through the scrub to the shore.

The boy leaned against the rock and rubbed the bruised flesh of his arm and watched Bardi's figure disappear from his sight.

Fidel walked on, feeling the rage slowly subside. He knew how close he had been to using the knife on the boy and how stupid it would have been here. He had gotten away with it on Crete, but in this place there were eyes everywhere.

Not even one full day I have been here, he thought, *and I almost killed him. What was it about him that made me want to do it?*

He thought about the calm certainty with which the boy had told him he must go. As if he had a right to say it. He felt the anger rise in him again at the memory and forced himself to be calm. He would find out about the boy, who he was and what he had meant by saying that he cared for the people.

Mora would be the one to ask. People talked when they drank and innkeepers always listened and remembered.

That night he listened as his father rambled back through his life, re-living incidents that had happened over sixty years ago. Finally the old man had risen to his feet and stumbled away to bed. Fidel stood in the doorway of the house and watched the blazing red, gold and black fireball sun slide swiftly into the sea, leaving almost the entire island in darkness.

As his eyes adjusted to the gloom he began to make out the soft glimmers of light of the oil lamps in the little houses. *Now it really begins*, he thought. *This is just as I remembered it. As if the world had died. No tavernas or cafes. Nothing. None of the noise and bustle of the big cities at night. Only the sound of the sea as it broke against the land.* He smiled bleakly. *You came here to escape prison and now here you are in another kind of prison.*

He went back in the house and stood for a moment looking at his father lying crumpled in the narrow bed. No one had called to see the old man and Fidel knew that they wouldn't now that he had come back. They all knew the son would care for the father.

After sitting outside for an hour leaning back against the stone wall in the oppressive air that never seemed to cool at night, he walked slowly down to the inn. As he pushed the wooden doors open and stepped inside he could smell the oil from the lamps on the tables.

Yole Mora was behind the counter talking to a very tall thin man. He stopped when he saw Fidel and half raised his hand. "Bardi," he said, "I was just telling Saur you have come back."

The tall man looked at Fidel intently and nodded. "I remember you," he said. "When you left your father would come in our boat sometimes."

"That is right," said Mora. "Saur's father was good to him." He looked at the space above Fidel's head and smiled his weak smile. "I think it kept him alive."

Saur shook his head. "There is no room for pity on a boat. He earned his place."

"No, no," Mora said quickly. "No one ever said Frado Bardi needed pity." His restless eyes moved over Fidel's face. "Wine?" he asked.

Fidel nodded and looked around the room. The men were all strangers to him, though some of the faces were oddly familiar. He raised his mug to them and they nodded their heads, then went back to their conversation, only subdued now, as if his presence had altered the atmosphere in some way.

He turned back to the men at the counter. "I walked the top today," he said. "Nothing seems to have changed here."

Mora nodded. "That is good. We don't need change."

Saur drank deeply from his mug and wiped his hand over the heavy moustache that covered his top lip. He shook his head slowly.

"Some things I wouldn't mind changing." He frowned. "The power that runs through the wires like on the boats that come over for the fish. That would be good."

"You mean the electricity?" Fidel asked.

"Yes," said Saur. "It would be something to have light in the houses without using oil." He thought for a moment. "And not to have to work a sail to move the boats…."

Fidel stared at him. "You do not have an engine for your boat—you still work with sail?"

Saur nodded. "Yes, we all use the wind to fish." He looked round the room. "None here have money to buy an engine."

The men looked up and nodded assent at his words. One of them stood up and came to the counter. He was short and broad in the body with dark hair that fell down over his ears in a tangled mass of curls. "I remember you, Bardi," he said. "You were the one that never spoke." He grinned at the others.

Fidel smiled. "That was a long time ago."

The man nodded. "True." He tapped his chest and smiled, revealing broken and stained teeth. "I am Salan. My father would go with yours sometimes when the sea ran with fish."

"I remember," Fidel lied. "Your father—he has good health in his age?"

Salan's face tightened. "The sea took him." He shrugged. "It was a long time ago now. We never knew how it happened. They said he got into the dark water and was lost."

Saur nodded. "It is an old story," he said bitterly. "The dark water runs far out and a man can think he is safe from it until it is too late."

"They never found anything?" asked Fidel.

Saur stared at him for a moment. "You were born on this island, Bardi. You should know that nothing is ever found that goes into that hell."

"You are right. I should have remembered," said Fidel. "The water is a living grave."

"I have three cousins," said Saur. "We shall be lucky to go into old age without losing someone to the sea."

Mora poured fresh wine for Saur and Salan and looked at Fidel who nodded. The innkeeper refilled his mug and carried a flagon over to the men sitting at the tables.

"When I was walking on the top today I met a boy. He was sat on a rock and looking out at the sea," said Fidel.

"Did he speak with you?" asked Saur.

Fidel nodded. "He did and I could make no sense of what he said."

Salan laughed. "That was the boy," he grinned. "Sometimes he speaks in riddles."

"Who is he?" asked Fidel. "I thought he was sick in his mind."

The two men exchanged glances.

Saur shook his head, his face suddenly cold. "Do not say that." He made a chopping gesture with his hand. "Ever."

Salan broke in. "Hold, Saur. He did not know, or he would not have spoken." He turned to Fidel. "The boy is not like us. He is different."

"I do not understand," Fidel said. He frowned. "How is he different?"

They were silent for a moment, then Saur placed his mug carefully on the counter and looked at Fidel. "The boy has the gift," he said.

"Gift? What gift?" asked Fidel. He looked at their serious faces. "What are you saying?"

"He knows what will be," said Salan. He nodded at Fidel. "It is the truth. He has saved lives on this island because of it."

"You mean he is a seer?" asked Fidel. "He knows the future?"

Saur nodded. "That is right. He has the gift."

Fidel looked at them, then laughed scornfully. "That is not possible. No man can know what has not already happened." He shook his head. "It is an act; a lucky guess that comes true and...." He stopped, suddenly aware of a silence in the room and that all eyes were fixed on him.

What is happening here? he thought. *They are speaking of something that cannot happen. No one can see into the future. Yet they all believe.* He looked round the room at the weathered, lined faces with the hard eyes that looked upon the sea and lived with it in all its moods. Were these men that would be fooled by a boy, not yet grown to a man?

Saur leaned towards him and Fidel was suddenly very aware that he had the great physical strength that some thin men possessed. "Do not speak of things you do not know, Bardi," he said coldly. "You are a stranger here." He pushed his mug across the counter to Mora who had rejoined them. "Again," he said curtly.

Mora stared at Fidel as he filled the mug. The weak smile of triumph hovered about his lips.

"It is not his fault, Saur," the innkeeper said. "He has no way to know how things are with the boy."

Saur grunted. The innkeeper thought for a moment, then nodded at Fidel. "There is something strange here, Saur," He nodded at Fidel. "If the old people are right in what they say, then Bardi came into the world the same way as the boy."

Salan frowned, then nodded. "That is right." He looked at the men sat at the tables. "Do you remember? How they say the boy's mother was found on the shore," some of the older men nodded, "and that he was cut from her body as she died."

One of the men nodded. "I heard she had died before they took him from her."

"No matter," Mora said impatiently. He pointed at Fidel. "It is told that Bardi's mother refused to bring him and was mad." He shrugged at Fidel. "It is only what is said, Bardi. I do not say that it is true, only they say she would not give you life."

The man at the table nodded again. "It is true. My woman has a sister who was there with Frado Bardi." He shook his head. "She said they could do nothing with his woman. That she broke the room and tried to hide from the birth for three days and then, when they brought the child out of her, she would not take it and she refused it milk." He thought for a moment. "They took it to a girl who had borne a dead child and she fed and cared for it as her own." He nodded at Fidel. "Frado left you with her for five years before he took you back to raise himself."

Mora nodded. "You see, you and the boy were not given an easy path into this world."

Fidel was silent for a moment, then shrugged. "Easy or hard it is all same when you are here." He picked up his mug and drank deeply. He looked at the man sat at the table. "My mother... did she die at my birth?"

The man shook his head slowly. "No. I think they said she lived three days." He tapped his head. "They say she went into some other place where no one could reach her. Then she just died."

There was a silence in the room, broken only by the soft hiss from the lamps. Then the door behind Mora opened and his wife came in and stood beside him. The innkeeper looked at her and frowned. "Have you no work to keep you from here?" he asked coldly.

The woman smiled. "Everything is as you wanted it."

Fidel noticed a sudden hush as she entered. The men at the tables and the counter stopped moving and turned their eyes away from her. It was as if she had drawn all the energy out of the room, taken it into her body and poured it back transformed into a raw, potent sensuality that flooded over them all. Then, just as suddenly, the movement and talking resumed. The woman looked at Fidel and smiled. "You are here again."

He nodded, conscious of all their attention and Mora's eyes on him. "I did not find anywhere else to go," he said evenly.

She put her hand up and ran it through the dark mane of her hair. He watched as the action strained the heavy breasts against the thin dress. Behind him he heard the soft inrush of Salan's breath.

Then the woman laughed, a full-throated sound that touched the nerves of every man in the room. "So we are the only choice," she said.

Fidel nodded. "You have no competition." He pushed his mug across the counter to her. "Another, please."

He watched as she lifted the flagon easily and poured the dark wine. He placed the coins in front of her. She ignored them and Mora gave a tiny hiss of anger and swept them up into his hand. Fidel lit a cigar and offered the pack to the others standing with him. Only Salan took one. Saur refused with a curt shake of his head and Mora simply looked away, his lips tight under the heavy beard.

It is only since she came into the room, thought Fidel. *It is all changed because of her. Before, men were just talking and drinking. Now, there is a tension that you could almost reach out and touch.*

He ran a hand over his face and looked at the sweat on it. "This is what I remember," he said. "How the nights are almost as hot as the days."

Saur nodded. "That is true." He looked at Salan, who nodded. "Yes, sometimes I lie outside the house at night to sleep," he said. "Inside, it is like an oven."

Fidel drew on his cigar and watched the tip glowing redly in the soft light of the room. The night wore away as they talked and drank and Fidel felt the dark wine stir his blood, so that every time he looked at the woman, or heard the harsh richness of her voice, he felt the overwhelming want of her rise up from his loins so powerfully that he could taste the musk-bitterness of it.

Finally, Mora slapped his hand on the counter twice. "Enough," he said loudly. "Finish your wine."

Fidel watched the woman for the last time as she moved through the room blowing out the lamps. She nodded to him as she came back to the counter, the huge eyes fixed on his for a second; holding him, then she was gone.

Mora followed them to the door and Fidel heard him sliding the bolt across behind them. Saur moved off down the track without a word. Fidel and Salan stood and watched the tall man as he faded into the darkness.

"He is not a man for words," said Fidel lightly.

Salan laughed. "He is not." He shook his head. "You should sail with him. Maybe two words or three." He grimaced. "It makes the day a long one."

Fidel smiled. "What of the innkeeper?" he asked. "He does not seem a happy man."

Salan was silent for a moment as he looked at Fidel speculatively. Then he looked back at the inn. "You have eyes in your head, Bardi. Did you not see his woman?"

Fidel frowned. "Yes," he nodded. "What of it?"

Salan gestured him to walk on. "She is his trouble." He lowered his voice almost to a whisper. "He is not man enough for her. It is known everywhere on the island. He wants a child from her, but," he shrugged and spread his hands wide, "it is not to be."

"Ah," said Fidel. "This is why he has such a face on him."

They had reached the well in the square and both men sat down on the low wall that encircled it.

"How did a woman like that come to be with Mora?" asked Fidel.

"His father... old Mora... bought her for him," said Salan.

Fidel looked at him incredulously. "What are you saying?"

Salan nodded vigorously. "It is the truth. The old man wanted grandsons and Yole couldn't get any of the women to live with him. So old Mora went and bought him a wife."

Fidel shook his head bewilderedly. "I do not understand. Explain yourself."

Salan smiled patiently. "Listen," he said. "This is the way of it. When Yole's bed remained empty his father looked about the island for a woman that would be a good breeder for his son. None of them would go with him, so he went to a woman that lives at the end of the island, the other side of the dark water." He cocked his head at Fidel, who nodded. Salan lowered his voice and leaned forward. "People said that she had a child years ago by one of the crew that came over to buy fish." He lowered his voice even more. "They say that he was a black." He leaned back and stared at Fidel. "A black!"

"What happened?" asked Fidel.

"Old Mora went over and saw her. You remember the size of him?" Fidel nodded again. "And that he never went out of the inn. That he could not move without fighting to draw breath into the body that he carried."

Fidel smiled, "Yes."

"Well, the old man had a mule and cart that was used to bring supplies for the inn from the boats. So he gets into the cart and goes over to the woman at the other side of the dark water."

"Wait, Salan," said Fidel, "how do you come by this story?"

Salan smiled conspiratorially. "The old women—they know everything that happens. And one of them used to clean the inn for the old man." He put his fingers up to the sides of his head and waggled them. "They have long ears."

"Go on," said Fidel.

"That is all. When he saw the girl, Lyra, he paid her mother money so that she would come and live with his son." He spread his hands. "You have seen Lyra; she was only sixteen." He ran his tongue along his lips. "Can you imagine her then—never been with a man. And having to lie with Yole Mora!" He shook his head disgustedly. "What a waste!" His face became serious. "Now the old women say that Yole is in hell with her—that their bed is cold—that Yole weeps while his woman has never known the real strength of a man inside her." He stared at Fidel, his eyes gleaming at the thought of Lyra Mora lying unsatisfied in Mora's bed.

"She has never gone with another man?" Fidel asked.

Salan shook his head grimly. "Bardi," he said very seriously, "you know the laws of the island. A man would be a fool to risk breaking them for her."

"Has no one ever tried?" asked Fidel.

Salan tapped his head. "Only in here." He grinned. "There is not a man on the island that has not pleasured Lyra Mora in his head, but," he paused and sighed, "that is all that has ever happened. "He shook his head sadly. "Ten years she has lived with Mora, and the old women say that he has broken her in, but never given her any pleasure. So, she has listened to their stories of the madness that men and women do to each other in bed that drives them wild and she has never known any of it."

"For a woman like her that is a sin," said Fidel.

"You are right, Bardi," said Salan. "If it were anywhere but here, then she could have many lovers to satisfy her." He stopped and shook his head at Fidel. "But here, every man wants her and not one can have her. And because this is the way of it, all are sick with wanting."

"And Mora—he knows how it is with the men here?" asked Fidel.

Salan spat into the dust. "He knows." he said flatly. "And he also knows that as long as we are all watching one another then not one man will touch her. Because if they were caught, then all the men on the island would join with Mora to beat the man to death." He tapped Fidel on the chest. "Certain death."

Fidel shook his head sadly. "What a waste."

Salan smiled broadly, the moonlight glinting off his broken teeth. "And now you, Bardi, you will join us in watching her. And having her in your head," he crowed.

"I will not waste my time with that," said Fidel.

"You wait," laughed Salan. "You wait till you see her moving in Mora's place. That body that has not known the wildness of the flesh and you think it could be you that teaches her it."

"And be beaten to death?" asked Fidel. "I do not think so."

"You will think of her," Salan said firmly. "When you are in your bed and you have no woman to use, then you will be with her in your head."

Fidel laughed. "Think what you will, then." He stood up and stretched. "I am away to sleep."

"Wait," said Salan. "There is one more thing for you to think on." He laughed softly. "This will make the night even hotter for you."

"What is it?" asked Fidel impatiently. He was beginning to find Salan's talk of Mora's woman tiresome.

Salan came closer to him and peered up into his face. "This is the best," he said gloatingly. "Lyra Mora goes over to see her mother sometimes." His eyes gleamed as he spoke. "Because it is on the other side of the island she takes the mule and cart."

"Well," asked Fidel, "what is so exciting about that?"

Salan held up his hand. "Wait," he said, "there is more. Saur said…." He stopped and nodded emphatically. "And you can believe him because he is not a man to lie. He was bringing his boat back to the island," he shrugged, "maybe from fishing; and he passed the inlet where the mother of Lyra Mora has her house; it is cut back into the cliffs there, and he swung in close to avoid the rocks, and when he looked to the land again he saw—." He paused and frowned at Fidel. "You have been to the mainland, Bardi, I have heard that the women over there, when they are on the beaches," his eyes glowed, "they are without shame."

"You mean… she was naked?" asked Fidel incredulously.

"Yes, yes!" said Salan eagerly. "Saur said she was in a bay, too small to even get a boat in and she was in the sea." He shook his head wonderingly. "Saur said he thought it was a fish when he saw her. Then he said she came out of the water and stood for a moment in the sun." He stopped, lost for a second in the vision of Lyra Mora naked in the sunlight.

"What happened?" asked Fidel. "Did she see Saur?"

"He did not know. If she did she never hid herself from him. Saur put the boat about and took it round the headland." He smiled briefly. "Said he nearly sailed the damned thing into the dark water he was shaking so."

"Is that all?"

"Is it not enough?" asked Salan. He paused, and then laughed. "Only that his woman told mine that Saur was like a wild thing when he got home and that he rode her many times in the night."

"Did he—Saur—ever go back again?" Fidel asked.

Salon shook his head. "No, and nor did any other man." He laughed bleakly. "When it was known that she was there, like that, it would have been death to watch her." He nodded warningly at Fidel. "Do not think to try it, Bardi. There are eyes everywhere."

Fidel shook his head slowly. "I would not be so foolish. Thank you for telling this, Salon."

He watched as Salon walked away down the track. Then he turned and went through the narrow streets to his father's house at the end of the track. He looked in at the old man, still in the same position, his breath wheezing in and out of the fragile lungs. He smoked another cigar, then settled down in the chair and waited for sleep to come. But it was as Salon had mockingly said; the image of Lyra Mora filled his thoughts, walking out of the sea, and naked and wet gleaming in the sunlight, staring unconcernedly at Saur. He turned over and over in the chair, desperate to rid his mind of her. Finally, he rose and went outside into the stifling heat of the night air and sat down against the wall of the house.

It was something he had not thought of when he had fled to the island. For whatever time he would have to stay he would be without a woman. He saw that very clearly now. All knew the laws and if he broke them he risked death. Her face flashed into his mind, the full lips drawn back over the white teeth and her long slanting eyes that had watched him at the inn.

He looked down over the tiny houses lit by the intense glow of the moon and huddled together like animals for safety in the night. He stubbed the cigar out viciously and threw it to the ground.

Chapter Nine

Lyra Mora sat on the bed brushing her hair with long slow strokes and thought about the man Bardi and how he had been in the inn that night. She had grown accustomed to the sly glances of the men of the island and the sometimes openly raw lust stares when they thought no one was watching. But Bardi was different. There had been a cool detachment in his eyes when he looked at her. Only once, when he had come to the inn for the first time earlier in the day and she had walked through to collect the flagons, had his eyes burned with a dark intensity that had stirred her.

The old woman that had come to clean the inn had said what a strange boy he had been, always so silent and always alone. And how he had left when he was still so young. With no thought to how his father would struggle to live without his son's strength to carry him. She felt a strange almost dream-like curiosity about him. As if she were in total control of whatever could happen.

When Mora came into the room she was still brushing the heavy, black hair. He stared at her naked body, the slow rise and fall of the big, firm-fleshed breasts as she used the brush, the long powerful thighs that formed the vee into her crotch and the wiry dark hair flaring up from her groin. She looked back at him, seeing the want in his face and felt a sudden heat move through her loins. She stood up and walked to the window as Mora stared, dry-mouthed, at the smooth dark flesh of her buttocks as she moved.

"I'll leave the shutters. It's too hot to close them," she said.

She turned back to him and felt a fierce need to have a man in her, any man, but knowing that it would have to be Mora and the almost inevitable frustration that would come with him, but not caring now, only to have his body tight on hers.

She lay on the bed and stretched out on her back. "Come to me," she said harshly.

He stared at her, his face working convulsively. "Why are you like this?" he asked. "What has made you this way?"

She reached out for him. "Do not speak." She stroked the bedcover. "Come."

Mora shook his head. "I know what it is." He gestured to the window. "It is the man—Bardi, Fidel Bardi; you are in heat because of him!"

Lyra smiled slowly and ran her hand down over her belly. "You are my husband; why would I want another man?" She beckoned. "Do it."

Mora's eyes burned into her. "Swear it is not him," he said.

She opened her arms and shook her head. "Only you."

He came forward then, and bending over her thrust his hand between her legs. She winced at his roughness as he forced his fingers deep into her, then pulled out his cock and fell on her, pushing her thighs apart and entering her without hesitation.

Lyra tried to match his frantic lunges as his loins pumped wildly. "No! No.... I am not ready!" she gasped, but he was deaf to her pleas and did as he had done countless times before, spilling his seed in her as she desperately tried to match his brutal heaving. Then, as suddenly as he had begun, he was finished, falling away and sprawling slack-bodied beside her.

There was a moment's silence in the room, then she turned her head and looked at him, her eyes cold and hard. "You have given me nothing," she said slowly. She pointed to her body. "I felt nothing." She raised up on her elbow and turned to him. "It is the same... always the same. Nothing."

When he was silent she reached out and shook him by the arm. "The women tell me they have pleasure with their men. Why do I never feel it with you? You rush to your pleasure... I have nothing," she grated. She pushed him to the edge of the bed and stretched her body out with her legs apart. "Will you touch me? Or have you no feeling left now?" she asked bitterly.

Mora did not answer and turned his face away from her. She clicked her tongue in anger. "Then be still while I do what you should have done."

She slid her hand over her belly and down the soft flesh of her crotch, slipping her fingers into her wetness. As her hand moved, gently at first, her hips began to rise and fall and her breathing deepened.

Mora looked at her fearfully. "It is wrong," he whispered. "It is a sin!"

"Be silent!" she hissed. "Or I will tell them all that I have to pleasure myself!"

He stared at her as she began to moan softly, then her head went back on the pillow as she rocked her hips and opened and closed her thighs on her hand as it plunged in and out. She moved faster and faster, then suddenly arched up, grunting in time to her frenzied heavings and then screamed out as her body convulsed and almost threw her from the bed. Finally, she slumped back, exhausted, her body running with sweat, and lay staring dull-eyed at Mora.

He put his head in his hands and began to weep.

After a few moments she sat up and spoke. "No matter. It is done with," she said coldly.

Mora curled up on the edge of the bed facing away from her. Lyra lay back down, staring at the ceiling and listening to his muffled sobs. A long time later, as she drifted into sleep, she thought of the man that had come back to the place where he had been born.

Chapter Ten

Now the island moved into the time when the sun burned out of a sky made yellow by its fire. People rose at first light to work on the land before the earth scorched their feet. Those that went to the sea had the boats in the water and away before the night had departed. The sheep grazing on the lower slopes would spend the middle of the day panting in the shade of the scrub, waiting for the sun to slide lower in the sky.

The only respite were the storms that would rage over the island with incredible ferocity; the rain pouring down in long hard bursts, churning up the black earth into a sticky mud that spread everywhere. They would stop as suddenly as they had started and afterwards a cooling wind would blow from the sea. Then it would be back to the savage heat again. It had always been like this as far back as they could remember.

Many years ago someone from the mainland had once tried to explain it, saying something about a geographical fault line and sharing the same climate as parts of Africa. He told them the long and complicated reason and the name for it. The islanders had listened to all that he had said and understood nothing. They simply called it the days of the furnace.

Fidel knew that he must try to adapt his life to the pace of the island. The only places that were not baking in the heat by early morning were a few of the sea caves on the north shore. He would buy a half flagon of wine, walk to them and sit looking out at the heavy, slow swell of the sea.

Sometimes, stupefied by the drink, he would fall into a heavy sleep. One day he walked to the cliff overhang where many years before he had killed the girl with the empty mind. As he stood under the huge ceiling of rock and looked around and remembered, the need for a woman grew swiftly in him and he wished desperately that she were here.

One day, when the boat came from the mainland, Fidel was waiting at the store when the provisions were being unloaded. He had ordered several boxes of cigars and had come down to collect them. He sat and watched the sacks of beans and the big boxes of tinned food carried from the boat and up into the store, followed by the cartons of sugar and dried peppers, the harness and tools, the cases with the bottles of olive oil and all the rest of the cargo.

Then he noticed Yole Mora waiting with his cart and mule. The innkeeper had arrived to bring the empty wine flagons down to the boat and pick up the fresh ones filled with the cheap wine that he bought from the mainland and sold beside the local brew. Fidel raised his hand in greeting, and Mora stared at him before nodding briefly. Fidel waited for two hours, while the boat was unloaded and Otem, the storekeeper, refused to sell anyone anything at all until he had checked everything that came off the boat and that it tallied exactly with what was on his order sheet.

It was only when Fidel had paid for his cigars that he realised that Mora had to wait right to the end for Otem to serve all the others that had come for their goods before he took the empty flagons from Mora and collected the money for the full ones. So the innkeeper would be away for at least two to three hours, Fidel thought, as he walked back up to the village. And he would never close the inn for that length of time—his greed for money was too well known. And the woman would be alone there.

He allowed the implications to slide round in his mind—the possibilities of seeing her and talking without the restraining presence of her husband hovering over them, the physical excitement of her body and the unspoken challenge in her eyes. Suddenly the stifling boredom of his daily routine faded as he contemplated the prospect of Lyra Mora, and the danger too if he started something that he could not control and that might sweep him terrifyingly into violent death.

He found out that the supply boat always came on Thursdays just after midday. Also, that if he walked to the village square and stood a few paces past the well he could look down to the shore and see if the boat had arrived.

The following Thursday he waited and watched as the cumbersome old vessel rolled in and settled on the shore. He threw down his cigar and slowly walked up the side street, feeling a shiver of anticipation run through him.

When he stood before the opened door to the inn he hesitated momentarily, then went through into the suddenly cool interior. The room was empty except for the woman was standing at the window by the counter looking out at the sea. She turned as he entered.

He smiled. "It is too hot to walk any more today," he said.

She moved back behind the counter and nodded. "Yes." She picked up a mug and looked at him. "Our wine?" she asked.

He nodded. "The other is just rotgut," he said.

She smiled coldly. "Mora likes the price he pays for it." She placed his mug in front of him.

Fidel picked it up and took a long drink, relishing the coolness. He placed it carefully on the counter and nodded. "That is the drink of life on a day like this," he said.

The deep green eyes considered him thoughtfully. "It is just another furnace day," she said. "You should not walk in it if you cannot stand the heat."

"You like the sun?" he asked.

"Yes," she said.

She walked over to the window and looked out again. She wore a plain, sleeveless faded blue dress that fastened down the front and ended just above her knees. The first two buttons were undone and he could see the full flesh of her breasts moving as she walked. Suddenly the room had the same charged tension that she had brought to it the first time he had seen her. "Mora is down at the shore for his supplies," she said.

Fidel lit a fresh cigar, making his movements slow and deliberate. "I know," he answered.

She turned her head and looked at him, the stunning eyes probing and evaluating. When she spoke her voice was harsh and deep. "They say you do not work, Bardi. Are you rich that you do not need to earn your food?"

Fidel shook his head and drew on the cigar before speaking. "It would not please me to work as they do," he said. He walked over to a table and sat down on one of the battered wooden chairs. "I lived as a beast in this place so that I might eat," he said quietly. "When I became a man I swore I would never be that way again." He looked at her through the cigar smoke that weaved and hung in the still air. "A man who lives like a beast becomes one."

She shrugged. "It is all they know. Would you have them starve?"

He shook his head. "It is nothing to me what they do," he said flatly.

"Yet you came back," she said, "to a place you have no love for, and people that are nothing to you."

He drained the mug and held it out to her. She walked over, took it from him and refilled it from the flagon behind the counter. Then she brought it back and went over to the window again where she stood staring out at the sea below.

"They also say you came back to care for your father," she said.

Fidel nodded. "That is true."

She frowned. "Then is it also true that you are still paying one of the old women to look after him?"

He nodded again. "Yes." He laughed shortly. "This place never changes."

"You should know that, Bardi," she said. "Everyone is known."

He looked at her and smiled, his lips drawing back from the glistening teeth. "Are you known, Lyra Mora?" he asked softly.

She turned from the window and stared at him. Suddenly the room was very quiet. "What do you mean?" she said coldly.

"You said everyone is known," said Fidel easily. "If that is so, then none of us have any secrets." He smiled again. "If I have none, then you have none."

Her lips tightened with anger. "I know that you did not come back to care for your father, Fidel Bardi," she said harshly.

He felt a tiny stab of panic and then relaxed. She could not possibly know what had brought him back to the island. "I have made you angry," he said quietly. "I am sorry."

She was silent for a moment, then her face relaxed and she shrugged. "It is of no matter."

"Then we are friends?" he asked.

She looked at him for a long moment. "Why would you wish to be a friend to me?" she replied.

"Because I have no friends here," he smiled. "You would be the only one."

"What of the men? Are you not friends with them?" she said.

He shook his head. "No." He turned the mug in his hands. "I am more than they are. I have seen the world and how people live in it." He smiled thinly. "How could I be friends with the men of this place?"

She nodded. "I can understand that. I have never been away from here, but I know there is a different life than this."

"Why do you not go over to the mainland?" Fidel said.

She shook her head. "You know how a woman lives on this island, Bardi." She grimaced. "When she is with a man she becomes his property. She has no say in how her life goes."

Fidel shook his head. "That is still the way of it."

Lyra nodded. "Yes."

"How long have you lived," he looked round the room, "in this place?"

She thought for a moment. "Just past ten years." Her eyes held him in their brilliance. "That is how long I have been with Mora." She smiled bitterly, her lips tight against her teeth. "Sometimes I forget how many… one year seems much as the others."

"To feel like that is not living," he said very slowly. "It is like being in a prison."

She held up her hand and shook her head, the black mane of hair flying round her shoulders. "It is not for you to say, Bardi." The huge eyes blazed into him. "Do not tell me what my life is!"

Fidel held up his hands in a conciliatory gesture. "You are right. I am sorry. I spoke without thinking." He stood up and walked over and placed the mug on the counter. "I will drink one more mug of your wine, Lyra Mora." He looked out of the window. "Then I will go to the sea…."

"You will swim?" she asked.

"Most days," he smiled.

"I love the sea," she said slowly. "When I swim I feel I am free of this place."

"I go where the cliff hides the sun," he said. "When I come from the water I can rest from the heat."

"I know that place," she said. "I have been there."

"I have never seen you," said Fidel.

"I do not go there now."

"Why not?" he asked.

She was silent for a moment, then looked at him, her face serious. "Mora does not want me to swim there."

Fidel frowned. "Why? The sea is calm. There is no danger. You are a long way from the dark water."

She shook her head. "That is not the reason."

He let the silence grow slowly as he watched her. Now would be the time to begin. To build a confidence between them. Something that she would share with him alone.

"What is the reason then?" he asked quietly.

She shook her head again. "It is not right to speak of it."

He shrugged. "Why?" he persisted. "It is only a place to swim. What harm could there be…."

She raised her hand to silence him. "I told you. Mora has forbidden me to go there." She paused and looked down at her hands resting on the counter. "It is between the two of us."

"He does not go with you to swim?" asked Fidel.

She shook her head. "He fears the water."

"So he stops you because he is afraid himself." He laughed shortly. "There is no sense in that."

"He does not forbid me because of the water." She hesitated for a moment. "He says there are too many eyes in that place."

Fidel shook his head slowly in disbelief. "You mean he is frightened that someone will see you?" he said incredulously.

She nodded. "Yes."

He laughed. "Has he never been to the mainland? Never seen the beaches over there?"

"Mora has never left the island," she said. Her face tightened. "He says he never will. He thinks the people over there do not keep good ways."

Fidel shrugged. "They do not think as he does. They are grown men and women and they do what gives them pleasure." He hesitated. "There is more I could say… but I would not wish to offend you."

She shook her head. "You will not do that, Bardi. No one says what I must think. I decide for myself."

He nodded. "It is only that things are so different over there. Many of the women go to the beaches without anything to cover them," he tapped his chest, "here." He paused and watched as her eyes widened. "And there are…." He stopped and shook his head. "It would not be proper to say more."

"I told you," she said curtly, "I decide for myself."

"You are sure?" he asked.

"Yes."

"It is this, then. There are beaches and places where men and women go together and they wear nothing. Everything is seen."

"This is true?" she asked wonderingly. "Men and women together… like that?"

He nodded. "What I have said is the truth. No one is ashamed and," he smiled broadly, "they are all very happy!"

She stared at him, the huge eyes gleaming. "It is hard to believe."

"I told you. It is a different world." He smiled at her. "You could swim there as you liked. No one would tell you what you could do."

He felt a sudden overwhelming maleness ballooning up through his belly as he pictured her lying naked on a crowded beach. "No one," he repeated.

She shook her head. "I do not need to go there…" she began and then stopped.

"What is it?" Fidel asked.

She remained silent, her eyes withdrawn and distant.

"What is wrong?" he persisted. "Do you fear to speak even in your own home?

"I have no fear, Bardi," she said, her lips tight with anger.

"Then what makes you like this?" he probed gently. "Why do you not finish your words?"

"Because you are a stranger to me and I have no trust in you," she said.

He shrugged. "You must think as you wish," he said quietly. "But know this, Lyra Mora." He tapped his hand on the counter to emphasize his words. "Anything that you said would stay with me."

The deep green eyes held him in their depths as she considered his words. Then she nodded. "You are right, Bardi. It is not a thing to make a secret of." She smiled. "It was when you spoke of the swimming… I have a place where I go…" she paused, "I can be free there." She shook her head. "Do you see what I have said?"

He nodded. "Yes. I know what it is like to want freedom." He spread his hands. "It was why I left this rock. To be free."

She frowned. "But you came back?"

"That is right." Fidel laughed shortly. "I had my reasons." He raised the mug and drained it. "Will you tell me where you swim, Lyra Mora?" he said. "Then we could escape for a time in the sea."

"Do not ask, Bardi. If Mora knew that I went there…." She left her words unfinished.

He smiled broadly. "It is nothing. I will go to the place under the cliff." As he turned to go he reached out and touched her hand resting on the counter. "Do not worry. What you have said is only for us to know."

As he walked down to the shore he knew that she would think of all they had talked of. There would be a bond between them now because she could not speak of it to anyone else on the island. And he had touched her hand. Only for a flicker of time, but he had felt the warm velvety feel of her skin under his and she had not wrenched her hand back or protested. He smiled, satisfied with all that had happened.

When he reached the cave under the cliff he sat on the rock floor and smoked a cigar and thought about Lyra Mora. When the images in his mind grew too vivid he stripped off his clothes and slid gently into the warm sea. He lay on his back, closing his eye s, relaxing down into the water, feeling the sun's warmth and the gentle motion of the sea on his body.

CHAPTER ELEVEN

The boy had felt the shadow just touching the island ever since the night of his dream. He had woken in terror from a sleep that held images of horror; in which a man that moved in darkness had taken the life of another man who lived in sin, then slaughtered one who served God.

Since that night the dream had lived in him and he knew that he had seen a great evil. Every day the feeling of dread had grown stronger as if the fear were a living thing that he could not control.

Then, he had waked one morning and the fear was upon him stronger than ever before and he knew that it would be with him that day. He had walked the shore for hours watching the sea gleaming under the pitiless glare of the sun, his mind confused and frightened. At midday he took the path to the top of the cliffs and sat on a rock and waited.

A long time later he heard a sound behind him. He looked round and saw a man walking along the track towards him. Suddenly, for a moment, it seemed to the boy that the sky went black and the land was plunged into darkness. Then, as he shook his head and looked again it was light once more.

When the man stopped and looked at him the boy had known his name and called to him. He had come closer and the boy had looked into the empty darkness of his eyes. The fear had rushed into him and he knew that here was the man from his nightmare, and that the horror had come to the island and he was very afraid. When he told him to go away from this place the man had taken hold of the boy and the dark eyes had filled with a killing rage. Finally, he had let the boy go and walked away down the track, leaving him slumped against the rock trembling and exhausted.

From that day he had watched the man Fidel Bardi moving over the island and it seemed to the boy that he brought darkness wherever he went. He knew that none of the people could see the darkness and that he was alone with the knowledge of the evil that was in Bardi.

The life that he had lived among the people was changed because of this. His terror was so strong that he could not share with them as before. One day he would be working beside them, the next they would see him walking on the high places, alone and silent, his face a mask of fear.

When they asked what troubled him he would turn away and make no answer. He would not stay in their homes to share the food with them and talk with the children as he had always done. He slept under the broken boat that lay near the dunes where his mother had been found. If there was rain in the night they would ask him in to the shelter of their homes. He would refuse, his eyes frightened and say that he had to be in the open under the sky where he could watch.

When the people gathered at the inn they would speak of the boy and say that perhaps his mind was lost. They talked of things not spoken of in years. The strange woman that had carried him and how had she come to the island and how the keen blade of a fisherman's knife had brought him into the world.

They began to question his power of knowing. One said he had heard Fidel Bardi say that it was not possible to see what had not already happened. That it was a trick he had watched in places where you paid to see such things done by clever people, who became rich by the doing.

Others protested at this. Had not the boy saved lives with his truth about the sea? That he had sent men out in weather truly from hell and they had lived to come back. And the times when people had gone to him with a thing that could not be made right between them and he had always shown a way so that all were content.

But doubt had been sown. And there was no way back from the doubt. The people had always thought of him as one of their own. Now, slowly, that was beginning to change. Every day that he did not work beside them in the fields, or take a place on a boat, moved him further away from them.

Then, one day, when the fish were running, but the sky was almost on the sea, they went to him and asked should they take to the boats.

As they waited for him to answer his face became troubled and he struggled to speak. Then, the words came and he said he did not know, that he could not see anything to tell them.

They asked again, saying they must have an answer, that he had always guided them and kept them safe and why could he not do so now?

He had clasped his head in his hands and seemed to be struggling against a powerful force that they could not understand. Finally, he looked at them and told them to go, but they must be watchful. They had asked what they might see to alarm them. He had only shaken his head despairingly and said he had no more to tell them.

They had grown impatient with this and had taken to the water, saying they would rely on their own judgement. As they went further out the sea was calm and they knew they had been right. Then, without warning the sky turned into a black mass that fell around them so that the world became one huge stifling darkness. Suddenly, they lost all sense of place and twisted and turned, trying to find a way out of the awful enclosed world. It lasted for three hours, reducing them to a terror they had never experienced.

Then, when they were sure that they were lost forever the sun swept the darkness away and they could see again. They called to each other to turn for home while they had light.

When they finally beached the boats it was seen that Lodino and his crew were missing. The fear was so great in them that no one would put back out to look for him. As the hours passed the families of the missing men came to the shore and stood straining their eyes out to sea. It was not until the new day was upon them that a boat was seen moving slowly, almost drifting, towards them.

Then the men went to meet them and securing a line towed them in. As Lodino's crew stepped ashen-faced to the shore they had the look of men that had seen their own deaths so close they had touched them. Lodino said that when they were surrounded by the darkness they had tried to find a way out, and had touched against the outer fringes of the dark water. The boat had begun to move into the Run and for two hours the men had fought frantically with sail and tiller to stay out of the death.

Then the light had returned and the water had let them go. They had taken the boat into safety and then collapsed, exhausted and weeping with relief. Many hours had passed before they had the strength to make for home. Even then, only two of them had worked the sails, while one sat slumped at the tiller as the rest blankly watched the water slide past.

Their people helped them up the track to the village and food and rest. Saur, who had been out with his brothers, looked around in the crowd. "Where is the boy?" he said. "Why is he not here?" He shook his head angrily. "Why did he let this happen?"

Otem, the storekeeper pointed to the top of the cliffs. "He went up to the high places to watch."

Saur smashed his fist hard against the side of his boat. "He should be here to see what he has done." He glared at them. "We could have died because of him. Why did he not tell us of the darkness?"

"We asked him. He did not know," said one of his brothers.

"Then why did he always know before?" Saur shouted. "Why did he let us go to die? Lodino almost went into the Run. You saw him just now. He has walked with death. It is marked on his face."

"Perhaps the boy has lost the power," said a woman.

Saur wiped his hand across his wet face and spat on the rocks. "Then why did he not tell us?"

That night the inn was full of what had happened. Those that had previously spoke out in defence of the boy now had little to say. The facts were too strong. Men had almost died because he had not seen what was about to happen. They had trusted him in the past and been safe. Now the trust was going as they talked about how strangely he been acting recently, his insistence on being alone so much and the refusal to join in the village life.

Fidel stood quietly and listened and picked the story out of the excited babble and waited until he caught Saur's eye. He nodded to the tall man who turned from his companions and pointed to Fidel.

"There," he said, "ask Bardi. He has seen places where tricks are done… things to make a man believe he has seen the impossible." He looked at Fidel and beckoned. "Come over to us, Bardi, and tell what you know of this."

Fidel picked up his mug and walked across the room. As he joined them the noise in the room lessened as they pressed forward to hear. He smiled. "What is it you would have me speak of?"

Saur frowned impatiently. "You remember the first time you came here and spoke of the boy?"

Fidel nodded.

"And you said that," Saur hesitated, "you had seen things done to fool a man… and that maybe the boy could do the same."

"Yes, I remember," said Fidel. "And you told me never to speak that way again."

Saur's face tightened as he stared at Fidel. "That is true. I did say that." He looked at them. "I spoke what I thought was the truth. Now I ask Bardi to tell what he knows. Then I will think again."

Fidel placed his mug on the counter. "I have seen things, that is right," he said. "In the big cities there are places to go where clever men and women do tricks they call magic."

He lit a cigar while they waited impatiently for him to tell them about a world that was beyond their understanding. "Sometimes they make a person vanish," he said.

"That is not possible," said Yole Mora quickly.

"You are right," Fidel said. "But they can make you believe that it is."

"I would not," Mora said.

"You are free to believe whatever you like," Fidel said calmly. "I am just saying what these people can do." He smiled at the innkeeper. "They always bring the person back before the end of their tricks. That is how clever they are. You think they have gone, then they are back."

"I would still not believe," Mora said staring just above Fidel's head.

Fidel looked at him thoughtfully. "Did you believe in all the things this boy told you before?"

Mora hesitated. "Sometimes. He was right many times."

"And when he spoke of the weather and the sea you believed him then."

Mora frowned. "I was not interested in that." He shook his head. "The sea does not concern me."

"It concerns me," Salan said harshly. The stocky man glared at Mora. "We go to her and trust our lives that she will not take us."

Mora nodded quickly. "You are right. I did not think." He spread his hands. "I work in these walls. I am not threatened by the sea as you are." He looked anxiously at Salan who nodded curtly to him.

Fidel continued. "Did you believe him today?"

"I did not hear what he said. I was at my work," Mora answered.

"I will tell you what he said." Saur leaned forward and rapped his hand on the counter. "He said we were to go, but we should be watchful." He turned to the men in the room and held out his hands. "How could a man watch for darkness in the sun's highest time?"

One of the men that had sailed with Saur looked up. "There has never been such a thing," he said. "It is not possible for night to enter the day."

"Tiran is right. This is what I am saying," Saur said. "The boy told nothing of darkness!"

Fidel nodded. "If he did not know then how could he tell you?" He turned back to Mora. "So, if you had heard what he said today, then you would have believed him because he was right in the things he said before."

"I suppose so," the innkeeper said slowly. "I am not sure."

"You are not sure now because of today," Tiran said. "That is the truth of it."

Mora nodded. "Perhaps."

"Then this is what I am saying," Fidel said. "Before, you believed. Now you are not sure." He smiled gently. "I do not believe the boy is the same as the people that I have seen. They get much money for their tricks. He does not." He looked all round the room at them. "All you do is feed and shelter him."

There was a silence as they looked at one another. Fidel could almost hear them thinking. They had trusted the boy totally until today. Now in just a few minutes Fidel Bardi had added to the doubt that was already among them.

He wondered what they would have said if he told them the boy had known his name without ever seeing him before. There had to be something different about him. Fidel thought perhaps he did have a power to see. He had heard it said that sometimes a man might have a gift that could not be explained.

Though, as he looked at them, he thought it might be very different for the boy now. It was a pity that none of them had been lost to the dark water. That would have turned their minds away from the boy completely.

Tiran drained his mug. "I am for my bed." As he went to the door he looked back. "I do not think I will ask the boy's word again."

Saur nodded. "We are the same in our minds on that, Tiran." The rest of the men looked at each other and slowly nodded.

"It is not for me to say," said Fidel carefully. "I do not share your danger, but surely you have enough knowledge of the sea to decide for yourselves."

As they left the inn some of the men nodded to Fidel and he knew that he had made an impression on them. He was no longer the outsider. They had asked for his knowledge of the world and he had shared it with them. He knew they would ask again. He was almost accepted back into the island.

As for the boy, he had failed them and men could have died. Now they spoke of him without respect. And Fidel Bardi had said a thing that many of them had thought for a time now. They did give him food and shelter, but now he hardly worked at all. Some of them thought his mind had gone away from him. Some even said he brings nothing to the island, why then should we care for him. And some whispered that he was not even come from island people.

Saur and his brothers made it known they would no longer have him in their boat. They said if he could not guide them away from danger as before then they did not want him at sea.

Others began to speak in the same fashion. Soon the boy became more alone than ever, only fed now by a handful that remembered how true he had been in the old days and refused to turn their backs on him.

Chapter Twelve

The daily rhythm of the island life continued under the boiling sun. Fidel walked and swam and it was on such a day that the storm had begun as he walked up from the shore. He knew that Mora would collect his wine from the store and Lyra would be alone at the inn. He quickened his steps as the first scattering of drops fell, then began to run as the skies went black and the drops became a torrent, bouncing off the rocks and striking the earth with such force that the dust flew up as mud.

By the time he got to the door of the inn his clothes were sticking to him and water was running off his body. He went in and stood for a moment, wiping his hands over his face, clearing the water from his eyes.

"You have brought the rain with you, Bardi." He looked up and saw her sitting at a table by a window in the empty room.

"Close the door or we will have the storm in here," she said. He turned and pushed the heavy door shut. She stood up and went behind the counter and poured him a mug of wine. Fidel shook his head spraying the water round him. He walked over and picked up the mug and looked at the woman. Her dark hair was drawn back and tied in a knot behind her head and she wore a thin green shift that left her arms bare. She looked at him as he drank.

"Have you just walked out of the sea, Bardi?"

"I swam this morning," he smiled. "I should have stayed there. I would have been no wetter."

"I have been in the water when a storm has broken," she said.

"Were you not afraid?" he asked.

She shook her head. "What is there to be frightened of? It is only noise and rain."

"What of the lightning. It can kill you."

She laughed, her eyes holding him. "That would be a quick death." She considered him for a moment. "Would you be afraid to swim with the storm?"

He looked out of the window. The rain was falling so furiously that it was like a wall that he could hardly see through, only the wavering outlines of the houses and the shore, as it cascaded off the roofs and went pouring down the streets in long rivers of black mud. Suddenly, thunder rolled off somewhere out at sea, followed seconds later by lightning that crackled and sliced through the gloom.

"Not if you were there," he said.

"Why would I make you strong?" she asked.

He smiled. "I am a man," he said. "Men think they are braver than women." he shrugged. "I do not believe it."

"So," she said. "So if I swam with you in a storm I would try to look as brave as you."

He grinned. "Even if I was not."

The thunder sounded again, nearer now. Fidel drained the mug and she refilled it. He nodded at the window. "How long will this last?"

She shrugged. "Sometimes a few hours... maybe a day... who knows?"

"I am trapped here then, until it stops," he said. He looked round the room. "There are worse places to spend time in."

Lyra looked at him reflectively. "Are there?" she said.

Fidel shook himself again and rubbed his face. "Do you have a cloth that I can dry myself?" he asked.

"I'll get one for you," she said and turned and went through the door behind the counter.

Moments later she came back carrying a large blue towel. She passed it to him and he rubbed his hair and face.

"May I take this off?" he indicated his sodden shirt that was plastered to his chest.

She nodded and watched as he tugged the clinging garment over his head and dropped it to the floor.

"What is that?" She pointed to the thin sheath hanging under his left arm.

Fidel took hold of it and lifting it carefully over his head placed it on the counter. She went to touch it and he held out his hand to restrain her. "Easy, it is as keen as a razor."

She picked up the sheath and gently slid the dull-glowing blade out of the covering. As she held it the light danced off the steel. She frowned at Fidel. "Why do you have this with you?" she asked harshly.

He stared at her for a moment, then smiled tightly. "It is a friend," he said quietly.

She ran her finger delicately along the edge of the blade. "How do you come to need a friend like this?"

He was silent as he rubbed the towel over his chest. She looked at the dark eyes, so dark now as to be almost black and she felt something alien about him. She had noticed it when he drank and spoke with the men of the village. That he was somehow apart. And it was not simply that he had lived in the outside world. He always seemed in control and had never shown the sly scarcely concealed lust that she had come to expect from the other men. Only once or twice had she seen his eyes burn into her, for just a second, then nothing. She also found him oddly menacing and she did not know why. But she had no fear of him.

"You would not understand," he said softly.

"What is there to understand about a knife?" she asked. She turned the blade in her hand. "It is not like those the men here carry. They have knives for work. This does not look like a thing for labour."

Fidel smiled easily. "You ask many questions."

She slid the blade back in the sheath and laid it on the counter. "And you have no answers."

He shook his head. "It is just that I have sometimes lived in strange places," he said slowly, "where the people are not always ready to listen to reason." He nodded at the knife. "It is good to have a friend then."

She looked at him silently while he dried himself. When he finished he placed the towel on the counter.

"Thank you." He indicated the wet trousers and shrugged. "They will soon dry in this heat."

It was true. The room was like an oven. Fidel wrung his shirt out and hung it on the back of a chair. Then he sat down and reached for the mug of wine. "You do not drink?" he asked her.

"No." She indicated over her shoulder. "Mora likes everything paid for."

Fidel smiled and reaching in his pocket placed a couple of coins on the table.

"There," he said, "now he has no reason to grieve." He pointed to the wine flagon. "If it pleases you, then drink."

She frowned for a second, then laughed throatily, her lips curving up in amusement.

"If he comes back now he will not believe that you paid for me to drink," she said.

Fidel tapped the coins. "Show him the money."

She shook her head. "Where it is money he believes no one."

"Drink, anyway," he said. He nodded at the deluge outside. "Look at it. He will be a long time down there, yet."

She picked up the flagon and filled a mug. He watched as she drank. When she put the mug down her lips were dark from the wine. She smiled. "That is the only good thing to come from this place," she said.

Fidel nodded. "The sun is a hell, but the wine loves it." He leaned back in the chair and she looked at the muscular compact torso as he stretched his arms above his head. She leaned forward on the counter and Fidel felt the breath catch in his throat as he saw the square-cut shift gape and the loveliness of the big, woman's breasts exposed, straining against the thin material. He stared at her openly and as she watched his eyes became very dark, almost red.

Suddenly, the stifling room was still and silent, the only sound the rain hammering on the roof and sheeting down the walls. He got to his feet and looked at the door, then at her. In three strides, moving fast, he was at the counter. She straightened up and stepped back quickly. His eyes blazed into her, his desire raw and urgent for her to see.

"What day do you swim?" he said harshly.

Her eyes widened in alarm. "You cannot go there!" she said.

"When?" he demanded.

She shook her head. "No. I have said that you cannot go there."

"Answer me," he said.

"Do you not hear what I have said?" she asked desperately. "He does not know that I swim in that place. If you are seen there he will have you killed!"

"He is nothing to be afraid of," Fidel said contemptuously. "No man tells me what to do on this island. I go where I please."

She pressed back against the wall, the huge eyes wide. "Please... do not make trouble."

"Then tell me." He took a step round the counter and she came off the wall and held up her hand.

"Do not touch me, Bardi," she said warningly. Her eyes flashed. "I am not a thing to be used!"

He stopped, then shook his head. "Do not fear. I will not harm you," he said slowly. "Just tell me the day."

Even now, with her heart pounding she was not afraid, only gripped by an almost unbearable excitement. "If I tell you, then you must promise not to go there when I do."

He smiled, his eyes gradually turning dark again, the redness vanishing. "And if I should forget the days?"

The huge eyes bored into him, the deep green gleaming in the overcast light. "I have told you what he will do." She gestured down at the village. "They are like animals. If he tells them to they will kill you."

"What day?" he asked.

"You are mad, Bardi," she said. "Have you heard nothing of what I told you?"

"I hear you," he smiled. "What day?"

She shook her head silently. "I can ask the old woman that cares for my father. She knows everything. She will tell me," said Fidel.

"If you do that, then in one day they will all know," she said.

"Then you do it," he replied.

She bit her lip and stared at him. "You will not promise."

"No." He moved back to the other side of the counter and picked up the knife and slung it round his neck, adjusting it down under one arm. He looked at her as he pulled his shirt off the chair. "Well... is it you, or the old woman?" He struggled into the shirt. "I do not say that I will go there. Only that you tell me the day." He shrugged. "It is a very small thing to know."

"You are a fool, Bardi, and you are playing with your life," she said. She waited for him to speak, but he remained silent, watching her.

"All right," she said finally, "let it be for you to decide." She picked up the mug and drank. "I go to my mother's house the first day after the rest."

He knew she meant the first day of the week. The islanders had always called Sunday the rest.

"I take her food," she said. She smiled coldly at him. "That is one of the reasons I am here. So that she can eat." She looked at him enquiringly. "You do not find that strange, Bardi?"

He shook his head slowly. "No. I live in this world. Nothing surprises me."

"Then you are lucky," she said bitterly. She looked all round the room. "I would have wished for my life to have trod a different path than this."

"You have much time before you," he said. "Today is one thing... tomorrow a life might be changed." He smiled at her." We cannot know."

"You think not," she said, her eyes intent on him. "When old Mora bought me for his son and I came here I knew then what every day would be."

"You are wrong," Fidel said firmly. "Things will change. Just be still and wait."

"It is easy for you to say," she said hotly. "You do not have to live with a man that...." She stopped and turned her head away from him.

"What is it?" Fidel asked. "What gives you such pain?"

Her fingers tightened round the mug. She shook her head slowly. "I cannot speak more. It is a thing that must be kept here," she placed her hand over her heart, "not for others to know."

Fidel looked at her. The tiny bond that had been established the time before when he had touched her hand was strengthened now. She had told him what day she swam. The knowing lay between them. In the keeping of it from Mora she would make a pact of silence in which they both shared. He knew he must not be as the men that craved her. Although she had known his hunger a moment ago, when he stood close enough to feel the power of her body, he had not touched her.

Even now, in her bitterness, her lips drawn back, mouth tight under the high cheekbones, the huge eyes almost slitted, she still exuded the overwhelming sensuality that he took with him into his sleep every night.

He walked to the window and looked out. The rain had begun to slacken and he could see the shoreline. There was a receding roll of thunder and he turned back to her and pointed out at the sky. "It is less now."

She nodded. "Soon it will stop. Mora will start back then."

Fidel sat down at his table. "I will finish the wine and go." He pulled a soggy pack of cigars and a box of matches from his pocket and took one of the cigars out. He looked at it and nodded, then opened the matchbox and frowned. "These are useless. Do you have any?" he asked.

She reached behind her and took a box off the shelf and threw it to him. He caught it and lit the cigar, drawing deeply on it, sending a stream of blue smoke spiralling up in the still air.

"He will know you have been here." She nodded at the smoke. "No one uses cigars as you do."

"Why should I care if he knows?" Fidel said. "Is this not a place to drink wine?" He smiled tightly at her. "I told you. I have no fear of Mora. Nor any of them."

He stayed another half hour then left, walking through the mud, feeling the last of the storm rain, thin now, falling on him, the cooling wind moving gently in from the sea, short-lived and soon to die, and then back to the intense heat. When he came to the well he stopped and looked back down to the shore.

Through the haze he could just make out the tiny figure of the mule and cart struggling and sliding up the track and he knew it was the innkeeper coming back from the store.

Suddenly, fragmented images of Mora and the woman coupling flashed into his mind, their bodies writhing, every sound and detail sharp and clear, her face taut with passion as Mora rode her, his loins pumping, her thighs opening and closing on him, her gasps and grunts, then the frenzied small screams as he brought her to pleasure.

He struggled to clear his head from it, remembering what Salan had told him—that the innkeeper had never been with her as a man should with his woman. Finally, it vanished and he bent over the well wall and spat viciously down into the long darkness.

Chapter Thirteen

Fidel had never had a definite plan for the taking of Lyra Mora. It was as if he had found all the pieces of the plan simply by chance, picked them up, and assembled them into a pattern of action, that if completed would bring success.

On his long walks up the goat paths in the shimmering light to the high places and during the slow hours of swimming naked, gliding through the warm blue-green sea, her presence had always been there, the incredible eyes seeing into him, taking him down in their deep green depths, her powerful body so absolute in its sensual containment, and always the danger of knowing that the having of her might mean the losing of his life.

Now he felt he had the pieces really into place. First, where she swam was far from the village so he had to get to her without arousing suspicion. He knew he could not travel overland; it was too far for him to go on foot in a day and he would be seen leaving. So he would go to the mainland on the store boat, or one of the boats that came for the fish, and the following day hire a boat and come back to the point where her mother lived.

He had to risk being seen from the island as he approached, but the old woman's house was set in remote country and he was sure that no one would have cause to be at that end of the island.

Then, the following day he could sail to the mainland and wait to get a ride back over to the island.

When he went over it in his mind the doing of it seemed easy. The thought of what she would do when she discovered him in her secret place intrigued Fidel. He had considered the possibility that she might refuse to be there with him although this did not worry him unduly. He knew her situation with Mora and was sure that alone in a private place she would give way to her body's hunger. Anyway, the uncertainty was much of the appeal of it. He welcomed anything that would break the relentless monotony that kept him confined to this searing mass of rock.

He waited, allowing the time to pass easily, taking his walks on the shore and the high places, swimming under the flat cliffs and going to the inn late in the day and at night. He began to fit back into the life of the island. They would include him in the talk as they drank their wine, going back to the time when he had lived on the island and what had happened then.

He told them of the outside world, things they could hardly understand and he would try to answer their questions. But the talk always returned to the island.

It was their world and he knew they would never change it for any other.

And the woman was always there, the eyes burning, watching him, revealing nothing, contained and powerful. Waiting.

When two moons had passed Fidel was ready. He let it be known that he was going over to the mainland and that if anyone wanted something brought back then he would try to bring it.

Saur asked hesitantly if he would bring him a small pack of the cigars like those Fidel smoked. Salan wanted a new knife that Otem at the store did not have in his stock.

He refused their money saying he was not sure of the cost, but he could get things cheaper in certain places. This impressed them as he'd known it would.

He left on the Thursday going over with the supply boat on its return trip. When it landed he took a room over a taverna in the docks and later that night hired a small boat from a fisherman at the bar. He stayed in his room for the rest of the night knowing that the hunt for the priest killer would still be going on and a fresh face might attract attention.

For the next two days he rose early and took the boat out to sea cruising along just in sight of the shore. When he came in he ate food at a cafe round on the other side of the docks and never stayed long in any one place.

On Sunday morning he rose at dawn and went to the beach where the boat was moored. He threw the bag with his food and drink into the stern and pushed off. The freshening breeze filled the sail and Fidel sat back at the tiller enjoying the swift rhythm of the little craft as it glided through the water. He watched the sea moving towards him in long irregular ridges, the bow rising on each crest, sending a fine salt spray flying into the air. The sun was warm now, but he knew it would be hotter when he neared the island.

It was just over two hours when he felt the movement change beneath the little boat and he immediately stood up and looked down over the side. The colour of the sea had darkened to a dull slate shade and Fidel knew he was on the outfringes of the dark water. He swung the tiller over and put out to sea, running for an hour before he eased cautiously back to see if he had passed the point where the power of the Run ended. When the boat sat smoothly and the water showed blue-green again he moved on, heading towards the island.

Finally, he saw the faint outline of the mass of rock on the horizon. He tacked across the sea until he was opposite the point where the old woman had her home, then began to ease the boat in to the land.

Suddenly he saw a thin plume of smoke rising in the air and knew it must be from a chimney. He looked at the shore searching for a place to put in, but the boulders rose sheer from the sea and he moved on round the outcropping of rocks until he saw a tiny opening barely wide enough for a boat to enter. He knew this would be the perfect place, well hidden from anyone looking from the land. He eased the little craft in and waited until it bumped to a halt among the rocks and then jumped over the side and slung a line over a rock, lashing it securely down. He stood up and looked around. It was truly a wild and solitary place where Lyra Mora's mother lived. Indeed, despite her warning to him, he doubted that anyone would ever come out here simply to watch the innkeeper's wife.

He started to climb up over the wet rocks moving to the high ground. As he reached the top of the cliff he dropped to the earth and looked over. Down below was a small stone house set up the cliffs above the rocks. Smoke rose from the chimney. He knew he had found Lyra Mora's mother's house. He moved back down to the boat and prepare to wait. He had food, drink and his cigars. The sun was hot and the night would be warm. He could sleep in the boat or among the rocks. He was ready.

Mora watched as Lyra led the mule and cart round to the front of the inn. He picked up the case of tinned food and the bottles of cooking oil and packed them tight up behind the seat. He shook his head as he looked at them. "The old woman will eat until I have no more to give," he said sourly.

Lyra climbed up onto the cart and took the reins in her hand. "You have what I give you, Mora," she said evenly. "That is more than a fair exchange for a little food." She shook the reins and the mule started forward. "I will see you tomorrow."

Yole Mora stood for a moment and watched them as they moved off up the track to the path that led to the high ground. "Just come back and tell me the old bitch is with us no more," he grunted, then turned away and went back inside.

As they reached the top of the cliff, Lyra felt the same sense of freedom that always came over her every time she did this journey. To be away from the confines of the inn and the sullen, brooding presence of Mora for just one whole day. Even the crushing heat did not bother her. She simply relaxed into it and let the mule make its own slow amble along the rutted track, its ears twitching at the clouds of flies hovering round its head.

She knew that Mora would be glad when her mother died and no more free food would leave the inn. She also wondered what she would do when that time came. There would be no need for her to stay with him then. Her mind wandered over the prospect of life without Mora. Where could she go and how would she live? She thought she could go over to the mainland and find some kind of work. Fidel Bardi had gone over when he was only a boy. She had listened when he had spoken with the men at night and they had asked him about the life on the mainland. Most of what he said she had not understood, but she was sure she could live away from the island.

Her mother had never spoken of the man that had fathered the girl, only to tell her that he had died at sea. The old woman that helped at the inn had told her that she had heard he was off one of the fishing boats, that he had stayed for a while and then gone. Also, she had said, her voice dropping to a whisper, that he was of dark blood. She had taken hold of Lyra's arm and stroked the soft sheen of the flesh, saying that must be the reason for the colour of her skin.

Lyra had grown up in the remoteness of her mother's home, surviving on fish caught from the sea and a meagre crop of corn grown on the patch of land behind the house. Her only contact with other people had been the times when her mother had taken her to the village to sell the fish to the boats from the mainland and the things given up by the sea—the twisted wood sculpted into strange shapes and rocks worn smooth by the pounding of the water.

Sometimes the men would throw them a few coins and take the stuff back to sell to the tourists.

She had seen the way the people of the village stared at them and she had always been glad to return to the little house cradled into the cliffs far away from their looks of pity and contempt.

When old Mora had come to her mother and asked for the girl to live as his son's wife there had been no question of refusal. The harsh uncertainty of their existence had meant immediate acceptance and guaranteed the mother would eat as long as she lived. The condemning of her daughter to a union with a man she had never met had not been considered. Survival was all.

So the girl had come to the house of Mora and worked as an unpaid slave, listening to the whinings of the son and the ranting of the father as the marriage bed remained childless. As time passed the old man had wanted to send her back to her mother but by then she had grown into a woman of such devastatingly raw beauty that the son was totally obsessed with her and although the seed he desperately forced into her body remained fruitless, he could not bear to let her go.

When old Mora died things had become easier for her. She had taken a stronger position in the relationship now that the son no longer had the massive presence of his father to bolster his weak authority. Also, she had become angered with his crude fumblings with her body that always ended with him spent and exhausted and her tense and frustrated. He had told her that this was how it was between men and women, that it was just to bring children that it was done.

But Lyra knew differently. One night, after he had used her and then slumped into a deep sleep, she had risen from the bed and gone outside. Angry and confused she had leaned against the wall and looked up at the diamond-bright blazing stars hanging in the velvet sky. Then she had heard a slight sound in the field behind the inn where the mule was stabled. When she listened hard she recognised voices and she had gone closer to the stone wall and peered through a break in the slabs.

As her eyes adjusted to the darkness she had seen Salan and his woman lying on the ground only a short span from the wall. Lyra had remained totally still and watched, heart beating wildly as Salan's woman had stripped off her shift and Salan had begun to kiss and caress her breasts while she had pulled out his cock and stroked it. Then she had opened her thighs and pulled him on top of her, sliding him into her body. Lyra had bitten her hand to stop from uttering a sound as they rode each other in front of her.

As she watched she realised that this was not how Mora was with her. Salan and his woman kissed, long slow kisses, tongues flicking into mouths and hands roaming each other's body. The woman arched her back and Salan cupped her breasts and teased her nipples with his fingers.

When Salan had started to move faster on her she had pushed him off and whispered, "No, not like that,"and rolled over on top of him. She had laughed and dangled her breasts before his face and reached down with her hand to fit him into her. He had pushed hard, twice, and she had squirmed and they had both laughed, then settled into a gentle rhythm, with gasps and squeals of enjoyment and Salan had gripped her broad buttocks as they quickened their movements and the sounds became frantic, and they both finally lunged to a climax, the woman collapsing on Salan and the both of them quite still for a long moment. Then they had risen, brushed the earth from their clothes and walked away, arms round each other.

Now Lyra knew that what Mora did to her was wrong. Salan had tended to his woman's needs and she had shared the passion with him. When she tried to make Mora do the same he said it was not right to touch each other in that way, and where had she seen it done? Lyra had replied that if he spoke of right, then surely it was not right for only one of them to feel the pleasure. She could not speak of what she had seen and Mora would not talk of it again.

Finally, she would wait until he finished with her and then touch her own body into a kind of release. At first he would try to stop her, clutching at her hands, but she threw him off violently, threatening to shame him before everyone. Then, to her amazement he would sit and weep, cursing his father for ever having brought her to the inn. The following day he would act as if nothing had happened. She had made herself learn to accept the daily routine of the life at the inn.

The only pleasure she insisted on was the weekly trip to her mother. Mora had readily agreed. He hated the old woman and was glad to forgo the long ride to the other side of the island. Then Lyra had said that she could not return the same day. It was simply too much time sat in the jolting cart. She would return the following day. Mora had grudgingly agreed.

He had seen the want in the faces of the men that came to the inn when they looked at his woman. He was also aware of the ruthless code concerning infidelity, and that so great was their distrust of each other that not one of them would dare move towards Lyra for fear of being found out and killed. And, although his jealousy almost drove him mad, there was a strange pleasure in having them all know that he could use her whenever he wanted.

But he made her swear that she would never speak of what happened between them in the bed.

The sun was high as she came to the narrow path that forked off away from the main track and led down to the stretch of rocks where her mother lived. She shook the reins over the mule's back and braced her feet against the board as the wheels bounced over the rough ground. She would be there in a little while now and could enjoy the precious time left in the day as she pleased. Her mother had lived a solitary life for so long that she would have few words to say to the girl that she had sold to the innkeeper many years ago. Lyra would tell her of the happenings at the inn and the old woman would grunt her acknowledgement, ask a question or two and that would be the limit of their contact.

She would accept the food, checking everything that came off the cart, then cook fish for them. When Lyra had eaten she would go to the shore and remove her shift and plunge into the sea. She loved the warm touch of the water as she slid easily through the clear depths, driving all thoughts of Mora, the inn and the daily drudgery from her like a soothing balm, totally embracing her and cleansing her soul.

She would swim for hours, moving like a great sleek fish, diving down into the depths, twisting and turning gracefully, exploring the underworld, and then rising and floating on her back, staring up at the huge expanse of burning sky. The sea took her and held her as she found the pleasure that she had never known on the land.

Sometimes, even when darkness came, she would stay in the water, reluctant to leave this other world of silence and beauty.

Today her mother was even more withdrawn than usual and Lyra was glad when the silent meal ended. She rose from the table to clear the dishes but her mother took them from her and waved her away. Lyra started to say she would help, then shrugged and went outside. She stood a moment in the warmth looking all round at the sea and cliffs. The only sound was the shrill cries of the seabirds circling high above the gentle waves and the water lapping the rocks.

She peered back inside the darkness of the house and saw her mother sat at the table totally engrossed with the tins of food.

Lyra spoke to her, but the old woman remained silent. Lyra waited, then shrugged, turned and started to walk down to the shore. She climbed over the huge rocks and descended to the tiny level where she always swam from. A long flat stone jutted out of the sea here and she sat down on it and let her feet dangle in the water.

Slowly, her mind began to relax into the solitude and she stripped off her shift, spread it out behind her and lay back, supporting herself on her elbows and gazing out at the endless expanse of sea.

Almost drugged with the heat she drifted into a semi-sleep. It was only when one of the birds swooped down, screaming, and flashed past her head that she sat upright with a start, thrusting her arm in the air to ward it off. She waited a moment, collecting herself, then moved forward to the edge of the rock and slid down into the water, going deep under the surface in a long glide, hands outstretched and legs moving slowly to propel her through the warm clear sea.

Finally, she broke surface fifty yards away from the shore and turned over on her back to hang suspended in the water, totally relaxed, barely moving with the ebb and flow, her mind empty, everything gone away, only the sun and the sea real to her.

Fidel had slept half propped up against a rock drawing the heat from it into his body. He had woken just after first light and lay a long time staring at the sky and wondering what would happen this day. He knew that Lyra should be here, it was her day to make the journey to her mother, and while he had been on the island she had never altered her routine.

He ate some bread and olives and drank wine. Then he walked cautiously through the rocks and peered out along the shoreline and up at the cliff top. There was no one anywhere, as he had thought. He went back into the rocks, sat down and lit a cigar and drank more wine. She should be here just before the sun was highest in the sky and he thought he would have to find a place to watch her and see where she swam.

He put the food and wine back in the boat and climbed from the rocks to the high ground and peered over at the old woman's house. There was nowhere on the shore in front of the house that looked like a place to swim from and he thought she must have a particular spot she used to enter the sea. All he could do was to stay hidden and watch the house until she arrived, then wait to see where she went.

He looked at the track leading down to the house and then back up it to the cliff top. That was the way she would come down. All he had to do was wait. Then he remembered her warning of what would happen if he were seen. Not that he thought anyone would follow her out to this forsaken place on the chance of catching her with a man. Still, it would do no harm to stay concealed. He looked at the sun. About four hours to go. He moved carefully back down to his place among the rocks and got the wine from the boat and sat down again.

It was only when the sun had moved directly overhead and was striking his face that he woke from the soft sleep that he had drifted into. He stood up and stretched, then moved once again through the rocks. As he reached the last huge boulder jutting up from the ground he stopped, heart racing.

Lyra Mora was lying naked on a long slab that hung out over the sea. He stood, scarcely breathing as he looked at her body, dark skin gleaming in the harsh light. As he was about to step out from the shelter of the rocks she sat up as a bird flashed past her head. Fidel waited as she paused for a moment, then went forward and down into the sea, going under and out into the depths. She reappeared away from the shore and lay back on the water, drifting gently with the pull of the sea.

He watched as the sun burned down on her and he felt his blood pounding. He pulled off his shirt and pants, drew the knife over his head and let it fall to the ground. Then he stepped out and walked to the slab. He had just reached it when she turned in the water and saw him. She came upright immediately, treading water and staring at him, her eyes wide.

He stood on the slab and smiled at her. "You chose well, Lyra Mora," he called. "This is a fine place to swim."

She looked all round the high rock walls. "You cannot stay here," she said fearfully. "You must go… now!"

His smile widened. "You were wrong to be afraid. No one will ever come here."

She swam slowly closer until she was almost under the slab. "What are you saying? Why would they not come?"

"Because they are all afraid." He looked down at her and laughed. "You do not see. It is simple. Did you never wonder why you saw no one here?"

She shook her head and frowned at him. "No."

"It is as I said. They are afraid to come here because they think they will be seen." He watched the uncertainty in her face as he spoke. "Think on what I say. They are all like frightened children. Wanting to be here and watching you, but terrified someone will see them." He smiled triumphantly. "And that is what keeps them away. Fear!"

She trod water, moving easily. "How can you be sure of this?"

Fidel laughed. "Would I risk my life to be here?" he asked.

She looked at him for a long moment. "I think you have no fear in you, Bardi." She laughed, her huge eyes gleaming, the full-throated sound echoing out over the water and waking a raw overpowering urgency in his loins.

He looked at the intense green of her eyes, her hair the colour of jet plastered wetly to her head; her sleek body shining in the brilliant light, the full breasts moving in the water, and the gentle swell of her belly that slid breathtakingly down into the dark hair of her crotch; the flaring hips that tapered into the long thighs and the powerful arms holding her upright in the sea.

He felt that nothing that had happened in his life right up to this very moment mattered at all, that there was only the two of them in this place, so isolated that they could be the only people on earth and this fire that had touched him the very first time that he had seen her at the inn, and all the rest of the times, and that was now raging almost out of control through his body, threatening to consume him, would not be denied.

He stepped forward right to the edge of the big slab and stood staring at her. "You know why I am here, Lyra Mora," he said thickly, almost tasting the acrid pungency of his desire.

She moved slowly back through the water away from him. "Yes," she said softly.

She watched as he ran his hand over his chest wiping away the sweat, and then down to the thick hair of his groin, his fingers brushing lightly against his suddenly erect phallus and she felt her need rise strong and urgent. It was as if time had stopped and they had no control over anything anymore, that they were just creatures of this burning land, without inhibitions or laws or morals, simply compelled to act by raw instinct.

"If I stay, you know what will happen?" he asked harshly.

She nodded, the water sliding down the curve of her neck and into the fullness of her breasts.

"Well?" he demanded.

She looked up at the sun that was almost white with fire against the endless sky and then back to the naked figure on the slab. The man that had none of the weak, sly shame of those that made her feel unclean as they took her with their eyes. The man that had spoken to her as if he knew what she was feeling as the man who shared her bed never had. She thought of Mora and the revulsion at what they did together sickened her and she felt a great anger, an energy, flash through her, that left her mind quite calm and resolved. As if this day had been waiting for her all her life.

"Then let it happen," she said and, turning, plunged deep into the luminous depths.

Fidel stood motionless for a second, then crouched and sprang far out from the slab, arcing his body into the air and down, sliding through the water cleanly. He could see her below, upright and moving gently, watching him as he descended. She moved up to meet him and he took her hands and pulled her to him and put his arms round her, pulling her tight against his body, feeling the soft spread of her breasts on his chest, his hands dropping down to clasp her buttocks and hold her loins hard into his erection. She began to move her hips against him, then suddenly broke away, her hair fanning out behind her like a black cloud, and pointed upwards. He nodded and she thrust down with her legs and began to rise up fast through the water.

Fidel broke surface just as Lyra was heaving herself up onto the slab. He gulped air into his lungs and reached up to grasp the slab as she turned and looked down at him. As he hung there she reached out to him and took his hand and pulled him up onto the rock beside her. He lay panting for a moment, and then turned over on his back and looked up at the sky.

"Fidel," she leaned over him and hesitated awkwardly as if his name was strange to her tongue, "you are sure?" She stopped uncertainly.

He reached up and pulled her down and kissed her, feeling the initial resistance, then her lips softening and opening under his. His tongue probed into her mouth as his hand caressed one of her heavy breasts. He kissed her harder and she responded fiercely, crushing her mouth against his and sliding her thigh over him and rubbing it between his legs. He stroked her rounded belly, then put his hand down to her crotch and gently explored the soft lips of her cunt. She murmured as his fingers moved inside her, probing and stroking and her hips began to rise and fall as a sexual heat she had never known before flooded through her body.

Fidel took her hand and placed it on his cock. "Touch me," he said. As she squeezed and gently pulled his huge erection he increased the pressure of his fingers inside her and she began to moan and move her hips faster. He laughed softly and slowly withdrew his hand. "Not like that," he touched his cock, "you must have all of this."

She stared at him, her face serious. "I... I have never known how it feels to be with a man...." She stopped and turned her head away.

Fidel smiled. "Then this will be your first time." He kissed her, tasting the sweat on her lips. Then he tapped his cock, sliding his fingers down its length and thrusting his hips up to her. "This will give you all the pleasure in the world."

She shook her head. "But when he did it there was nothing," she began.

Fidel put his hand over her mouth. "Stop. Do not think of that." He kissed her again, biting her lips gently and she pushed her tongue deep into his mouth.

Suddenly she broke away and stared at him, her eyes wide and hot. "Now!" she said hoarsely, "Do it now!" She began to turn over onto her back as like all the times with Mora, but Fidel stopped her.

"No," he shook his head and pulled her on top of him. "Like this."

She remembered how Salan had done it in the field behind the inn and the pleasure his woman had taken.

"Yes," she said eagerly, and swung her leg over him, opening her thighs as he reached down and took hold of his cock and gently eased it up just inside her cunt. He pushed up slowly and she gasped as he filled her. Then he started a slow rhythm that she began to match, gradually moving faster. He fondled her breasts, pulling hard at the nipples as her breathing quickened. She leaned back on him, lips drawn away from her teeth, eyes slitted, neck cords standing out under the skin, sweat pouring off her face as she watched the thick shaft of his cock drive in and out of her. Then she began to moan in time to the tempo of their bodies and he knew she was close.

"Is it near?" he asked.

"Yes! Oh, yes!" she gasped, "Oh! Oh! Yes! Yes!"

Suddenly she fell forward on him, pumping her hips wildly. "Now! Now! Oh! Yes!" she screamed desperately, her feet scrabbling frantically for grip on the slab.

Fidel clasped her buttocks as she writhed furiously in the savage ecstasy of her orgasm. Every day of the eight months he had not had a woman erupted out of him, every day of seeing and wanting her so badly that the pressure had built up until he had been almost mad and the trigger that had set it all off had been the wild loneliness of this place; and the scorching fireball in the sky. And then, finally, the woman in the shining water who had been waiting for him to unlock and explode the senses of her body.

Lyra felt him flooding into her, filling every part of her being as she matched him in the frenzied violence of their coupling that went on and on until they finally came to a shuddering halt, the rigid-nerved tension draining away; and she fell to the side of him and turned over on her back.

After a moment she spoke. "The old ones were right," she smiled, her voice hoarse and shaking. "They said it was a pleasure you could hardly endure… like dying and being born again." She laughed, deep in her throat and touched his slackening cock. "So strong... and now... nothing!"

Fidel propped himself up on his elbow and looked at her sweat-slicked face. "Do not worry," he said, "in a little while he will be ready again." He reached out and stroked her belly, running his fingers down into her pubic hair. She put her hand over his and pressed it hard into her crotch, murmuring softly with pleasure.

They lay talking softly and relaxing in the heat until Fidel felt his desire returning. He sat up and looked down at her. She smiled and reaching out took hold of his cock and squeezed it.

"I saw it begin to come back to life," she said and leaning down she kissed him hard, her tongue probing and flicking.

"Will it be as before?" she asked. "Will you make me a madwoman?"

He laughed. "I think you were that before I came back to the island." He touched his cock. "It was this that set you free."

She reached up and pulled him down onto her body holding him hard against her. "Do it," she said. "Make me mad again."

Fidel pulled back and began to kiss her breasts, cupping their ripeness in his hands and gently biting the erect nipples.

She moaned and arched her back, pushing her body up to his mouth. Then she took hold of his cock. "Pleasure me with this."

He shook his head. "No. This time it will be different." He moved lower down her body and kissed her belly, sliding his tongue all over the plump skin.

She moaned softly and pushed her hips up to his mouth.

"Do it," she said urgently. "I want it now!"

Fidel took hold of her thighs and pulled them apart. He put his mouth down over her crotch and slid his tongue into her cunt. Lyra stiffened, almost drawing away from him, but Fidel held her firmly.

"Lie back," he smiled, "this will make you mad." He put his head down between her thighs again and kissed the soft flesh of her cunt with tiny sucking kisses. Her body began to rise and fall and her breathing deepened.

"Yes!" she said hoarsely. "Oh, yes!"

Fidel opened the lips of her cunt wide with his fingers and put his tongue deep into the wetness, probing gently all over the warm flesh. As he felt her hips thrust harder he stiffened his tongue and thrust it harder in and out of her cunt.

She took hold of his head crushing it into her crotch. "Oh yes!" she gasped. "Yes! Do it! Now! Now!"

He tasted her juices pouring over his tongue and he held her hips as she bucked and writhed. Finally, she relaxed and her body slumped to the ground.

Slowly she opened her eyes and looked at him. "That was another kind of madness," she said and laughed. "If they could see what we have just done they would put us in the dark water to die." She reached out and gripped his erect cock. "Shall he have the same?" she asked.

Fidel nodded and lay back as she began to run her tongue up and down the length of his cock. He groaned with pleasure as she bit the tip before closing her mouth over it. She cupped his balls in her hands and gently squeezed and stroked them. Fidel spread his legs wide and braced his feet against the rock as Lyra sucked harder, her tongue teasing the straining head of his cock.

Suddenly he reared up caught in the spasmodic lunges of his orgasm. Lyra threw her body across his thighs to hold him down. When he had finished she leaned forward and kissed him, and he tasted the sweat of her lips and the juices from his cock on her mouth. Then she fell back and stretched out on the sand.

Fidel sat back against the rock and looked at her. "You do not care who sees you now," he smiled.

She shook her head, the wet hair swirling about her shoulders. She smiled. "No. I do not care. It is nothing to me."

She stood up suddenly. "Come." She pointed out at the sea. "Swim… if you are sure that no one would come here then we have nothing to fear." She ran down to the flat rock and dived into the water, going far down and turning over and over before gliding back up to the surface.

She beckoned to him and Fidel got to his feet and walked to the rock where he sat down on the edge, then slid in to the warm sea. They swam for a long time, moving through the hours of the day almost as if they were part of the wildness of the place. Finally, when the sun began to fall to the far side of the mountain they came out of the sea and stood on the rock.

Lyra ran her hands over her body flicking off the water and then reached for her shift. Fidel caught her by the arm and pulled her to him, kissing her and feeling her mouth open under his.

He drew her up to the big rocks and pushed her back against the stone. She put her arms round him and crushed her body against his. As he put his hand down to her crotch she opened her legs and guided his cock into her body.

"Yes," she said urgently. "Again… do it."

Fidel drove in and out of her, almost lifting her in the air with the force of his lunges. She grunted and clasped his buttocks, grinding her crotch desperately against his cock. They came swiftly, the feeling too powerful to hold in check, she screaming hoarsely and Fidel ramming her hard into the rock as he spent. Finally, he stepped back away from her and drew a long shuddering breath. "You will make me old before my time," he said.

She shook her head. "Not you, Bardi," she smiled, her eyes huge in the failing light, "not you."

When the darkness was complete Lyra went into the house and cooked fish over the fire whilst her mother watched silently. When the food was done she piled it on a platter and looked at the old woman. "Do not wait for me. I will sleep outside tonight."

Her mother stared at her, the deepset eyes indifferent in the lined face and turned away without a word.

They sat in a sheltered place among the rocks, hidden from the sea and the land and ate the fish and drank the raw wine that Lyra had brought with her from the inn. When the food was gone Fidel leaned back against a rock and lit a cigar and looked at the woman lying before him on the sand. "What will you do now?" he asked.

She looked up in surprise. "What do you mean?"

He flicked the ash from his cigar. "Now that you are not Mora's woman anymore."

She was silent for a moment, then shook her head slowly. "I don't know… I had not thought to do anything."

He blew a plume of smoke into the air. "Out there…" he waved the cigar at the sea, "is another world. You can be free and do whatever you wish."

Her mouth tightened. "Why should I leave here to be a slave in a land where I would be a stranger?" She propped herself up on her elbow and regarded him. "I have nothing—not money or shelter—what would I do away from this place…? How would I live? Where would I go?" She made a slashing gesture with her hand. "Mora has me… it is the way on this rock and it holds me."

Fidel took another drink and felt the wine move in him. Something very small tugged at the corner of his mind. "Suppose," he said slowly, "Mora was to leave the inn and you were to remain?" He stopped, his mind probing a far-off and ill-defined possibility.

She frowned at him. "He would never leave." She shook her head firmly. "It is his life."

Fidel drank more wine. *I can drink all night and I won't be drunk*, he thought. *It is like the wine has opened my mind to a thing that, as yet, has no form, but is there waiting to tell me something that I have to know.* "You did not answer my question," he said quietly. "If there were just you, would the inn be yours? Is that the law in this place?"

Lyra shook her head impatiently. "Why do you not hear what I say... he will never leave."

Fidel cut her short. "Enough! I heard you. Just tell me the law. Does the woman take the man's possessions if he is not with her any longer?"

"I don't know," she said. "I suppose so." She thought for a moment. "Salan's brother went into the dark water and the house they lived in was her's afterwards." She nodded. "Yes, the people met and said it was the way of the island... She lives in it until she takes another man. Then he is the owner."

Fidel drew on his cigar and looked at her. *She would be worth the risk*, he thought. His mind looked at the other side of the possibility. *You would be killed if you were found out. It would have to be done in a way beyond suspicion. With a cool head and a careful plan. But there is always a risk.* The wine swirled up through his mind... *and the danger is always part of the pleasure.* He leaned forward and regarded her intently. "Listen... listen to what I say and do not speak until I finish."

She stared at him. He went on. "Suppose Mora died." Her eyes widened. "If he were dead then you would be free to live as you please. And you would have a living from the inn." He smiled at her, the teeth-glistening smile. "No one would ever own you again."

She stared at him for a long moment, then shook her head and frowned. "But he is alive." Her lips curled contemptuously. "He does no work to wear out his body. He will live forever."

The idea sat firmly in his mind, the details had taken shape and had form now. "When we spoke at the inn a time ago you said you knew how your life would always be."

She nodded. "I remember." She grimaced. "Nothing has changed."

Fidel spread his hands wide. "How can you say that?" He laughed. "We are here and you have betrayed your man. I would say you have begun to change your life now."

Lyra smiled slowly. "That was you, Bardi." She stroked her hand down her body. "You made me alive as other women. But I am still not free... and we can never do this again." She looked around her. "Someone will see that we are both away from the village at the same time and that will be the end of us."

Fidel shook his head. "I thought that now you would have the strength to live as you please."

"Not while I am the woman of Mora," she said.

He put his head back against the rock and looked up at the incandescent sliver of moon that hung in the dark sky. "And what if he were dead?" he said very slowly. "How then if you had no man... no one to own you."

Lyra stared at him. "You make no sense with your words, Bardi. You speak and you say nothing." She made the dismissive gesture with her hand. "I will tell you what is true and that is while Mora lives I am his to do with as he wishes."

Fidel was silent, still looking up into the sky.

Lyra waited for him to speak, then leaned forward and shook his arm. "Why do you not speak, Bardi?" She laughed bitterly. "Have you no answer for me now? No talk of how I am free just because we have lain together, and...."

Fidel held up his hand to halt her. "Stop," he said softly. "It was only that I wondered how the law was in this place... that is all. I will not speak of it again and cause you pain."

They lay under the huge mass of the sky and she moved restlessly in her sleep, calling out things that Fidel did not understand, until she woke suddenly and sat upright, turned to him and called him Mora, then as recognition dawned in her eyes she mounted him in a frenzy that went on and on until Fidel thought she would go mad.

When the first light touched his face Fidel woke and dressed. He shook her gently and told her that he had to get to the boat and take it back to the mainland. She nodded and held him briefly and told him to go.

As he sat on the deck of one of the boats going over for the fish he thought about the woman. He had never known anyone like her. Not even some of the rich ones that were like animals when they were naked, willing to do anything to feed the hunger between their legs. He had used all of them and had always been in control, but Lyra was different. She had matched his power when they were mounted, and he had felt the strength in her body and she had treated him as her equal in all things. He thought, with a cold contempt, that Mora was a fool who did not deserve the woman who shared his name. He thought a lot about the innkeeper as the boat moved through the water, and when it finally slid to halt at the island he had formed a plan that would free the woman from him forever.

Chapter Fourteen

Over the next few weeks Fidel continued his daily visits to the inn, but now he always was careful never to go when Mora was absent. He talked to him about the island, things that Mora knew and could expand on. At the same time, when Mora asked him how things were done on the mainland Fidel gradually gave him the impression that the mainland could not compare with the island in matters of honesty and trust between people. Mora had listened to this with much satisfaction, pointing out to Fidel that that was the reason that he had never moved off the island.

He would stare just above Fidel's head and ask him what was the point of leaving a place where you were known and trusted to go and live amongst strangers that would cheat and harm you?

Fidel had agreed and said that was one of the reasons that he had come back to the place where he had been born, to live among his own kind. Mora said he had known this, but had not wished to offend by telling him. If Mora ever wondered about why Fidel never mentioned Lyra, or hardly spoke to her when she appeared, he did not speak of it.

When Fidel was certain that Mora counted him as a friend he moved into the second part of his plan to take Mora out of Lyra's life forever.

He knew the days when Mora went down to the store to collect his goods that came over on the supply boat. The innkeeper had to go down the track and then fork to the left along the cliff path. Fidel had watched him many times from the rocks below and knew that Mora never hurried, he simply let the mule take its own pace. From the high cliff he then descended onto the track that took him down to the store. Fidel had timed him, counting the minutes and checking them against his watch. There would be time enough.

The day had broken with a sullen overcast sky and heavy seas that had made the men fight with the sails as they struggled through the water. Fidel stood outside his house and watched the little boats as they rode the incoming waves and then gradually faded out of sight into the horizon.

He went back into the house where the old man was crumpled on the bed, rasping out some unintelligible sound that Fidel ignored. He emptied his pockets of money and cigars, anything that might identify him. Then he took off his watch; he was the only one on the island that owned one. If he lost it, it would mark him as surely as a brand. When he was ready he took a drink of the stale wine from the jug on the table, grimacing at the sour taste, and went out without looking at the old man.

He walked through the scrub behind the house and up onto the high ground where he could look out over the sea. There was time enough, almost two hours before he needed to be in the position. He found a space by a rocky outcrop and sat down facing away from the track. He did not expect to see anyone at this hour, but it would be dangerous to take the risk. He looked at the ground by his feet and picked several small rocks, discarding each one in turn until he had the one he wanted, turning it over in his hands, feeling the sharp splintered edges, then slipping it in his pocket.

As the morning wore on the sun broke through the clouds shafting the land with light before vanishing behind the next dark mass. He stood up and walked along the track, following it until it sloped down behind a bank of ground for a short distance, then picked up the main path to the beach. Fidel had walked the ground many times and knew that this place, behind the high bank, was totally hidden from the land. If it were to be done this would be the place. He went to the cliff edge and looked over at the jagged rocks rearing up from the sea far below; then he walked back to where the track entered behind the high bank and sat down to wait.

When he heard the squeal of an axle and the hoarse breathing of the mule he stood up and, leaning back on the bank, held up his right foot and clasped it with his hand. As the mule and cart appeared he limped forward and stood by the track.

Mora looked down at him, then heaved back on the reins. "Hold," he said and slammed the wooden brake block onto the wheel.

Fidel hopped forward and held onto the side of the cart. "It is good that you came this way, Mora," he said wincing with pain.

Yole Mora frowned. "What is it, Bardi? What has happened?"

"I fell back there," he gestured back up the track. "This damned ground is only fit for goats."

Mora shook his head. "I think it is not only the ground, Bardi," he said pursing his lips. "It is known that you walk the island when you have much wine in you." He wagged his finger at Fidel. "One day you will go over into the sea and that will be the end of it."

Fidel hopped on one foot and nodded his head. "You are right, Mora. It is true that I have wine in me." He gritted his teeth and groaned. "There is much pain… can you take me to my house? It is not far."

Mora stared at him for a moment, then shook his head. "I cannot do what you ask, Bardi. I have my supplies to collect from the store," he said slowly as he looked above Fidel's head. "If I were to take you back now I would not be done with my supplies till after the night was upon us."

"Then take me with you to the store and I will wait for you there. You can take me back after you have your goods," Fidel said.

The innkeeper motioned behind him. "You will have to sit in the back. There is no room for us both up here." He watched as Fidel struggled up into the back of the cart, making no attempt to help him. "Are you ready?" he asked and without waiting for an answer he shook the reins and clucked his tongue at the mule who lurched forward.

Fidel clung to the sides of the cart to steady himself. He waited until they were almost to the middle of the track that was hidden from the land side, then stood up and reaching past Mora heaved on the brake handle. The cart rocked to an abrupt halt and Fidel caught hold of Mora by the shoulder and wrenched him round in the seat to face him.

"What are you doing, Bardi?" cried Mora. "Why do you do this?"

Fidel tightened his grip on Mora's shoulder and lifting him out of the seat he spoke directly into his face. "Listen to me, innkeeper. I, Fidel Bardi have lain with Lyra… I have made her a real woman and now she knows the pleasure a man can give her."

Mora's eyes opened wide and his face convulsed with shock and anger. "What are you saying?" he gasped, squirming in Fidel's grip. "You are mad! You lie! It is a lie—she would not do that with you—not you!"

Fidel laughed savagely. "Who else but me, you fool! Do you think she would give herself to any of the animals on this hellhole… it had to be me!"

Mora struggled furiously, but Fidel held him tighter. "The first time was at the old woman's, her mother's… we stayed all day in the sea and then at night we were in the rocks."

The innkeeper's face darkened with rage and the words rushed from his mouth in a torrent of hate. "You will be killed! And her as well... the bitch! I will tell them to beat you and put you in the dark water... you will both die for this!" he screamed.

Fidel shook him and then looked right into his eyes. "Look at me properly, Mora... look at me for the first and last time!" He pulled the jagged rock from his pocket and smashed it down on Mora's head. The mule lurched forward, almost throwing them from the cart as Mora slumped down in the seat, blood pouring from his wound. Fidel jumped from the cart and reached for the reins and pulled the mule round until it faced the cliff edge. Mora's eyes opened wide in terror as Fidel released the brake and slapped the reins across the mule's hindquarters and the beast moved forward a few steps and stopped at the edge.

Mora opened his mouth to cry out, but Fidel lunged at him and struck him again. Mora crumpled on the floor of the cart, his hands over his head trying to shield himself from the blows.

When Fidel stepped back from him the innkeeper lifted his head, and spoke through the welter of blood. "You will both die... both die," he gasped.

"I think not," said Fidel. "You will be the one to die!" He struck the mule hard and slapped the reins, but the animal remained still, its eyes rolling in terror.

Cursing, Fidel drew the knife from under his arm and jabbed it hard into the mule's rump. The beast gave an agonized bray and lunged forward, started to go over the edge and fought for grip on the soil. Fidel stabbed it again and flung his body behind the wheel and heaved.

The mule began to slide over, its forelegs already clear of the edge. Fidel strained against the wheel, his feet fighting for grip on the earth, then as the mule began to go over Mora flung himself out of the cart and sprawled on the ground beside Fidel. The mule gave a bellowing roar as it plunged down, followed by the cart. Mora started to crawl away, but Fidel seized him, lifted him up and moved to the edge. "No... no, Bard... no!" Mora babbled, struggling to free himself. "No, no!"

Fidel swung him high in the air and threw him far out over the cliff. There was only the sound of a thin scream, then nothing. Fidel dropped to the ground and looked over the edge. Far below he could see the mule sprawled on the rocks. It had been broken from the shafts as it fell and lay a short distance from the shattered remains of the cart. Mora had landed almost on the cart, his body wrenched into a grotesque shape, legs splayed and trunk twisted.

Fidel knew he must move quickly now. He checked his clothes for blood, then started up the bank and across the scrub, retracing his steps until he came back down onto the ground behind his house.

Once inside he stripped off his clothes and rechecked them for any signs of blood or the struggle that might give him away. Then he put on a pair of old trousers and went outside and carried some rocks from the ground behind the house round to the front, where he began to split them in rough tiles for the roof.

When he had cut a few he climbed onto the roof and started to fasten the sagging timbers. As he worked he could see the old women in the street and he knew that they would notice him. They would be the alibi he would need. When Mora was found it would not be possible to say the exact time he had gone over the cliff and Fidel would have been seen working on his father's house. This would be enough to put him above any suspicion that Mora's death was anything but an accident.

He worked on steadily through the heat, only stopping to rest briefly and drink wine from the jug and eat fruit. It was just after midday when he heard the excited babble of voices and he looked down the street and saw the women talking and gesturing excitedly.

He carried on cutting and fixing the tiles until he heard his name called and saw one of the crones shuffling up to him. "Bardi, have you heard?" she shrilled.

Fidel straightened up from the pile of rocks and wiped the sweat from his face. "Heard what... what are you saying?"

"It is the innkeeper, Mora—he is dead." Her eyes glittered excitedly. "He went over the cliff."

Fidel frowned at her. "Dead?" He shook his head. "I do not understand. When...?"

The old woman cut him off. "He went over the cliff... he was in his cart going down to the store... the mule must have run wild." She came so close to Fidel he could feel her foul breath on his face. "They say it is all smashed. The mule... the cart," she paused, "and Mora, all to nothing."

Fidel stepped back from her. "How do you know this?" he asked.

She flung out her arm and pointed down to the other women. "They have come up from the shore... some of the men told them; they are bringing Mora back to the inn." She moved closer again and lowered her voice. "I do not think his woman will be in grief long for him," she nodded her head knowingly at Fidel. "They were not as a man and woman should be."

Fidel dropped the hammer by the split rocks and wiped his face. "It is a bad way to end a man's life."

She nodded and caught his arm. "Will you go to see him? They are bringing him up to the inn."

Fidel nodded. He had knew he must go, to stay away from such a thing might cause suspicion. "Yes, I will go," he said shortly.

She tugged at his arm again. "One of the men said Mora is not fit to look on." Her mouth twisted convulsively. "They said he is less than whole."

Fidel pulled free from her grasp. "I will go now," he said. As he started walking down the track she called after him. "When you come up again tell me what you saw… I cannot get down there to see for myself."

Fidel did not answer. There were people already moving in the direction of the inn and he knew the news had spread. He heard his name called and saw Salan waving to him. "Bardi, Bardi, have you heard? Mora went over the cliff with his cart," he called.

Fidel stopped and waited for Salan to catch up with him. "One of the old ones just told me," he said. "Is it true… that he is dead?"

Salan nodded. "Yes, it is true; they are bringing him to the inn now." He pointed past Fidel. "Look."

Fidel turned and saw a group of men carrying a body up the track.

"Let us go down… they will go the inn," Salan said. He gripped Fidel's arm. "Come."

A crowd had gathered talking excitedly when Fidel and Salan arrived at the inn. They fell silent and parted to allow the body to be carried inside, then thronged into the big room, struggling to see. Mora was laid out on the floor and one of the men tried to straighten his twisted body. He looked up at the people and shook his head. "Look at him; it is as if he had been taken by the dark water."

Just then the door to the rear opened and Lyra Mora came into the room. The men stepped aside for her and she stood silently looking down at the body. After a long moment she stepped back and spoke. "Pull two tables together and put him on them."

The men looked at each other, then one said, "You do not want him," he hesitated and pointed to the door leading to the private part of the inn, "in there with you."

Lyra shook her head. "No, do as I say."

After a moment's hesitation the men picked Mora up and held him while the others put two tables side by side, then carefully laid him across them and stepped back. "He went over the cliff," said one of them. He spread his hands. "How could that happen? He must have done such a journey many times… many times…" he nodded at the body, "and then this."

"The mule must have gone mad and dragged him off the track," said Salan. "The way can be treacherous up there; it only takes a slip of the foot, and…." He stopped and nodded to Lyra.

"Your pardon, Lyra Mora, I do not mean to cause you pain."

She shook her head. "I am not offended, Salan. What you say could have happened."

Salan nodded, then turned to the gathering. "Will the women help Lyra Mora to prepare her man for the ground?" he asked.

Lyra held up her hand. "I do not ask for help. I will do what has to be done myself."

There was a murmur among them, then one of the old women stepped forward. "It is the custom for the women of the island to tend the dead," she said.

Lyra stared at her, the huge eyes cold and flat. "You all heard me. I want no one to help." She went behind the counter and picked up a large towel and draped it over Mora's head and upper body, then looked at them all. "This place will not be open until Mora is in the ground."

There was silence in the room, and then one of the men spoke hesitantly. "He should lie here for a day, then go to the ground."

She nodded. "Let it be so then."

As the people walked back to their homes they talked of how the woman of Mora had shown no tears. It was as if they had brought a dead dog to her for all the grief she showed. But then they said, "What could you expect from her?"

She was not of the island people; they all knew her father had been a black off the fish boats that had gone with the old woman on the far side of the island, and then deserted her just as quickly.

Fidel carried on working on the roof. He knew he had to act as if the tragedy was of no concern to him. The people stood in their doorways and in the streets talking of the fate that Mora had met on the rocks. No one expressed much sympathy for the innkeeper; he had not been a man to warm to. More was spoken of his woman, and how she had been when she had looked on Mora in his death agony and had shown nothing, no tears or any sign of her loss. The old women nudged one another and nodded knowingly, what could be expected from her, they said, after all it was known that Mora had never made her a real wife. And now, according to the island's law the inn was hers.

Some shook their heads at this and raised their voices in protest. The truth was that she was not of the island people, the black had made her mother with child and then gone away and never returned. Why could the inn not be for all the people that were born of island stock?

Then someone asked who would tell the woman of Mora that she was not wanted. There was silence at this. Lyra Mora would know the law of the island; that when a man died his belongings went to his woman, and they were sure that she would not stand for any attempt to deny her rights.

The talk moved on to how Mora had died. "How could it be," they asked, "that a man that had made the journey from the inn to the shore for many years, and must have known every rock and scrub along the way, could have gone to his death in such a way?"

"Maybe," someone said, "it was just because he had done it so many times that he had grown careless of the rough ground underfoot, and let the mule wander off the track. Or perhaps the heat had taken him into sleep as the cart moved along the track, and he had gone before he could wake."

After much discussion, which led them no closer to the cause of Mora's death, they took to their beds.

Fidel watched as the lamps went out one by one in the little houses until the night had spread its darkness over the island. He sat on the ground outside, and drunk his wine and smoked a cigar, and waited a long time until he could hear nothing but the sea breaking on the land.

The heavy clouds moved steadily across the sky hiding the moon's light from the island. *That is good*, he thought. *To be seen out in the open tonight at this hour will be enough to bring death to me.*

He extinguished the lamp on the table, walked over and looked at his father hunched on the bed. *Better you were out of this world, old man*, he thought. *This life has no pleasure for you.*

He opened the door slowly and stood a moment before stepping out into the street. Moving carefully he took the path up away from the village and worked his way slowly down to the back of the inn.

As he walked through the broken ground he could see no light from the building and he wondered if she would hear him. He stood close to the wall and tapped gently on the window and waited.

After a short while he tapped again and heard a bolt drawn back and saw Lyra Mora in the doorway. She stepped aside and motioned him in. As he stepped past her she spoke. "Tread softly, there can be no light until I close the door."

Fidel went through into the room behind the main bar. Lyra closed the door gently. "Wait, I will light the lamp," she said.

When the flickering flame gave light to the room Fidel saw that she was still dressed. "You did not sleep," he asked.

"No," she said. "I knew you would come."

"I had to," said Fidel. He took a step forward and she held up her hand and shook her head.

"Wait." Her eyes burned into him. "Speak the truth to me. Do not lie."

Fidel nodded slowly. "Not to you... not now."

"You killed him... you killed Mora.'"

He was silent for a moment, then he nodded, "Yes."

"Why?"

He smiled gently. "You wanted to be free... now you are, I set you free."

"You did that for me?" Lyra said, "You took his life from him?"

Fidel nodded again. "You do not grieve that he has gone?" he asked.

"Grieve?" She shook her head, the dark hair swirling round her shoulders. She laughed harshly. "What could I have to grieve for?" She turned and pointed into the bar "That which lies in there... he was nothing alive and he is nothing dead."

"It is done... you have a life now," he said. As they looked at each other the room suddenly seemed smaller and filled with an almost stifling tension. She moved closer to him, so near that he could smell the fragrance of her body and he felt his loins tighten and ache for her. She smiled, the green of her eyes intense in the half light. He reached out and pulled her to him, feeling the full softness of her body against his, mouths clamped together and tongues probing.

Suddenly, she broke away. "Wait," she gasped and drew the dress up over her head revealing her nakedness. Fidel stripped off his shirt and pants, threw them from him and pulled her down. Their bodies strained, scalding with the rage of want, tearing away all caution, inflamed by the death lying on the tables in the next room. Lyra pumped her hips at his cock as he slid in to her. Then, arching her back as her hands fed her breasts to his mouth, his head right back, guttural sounds erupted from her as Fidel drove into the savage rhythm that rocked their sweat-drenched bodies. Fidel held his hand over her mouth to stifle her screams as her body bucked frantically into its shuddering climax, then nothing, only the release that left them lying side by side, drained by the violence of the act.

Slowly, Lyra stood up and looked down at him. "You must go, Bardi," she said, struggling into her dress. "There are eyes everywhere in this place... if you are seen here now it will be death for us both."

When he had dressed Fidel stood by the door and waited for her to open it. "You have no fear to be with that," he gestured at the other room, "now you know how he came to his end?"

"I never feared him alive," she replied. "I am no different now." She pulled the door back and stood to one side. As he moved past her she touched his arm. "Do not come to the inn again until he is in the ground," she shook her head warningly, "and do not come when I am alone... not yet."

He nodded and went silently up the scrub ground looking all round him to be sure that he was not seen.

Most of the people trudged up the long track to where the islanders laid their dead to see Mora put beside his father. When the box was in the ground they stood and waited for his woman to speak, as was the custom at this time, to say something of his passage through life, maybe to praise him, or relate a story to dignify the solemnity of the occasion.

Lyra Mora simply handed a few coins to the two men with the broad-bladed shovels who would heap the black earth into the hole and turned away to walk back down to the village.

As the rest of them followed some way behind her in little groups of twos and threes, the talk was all of how she had shed no tears, or shown not a sign of sorrow at her man's passing.

"Indeed," they said, "the life between them must have been as barren as the earth of the island."

Chapter Fifteen

The big map was spread out all over the polished desk surface. The three men stood round it staring down at the mass of lines and curves and tiny words set against the different coloured backgrounds. There was a long silence as they studied it intently. Then one of them shook his head and stepped back.

"No. There is nowhere." He looked at the other two. "Anywhere of worth has been taken and used." He smiled ruefully. "We have done our share in the taking as well."

He looked up at the chart which ran the entire length of the wall behind the desk. It was covered in symbols of the company's name proclaiming their holiday homes. He waved his hand at it. "There we are, gentlemen. All our creations." He sighed regretfully. "We always knew it would end. I guess we never thought it would be now."

The three men were the directors of one of the richest holiday home builders in the islands. They had foreseen the boom in the demand for homes in the sun and built accordingly. For years their name had been a byword for excellence in their business. Now, at last the well had run dry. All the land that had any potential had been used. It would merely be a question of maintenance to their existing properties in the future. Profits would slump and they knew it.

Suddenly one of them leaned over the map and ran his finger over the surface. He looked up at them and frowned. "It is not here," he said. He looked again and shook his head. "No, nothing."

Paulos Passayannis, the senior director, a heavy built man with wavy silver hair came round the table and stood by his side. "What is it?" he asked.

The man pointed his finger down at the map. "There is an island, just here," he said, "only this map does not show it."

Passayannis shook his head. "That is not possible. This is the latest map supplied by our survey department. Everything of importance will be on it, Constantine."

Constantine Melas bent his head to the map again and studied it even more closely. "It is not."

He looked at the third man. "Do you know the island, John?"

"Yes," said the man slowly. He turned to Passayannis. "It is not on every map, Paulos." He gestured at the wall chart. "Look at our projects. They are all on reliable ferry routes and accessible to our buyers. This place, this island is so far from anywhere that no one ever bothered with it. The travel times were not favourable..." he frowned, "and I think I heard that the terrain was very rugged." He paused. "Also there was talk of a stretch of the sea close to the island that had taken down many boats... something about water running the wrong way."

He spread his hands. "There were other places easier to reach and with all the right requirements. I don't really know more than that."

Passayannis leaned over the map. "An uncharted island," he said slowly. "This is interesting."

He waved his hand over the area. "Can we get a map showing the exact locale of it?"

John Demetrios nodded. "The survey people will have one somewhere in their files." He tapped his hand on the map. "They probably thought this was the best to date."

Passayannis took out a gold topped fountain pen and wrote swiftly on a small pad. "Have a map here in three days. Get every scrap of information on this island that can be obtained." He looked at them. "You know what I mean... climate, terrain as far as can be estimated without actual surveys; population, access to shipping—anything that we can use." He turned to look again at the wall chart. "Maybe there is something more we can do, gentlemen."

In three days the required information, land records, written reports on the island, though these were almost too brief to be of use, and the few actual sightings that were available, lay on the big polished desk.

John Demetrios looked at them. "There is not much to go on."

"No matter," Passayannis said. "All we can do is look at what we have."

He shrugged. "If we feel there is something to be gained then we take the necessary steps."

The three men gathered round the table and opened the file. They went methodically through everything that it contained, exchanging the papers with each other so that nothing would be missed.

Finally it was done and the file re-assembled and placed back on the table.

Passayannis broke the silence. "This is amazing," he said slowly. "This place... not even on some of the marine maps." He looked at them and shook his head. "I cannot believe that someone has not carried out preliminary investigations." He tapped the table emphatically. "Look at it. It is quite unique, alone out in all that sea. Why?"

He stood up and went over to the wall chart and looked at it. "Not even shown on here... we have many competitors... why have they not looked at this island?"

Melas frowned. "Maybe the same reason we never did." He shrugged. "Perhaps they thought the place was just too far from anywhere. Too many problems with any considered building work... who knows "

"I think at that time there was land everywhere for all of us," said Demetrios.

"That is why we never bothered with the place." He pointed to the wall chart. "And if it was not shown then perhaps we never knew that it existed."

Passayannis waved the others to the leather armchairs. When they were seated he took out a small gold cigar case and handed it round. When they had lit up he sat back and looked at them.

"I have spent the last three days considering this situation," he said. "These," he indicated the file on the desk, "show us that the island has potential for our business." They nodded in agreement. He tapped the ash from his cigar. "What I am asking you to consider is something we have never attempted before."

Melas and Demetrios stared at him. Passayannis had always been the innovator, always prepared to change and try something new and he had been right so often in a business fraught with risk that they had come to accept whatever he might suggest. Now they waited for him to speak.

"This island that is something of a mystery to us... this place that may have no use at all," he spoke slowly as if wanting to have their maximum attention, "or could be something so wonderful that it could never be achieved again." He nodded at their puzzled faces. "Let me explain what it is that I have thought of." He pointed to the wall chart. "There is what we have done over a twenty-five-year period. All first class homes and satisfied customers." He smiled warmly at them. "We have a well-deserved reputation for quality products."

"Paulos, where is this leading?" asked Demetrios. "We know what you are saying is true, but what are you getting at?"

The big man held up his hand. "Just this. Suppose," he stopped and shrugged, "just suppose that the island is favourable to our requirements. But with one huge difference."

"Such as?" asked Melos.

"This." He looked at them intently. "Instead of us building homes and selling them suppose we sold the entire island."

Melos frowned at him. "I do not understand, Paulos."

Passayannis laughed softly. "You see. I said it was so wonderful that it had never been done before." He smiled at them. "Consider this. A private island. Its own security personnel. Helicopter launch pads to each dwelling. Homes built to specifications never achieved before. The finest fittings used everywhere. Heated pools with total privacy. The latest in television and communication developments beamed to the island."

Both the men sat forward. "It's never been done like that…" said Demetrios. "An entire island." He turned to Melas. "Would it be possible to buy an island and do what Paulos is telling us, John?"

"It is possible to buy an island, yes," said Melas. "But this place we know nothing about. Who owns it? What kind of people are they?" He spread his hands. "Would they even consider selling their homes?"

Passayannis nodded. "You are right, John. All that I have said is purely hypothetical." He smiled again. "All I ask is that you consider it. Of course there are many facts to be established. What I propose is that we send one of the survey team over this island in a helicopter and bring back the usual photos for us to study the terrain and shoreline. A general impression of the place. If it is favourable then we could go further." He faced them squarely. "Now, I need to know your thoughts on what I have said."

Demetrios and Melas looked at each other. Passayannis had been the leading figure in the company for so long that they found it incongruous now that he should ask their permission for a project. Yet, what an undertaking, something staggering in its vision.

"These homes, Paulos," asked Melas, "who would buy them if they were as priceless as you describe them?"

Passayannis smiled at him. "John, there are people in this world that have the money to do whatever they like." He drew heavily on his cigar. "Heads of state that have left their countries in financial ruin while their own fortunes sit in Swiss banks... the faceless men behind the multi-nationals... motion picture people... the heads of finance houses...." He nodded at them both. "There are always people prepared to pay for exclusivity. And this island would provide just that." He nodded. "That would be the single most important selling feature. Total exclusivity... security round the clock amid magnificent surroundings."

There was a long silence in the room broken only by the hum of the air conditioning. Then Melas sat forward. "I speak now without any idea of costings," he said quietly, "but the overall figure would have to be far in excess of anything we have done before." He looked at Passayannis questioningly.

The big man nodded. "Of course you are right, Constantine. But suppose we sold every single dwelling for a sum well into the millions. And just say that this island could support... maybe between forty to fifty exclusive homes."

Melas picked up a calculator from the desk top and swiftly punched in several numbers. He looked at the others with raised eyebrows and then handed the calculator to Demetrios who stared at it.

Passayannis smiled. "A formidable figure, no?" He clapped his hands together gently. "The challenge would be one that we have faced before. After all, we are builders. That is our business. The only difference would be the size of the project."

Demetrios nodded. "You are right, Paulos." He took a pen from the desk and began writing on a pad. "The location would be a challenge. The transport of materials is always a problem, but with a site so remote it would be vital to have them running as smoothly as possible."

Payassannis held up his hand. "First, we must know if the island is suitable for our intentions. Let us wait until we have the aerial pictures. If it is favourable then we could make enquiries as to who owns the land."

He stood up and walked over to the window and looked out at the immaculately tended gardens, then turned back to them. "I find it almost impossible to believe that our competitors have not seen this island," he paused, "and may well be at this moment thinking as we are. Therefore, the emphasis must be on the strictest secrecy regarding our intentions. No word to anyone at the moment until we know all the details that we have to know."

CHAPTER SIXTEEN

The people had watched as the squat machine with the spinning blades and the strange chu-chu sound hovered and whirled above the village, then circled the island many times, swooping low over the landing shore and the crop fields.

They had seen one man leaning out and pointing a black box object many times as the machine passed to and fro. Then, as suddenly as it had appeared, it soared high into the sky and vanished.

Fidel had seen it and felt a flicker of fear as he wondered if it came from his past. Then he'd shrugged it away. That was all too long ago to concern him now, probably some kind of population check or scheme that would come to nothing.

One moon later the machine came back. It hung in the air over the shore, steadied, then set down carefully on the ground. A man wearing a dark suit and clutching a fat briefcase scrambled awkwardly out of its body, looked around him, then started walking slowly up the track that led to the village.

As he drew near to the group of women that had watched the machine as it landed he called out to them. "Who speaks for you?"

They stared at him, then jabbered among themselves while he waited. Then one of them stepped forward and spoke haltingly to him. "Fidel Bardi..." she pointed up the track and repeated the name, "Fidel Bardi..."

The man stared at her uncomprehendingly as she pointed again. Then one of the other women beckoned to him and began to walk up the track. She looked over her shoulder at him and beckoned again.

"All right," he said. "You go… I will follow."

The woman led him up the track with the others following until they reached the square. Then they turned and went further up to the last few houses at the top of the village. The leading woman turned and gestured at one of the dwellings.

"Here?" asked the man. "This one?"

The women nodded vigorously. He stepped forward and tapped on the door. After a moment it swung open and a dark-haired man dressed in a white shirt and tan shorts stood looking at him. "What do you want?" he asked harshly.

The man put his briefcase on the ground and mopped his face with a large white handkerchief. "Do you speak for these people on this island?" he said.

The man stared at him. "What is it to you?" he asked.

The man picked up the briefcase. "My business is for you to hear in private." He nodded at the house. "May we go in?"

The man paused, then stood aside and he entered. He stared at the old man lying on the bed who struggled to sit up, then fell back moaning softly. The dark-haired man pointed to a chair. "Sit down." He glanced at the old man. "Be quiet," he said. The noise subsided and he turned to the man with the briefcase. "I am Fidel Bardi," he said.

He crossed to a jug of water on the table and poured some into a mug and handed it to the man who drank gratefully, then wiped his mouth with a handkerchief. "Why are you here?" asked Fidel.

"First, I have to know if you are the one that speaks for these people?" the man said.

Fidel smiled thinly. "There is no one else here that will speak to you."

The man stared at him. "You have no council or elected legislative body on this island?"

Fidel shook his head. "Nothing. When there is a thing to be decided it is talked over until it is done."

"So there is a kind of," the man hesitated, "committee."

Fidel laughed shortly. "There is nothing for you to talk with." He tapped his chest. "You say what you have to say to me then I will tell them. That is how it is."

"Do you have some kind of official document that gives you authority to represent the people?" asked the man. His plump smooth-shaven face was running with sweat and he began dabbing it with the handkerchief.

Fidel walked to the door and opened it. The old women were still standing outside. When they saw him they moved closer. He looked at the man and gestured at the women. "Go and waste your words on them," he said. "They will listen to all you say and understand nothing. Then they will leave you standing in the road and go on with their lives." He shrugged. "That is how they are."

The man stared at him, then nodded. "If that is how it is then we will talk." He opened the briefcase and took out a thin pile of papers that he placed on the table. Then he began to speak.

Fidel sat down on a stool and listened very intently. He did not want to miss a word of what the man was saying because it was so amazing. He wanted to buy everything. The houses they lived in and the land they planted. The shoreline and the mountain. The entire island. The company he represented would pay excellent money for it all. All fees and expenses would be taken care of. If they were reasonable people then they would be treated very generously.

Fidel listened as the smooth voice, that was now on familiar ground and having momentarily forgotten how unbearable the heat was, explained how good it would be for all the people that had worked so hard all their lives. How they would be rich beyond their dreams. What they could do with their wealth. How his company would be willing to advise them on how to make their money grow even larger. And all Fidel had to do was to explain this good fortune to his people.

The man smiled warmly at Fidel and said that he would be paid handsomely for his services. And there was something more. He nodded seriously and lowered his tone. No one was to speak of this to anyone outside of the island. That was the most important fact of all.

As the smooth voice spun its practised phrases into the room Fidel heard only one thing; the sound of a miracle settling around him. He was surely blessed now. Not only could he escape from his prison up here in this fortress, but he would have money to do whatever he liked for the rest of his life.

He held up his hand. The man stopped speaking and looked almost resentful at being halted in the flow of such oration. Fidel smiled. "Thank you for telling me this."

The man nodded and started to reach for the papers on the table.

Fidel held up his hand again. "Please, I have a question for you."

The man stared at him, then nodded. "Go on."

"There are others… others who wish to do as you… to buy our land?" Fidel asked.

The man reached for the handkerchief and began to wipe the sweat that had suddenly appeared again on his face.

Fidel went on. "You wish to turn our homes into a place for the rich to enjoy?" He nodded. "I understand. I have seen such things before."

"Only if the site is acceptable to us," the man began.

"Listen," Fidel said firmly. "Do not think you can come here and frighten us into giving up our land." He smiled tightly. "These are a primitive people. They will not bend to your wishes. If I say no to them they will never sell."

The man held up the hand clutching the now soggy handkerchief. "Excuse me. I did not wish to offend you in any way. Perhaps I did not make myself clear."

Fidel leaned forward. "Let us speak the truth now. You want our land. It will be of great worth to you. And you do not want anyone else to have it." He smiled again. "Is that not the way of it?"

The man studied him for a moment. "You are a blunt man to speak business with," he said.

Fidel remained silent. The man picked up one of the sheets of paper and glanced at it. He held it up for Fidel to see. "Do you...?" he stopped and looked at Fidel embarrassedly. "Forgive me, but do you read?"

Fidel nodded and the man gave him the paper. Fidel saw that it was an agreement to preliminary surveys to take place on certain land left vacant, and dated.

"If you would sign this then we could proceed," the man said.

Fidel put the paper back on the table. "That will not be necessary. You can do whatever you have to. I will explain to the people what is happening. Then when you have finished you will tell me if you are ready to buy our land."

The man shook his head. "That is not how things are done. We must have authorisation to survey."

Fidel shook his head. "No," he said firmly. "I will not put my name to a paper until it means that we are selling the land."

The man picked up the paper again and held it out to him. "My company will do nothing without proper written authorisation. That is the law," he said.

Fidel ignored the paper. "I have told you what I will do. If you cannot work without a piece of paper then perhaps others will not feel the same."

The man stared at him, then shrugged and slowly mopped his face. Finally he put the paper back in the briefcase. "It will be against all the regulations, but I am sure my company will make an exception in this case." He stood up and reached for his briefcase. "There is just the one thing that I have mentioned. Nothing of what we have spoke of in this room must be made public." He leaned towards Fidel and looked at him very seriously. "Give me your word on that."

Fidel smiled understandingly. "Of course. You will be the only one that makes—a survey you called it, yes… the only one to see our land." His smile grew wider. "And the only one we will deal with if you are happy with what you see."

Chapter Seventeen

When the man had shaken his hand and left, accompanied down the track by the cackling old women, Fidel sat in his father's house and slowly smoked a cigar and contemplated the wonder of it.

That night he went to the inn and told the men that they must bring all the people to the square the following evening. He said the man that had come to the island in the helicopter had told him to tell all the people something very important. He refused to answer their questions, telling them to wait until they were all together.

The next night he waited for almost an hour as they gathered in the square. When he stood up on the low wall and held up his hand all eyes turned to him and they fell silent.

"Listen to what I have to say," he began. "Do not ask me anything until I have finished speaking."

He paused to be sure of their attention. "You all know that a man came over from the mainland and spoke with me. He said something that can change all your lives."

A voice called out. "What are you saying, Bardi?"

Fidel shook his head. "Not until I finish." He took a scrap of paper from his pocket and held it up for them to see. "On this is the name of the man that wishes to give you all a great sum of money." He watched as their faces came alive with interest. "He asks that you sell your homes to him. All of us on the island. He will then build new homes for everyone and you will all have money to do as you wish."

The faces stared at him blankly for a moment, then Saur stepped forward and stood before Fidel. "What are you saying, Bardi?" he asked harshly. "What is this foolish talk?"

Fidel stepped down from the wall. "It is as I have told you, Saur. They wish to buy all the houses on the island."

Saur frowned. "You do not make sense, Bardi. Why would this man take our homes and then build us new ones?" He turned to the crowd. "This sounds like a man that has lost his senses!"

Fidel shook his head. "Wait, Saur. There is more to tell. When they have bought our homes they will build places on the island for the rich to come and live. They need our land so that they can build these places. Then they will build new homes for us as well." He held out his hands to them. "Think of this. You will all have enough money so that no man will ever have to work again." He pointed out at the sea. "That would never take another father or son from his family."

He swung round and gestured at the fields above the village. "Who would wish to labour under the sun up there? Not one of you. Now you have the chance to stop because this man has come to set you free from all that."

He looked at their faces. Harsh, lined by the sun and wind, old beyond their years. Bodies worn with toil. Existing on the edge of starvation and dependent on the whims of the sea and the hell of the sun for their survival. Living by a centuries old code of behaviour that would never be allowed anywhere else in the civilised world.

He struggled to suppress the sudden anger that flared through him at the thought they might throw it all away through fear and ignorance. What he needed now was patience and a cool head to allay their suspicions of anything that came from the outside the island.

"Listen to me now," he said to them. "This is a thing that must be talked over with a steady tongue. Only think of what you will gain from all this. Freedom from work. No more hunger for the children when the crops are poor or the sea is empty of fish." He nodded forcibly. "It is true that I have been away from my home for many years. But I remember all those things. Times when we went without food and wore rags because we were so poor."

He turned and pointed up the track. "There is a man lying in a house who cannot work now because he has given all his strength to the years when he struggled to feed his family." He laid his hand flat on his chest. "That man is my father. You all know Frado Bardi." A murmur ran through the crowd. "A good man... as many of your own old people are. Now if we all can see the wonderful thing that has come to this island, then we can make sure that they live the rest of their lives in comfort."

He watched as they turned to one another, talking fast in the island language, some of them nodding their heads at him as they spoke. He began to walk among them, stopping to answer questions or reassure them on some point.

Salan caught him by the shoulder and looked at him, eyes shining excitedly. "It is true... there would be money for new sails?"

Fidel laughed, conscious of their sudden attention at the mention of sails for the boats. "Sails?" he exclaimed. "Why would you need sails, Salan?" He clapped him on the back. "Only men that have to work need a sailboat."

Salan frowned. "Not work? What would I do... how would I live?"

"With your money. You would live without work because you would be rich!"

"But I have always had a boat," the stocky man said. "It would not feel right to be without one."

"Then have one for pleasure," Fidel laughed, "Sail the sea when you wanted to. Enjoy the boat. Take it out when the sun is high. Take a flask of wine and food. Live like a rich man."

Salan stared at him, then grinned hugely. "You are right, Bardi." He looked at the men round them. "I, Salan, could do all that Bardi says... because I would be rich!"

He seized his woman and whirled her through the crowd in a wild dance. People parted before them, laughing and hooting.

The mood of excitement and wonder spread amongst the people and Fidel climbed back up on the low wall and held up his hands.

"Wait," he said. "Go to your homes and talk with each other over what you have heard here. Then, if you are all agreed, I will tell the man when he returns that he can send his people over to look at the island, to see if it is what they need for their plans."

He watched them move slowly away until only Saur was left in the square. After his first question to Fidel he had leaned against a tree and ignored the rest of them. Now he slowly walked over to where Fidel was standing. Fidel watched him, feeling the unease he always experienced with Saur. The tall man had an air of scarcely suppressed violence about him, and Fidel had once seen him hurl a dog over the cliff top to its death because it had snarled at him as he passed.

Now he waited until Saur stood before him. "What is it?" he asked.

Saur stared down at him, the cold slate-grey eyes probing. "Why were you the one that they chose to speak for us, Bardi?" he said.

Fidel smiled easily. "I was here when the man came. He spoke to the old women and they brought him to my house because they did not know what he wanted."

Saur was silent, still staring. Then he spoke, his voice low. "Know this, Bardi. I trust no one. If there is something between you and these people that is being hidden then I will find the truth." He leaned down, his face almost touching Fidel's. "And if you think to gain by using us then I tell you that I will put you into the dark water."

Fidel stepped back from him, suddenly very conscious of the blade under his arm. "You are wrong to think that, Saur," he said evenly. "I have no more to gain than any of you. We will all have the same from this business."

Saur regarded him for a moment longer, then nodded. "For your own sake, may it be as you say, Bardi," he said curtly.

The next day the people told Bardi that they all agreed to the man looking at the island. Three days later the helicopter came back with the same man. This time he came straight to the house of Fidel Bardi where they agreed the permission for the survey to begin.

The following day two helicopters brought sixteen men and field survey equipment to the island and the work began.

The men worked all through the heat of the day, sweating their way up to the high ground with large tripods and measuring devices. They used small black machines that they spoke into to communicate with each other. After the high ground they moved along the shore and then the entire village area. At night they slept in a huge tent that one of the helicopters had brought. They never went to the inn and were up at first light to begin. After four weeks of unceasing work they were finished.

Fidel watched them on the last day as they loaded the equipment into the helicopters and took off, circling the island once then straight out to sea and the mainland.

Chapter Eighteen

The survey was written, the land and air photographs developed, and the entire report was placed in a company folder and taken by two of the security people to the directors' offices and handed it in to the secretary, who took it in to the special meeting that Passayannis had called on receipt of the report.

Passayannis handed copies of the report to Demetrios and Melas. He placed the third copy on the desk. "I have read the report already." He laughed at their surprise. "I could not wait." He nodded to them. "Read it yourselves."

The two men read the report in almost total silence. When they had finished they sat back and looked at each other.

Passayannis finally spoke. "Perfect. It is perfect." He looked at them and shook his head in awe. "This place is simply right for us. And to think it just sat there all these years." He nodded at the survey copies. "These could not be better. The terrain is rugged so each dwelling will be almost naturally hidden from the next." He smiled warmly. "The element of privacy, gentlemen. The shore line is one of almost continuous rocks so we will have to create a harbour for the yachts and the supply boat that will service the island."

"When will we have costings for the project?" asked John Demetrios.

"They are being calculated as we sit here," Passayannis replied. "When I saw the survey I acted right away." He shrugged apologetically. "Please, my friends, do not think I wanted to act without consulting you, but speed is our ally in this matter. We must know the financial side in order to go ahead with this work."

They nodded agreement.

Then Melas frowned at them both. "You speak of costings, Paulos, but how will we know the price to be paid for the homes of these people on the island? How can that be included in the figures?"

Passayannis smiled. "That is true, Constantine. But we have bought from people like these before. They are not used to money. What is a figure of no significance to our accountants is true wealth to them." He threw his hands in the air. "It will be next to nothing in the final costings."

"How will this be done... this buying of the properties?" asked Melas. "Have these people documents to prove their right of ownership to their dwellings?"

Demetrios nodded firmly. "That is right. Sometimes these people that live in country regions can be difficult to deal with."

Passayannis smiled reassuringly. "This is nothing that we cannot handle." He lowered his voice. "I have made enquiries concerning that aspect. It seems the people on this island can declare that they own their properties by right of occupation. It is legal simply because they have lived in the same house for a certain period of time."

"They need no documents to prove this?" asked Demetrios.

Passayannis shook his head. "None. The law in this instance recognises their right to valid ownership."

"How do they sell without proper papers?" asked Melas.

"The standard sale papers are used. Their legal agent attaches a photograph of his client to the papers and a seal is stamped over it. The agent then dates and signs it." Passayannis clasped his hands together. "It is all legally binding."

Melas frowned slightly. "I hear what you say, Paulos, but a good lawyer might find ways through it," he looked at Demetrios, "to our cost."

Passayannis smiled broadly and leaned forward. "What you say is true, John. However, with a prize such as this almost within our grasp we shall take no chances of allowing that to happen."

The other two were silent as they waited for him to go on. The big man's eyes narrowed.

"There is a man that lives on the island. He was the first person our agent spoke to. Apparently no one else will talk to outsiders. This man has travelled and is..." Passayannis hesitated for a moment, then shrugged, "less primitive than the rest of them." He smiled coldly. "Our agent says he has a very realistic attitude to what we are proposing. Told him that he is the only one that we can negotiate with and if we do not accept that then he will go to other developers."

"He is serious... this man?" Demetrios asked.

"Our man said he seemed to be very certain of what he said. He also said he does appear to have influence over the islanders and that is what we must have. So we shall bring him in to our team with the utmost secrecy."

Passayannis tapped the file. "Regarding the legal side of this we shall have the man on the island find a lawyer to handle the sale of the houses."

Melas stared at him surprised. "Why?"

"There is a man who runs a small legal agency on the Turkish side that has been useful to us in the past," said Passayannis. "He will make sure there is no way that the contracts can be challenged once they are finalised. He will be the one that the man on the island uses to represent his people."

Melas frowned, then nodded. "Yes, I remember the Turk." He laughed shortly. "He is a man that places a high value on secrecy."

"His name will be given to this man who will wait for him to arrive." Passayannis smiled at them. "Of course, we will have seen that he is fully prepared with all the details before that happens. Everything will be ready for him. There must be no possible chance for error." He stood up. "The next move will be our agent talking to the man." He shook his head and smiled. "We really must find out this man's name, and then we can start the house sales moving."

Chapter Nineteen

As the long days wore slowly away, Fidel had begun to wonder if the dream would ever become a reality.

Then the small dot had appeared just over the horizon and gradually taken on the familiar shape of the helicopter, circling and finally settling on the high ground above the village.

The agent had jumped out and walked quickly down to Fidel's house. Once inside he had taken a drink of water, sat down and opened his briefcase.

"My company has looked at all the findings relating to the possible purchase of the land on which all the dwellings stand, and also the total area of the island," he said. He mopped his face and smiled wanly. "How do you stand this heat?" he asked. "I have just stepped out of an air-conditioned helicopter and I'm exhausted already."

"It is a thing we are born to," said Fidel.

The agent shook his head. "Incredible." He took another drink and set the mug carefully on the table. "You are willing to act for the people here?"

Fidel nodded.

"Then we must begin with the purchase of the houses." He took a slip of paper from the briefcase and handed it to Fidel. "That is the name of the lawyer who you will choose to act for you."

Fidel stared at him. "We do not pick our own man?" he asked.

The agent settled his bulk on the small chair and sighed. "No." He tapped the paper in Fidel's hand. "That is the man who will make sure that everything will be done to our satisfaction." He looked hard at Fidel. "Your satisfaction and my company's. We will both be happy."

Fidel smiled coldly. "This man will make certain that you have the best deal. This is what you are saying."

"No," replied the agent shortly. "What I am saying to you is that if you can make this end of the business go as smoothly as possible, then my company will see that you are well rewarded." He leaned forward and tapped Fidel's arm. "Very well rewarded."

Fidel nodded. "As long as we are clear on that point."

The agent took out papers and placed them on the table.

"This is the standard form of purchase that will be used for the house sales." He ran his finger down the paper, muttering under his breath as he did so, then looked up at Fidel. "There is nothing here to confuse anyone."

Fidel laughed harshly. "The people here cannot read so they will not know what they are looking at!"

"None of them?" asked the agent, incredulously. "Not one person on the island?"

Fidel pursed his lips. "Maybe the storekeeper." He shook his head doubtfully and indicated the paper. "Even he would not know what that means."

The agent sat back in his chair and stared at Fidel, then slowly smiled. "Then there should be no trouble with our negotiations."

Fidel looked at the name on the slip of paper the agent had given him and raised his eyebrows slightly. "A Turk?"

"You have no objection to him?" asked the agent.

Fidel shook his head. "None at all." He grinned at the agent. "With this kind of business he is just the man you need."

The agent's lips tightened, but he said nothing. Then he produced a notebook from the briefcase and looked hard at Fidel.

"Now we have to make sure that if your people sell their homes to us they realise they must leave the island immediately. We need to have them away as soon as the papers are finalised." He tapped the notebook emphatically. "They cannot stay."

Fidel shook his head. "No... I have told them a different story. If it is changed then they will never sell. There will be no homes for the rich built here. Ever!"

The agent flinched as if he had been struck. "What are you saying?" he said. "We have the surveys and the...."

"If you tell them to go then you have nothing," Fidel told him firmly.

"Then what do we do?" asked the agent, his face distraught. "My company is preparing to put this project into operation...."

"Stop," Fidel held up his hand, "calm yourself. Listen to me. This is what must happen." He leaned closer to the agent and lowered his voice. "They must not be told that they have to leave the island." He shook his head firmly. "They will never sell if they know they have to leave."

"How will we buy their homes, then?" asked the agent.

"Simple," said Fidel. "We do not tell them until they have sold."

"Then how are you so sure that they will sell?"

Fidel smiled slowly. "Because I have told them that you will build them new homes here on this island after they have sold you their homes."

The agent stared at him aghast. "You told them we would... build them new homes," he stumbled over his words in his agitation. "You promised that we... my God! How could you do that? We want all the land here, not just the houses, you knew that and...."

"Enough," Fidel said sharply. "Do not act this way. You must have this island and I will give it to you. All you have to do is listen to what I say."

The agent sat forward, his hands gripping tight to the edge of the chair, waiting.

"That is better," said Fidel. "Now in the first place you do not have to tell them anything. I will talk to them." He held up the slip of paper. "Then the Turk will come here and do what is necessary." His face became serious. "Then they will be without homes and have no right to remain on this island. Is that not the way of it?"

After a moment the agent nodded. "Yes... we would own all the land," he said slowly.

"Then you would have the power to have them removed," said Fidel. "A company as powerful as yours would have the means to take them off the island." He smiled at the agent. "Once the sales were done you would have finished your part. It would then be for others to make them go." He spread his hands out wide. "Am I not right in this?"

The agent considered for a long moment, then nodded. "Yes. They would have no rights to remain."

"Then know this also," said Fidel. "There are some among them, especially one named Saur..." he waited as the agent wrote down the name on his pad, "who will not wish to leave without making trouble." His mouth set grimly. "Your people would have to deal with him very strongly. You understand?"

The agent had recovered his composure now that he could see the problem disposed of. "Yes. We have the people and the methods to handle trouble makers. Now that I know what is required the correct steps will be taken."

"Then may we pass on to the matter of what I shall receive for my services?" asked Fidel.

"Of course." The agent reached for his pen and pad again.

Fidel lit a cigar and offered one to the agent who shook his head. "I have given this much thought," said Fidel seriously, "and if the business goes through then I will have to remain on this island."

"Why?" asked the agent. "You will have much money. You could go wherever you like. Why stay in this Godforsaken place?"

Fidel smiled. "I thought when you have finished this island would be a paradise. A place where any man would be happy to live."

"Yes, but why would you wish to stay?"

"Because it would not be safe for me to go where they could reach me," said Fidel.

"Reach you?" asked the agent in puzzlement. "Who do you speak of?"

"The people that you will put off this island," said Fidel. "I told you there are some who do not behave in a civilised manner. They will want to do me harm—even kill me if they can."

"You are not serious," said the agent. "Surely they would not go that far?"

"It is my life," Fidel said calmly, "so I am very serious. Yes, they would go that far. The only way I can stay alive is to remain here."

"Then that is what you must do," said the agent. "Stay on the island."

"I shall," said Fidel. "In the house that you will build for me."

The agent stared at him. "You want a home here?"

"Where else would be as safe as this?" asked Fidel. "If you are building homes out here in this sea then the people that will live in them will be only the very rich ones. They will want to live the way that the rich like to live. When you have done this island will be like a prison." He laughed shortly. "An expensive prison where no one that does not have big money will ever be allowed in. Much security to keep the rest of us out. Those that you put off this place will never be able to get back." He nodded. "This will be the only place where I will live in safety. Do you understand what I have said?"

The agent nodded. "Yes, I see that you are right." He shuddered. "They are indeed a savage people."

"They are," agreed Fidel. "Now, as to the home that you will build me, and the money that I will receive for my services to your company."

The agent straightened up, pen at the ready. "Yes?"

"The home will be on the other side of the island," Fidel said. "I have drawn a map showing how and where it is to be." He stood up and crossed to the wooden box set in the wall, opened it and took out a folded sheet of paper. He handed it to the agent who looked at it. "You will see that it is not close to anywhere that would upset any of the rich ones." He smiled. "I am out in the wild country."

"It is not a grand house," said the agent. He shook his head. "Not considering that you might have demanded something much larger in the circumstances."

"That is not my way," said Fidel. "I shall be satisfied with this and the money." He looked at the agent thoughtfully. "The legal papers for my house," he said, "I shall not use the Turk for that."

"Why not?" asked the agent. "He is a capable man in this work."

Fidel nodded. "Of that I am certain. As surely as I am certain that he is your capable man."

"You are wrong to say that," protested the agent. "Your papers would be standard contracts with nothing against your interests."

"Then you will not mind that I find my own man," said Fidel firmly.

"It would make the business more simple if you used the Turk," said the agent.

Fidel slapped his hand sharply on the table. "I have told you no and there is an end to it."

After a moment the agent shrugged his shoulders. "As you will."

Fidel smiled. "Good. Now to the sum of money that you will pay me." He reached out and took the pen and pad from the agent's hands and carefully wrote a figure on it and handed it back to him.

The agent looked at it, and then at Fidel. "This is a very large sum of money," he said.

Fidel nodded. "That is right, but not when you compare it to the value of this island when you have finished all the work and sold the houses."

"It is still a great deal of money," the agent said stubbornly. He wiped the sweat off his face and looked down again at the pad and shook his head. "I cannot say that this is acceptable."

Fidel remained silent.

The agent tore the paper out of the pad, folded it and placed it in his briefcase. "This will have to be put before the accountants." He pursed his lips and shook his head again. "I do not think they will agree to it."

Fidel slowly stubbed out his cigar on the table top, grinding it down until the charred leaves were crushed into a powdery smudge. Then he stood up and walked to the door and opened it. He stood back and looked at the agent.

"Then we have nothing more to discuss," he said quietly. "I will say goodbye to you now."

The agent stared at him amazedly. "What are you saying?" he said. "We have much more to discuss... why are you doing this?"

Fidel walked over and stood in front of him. "Listen carefully," he said in the same quiet voice, "go back and tell your masters that there is nothing here for them because you," he leaned down and poked the agent gently in the chest, "were too proud or too stupid to give a little to gain much."

"It is not for me to say what they will give you," protested the agent. "I am only an employee of the company...."

Fidel raised his hand. "Do not insult me with this." He laughed harshly. "Am I to believe that people with enough money to buy an island, and make it into a playground for the rich, do not have enough to pay the cost of making sure that everything is done in secret? That there are no others to bid for the island because I have said that you will be the only one. And that no one else has the power to do this." He tapped his chest. "Only me."

"But I do not have the authority to say yes to this...." The agent wrung his hands and then mopped his face again.

"Then tomorrow I will take a boat to the mainland and tell the others who work as you do that this island is for sale," said Fidel decisively.

"Wait... wait," the agent's hands fluttered agitatedly in the air, "do not say that. Now that we have come this far we cannot stop." He looked beseechingly at Fidel. "Please, let us sit down and talk." He turned and took the scrap of paper with the sum of money written on it from the briefcase. "Look," he held it out to Fidel, "there is no need for me to take this back." He picked up the pad and wrote some figures on it. "See, I am working out what I think they will go to."

He motioned to Fidel. "Sit, please, I ask you."

Fidel looked at him with contempt. Where, minutes before, there had been a man confident of the absolute power of his position, there was now a panic-stricken creature, desperate to appease someone he had previously regarded as scarcely one step up from the islanders.

"All right," he said slowly. He sat down as the agent nodded and tried to hold a smile on his face.

"Good, that is good," he intoned. "Just wait while I do this." He bent back to the pad and scrawled more figures on it. Fidel watched the podgy fingers guiding the pen as it raced over the page.

Finally the agent straightened up and held out the pad to Fidel. "See? It is as you asked for," he said.

Fidel glanced at the mass of figures, then gave the pad back to him. "These mean nothing to me. All I want is the sum I asked for," he said.

The agent nodded desperately. "Yes, that is what I have written." He held up the pad and tapped the figures. "Here, as you wanted."

Fidel shrugged. "They are just numbers on paper to me." He smiled coldly. "Tell your masters that I do not want to paid with a cheque. Bring me the money in notes."

The agent looked aghast. "I could not travel with such a sum," he protested. "It would not be safe."

"Then do not come alone," Fidel said. "Bring people with you to see that it arrives here," he tapped the table, "to me."

The agent slumped on the chair. "Business is not conducted like this, Bardi," he said weakly. "I am not accustomed to working in this fashion."

"Do not worry," smiled Fidel. "You will never have to do this again. And think how much your people will reward you because you found the one man who can give them the entire island." He clicked his fingers suddenly. "Ah, there is one more thing that I shall want."

The agent blanched. "Not more money," he said. "I thought we had settled the figure?"

Fidel laughed. "Calm yourself, my friend," he said. "No, not more money. Just a small boat."

"A boat?" asked the agent apprehensively "What kind of boat?"

Fidel stroked his chin thoughtfully. "Something like those I have seen in the harbours on the mainland. With a cabin for a man to hide from the heat of the sun and maybe sleep. And with an engine, a good one, not a cheap piece that fails after a couple of summers." He nodded. "Maybe something German."

The agent nodded tiredly. "I know what you mean," he said. "Leave it to me." He shrugged. "If you are not happy then you can change it."

"Then we are agreed on everything now," said Fidel.

"There is only the matter of the house purchases," said the agent. "I will arrange for the Turk to come here and begin." He wrote on his pad. "You will assist him in this?"

Fidel nodded.

"Good." The agent heaved his bulk to his feet. "There is nothing else we need to discuss now."

He picked up his briefcase and walked to the door, then turned and looked at Fidel awkwardly.

"Forgive me, Bardi, but I must ask you," he said hesitantly. He nodded at Frado Bardi who lay on the couch sleeping fitfully, "There will be the question of who owns this house." He looked round the room, then back at Fidel. "It will be the face on the contracts that will legally be regarded as the owner." He mopped his brow. "It would be well if that face were yours."

Fidel nodded slowly. "I understand."

He watched the agent hurrying down the street, dust spurting up from his shoes, then disappearing round the corner. He went back inside and closed the door. The old man stirred suddenly, muttering a name, then falling back into sleep. Fidel sat down, lit a cigar and watched his father for a long time while the shadows crept into the room.

Chapter Twenty

Now every day the island was full of the talk of the great thing that was going to happen. People all over made plans of how they would live when the money came to them. Where they would have their houses built, and what kind of new boat would sit outside in the water waiting to take them over to the mainland if they decided to go. Because they would have money and be as good as any of the people over there. Money, they declared knowingly, or rather the lack of it, was the only thing that had always stopped them from doing things before. Now it would be different. Some of them drew rough maps of the island marking places with a cross where they would have their new home. To show to the men that came to build. "Better to get it right now than risk losing a good spot later," they told each other.

After the work of the day was finished the inn would be packed and the talk would continue far into the night. Fidel had now reached a position of official spokesman for the islanders and they would ask him the same questions again and again. How would the money for their houses be paid? They had heard that people with money carried little pieces of paper with their names written on them and they could make their mark on the paper and it would serve as real money.

The islanders demanded real money, solid coins that a man might hold in his hand and know their worth. "What good was a piece of paper that had no strength to it? No," they told Fidel loudly. He was to tell the man who spoke for the rich ones that they would only deal in coins.

As their intake of the harsh wine increased, their demands for bigger houses and more land grew. They would bring scraps of paper torn from packing cases, or old newspapers from the boats that came for the fish, and lay them out on the counter top at the inn and scrawl uneven lines of room plans that wandered all over the paper, with huge areas outside the lines that indicated the land they wanted. The land would lie barren because they would be rich and have no need to work it, but a man of wealth should have something to show and the land would do that for them.

Fidel listened to all that was said in the big room. Questions about money from men that had never had more than a handful of coins in their lives, and who could hardly count above the number of fingers on their hands. And who, even if any of it had ever come true, would have never been able to break their iron-grained habits that bitterly begrudged every coin that left their pockets. He thought contemptuously that they would have been happy to live in hovels with their newfound wealth than spend any of it. But he listened patiently as their tongues loosened and the air thickened with still-born dreams.

Only Saur never spoke to him, other than a cursory nod to acknowledge his presence. Sometimes Fidel would look up from answering a question and find the thin man's cold eyes on him. It was as if Saur was outside of the rest of them, simply waiting and watching Fidel until the time came for him to act as his violent nature dictated.

Fidel made a mental note to tell the agent to make a special case of Saur, to have him taken away immediately the sales were finished. Maybe to hold him somewhere so that he could not get back to the island at all. Even to have him killed, perhaps a drowning accident on the way over to the mainland. *Anything*, he thought, *was possible when there was huge money involved.*

He told them that he had engaged a man that dealt in matters of the law. They asked him what the law was to them— they had lived by their own laws for as long as anyone could remember. Why change now? And why have someone from the outside world? Why could Fidel not do it? Why should they pay an outsider when he could do it for nothing?

Fidel said that things were not done like that. The laws of the outside world were many and treacherous. A man might be ruined if he did not have someone with sound knowledge to make the best money for them. He smiled and said the man was a Turk, who had no love for the rich people that wanted their land, and that he would make them pay the highest prices for it.

They had laughed at that and told each other the Turks were known for their strength in business.

Then he said the Turk was so clever that he would even make the rich ones pay for his services; it would cost the islanders nothing.

They had whooped and patted Fidel on the back at this and said it was indeed a fine stroke to think of hiring a Turk.

He explained about them having to have their pictures taken to prove that they were the rightful owners of the property. That the picture would be fastened to a paper telling of the sale of their home and that they would then make a mark on the paper. "What kind of a mark?" they asked.

"Anything you like," said Fidel. "A cross or a shape of a boat, whatever you think best. It doesn't really matter as long as the picture is there."

"And the money, when will the money arrive?" they asked, the room suddenly quiet and still as all eyes turned to Fidel. He looked round at them all and smiled his tooth-glistening smile. The money would be theirs directly the last house had been sold. That was why it was so important that nothing happened to slow the proceedings.

"And our new homes, when will they be built and where will we live while this is happening?"

He explained that they were to stay in their homes until the new ones were ready for them to move into. They could go and watch as they were built, maybe make suggestions or change things as they liked.

Fidel thought about the photographs on the contracts. His would be the only face not on one. He remembered what the agent had said as he left. The man had made it plain that only the face would be recognised as the legal owner.

But Frado Bardi was still alive and it was his house in which his son lived. The old man was known to everyone on the island and it would be his face that went onto the contract. Fidel would have no right to any money that came from the developers. It would go to a man that lived almost all his waking time in a different world, inhabited by people and events from his past. He would not even know what the money was if it were given to him. It would be the correct thing for his son to have control of the money, but Fidel had heard that before that could happen it all went to a court hearing and might take many months to allow the power to turn to him.

He had suddenly felt a hatred for his father surge through him, the ferocity of the emotion making him tremble, and struggle to regain his control. He tried to think it through clearly. The agent knew that he was the only one that could persuade the islanders to sell. But the agent might not be coming back in the near future, if at all. The Turk would arrive and the purchasing would begin. Fidel would accompany him to meet the people where he would take the photographs and prepare the contracts. His father would be treated as the rest of them. Legally, Fidel would have no house to sell. He would not be included in any way that would give him a right to any money or land. In the legal terms of the proceedings he would simply not exist.

This particular night he had come back from the inn late and sat on the ground outside the house, drinking wine and looking up into the vast silence of the night sky that went on forever, and let his mind examine the situation.

Gradually, all the small details fell away until he faced the solution. While his father lived he had nothing. The old man might just be the one thing that stood between him and a life that could be lived in ease, with money to support him forever.

The wine beat a tempo in his head that marched to the logic of the solution. He stood up and stretched, breathing deep, drawing the heavy air into him, every muscle and sinew in his body vibrant with life. A great ecstasy of anticipation swept through him.

He went into the house through the open door and stood very still in the darkness, listening to the ragged flutter of his father's exhausted lungs as they dragged life into the frail body.

Fidel lit the small lamp that stood on the table and waited as the tiny flame slowly grew and threw a flickering light into the room. Suddenly his father stirred and turned his head and looked at Fidel. His eyes were clear and unblinking and they knew his son. He spoke on the faint outrush of his breath.

"You are Fidel."

Fidel moved closer until he stood beside the bed looking down at his father. The old man stared up at him and slowly frowned. "Why did you come back?" he asked.

Fidel knelt down and smiled, his lips drawing all the way back over the white teeth. "I had to come, Father," he said. "I had to hide. So I came home. Back to this place."

His father's eyes closed for a second, then, "Why?"

"Because," he moved his head closer, "because I killed two men, Father."

He waited, watching, as the impact of his words registered in his father's eyes. They widened in a dawning horror as the old man shook his head as if to deny what he had heard.

"What are you saying?" The words trembled from his lips.

Fidel looked at the ravaged face. "I told you. I killed two men."

Flecks of blood flew from the old man's lips as he spoke. "Why did you do it?"

Fidel's face hardened. "They set themselves against me." He shook his head. "I had no choice."

His father closed his eyes. "You are evil." He drew a long struggling breath. "Your mother was right. She wanted you brought without life. That is how it should have been."

The long fingers of the moon's light slid gently into the room. Fidel moved even closer. "Listen," he said, "one of the men I killed was a priest."

His father opened his eyes and stared at Fidel in horror, then turned his head to the wall away from him. "Go," he whispered. "Leave."

Fidel shook his head slowly. "I cannot do that, Father. This is my place now. I must have it." He stood up and took his coat from the back of the chair and spoke very quietly. "While you live I have nothing." He knelt down by the bed again and reached forward and touched his father's shoulder.

The old man recoiled from him. "Leave me!"

Fidel smiled gently. "Father, I bring you a gift." His eyes were very dark as he looked at the old man, so dark that they were almost red in the flame of the lamp. He could feel the blood boiling in his head, emptying his mind of everything, save that which he knew had to be done. The light crept out of the room as long clouds swept across the moon, bringing a sudden darkness to the land. Fidel looked at the man who had given him life. He felt nothing, only the great power that tore everything out of his mind, leaving just the one act that would truly set him free.

"The gift that I have for you is sleep," he said.

His father stared at him confusedly. Fidel reached forward and gently pulled the stained pillow out from under his father's head.

"A sleep that you will never wake from," Fidel said. He waited a second longer, just enough to see the horrified understanding flood into his father's eyes. Then he smiled tenderly at the old man and leaning forward put the coat over his face and pressed down hard.

For one moment there was nothing, then his father reared up off the bed, throwing Fidel back. The old man struggled to get up, but Fidel slammed him back down and knelt on his chest. He bore down again with the coat and for a few seconds his father fought with surprising strength. Then, suddenly, as if all the power in his body had switched off, he became still, and Fidel leaned down on the coat and held it on his face; until he could feel no movement under his hands.

Slowly he sat back and looked at his father. The old man's face was relaxed into a shrunken mask, staring blindly at a world that had left him.

Fidel reached out and gently closed his eyes. "Goodnight, Father," he said softly. He placed the pillow back under his father's head, walked to the window and stood looking out over the sea.

After a while he made coffee and sat in a chair until the first sun brought the dawn.

When the old woman arrived to see to his father he let her in and told her that Frado had died in the night. She went over and looked at him, then said it was a mercy that he had escaped from a body that had only given him pain.

She nodded at him and said her son made the coffins for the people and he would make one for Frado Bardi if Fidel wished. He thanked her and said to tell her son to do that. Also, she could take any of the old man's clothes and boots that she wanted. Anything that her son might use, or any of the people of the village.

They put Frado Bardi in the hard ground behind the mountain that dominated the island and where the dead had been laid for centuries. Most of the people came to respect his passing. He had not been a man for close friends, but he had served the village well enough and lived a just life.

As the rough-hewn box was being lowered into the earth the boy stepped through the crowd and came up to the graveside. He stood quite still for a moment and then put his hand flat on the top of the coffin where Frado Bardi's name was cut into the wood. The men holding the ropes round the coffin stopped and looked at him.

"What is it?" one of them asked.

The boy did not answer for a moment, then turned his head and stared at Fidel. "This man," he looked at the coffin, "was not ready to die," he said.

"What are you saying?" said the man. "Frado Bardi is dead. He must be buried."

The boy shook his head. "His spirit is not at rest." He ran his hand along the top of the coffin. "He did not come to his end in peace."

Fidel stepped forward. "Enough of this," he said harshly. "Let the dead be treated with respect."

He turned to the crowd. "My father lived a just life. Is he not to be allowed to lie in this ground because of this boy's madness?"

The men with the ropes looked at the boy. He shook his head again. "No. This must not be. He cannot be put to rest." The colour drained from his face and he faltered and swayed, steadying himself against the coffin. "Until the truth is known."

"What is wrong with you?" asked Fidel. "Have your senses left you?" He gestured to the men holding the ropes. "Do your work."

They looked hesitantly from Fidel to the boy. Fidel took the rope out of the man's hand. "Do as I say!" he said angrily. "Let this boy play the fool if he will. My father must be put to rest now."

He began to lower his rope and the coffin lurched to one side. The men hastily let their ropes down in the grave until the coffin bumped against the hard earth.

As they drew the ropes back under the box and coiled them into their hands Fidel nodded at them. "Thank you," he said.

The boy remained standing by the grave staring down at the coffin. Fidel picked up a handful of the stony earth and tossed it onto the coffin. "May you rest in peace, Father," he said.

He stood for a moment in silence, his head bowed, then moved aside for Salan to come forward and do the same. As he did so Salan glanced at the boy, then back at Fidel, frowned and shook his head. Fidel nodded to him. He waited as the rest of them filed past and murmured their condolences. Finally they were all gone and only the boy and Fidel remained.

He pulled the spade out of the pile of fresh dug earth and began to fill the grave with it. The boy stood back from him and watched silently. Fidel continued till the grave was half full, then stopped and turned round.

"Why are you still here?" he asked, feeling the anger that the boy always aroused in him beginning to rise and wondering why it was so powerful. What was it in this man-child that the people had always found so strange and wonderful, that he had hated the very first time that he had seen him up on the high ground? Where he had known Fidel's name, and told him he would bring evil to the island. He looked at the slight body and the thin face with its haunted eyes that flooded with fear as they stared back at him.

"Well...?" he said. "Why do you not speak? You spoke when all heard your madness... speak now!"

The boy looked at him, then down at the earth in the grave. "Your father should not be there, Fidel Bardi." He shook his head very slowly and closed his eyes. "You are with him, I can see you... he is weak and you are close to him...." He stopped and put his hands up to his head and groaned softly. He remained like this for several moments, quite still and hardly seeming to breathe. Then he opened his eyes and looked at Fidel in horror. "You," he said, his voice shaking, "*you* took his life." He stepped back from Fidel. "You killed your father... you, his son, killed him!"

"You are mad," said Fidel contemptuously. "They said you are living in a strange fashion." He laughed harshly. "Now I see it is because you are mad in the head."

The boy shook his head desperately. "No. I saw it. And now he is down there," he pointed to the grave, "and you did it." He backed away and put out his hands as to ward Fidel off. "You are the one they said would come, Bardi; you are him." He stumbled and almost fell. "I knew… it was told to me… I heard it over and over again."

Fidel laughed again. "Better they take you and put you somewhere where you will come to no harm," he said. "If you stay here they will call you the island fool!"

The boy turned from him and began to walk away, stumbling on the broken ground. Suddenly he stopped and turned to face Fidel. He raised his arm and pointed up at the sky. "There will be darkness all over this land," he cried. "It will rain death on everyone. None will be spared."

Fidel raised the spade threateningly. "Go, fool," he said. He nodded at the grave. "Go before I put you down there with him!"

He watched as the boy, his face contorted with terror, ran down the track towards the dunes and was lost to sight.

Chapter Twenty-One

One week later the agent came back for the last time. He sat in Fidel's house and told him that the Turkish lawyer would arrive in three days. His name was Kemal and Fidel was to help him in any way that he asked. The agent said Kemal was not a man to waste time, so if Fidel could gather the islanders together, as many at a time as Kemal could handle, then that was what he should do.

Fidel agreed. He told the agent there would be no hindrance on his part. The agent gave him a contract and told him to get his father's name and photograph on it. Fidel had taken the papers from him and said his father had died and the picture on the contract would be his. The agent had smiled thoughtfully and said he was saddened to hear of his loss, but he should take heart because now the house was his and he would be doubly rich. First, from the money the company was paying him for his part in the house sales; and now the sale of his own house. "Indeed," the agent said, "the Lord worked in strange ways."

Fidel had agreed. He had lost his father whom he had loved dearly, but with his death the old man had made him rich. He had said many prayers for his father's safe journey to be with his God. He also told the agent that the man, Saur, was almost certain to make trouble so they should think about stopping him before he began.

The agent's face had tightened and he wrote something on his pad and underlined it strongly. He thanked Fidel for telling him. Then he glanced around, put his finger to his lips and reached down into his briefcase and pulled out a thick plastic square-cut bag. He placed it reverently on the table and silently motioned to Fidel to open it. Fidel did so and saw the hundreds of tightly packed banknotes crammed inside.

The agent waited while Fidel carefully counted it out on the table, separating the notes into their different sizes. Finally he was done and told the agent the money was exactly right.

The agent said it was a very large sum of money to have loose and should really be in a bank, and that he could recommend a good one if he liked.

Fidel smiled and said the money would be safe with him and he would make his own arrangements for its safe keeping.

The agent shrugged and said it was his responsibility now.

On the third day the Turk arrived in one of the company helicopters. The old women directed and accompanied him to Fidel's house where he introduced himself as the lawyer. Kemal refused water and produced a pile of contracts and a single lens reflex camera and asked if they could begin immediately.

Fidel looked at him. Kemal was of spare build with grey hair brushed back from a small hooked nose and expressionless brown eyes set deep under jutting brows. The eyes seemed to have no life, until he spoke of business when they glowed softly as if lit from within. He told Fidel that the helicopter would be back at night to take him away until the next day when he would return. He said he expected to finish everything in three days.

Fidel took him down the track to the shore where he had told as many of the people as he thought the Turk could handle in one day to gather. He made them form a line while the Turk worked smoothly and calmly through them, all the time refusing to answer their endless questions about money and the new houses.

Fidel watched them as they scrawled their marks on the contracts, some making crosses, others tiny crude drawings of boats or mules, anything that they could manage with the black pen that the Turk put into their hands. They stood, desperately self-conscious as he pointed the camera at them, relaxing into embarrassed laughter when he waved them away when the picture was taken.

The work was finished on the afternoon of the third day. The Turk spoke into his tiny hand-held phone and two hours later the helicopter landed on the shore. He nodded shortly to Fidel, advised him to leave the island quickly, climbed in and was gone.

It was done. Homes that had seen generations of the same families born and die within their walls had been sold into the possession of a giant institution that the people would never even know the name of. They celebrated to such an extent in the inn that night that many of the men could not handle their boats the following day and stayed home.

"No matter," they said. "We are rich. Soon we will have no need to work at all."

Two days later Fidel went down to the shore and waited to go over to the mainland on one of the boats that were buying fish. Suddenly, Saur appeared running down the track towards him. Fidel watched tensely as the thin man approached.

"Where are you going, Bardi?" Saur asked.

"I have business on the mainland," said Fidel.

Saur shook his head. "No." He jerked his thumb back at the village. "You have business back there now."

"What are you saying?"

"The boy is your business now, Bardi," Saur said grimly. "He is telling everyone that we could not sell our homes to the Turk… that it was not right by law." He nodded at Fidel. "You must stop his mouth before the fear spreads to all of them."

"Where is he now?" asked Fidel.

"At the well," said Saur. "When I came to find you more people were coming to hear him."

Fidel turned and began walking back up from the shore, Saur keeping step with him.

"Why did you not tell them that he knows nothing?" asked Fidel. "That he is not right in his head?"

"No, Bardi," the thin man said harshly. "You are the one that told us that if we sold our homes we would be rich." He smiled bitterly. "Now you must see that it comes true."

When they arrived at the well there was a crowd gathering. The boy was stood on the low wall and talking to them.

"You must see that it is wrong. You cannot sell your homes. Where will you go? What will become of you?" He stopped as Fidel and Saur pushed their way through the crowd and stood before him.

Fidel turned to face the people. "This is wild talk," he said. "Do not listen to him. You have all signed the proper papers and you will be paid for your homes." He turned to the boy. "What are doing? Do you not want them to live without the work that makes them old before their years?"

The boy was silent, the gentle eyes staring at him with the same intensity as when he had confronted Fidel at his father's grave.

When he finally spoke his voice was slow and halting. "You do not do this for them." He stopped and closed his eyes as if listening to something. "There is much you have not told us." He paused again. Then said, his voice firmer now, "Much you dare not tell us." He faced the crowd. "Ask Fidel Bardi if what I say is not true… that he hides the truth from us… that if we do as he says we will never live on this island again!"

Fidel looked at the sudden anxiety and doubt in the watching faces and knew that he must stop it now before the boy's words spread panic among them.

"This is a madness," he said. "What are we all listening to? The wild talk of a boy that says he can see what will happen?" He laughed contemptuously. "If that is true then why does he not do that?" He turned to the boy and opened his hands. "Tell us what it is you can see so that we all will know."

The boy shook his head slowly. "It is not clear… I do not have the words for you… but there is something terrible waiting… I cannot see…." He stopped.

Fidel shrugged. "There, it is as I said. A madness that comes upon this boy so that he feels he must put it on us."

Saur put up his arm to hold their attention. "I am with Bardi in what he says." He stared at the boy. "I do not forget when you almost let us go to our deaths. The sea could have taken many that day. We trusted in what you said and you were wrong."

"I could not see," the boy said desperately. "There was a darkness between my eyes and the truth."

He looked at Fidel. "It was you…." He stepped back from Fidel. "You have the darkness in you." His eyes were wild as he spoke. "You are the evil on this land."

"You do not know what you say," said Fidel. He shook his head sadly. "We should feel pity for this boy, not anger. He should go over to the mainland. They have places where he could be cured of this sickness." He smiled at them. "Go about your business." He waved his hand at the boy. "This is nothing."

He turned and walked away. When he had gone almost to the end of the track he heard footsteps behind him and turned. It was Saur.

"What now?" asked Fidel. "Not more madness."

Saur scowled. "You would do better to heed the words the boy is telling them, Bardi. He is still there and they are still listening."

"Do they believe what he tells them?" asked Fidel.

"I do not say that, but they have not gone from the place," said Saur grimly.

Fidel was silent as looked at Saur. He wondered how far the man would go to silence the boy.

"Do you think they will heed what he says, Saur?"

"I do not know," Saur replied angrily. "Why do you ask me something I cannot answer? I have told you what I do know. They are still there and still listening."

"Walk with me, Saur," Fidel said. He turned and began treading the path down to the shore.

After a moment Saur followed him. "What will you do, Bardi, if he does not stop his mouth?"

Fidel smiled gently. "What would you do?"

Saur did not reply for a moment, then stared at Fidel. "I tell you this, Bardi. I do not want to be robbed of the chance to never work again." He looked out at the sea. "I have had my fill of that bitch." He stopped and faced Fidel. "I will go as far as you. Anything that you do I will match."

Fidel felt his instincts awaken as he looked at the grim face before him. "Anything, Saur?" He smiled again. "That might be hard to do."

"Do not think to make a fool of me, Bardi. I have said what I will do." Saur moved forward until they were almost touching and Fidel could sense the anger in him. "Tell me what I know is in your mind," he said softly.

"What is in my mind is to find him and talk with him." He held up his hand to stop Saur's protest. "Then, if he will not see reason," he paused, "then, I will end his life," he said, calmly.

Saur smiled, his eyes glinting, the unfamiliar action splitting the deep lines of his face. "Yes." He nodded. "I will do that with you." He placed his hand on Fidel's arm. "I am with you, Bardi. We will rid this island of the fool." He put out his hand and Fidel took it. They did not shake hands, but stood for a brief moment, joined in their mutual pact of blood.

Then Fidel stepped back. "We must do this so that no blame falls on us when he is gone."

Saur nodded. "It must be so."

"Where does he go in the day, Saur?"

Saur thought for a moment. "On the high ground, they say. He walks back and forth on the top. He looks for something...." He shrugged. "No one knows what it is."

Fidel nodded. "Three days from now we will talk to him. Wait until he is out of sight of the village. Then you come up from the shore and I will wait on the high ground, so that he will be between us."

"Whatever you say to him he will not heed," Saur said. "His mind has gone from him. All he sees are things that frighten him." He held out his hands in front of him and made a snapping gesture. "That is all he will understand," he said harshly.

"We will try to make him see reason first," said Fidel. "Then, if what you say is right we will be ready."

Saur nodded. "I will be ready, Bardi."

"Leave me now," Fidel said. "We should not be seen together until this matter is decided."

He touched Saur lightly on the shoulder. "Three days."

The pace of life on the island had changed almost overnight when the people sold their homes. Men sat on the rocks at the shore and drank wine, becoming too fuddled to stand, and slept out in the heat of the day.

The boats were left beached high on the sand, or further up behind the dunes. Those that did work came back from the sea when the sun was overhead, laughing, with their boats only half full, saying the fish had run from them. Fields lay untended and a strange dreamlike mood lay over the land.

On the morning of the third day Fidel rose early and made coffee. He sat by the window and looked out over the sea. The heat was already thick and suffocating and he knew by noon most of the people would seek the shade of their homes. He took his coffee outside and leaned against the wall and smoked a cigar. He wondered where Saur was at this moment and what he was doing.

Fidel had no doubts that the man would do exactly what he said he would do about the boy.

He thought how strange to find such an ally in Saur who never hid his enmity towards him. But then, he was like that with everyone on the island. His violence was known and people were cautious round him. He wondered where the boy would be on the high ground at any particular time. They had to wait until they could not be seen from the village.

He went back inside and took the knife out of the sheath and stroked it gently along the stone, bringing a line of light to the razor edge. When he was satisfied with it he wiped the blade with a rag dipped in the oil from the lamp. Then he slid it back into the sheath and slung it carefully round his neck, positioning it so that it lay just under his left arm. He finishing smoking the cigar and drank the rest of the coffee. He was ready.

Saur walked slowly along the shore, picking his way among the rocks. He looked to the high ground as he went, searching for the figure of the boy. He glanced up at the sun and thought it time for Bardi to have left his house and started out. He wondered about Bardi and what he would gain from the company that had bought their homes. Fidel had told the people that he would get no more than they, but Saur knew he was lying. There had to be more than just the price of the old Bardi's home for him. He was being too useful for a house price. He thought how suddenly old Frado had died, just before the Turk came to buy their homes, and just in time for Fidel Bardi to have a home to sell. He grinned savagely at the thought of the son killing the father so that he could inherit and sell within a few days. And now there was the boy to deal with. He hoped Bardi would not waste time trying to change his mind for him. Better to make an end of it right away.

Chapter Twenty-Two

The boy walked slowly along the track that went all the way to the end of the high ground. There were small tracks leading off the main one, but they were hardly used and they only led to the more remote corners of the island. As he walked he struggled to make his mind clear of the images that haunted him and gave him no rest. When he tried to sleep at night the horror grew stronger, and always it was Fidel Bardi that came out of the darkness, smiling and talking to him as the fear rose up to engulf him. He would sometimes wake screaming, and at first some of the people would come running to the old boat on the dunes to see what was wrong. But now they left him alone.

He knew they thought his mind had gone away from him and that he no longer had the gift of sight. And he could not make them see that the evil was here all around them.

When the old man Bardi had died the boy had been wrenched from sleep and plunged into a waking nightmare as a corner of the darkness had lifted and given him a glimpse of the evil that was happening. And the image had returned again and again, as if to mock his failure to make the people see what was among them.

The strongest picture was the one he could never clearly see, but knew was there waiting to happen in all its horror. He tried to face it, but it always came in shadow with the stench of heat and burning, but never plain enough for him to see. Today when he woke it had seemed that the world was still in darkness. Even when he had crawled out from under the boat, and looked out over the sea into the blinding light, he could not lose the feeling of despair that bore down on him. Now, on the high ground the sun seemed to lay over the land like a stifling blanket that drew the strength from his body, and left him weak and almost stupefied.

He walked on over the stony ground and through the spindly pines that had struggled up out of the poor soil, on until he had left the sight of the village far behind. It was then that he noticed the tiny figure far below, and some way in front of him moving steadily up the side of the mountain. As the boy carried on walking and gradually drew closer he recognised the tall thin man as he appeared at the top of the track. It was Saur and he stood still, waiting.

The boy felt a sudden terror rush through him. Almost as if the foreboding that had gripped him when he woke at first light had taken form and was here now. He halted and waited, tense and afraid. Saur took a couple of steps along the track and stopped, staring at him.

The boy called out to him. "What is it… what do you want, Saur?"

The tall man stood and looked at him silently.

The boy called again. "Why are you here…? Speak!"

Again there was no sound or movement from Saur. Just then a cloud moved across the sun and a huge shadow began drifting over the land. The boy shuddered violently as the darkness touched him. He turned to flee from Saur, then stopped, frozen where he stood. At the far end of the track stood Fidel Bardi smiling at him. He began to tremble as Bardi began walking towards him. His nightmare had come out of the darkness and was alive and with him.

When Bardi had come within a few paces he stopped and smiled again.

"Do not be afraid," he said. "We mean you no harm. All we want is to talk with you."

The boy looked at Bardi, then turned to see Saur had moved closer.

"Why do you speak in this place?" he asked. "Why not in the village so that all may hear?"

Bardi shook his head. "Our words are not for their ears." He gestured at Saur. "Just the two of us are speaking for them."

The boy half turned so that he could see the both of them. Bardi held up his hand to halt Saur before he came too close.

"You see? We have no anger in us for you. We just want you to see that the people have sold their homes and soon they will be able to live a better life than ever they dreamed of." He nodded at Saur. "Is that not right, Saur?"

The thin man nodded silently, staring at the boy.

"But if you raise doubts in their minds then you will only make them unhappy," Bardi continued. "You must give us your word that you will be silent from this day on." He smiled the tooth-glistening smile at the boy. "Go back to living under your boat that never knows the sea's hand."

Saur smiled contemptuously. "Yes," he rasped, "go back to being the island's fool."

The boy stood silent for a long moment, then looked at Bardi. When he spoke his voice was very clear. "You did not come here to talk, Bardi." He looked at Saur. "And this one that you brought with you." He glanced up at the enormous darkness moving overhead. "You even shame the sun."

Then, without warning, he whirled round and ran off the main track and into the thick scrub.

Fidel swore and started after him with Saur close behind. As they ran the thin man drew level with Fidel and touched his arm.

Fidel looked at him. "What is it?" he asked.

Saur pointed ahead. "Let him run!" he said. He pointed again. "He runs to the place of the dark water!"

"Where do you mean?" asked Fidel watching the boy as he ran ahead of them.

Saur gestured angrily. "There," he said pointing again, "there, the ground lies over the dark water." He began to angle away from Fidel. "Catch him between us," he shouted. "Trap him above the water."

It was true. In his panic the boy was fleeing towards the high ground that fell sheer down to the boiling sea of the dark water.

The sky filled with the huge cloud as if the day had almost gone into night. The stray shafts of light that filtered through were enough to see the boy as he ran desperately from them. Saur was now a hundred yards away from Fidel and waved to him to in crease the distance between them so that the trap was even wider.

The boy looked round once, saw what they were doing and swerved to one side, then realised that he was moving towards Saur, and went back to his original line. He ran on, looking from side to side frantically for a way of escape, then began to slow down and move in a zigzag fashion.

Fidel watched him for a moment; then realised what he was doing. The boy had seen that he had come within sight of the cliff edge and that he had nowhere to go now. Saur started to close the angle now, and Fidel did the same.

It was a classic hunting routine. Pursue the prey until it has nowhere to go, and so traps itself.

The two men slowed now. The boy stopped, stood still, then ran one way for a short distance, stopped again, then ran back as the men drew closer.

Finally, he halted, and stood watching them. It was as if he realised finally, that the act had to be played out to its end, here in this desolate place.

Fidel spoke first, struggling to regain his breath. "Why did you run?"

The boy stared at him silently. Suddenly Saur lunged at him and struck him a heavy blow to the side of his head. The boy fell back and slumped to the ground. Fidel stepped forward and caught him by the arm and dragged him almost upright.

As Saur moved to strike him again Fidel blocked him and said, "Wait!"

The boy looked at him, his eyes filled with pain and fear. He shrank back.

"You are him," he whispered. "Your name is not Bardi... you are the one born in evil... the one they said would come...." His voice trailed away as his eyes remained fixed on Fidel.

"What is this?" snarled Saur. "What fool's talk are you saying?" He looked at Fidel urgently, the bloodlust raging in him. "Why does he say you are not Fidel Bardi?"

Fidel shook his head. "He is mad, Saur." He caught the boy by his hair that fell to his shoulders and jerked his head up. "Answer now and save yourself," he said. "Will you be silent and talk no more with the people?"

The boy tried to wrench free from Fidel who flung him to the ground. "Give us your answer!"

He looked at Saur who nodded. "I am ready, Bardi."

The boy struggled to get to his feet, then suddenly went rigid, his body crouched over, head twisted, looking at something beyond them. He gave a soft cry of abject terror and shook his head frantically.

"No! No!" he screamed out.

"What is it?" said Saur. "Are you really mad?"

The boy tried to speak, the words choking in his throat. Finally, his voice trembling, he spoke. "You are he... the one whose face I could never see when I dreamed." He caught Saur by the arm and shook him. "You must listen to me," he begged, "It is he... Abaddon... the Destroyer...."

Saur frowned and turned to Fidel. "What is this, Bardi?" He looked back to the boy. "Why does he call you that name?"

"He will destroy the land," the boy babbled. "He is from the world of the evil."

He twisted round and tried to get behind Saur. "Great darkness will come to this place and death will follow."

Fidel looked at him and knew the time had come. He was beyond anything that they could say now. He touched Saur on the shoulder and the thin man turned his head and looked at him. Fidel jerked his chin at the boy and Saur's face set like a trap. He nodded grimly.

"Pick him up," said Fidel.

Saur reached down, took hold of the boy's shirt and lifted him effortlessly to his feet. Fidel pulled out the blade and held it up for a moment, the steel glinting in the gloom.

Saur swung the boy round to face Fidel. "Do it, Bardi... do it now!" he said harshly.

Fidel stepped forward and slammed the knife into the boy's body, just under the ribs. The boy gave a gasping scream and stiffened in Saur's grasp. Fidel twisted the blade and levered it upwards, cutting and sawing with it.

The boy lifted his head and stared at Fidel, his eyes agonized. As he slowly began to slump forward he spoke for the last time. "Abaddon!"

Saur threw the body away from him and stepped back. "It is done, Bardi." Fidel looked down at the boy who lay half on his face in the scrub grass.

"Turn him over, Saur." The thin man frowned at him. "The grass," Fidel said, "he will bleed into the ground. It might be seen."

Saur nodded and slid his boot under the body and eased it over on its back. The boy's blue eyes stared up at the black sky.

Saur laughed mirthlessly. "He does not see now, eh, Bardi?"

"No," said Fidel slowly, "his gift had died with him."

"We must not stay here," said Saur looking round. "We have to put this," he nodded at the body, "into the dark water." He pointed over at the cliff edge. "Just along from here the water runs strongest. We must drag him to that place."

"Not drag, Saur," said Fidel. "The blood will mark the ground. If they look for him it could tell a story. We must carry him."

Saur nodded. "You are right to say that." He bent down and took hold of the boy's feet. "You take his head. Do not let the blood touch you."

They carried the body slowly, stumbling over the broken ground to the edge. Fidel peered over and saw the sea boiling in far below and smashing against the rock wall, and then folding under and turning the water almost black with its power as it thundered underneath back to the sea.

Saur smiled bleakly. "Put him with the others that went before him."

They held the slack body suspended over the edge. Suddenly, Saur gasped and recoiled, almost letting go. "Look," he said, his voice shaking, "his feet...."

Fidel saw the small wounds in the boy's feet oozing blood. Saur spoke again.

"The hands, look at the hands… they bleed!"

It was true. The same shaped wounds were leaking blood from the hands.

"Let him go," said Fidel harshly, "Do it now!"

As the body fell it turned once in mid-air and stayed that way, as if looking up at them, then hit the water and was gone. Fidel tried to look for it among the hell of movement below, but could see nothing.

Saur touched his arm. "Come, Bardi. Let us leave this place."

When they were back at the main track Fidel stopped. "We must not be seen together this day."

Saur nodded. "I left my boat down among the rocks. I will take it out to sea and land on the shore as if I have been out for fish."

"Good," said Fidel. "I will go to the inn and let myself be seen there."

As he turned to leave Saur held up his hand. "A moment, Bardi." He frowned at Fidel. "What did he mean when he called you that name?"

Fidel shook his head. "I do not know." He shrugged. "His mind was gone, Saur. You saw how he was. If he had been right in the head he would have lived."

Saur stared at him. "A long time ago… many years… after you had gone, Bardi, a man came to this island to tell us of a faith that he said we could live by."

Fidel frowned at him impatiently. "Now is not the time for this, Saur; we should not be here."

"This will only take a moment," Saur said. "Just listen while I tell you. This man tried to make us know of a man he called Jesus…."

"I know of that," said Fidel. "It is only another way to control people. There is no truth in it."

"Maybe you are right," Saur said slowly, "but that is not what I have to say." He made a dismissive gesture with his hand. "You know we have never needed to pray to anything. We go to the sea and if she wants us then all their prayers will change nothing."

Fidel waited silently for him to continue.

"This man that came… he told us many things." Saur tapped his head. "Some thought he was mad the way he spoke of this Jesus he called a god."

"I have told you it is all lies," said Fidel. "A man is a fool if he believes in stories from the old times." He laughed shortly. "There is no way to say that any of it is true."

"Maybe what you say is right, Bardi, but that is not what I am telling you. This man spoke of the other side of his god." Saur paused as he searched his memory. "What he called the dark ones that would destroy all the good in the world."

"What has this to do with me, Saur?" asked Fidel.

Saur stepped closer and fixed him with the cold slate grey eyes. "Only that he called the dark one the same name that the boy called you. Abaddon." Saur nodded firmly. "He said that he was the destroyer. That he brought destruction with him."

"Surely you did not believe this, Saur?" asked Fidel. "You said yourself the man was mad. So why should you care what a boy with a sick mind says?"

"I believe in myself," said Saur harshly. "Nothing else. But why, when he was dying did he call you that name? The name of a thing that destroys!"

Fidel shook his head. "I have no answer for you. Only that the boy must have been as mad as the man that wanted you to believe in dead stories."

"But how would the boy have known about this thing… this Abaddon?" He thought hard. "The man came to us the year that you left… just after you left. The boy was not even born then so he could have never heard the name."

"Saur," Fidel said firmly, "I cannot tell you what I do not know. Maybe the boy's sickness made him dream things." He threw his hands up. "I only know we must not stay here." He looked up at the sky. "Let us go while there is still the darkness to hide under."

When Saur had left, taking the track down to the shore, Fidel looked over the edge and down at the dark water for the last time. He wondered about the name the boy had called him and how Saur had recognised it from the ramblings of a preacher many years ago. Abaddon. It had a strange sound to it, he thought. A name from a different time. Almost like a curse.

The boy was not missed for several days. Since his way had become so strange to them the people were not alarmed when he was not seen in the village or up on the high ground. A few of them went out to look for him, but the excitement over the new life about to begin kept everything else from their minds. Anyway, it was felt that he had gone away from his mind and never returned.

They spoke of the strange way that he had taken against Fidel Bardi, who had done so much by speaking for them to the rich people that bought their houses, and had helped them deal with the papers that the Turk had brought with him. Bardi was doing all this just to see that they would have a better life. Not for his own gain.

When no trace of him could be found, they thought he must have fallen into sea and drowned. As Saur pointed out, the boy was always up on the high ground and much of the edge was treacherous and could turn a foot easily. One slip and a man might be gone and never seen again.

Chapter Twenty-Three

Then men arrived on a large boat with huge machines that they drove down a special ramp that had to be built from the boat to the shore. The people came to watch and ask questions. Were these to build new homes for them?

The men never answered them. More materials arrived and big steel sheds were erected on the shore to house hundred of bags of cement and piles of timber. Special locks that had no keys, only a round dial on the face, were fitted to the doors.

The people went to Fidel and asked when were their new homes to be started. He told them that a certain man would come any day now who would have the answers to all their questions. Just be patient. Their time was almost here.

Fidel knew that he had to leave now. When the man he had told them about did arrive, it would be to tell them they had to leave the island and never return. He knew the fury that would erupt when they realised what had happened. That when they protested, and said where were the new homes they had been promised, the man would point to the fine print in the contracts they had signed. In the complex language it said that each houseowner gave legal right to the buyer to occupy and own the island; because in law it was acknowledged that as no one else had title to the island, the islanders were assumed to own the island collectively between them. So by selling all the dwelling places on the island, they were legally selling all the ground of the island. And nowhere in the fine print was there anything that said the company would build new homes for the people.

He rang the agent and asked him to send a boat for Lyra Mora and himself to go over to the mainland. Once there they would go all the way to Athens.

It would be wise to go as far as far as they could from the island when the people were told they could no longer remain there.

He had a phone number to ring the agent when the people had been cleared from the island. They could return and live there while the construction work was under way. The agent told him proudly that the company was going to make this project the crowning achievement of its career. Only proven top class contractors would be hired and all work undertaken had to be finished in the stipulated times. "Already," he had confidentially remarked to Fidel, "the company has put out the most discreet enquiries to certain people they considered might be interested in a home on the island. The response," he nodded, "has been very favourable. If it continues the dwellings will be sold before they are built. You, Fidel," he said enviously, "will be very fortunate to own a home on the island. It will be better than money in any bank."

The three boats carrying the security personnel arrived at the island early in the morning of the day of the rest. Fidel had told the agent that it would be the one day when they would all be together in the village. The men formed into squads and marched up the track and stopped at the well. Then they went in parties of three to each house and told the occupants they had three hours to pack and move. Ferries would arrive at the island to take them and whatever they chose to bring with them over to the mainland.

There was baffled amazement from the people. Fear as well, as the men told them calmly and patiently that they had collectively soid the entire island. It was no longer their land. They had to leave.

Panic swept through them. They said they did not understand. The men showed them documents, taken from leather cases, pointing to sections of the print and explaining that it was all here, that they had sold the land to the company and must now go. The people stared uncomprehendingly at the papers, telling the men that they could not read. The men shrugged and said that was not their concern. They were there to see that the island was vacated.

Then someone said to fetch Fidel Bardi. He would know what had happened they told the men. Bardi was the one that had spoken for them and helped the Turk when the photographs were taken and they made their marks. Two of them ran to Bardi's house and banged on the door. When there was no answer they forced their way in. The house was empty and Bardi's clothes were gone.

When they went back to the others and told them there was a stunned silence. They looked at each other fearfully. Where was Bardi and what could it all mean?

Just then Saur came down from the high ground. He had seen the boats coming in and demanded to know what was happening.

The people told him and said that Fidel Bardi was not in his house and it looked as if he had left the island.

Saur's face went like stone and he was silent for a moment, then he swore a terrible oath and raged at them; did they not see what had been done?

They stared at him baffled and he swore again and said that Fidel Bardi had tricked them into selling the island and gone from them now to escape their anger. They did not understand him and crowded round saying that they were going to have new homes and money and a life free from toil.

Saur held his arms in the air and told them to be silent. Could they not see why Bardi was not here? Did they see why he had fled the island before these men arrived? That he was a thief that had helped to steal the island. Saur took a deep breath and his face darkened with blood. He would kill Bardi for what he had done, he said. Then he looked at the men that had come to take them off the island. "And any man that comes to my house and tries to enter, then I will kill him as well."

The men were not impressed by his threat. They had done this kind of work before, though never on such a large scale, and knew that there were always one or two people that gave trouble. When you took them away from the others the resistance soon vanished. After all, these were people that had no knowledge of the outside world.

The company intended to take most of them to a large gypsy camp on one of the big islands and land them quietly, confident that when they were amongst people like themselves they would settle down and make a fresh life, or disperse of their own accord. The rest would be dropped off at various islands in twos or threes. No one would care what happened to them. The world was full of people living on the edge of existence and they would soon vanish into the army of the dispossessed.

The man with the papers told them that it would be better for them to go to their homes and gather whatever they wanted to take. He looked at them warningly and said not to try to fetch furniture or any large items. That would all be collected later and sent on to them when they were settled.

Saur said he would go to his house and that if they came for him there would be death on the island. He looked at the others and said they should all do the same. Some of the people began to agree and the men moved in among them and said they should not listen to Saur. It would be better for them not to cause trouble because they had the law on their side, and people that went against it could find themselves in prison.

Then everyone split into groups and began to go to their homes, talking confusedly and in great distress. They had seen the papers the men had shown them, with all the writing and the signs, and they all looked very important and real. What could they do, they asked each other, and where was Fidel Bardi? Surely Saur could not be right? That Bardi had done something so wrong... to make them sell their homes and then have to leave the island. Where could they go... most of them had never been off the island... what would happen to them?

As the morning wore on little knots of people began to appear on the shore carrying sacks and bags filled with their belongings. Others remonstrated with them to change their minds and stay, but the security men gently herded them apart and wrote down their names. Once this was done the people began to feel that they had no choice in what was to happen. They began to tell each other that they had sold their homes and signed the papers and now they must obey this law that had snared them.

Meanwhile, Saur had gone to his home after spitting in the face of one of the security men and challenging him to fight back. The man had turned round and walked slowly away. Saur had cursed him for a coward and said he would be in his house if they wanted him. As he left, one of the men took a slip of paper from his pocket and looked at it, then nodded his head after Saur's retreating figure and said something to his companions.

By the time the two big ferries pulled in to the shore almost all the people were waiting for them. Many of them were in tears and held each other desperately as the men marshalled them aboard.

Some tried to take their dogs with them, but these were found and put back on the land. Some of the women were pregnant and the security men made sure that they had seats and were comfortable. Everything was done as quietly and swiftly as possible. In one hour the ferry was loaded and backing out to sea with the people standing at the rails and staring desolately at the island as it slowly receded from their sight.

When the second ferry slid gently in and docked, the security men had rounded up the last of the islanders. Some were still protesting and calling for Fidel Bardi to be found and explain what was happening. Those who shouted the loudest were kept away from the others right up until time to board, then they were unceremoniously pushed onto the boat and told to sit down and be quiet.

When the ferry was just a blur on the horizon the remaining security men, those that had not left with the boats, took the lists and ticked all the names off once again. Then they compared lists to be certain that all the people had left. Only six adults and four children were still on the island, Saur and two of his cousins and their wives. They had refused to leave their homes and had shut their doors to the security men.

Now the men marched up the track and split apart at the well. One column went to Saur's house and the others to the cousins'. Saur watched them coming through a window and brandished an axe at them, saying he would fight them to the death. The men banged on the door and called to him, saying to come out and behave properly, that the house was not his now and he should leave. Saur cursed them and said they should try to make him leave.

The men spoke together for a moment, then three of them went back down the track to the shore and picked up an empty oil drum. They carried it back to Saur's house where four of them took hold of it and slammed it into the door. At the third attempt the door fell inwards and the men dropped the drum and stepped back. Saur appeared in the doorway holding the axe, cursing vilely, and inviting them to try to take him.

The man commanding them said he would ask Saur for the last time to come out and leave.

When Saur shook his head the man nodded to one of the others, who took a short wooden club from his pocket and threw it at Saur with great force. It struck the thin man in the face and he reeled back, almost falling. Immediately the men charged into the room and threw him to the floor. He struggled violently and had almost got to his feet when one of the men holding him let go, and stepped back driving his boot into Saur's groin. Saur screamed in pain and fell forward, whereupon the man, whose face Saur had spat in, stepped up and kicked him hard in the head twice. Saur crumpled down and lay still.

"Pick him up and take him to the shore," said the leader.

They carried Saur outside and half dragged and half carried him down the track. When they got there he was thrown face down on the ground and two of them stood over him.

Saur's cousins were rounded up and decided that they did not wish to fight to stay on the island. Saur's wife joined them and they were escorted to the shore with the weeping children and placed in one of the security boats.

The men made one last sweep through the village going from house to house checking that everyone had boarded the ferries. It was when they were doing this that Saur escaped.

The men watching him had relaxed their guard and were smoking and chatting. Saur had regained his senses and lain still gathering his strength. When both the men had turned to look up at the mountain he acted. Springing to his feet he smashed his fist into the back of the head of the taller one who fell as if shot. The second man tried to grapple with Saur, who simply picked him up and threw him violently to the ground where he lay groaning.

Saur then began to run along the shoreline as the men up in the village looked down and saw what had happened. As they began to stream back down the track, Saur waded out into the water, climbed into a small boat and hoisted the sail. The wind filled it immediately and Saur brought the boat round and put out to sea. The men stopped as the leader called to them to let him go.

As he worked the tiller, Saur turned and looked back at the shore. He stood tall and put his hand to his mouth and shouted something to them. They could not hear properly, but watched as he made a fist and shook it, his face convulsed with anger.

Afterwards, on the security boat, when the leader asked if anyone had heard what Saur had shouted one of the men stood up and said that it had sounded like a name. He could not be sure, but it had sounded like Bardi.

The leader wrote something in his notebook, tore the page out and attached it to the papers that had been shown to the people. The men climbed into the boats and began the long trip back to the mainland.

The clearance was over. Only the tiny, crude houses remained as mute testimony that anyone had ever lived on the land, and even they would soon be gone as they were destroyed to make way for the new breed of people that would inherit the island.

The company accountants balanced their books on the transactions with enormous satisfaction. They were set to make profits on the completed project that would be unequalled anywhere in the history of development schemes. The incidental factor that in the working of this financial miracle they had totally destroyed a unique way of life simply did not occur to them. Nor, if it had, would it have mattered.

Fidel had been in Athens one week when he rang the agent to check that he could return to the island. The agent said he could come back when he liked as the building work was well under way now. Fidel asked him how long such a huge undertaking would last. The agent said not as long as Fidel imagined. The company had years of expertise to call on and a huge labour force backed by massive finances.

Just before Fidel rang off the agent said there was one more thing. He didn't know whether Fidel would be concerned, but the man Saur that they had talked about had badly injured two security men before escaping from the island in a small boat. The agent also told him that the man in charge of the security detail had said Saur had screamed a curse and a name back at them as he sailed away from the shore. The name had been Fidel's.

Fidel put the phone down thoughtfully. So, Saur was loose somewhere and full of hate for him. He was not surprised that Saur had eluded the security men. And Fidel knew that Saur would try to find him. He had to get back to the island and trust that the company's security men would be ready for any attempt by Saur to return if he thought Fidel had taken refuge there.

Chapter Twenty-Four

Fidel and Lyra went down from Athens into the Peloponnese and travelled by fishing boats to one tiny island after another, until finally he had to hire a man to take him over to the island.

The man told him that there was nothing there now; that all the people had gone; and he had heard that a big concern were building houses all over the land. He also told Fidel that the men on the island were keeping everyone away and they would not let any boats in.

Fidel had said he had business on the island and shown him money. The man had shrugged and taken it. Fidel then booked Lyra into a small hotel in a quiet area and told her to wait while he went back to the island and saw how things were now and where they could live.

When the little boat grated up on the shore it was late in the afternoon, and the man said that Bardi must be off the boat quickly as he had heard there was a sea of dangerous water close to the island, and he did not wish to find it when the light was failing.

As Fidel stood watching him leave he heard voices and turned to see two men wearing dark green short-sleeved shirts and pants walking quickly down the track. They stopped a few paces away from Fidel.

One of them, a heavy-set man with a small neat moustache, held up his hand. "What are you doing here?" he asked. "This island is private property."

Fidel jumped down onto the shore. "I know," he said. He motioned to one side. "May I speak with you?"

The man frowned and looked at his companion who stared at Fidel, then nodded.

Fidel walked away from the boat until they were out of earshot. He turned to the man and smiled. "My name is Fidel Bardi."

He waited while the man shook his head slowly, then a look of comprehension crossed his features. "Yes," he nodded firmly. "We were told you would be here, sometime." He tapped his chest. "I am Lannon... I look after the security."

Fidel looked up at the empty space that had been the village. The whole area had been cleared and he had to look hard to remember what had been a place where people had dwelt for so long.

"You have really started," he said slowly. He pointed up the track. "I was born there... now it is gone."

Lannon nodded and smiled. "You should see the other side of the island. They are putting in roads for the machinery to get over there and begin clearing the land." He looked all round him. "Six months and you won't know this place."

"Do you patrol the island?" asked Fidel. "I mean for security purposes... to keep away intruders?"

"You saw how quickly you were stopped," Lannon said, seriously. "We were watching you when you were a long way off shore." He shook his head. "There was no way that you could have got off the boat without being stopped."

"What about at night?" Fidel asked, thinking suddenly how Saur had lived all his life with small craft and to bring a boat out of the sea in the darkness among the rocks would be nothing to him.

"At night," Lannon said. "Yes... we have a team working right through the whole twenty-four hours."

"That is good," Fidel said. He paused, wondering if the man would have been told about Saur.

"There is someone that might try to get onto the island and make trouble."

The man's face hardened and he stared at Fidel. "No one will make trouble on company property while we are here," he said grimly. He tapped his chest. "I have worked for them for fifteen years and we have a very strong team in this place. More than anywhere else I have been." He stepped closer to Fidel. "This someone you speak of... he has a name?"

"Saur," Fidel said slowly. "His name is Saur. He is a man that has madness in him and will do harm to anyone that stands in his way."

Lannon shook his head firmly. "No," he said. "You are wrong." He smiled bleakly at Fidel. "We cleared this land in less than one day of people that had lived all their lives here. One man," he snorted contemptuously, "will be as nothing to us."

"I heard that he beat two of your men when you were clearing the island," said Fidel. "Did they think he was nothing?" he asked calmly.

The man was silent for a moment as he looked hard at Fidel. "Yes," he said slowly, "that did happen. The men you speak of were not regular personnel, and they have been discharged." He smiled coldly. "They were negligent in their duties. There is no second chance when that happens." He gestured behind him. "The people that are here now will not fail in their work."

He pulled a small leather-bound notebook from his shirt pocket and drew a thin pen from its spine. "This man that made the trouble… what did you say his name was?"

Fidel nodded. "He is called Saur." He shrugged. "I do not now how it is written."

"It is enough that I have his name," Lannon grunted. "What is the look of him?"

The image of Saur came flaring into Fidel's mind… the cold eyes and hard mouth set in the hostile face.

"He has the look of a man that seeks trouble… when you see him you will know."

Lannon frowned. "Not enough… I must have all of him… is he tall or short… has he power to his body?" He stopped and shook his head, "Of course he is strong… he got away from two of the men on the beach." He tapped the notebook. "You see what I mean? I need a picture for my people so if they see him they will be ready."

Fidel nodded. "I understand." He thought for a moment. "He is a tall man… taller than you or I. He has great strength in him though he does not look a powerful man. He has the face of a man born for anger… dark hair down to his shoulders and eyes that hate what they see."

The man wrote carefully in the notebook. Fidel waited silently until he finished, then picked up his bag and slung it onto his shoulder. "I was told you would have a place for me to stay."

Lannon's face relaxed slightly and he nodded. "That is right." He thought for a moment. "Yes, we can put you in with the construction people." He looked at Fidel. "They all have their own quarters, beds, showers and a dining area." He cocked his head at Fidel enquiringly.

"How many people are working here?" asked Fidel.

"Why do you ask?" said Lannon. He pursed his lips, then said, "Two hundred and fifteen. There will be more later as the work progresses."

Fidel nodded. "That is a great many to share much time with." He shook his head. "That is not for me." He smiled gently. "Where do you stay? You are security people... you have a separate place from the rest?"

"No, it would not be possible for you to live with us," Lannon said shortly. "Our position in this work means that we must keep apart from everyone." He shook his head firmly. "We have to keep to the rules of the company."

"Then you will have to find me somewhere on my own," said Fidel.

"I cannot do that." Lannon waved his arm at the work going on up the track behind him. "I do not have the time to provide shelter for one man." He stood taller. "My days are full with making this place safe from intruders."

Fidel put his bag down on the ground. "Then we have a problem. I will not live with so many—all I ask for is a place on my own and you say that is not possible."

"I have already said that you can share with the construction people and you say no." He shrugged. "You will have to find your own place." He smiled thinly. "Why don't you sleep on the beach? It is warm at night." He looked up at the sky. "This damned place is never cold." He turned to rejoin the man waiting for him.

"Hold," said Fidel. "I do not think you understand about me." He moved closer to the man. "Listen to what I say. I ask that you make contact with your head people and tell them that I am here on the island." He shook his head. "I do not wish to make trouble for you," he said quietly. "Maybe it is that you have not been told enough about me. If you speak with them they will give you all that you need to know." He smiled gently. "I do not say this to give offence, only so that you do not make a mistake that might do you harm."

Lannon stared at him, then nodded abruptly. "All right. I will do as you ask. You stay here while I use the mainland phone up in the security block." He held up the field telephone. "These are good only here on the island."

Fidel nodded. "I understand. I will wait for you." He sat down on a rock and lit a cigar as the man went back to his companion and spoke to him, indicating Fidel, then strode off up the track. Twenty minutes later he came back, picking his way carefully over the broken ground.

When he reached Fidel he stood for a moment looking at him. "I have spoken to certain people and the situation is clearer now." He smiled tightly. "My instructions are that you are to be given any assistance that you ask for."

Fidel smiled and stood up. "Good. Then I ask that you find me a place away from the work area."

"We have no accommodation other than what I have told you," Lannon said. He shrugged his shoulders. "It is not that I do not wish to help you, we just don't have anything else on the island."

Fidel turned and pointed to the far side of the island. "Over there," he said slowly, "is a house down by the sea. A woman lived there on her own for a long time." He turned back to the man. "It would only take a little work to make it fit for me."

Lannon pulled out his notebook again. "I know the place. My people said it is a ruin now." He tapped his pen against the notebook. "I suppose we could make it right for you... put a kitchen and shower in; do what needs to be done." He looked at Fidel questioningly. "You would not want it to be a palace?"

Fidel smiled. "No, just so that I can cook and sleep there." Lannon wrote quickly in the notebook, pursing his lips and nodding to himself. Then he snapped the notebook shut and put it back in his shirt pocket. "Anything else?" he asked.

Fidel nodded. "Yes. I would like a machine so that I do not have to walk everywhere, something that will not be broken by the stones in the ground."

"You need a four-wheel drive. A pick-up truck would suit you best... you could carry supplies... all that you need from the stores... food and oil for your cooking... you will have to cook with an oil stove." He waved his hand at the horizon. "You are so far away and we will not be putting power over there for some time."

"I am happy with the stove... it will be fine," Fidel said.

Lannon nodded. "Then we are settled." He pointed back up the track. "If you come with me I will get the truck for you and some food and all that you need." He looked sternly at Fidel. "I cannot start the work on the house today... all the men are at their places now. Tomorrow I will send a team over there to begin." He shrugged. "That is the best I can do."

Fidel smiled. "That will be good. If I am not settled in then I will not have to move anything out."

"That is right," Lannon said shortly.

In less than an hour Fidel was bumping his way in a large pick-up truck over the rough tracks as he made his way to the far side of the island.

When he came in sight of Lyra's mother's house, he realised that Lannon had been right in his description of the dwelling. It was indeed a ruin, with the roof almost gone and the windows fallen out. The ground all round was covered with the fast-growing scrub and small trees. None of this bothered him. The builders would do what had to be done to make it habitable. He went inside and began throwing the few pieces of rotting furniture outside. When the sky had darkened with night he stopped and ate the meat and bread he had brought and drank the wine. Then he chose a place where the remaining roof gave some shelter and lay down to sleep.

The next day the men arrived to work on the house. They ripped off the roof and completely gutted the interior. Three of them put in fresh roof timbers and laid new slates. The others divided the interior into a kitchen and a shower, with a pump that worked off a large battery, and one slightly larger room.
The man in charge told Fidel that there was not space enough for more accommodation, and that he supposed he would not wish to stay there when he could have a new house built for him later. Fidel agreed, just so that the place was sufficient for him to live in while they were converting the island.
In four days the work was done and Lannon drove over to see him and ask if he were satisfied with the house. He said he had received a letter instructing him to see that Fidel Bardi had all that he required and that he should given priority treatment. The man looked at Fidel with a new respect as he recounted this to him. He said Bardi would be informed as soon as they were ready to start building his house and that he could choose all the fittings and furnishings himself.
Fidel thanked him and said that he would be going over to the mainland in a couple of days to bring his woman back with him. The man had frowned, then asked him to repeat his words. Fidel did so, speaking slowly this time.
Lannon hesitated, then said bluntly that the company policy made it clear that no women were allowed to be living on a site. He said they were very firm on this; there had been trouble in the past when women had been involved in situations that had caused the work to suffer, domestic troubles that had flared into violence with all the resulting upset.
Fidel smiled slowly. "That will not happen," he said. "We will be here." He waved his arm at the land and sea. "None of your people will have cause to come this far from their place of work. Besides," he smiled again, "you have your security to see that we are not disturbed."
Lannon shook his head. "It goes against all the rules, Bardi. If I let one woman in, then others will want to follow."

"Not in this place," said Fidel. "Out here we are different; there is nothing here for your people." His face tightened. "I would think you are a man with enough power to make them live by your word on this matter."

Lannon was silent for a moment, then, "If you tell me that you will live over here, and not bring her into the working area, then I will agree to her coming over from the mainland."

Fidel nodded. "Yes, I will do as you ask." He hesitated. "What of the time when I come to the store for my supplies? I would not want to leave her here."

"You see," said Lannon, "it begins already; the problems, then… Wait… I have it. Your things will be brought over to you; that will make it easier for both of us."

Fidel smiled. "So, it is done. You have made the problem go away."

Lannon grunted. "I hope you are right, Bardi." He hesitated "Your woman… she will be all right in this place?" He shook his head doubtfully. "It is far from anywhere."

"That is of no matter," Fidel said. "She was born on this island. You know where the inn stood?"

Lannon nodded. "Way up on the hill."

"The inn was hers," Fidel said.

Lannon rubbed his finger over his moustache. "I heard something about that place," he said slowly. "There was a man killed… he went over the cliff and died." He looked at Fidel thoughtfully. "Was he connected to the inn in some way?"

"That's right," Fidel said easily. "He was the innkeeper."

"Then how did the woman…?"

"She was his wife," Fidel said evenly. "When he died the place went to her." He smiled at Lannon. "That is the law here."

Lannon shrugged. "Do not be offended, Bardi, if I say that from what I heard of this place the laws seemed to be made for people living in the dark ages."

"Maybe that is true." Fidel smiled at him. "The people chose to live by their own rules. It suited them to do so."

Lannon nodded. "And now the woman lives with you," he said.

"That is right," said Fidel coolly. He wondered why Lannon was showing an interest in what had happened at the inn and with Mora, then thought it was probably just the man's work that made him curious about people. Anyway, he told himself it was all gone now and there was no way that any suspicion could ever link him with Mora's death.

"Strange how life works out," said Lannon. He grimaced. "My wife was with me for twelve years, then she left me for a teacher."

"I'm sorry," Fidel said.

Lannon smiled sourly. "I'm not. I was glad to see her go." He nodded at Fidel. "All right, Bardi, bring her over… just don't make trouble."

The next day Fidel brought Lyra to the island. When she stepped from the boat and looked up at where the village had stood she turned to him in amazement. "It has gone, Bardi, all of it, gone."

"As I told you," he replied.

They walked to the truck and Fidel slung the cases in the back, conscious of the eyes watching Lyra. *It will be a good thing that we are so far from this place*, he thought. *So many men living without women and seeing Lyra among them would drive them mad.* He gunned the motor and manoeuvred the vehicle up the track and onto the high ground.

The light was fading from the sky when they arrived at the little house among the rocks. Lyra could hardly believe what the builders had done. When they had eaten Fidel went outside and walked down to the sea. He lit a cigar and gazed out at the moon's reflected light shimmering back from the water; then turned and looked at the dark mass of the high rocks behind the house.

He remembered what Lannon had said about how no one would be able to land on the island undetected. Then he thought of the hate that Saur carried in him, the hate that shaped the man—that same hate that was now turned to him. He knew that he could never rest while Saur lived and he knew that Saur would come back to the island. *This place is still a prison*, he thought. When he finished the cigar he went back inside and bolted the door and windows.

The building work went ahead with great speed. Machines cleared huge swathes of land, opening the way for the gangs preparing the footings for the houses. Pilings were driven deep into the soil, smashing their shafts through rock undisturbed since the earth's gigantic upheaval that had resulted in the island's birth. With the arrival of the ferries carrying an army of workers the island was never still, as the work continued under the huge lights switched on once night fell. Mixers turned non-stop, feeding concrete into the open lorries that crawled slowly along the new built roads, taking it to the sites. Huge generators fed the power tools, and the air was filled with their whining and shrieking sound.

The supply boats would sometimes lie at anchor out at sea, waiting their turn to move in and unload the tons of materials that were stored in the big metal sheds that were never allowed to be empty.

The roads were laid, drying under the heat of the sun almost as soon as the tarmac was poured. Many of these roads would be destroyed by the volume and size of the machinery that would use them during construction, and would have to be laid again once the homes were complete. All this had been accounted for in the costing of the work. It underlined the company policy for the project. Everything to be of the highest standard to justify the enormous prices that would be demanded for the properties.

As each site became ready for the building to begin, individual teams, composed of all the trades required for its total construction were assigned to each house and would remain together until it was completed. With the back-up of the required power supplies and all the materials available this ensured that there would be no stopping until the work was completed.

The company flew in communication specialists to install the most sophisticated systems of television and computer available. With these in place the residents would be able to reach any part of the world with the most powerful and private internet programmes.

All financial dealings could be carried out with the computer using a lock-in process that guaranteed total secrecy. Huge financial empires could be controlled and manipulated from the island, safe in the knowledge that every move was safe from any competitor's eyes.

Once the footings and the essential services were in place the client would be invited to work closely with the team building their house. An interior designer's services would be offered, advising on all aspects of furnishing, from carpets to furniture and fittings throughout the building. The company would use the finest and most expensive suppliers for all the materials required to transform a house into a home. Landscaping would follow, trees and shrubs planted, and a helicopter pad constructed behind every home.

Down on the shore a maintenance block would be built to house the specialist staff, who would live on the island and ensure that if problems arose they would be dealt with swiftly.

Behind them would be the security block housing a small force of security men trained to patrol the island twenty-four hours a day. It was feasible that some of the clients might be people that had built up immense accounts in foreign banks, before leaving their countries in abject ruin. It was possible that some of their erstwhile subjects might be tempted to exact swift and summary justice on them without recourse to the law. That security was paramount had been one of the strong selling points, and the island was impregnable.

When the work was completed the rock in the sea would be a fortress, inhabited by some of the richest people on earth.

Chapter Twenty-Five

Fidel would sometimes make short trips up to the high ground and look through the glasses that Lannon had given him at the army of workers on the sites. At first it had seemed to him like a madness of movement, but he had soon realised that there was a relentless logic to their actions.

Sometimes at night if the wind was in their direction they could hear the continuous noise of the building and they would go outside to listen. Fidel asked Lyra where she would like their house to be built and she asked why they could not transform where they were, the old place where she had spent her childhood.

Fidel had looked around at the area he had come to know well, thinking that if Saur did come it was best that Fidel confronted him on familiar ground.

As the weeks became months the builders could not only be heard, but also seen. The piling and footing work was completed on the sites only a half mile from the little house in the rocks and Fidel knew it would soon be their turn.

Already, four of the houses were occupied, the helicopters whirling their owners in and out of the island. Lannon told Fidel that every home on the island was sold even before it had been built; he went on to say that the only regret the developers had was that the island was not larger.

Sometimes they would see one of the helicopters circling before landing and Fidel would wonder what the islanders would have made of the transformation of the barren place they had struggled to exist in for so long.

Once or twice some of the rich people would drive over the high ground in their huge gleaming four wheel drive machines that never got dirty, and look down at the little house, and if they were outside the people would wave to them.

When Lannon was asked who lived in the house among the rocks, he said that they were two of the original islanders that had not sold their homes to the company and had assisted them in the purchase of the island. The company in return was going to build them a small house as a token of their gratitude.

The rich people thought it was wonderful that real islanders were still living among them, and Lannon told Fidel that they were welcome at any of the parties that the rich people held at their pools. He also told Fidel to be careful. "Sometimes the rich are not nice people," he had said. Fidel had smiled inwardly, remembering the wealthy ones that he had known before he came back to the island. *People are all the same*, he thought. *It is just that the rich have the money to do as they please*. And anyway, it might be interesting to go and mix with other people; it had been five months since he had brought Lyra to the island and days had begun to seem very long to him isolated so far from other human contact.

He asked Lannon when would be a good time to meet them, and Lannon said they held parties on Saturday nights and he would ask to see who was hosting the next one.

A week later the security chief drove over and brought their supplies to them, and told Fidel that the German who had been the first to move on to the island would be opening his house to his neighbours on the following Saturday night. He had told Lannon to tell the people in the little house in the rocks they would be welcome.

When Fidel told Lyra she said she would go to meet these people that had bought the island and see if having so much money made them different from other men. Fidel laughed and said they were just greedier.

Lannon gave Fidel a plastic card, saying that as soon as he entered the drive to the German's house he would be on the screens in the security block and watched. When he came to the gates at the house he had to feed the card into the checkpoint and wait. When the buzzer sounded the steel arm across the entrance would lift and he could drive on. Once inside the house the screens would blank off and only cover the perimeter of the property. They were also controlled from the house and could be blanked whenever the owner wished.

Lannon said sometimes they would not wish the security people to see what they got up to, but he shrugged; he did not care; they paid a fortune for security; they could do what they pleased.

As they drove up the track and moved onto the high ground Fidel glanced at Lyra. "Listen," he said, "these people we will see tonight… they will not be like any you have known before."

"How are they different?" asked Lyra puzzled.

"Sometimes…." He paused. "Sometimes the women are cruel… they do not always like how they are, or the men they live with, so they do things to hurt people."

Lyra frowned. "I would not let them hurt me." Her eyes glinted. "It would be a fool that tried to make me suffer." She patted his leg. "Do not worry, Bardi, no harm will come to me."

He nodded. "Just be careful!"

He drove down the fresh tarmac road and turned into the driveway leading to the house. As he did lights flashed on all the way along the drive, and he knew they would be looking at him down in the security block right now. It gave him a strange feeling to know that they were probably checking his face against any records they would hold and he thought it was good that he was not on police files anywhere.

As the arm on the barrier lifted he drove through and carefully positioned the truck in the big parking area, slotting it beside a black Ferrari and a Rolls Royce. He heard the sound of laughter, and the splash of water, and they walked round to the rear of the house and saw a crowd of people gathered in the gardens by a huge pool. As they drew near, a short man with greying hair cropped to his head and wearing swimming trunks came to meet them. He smiled and held out his hand.

"Good that you came," he said. "I am Schultz… Ernst Shultz."

Fidel shook his hand. "Fidel Bardi," he said, "and this is Lyra."

Schultz smiled again. "Pleased to meet you, Lyra." He turned and held up his hands. "One moment, please," he called out. "May I have your attention?" He patted Fidel on the shoulder. "These are the people I was telling you about. They lived on the island before we got here… now they are over… right over, out of sight on the other side."

They crowded round Fidel and Lyra, asking questions about how life had been on the island, and how they had lived so far from the mainland.

Fidel answered as best he could, whilst Lyra spoke in her halting new language, sometimes stumbling, and then trying again.

"What language did you people speak before you learnt English?" asked a large woman sitting in one of the poolside chairs. "I mean, was it a kind of Greek, or maybe Turk?"

Fidel smiled at her. "None of those. I went away from here when I was young... about fifteen, and I had to speak like everyone else on the mainland to get work." He nodded at Lyra. "She has only been on the mainland for a little while, so she still finds it hard to use your language."

"Could we hear it spoken... the island language... could you speak to her so that we could hear what it sounds like?" the woman asked.

Fidel nodded. "Lyra," he said, "they wish to hear the speech of the island... say something to me and I will answer so that they can know how the people that lived here sounded."

She smiled and nodded and spoke in the guttural, hoarse cadence that rose and fell almost too fast for Fidel to follow. When she stopped and looked at him enquiringly he shook his head and replied, albeit much slower. Then he looked round at them. "That is the language of this place."

Schultz clapped him on the shoulder. "Wonderful! I have never heard anything like that, and I have travelled all over the world." He beamed at them all. "Well, it looks like we bought ourselves a unique chunk of real estate here." He turned to the little woman sitting behind him. "What do you think, Elsa; have we got ourselves something rare?"

She nodded. "You paid enough for it. It ought to be special." Fidel looked at the tiny woman with the body of a girl, flat-chested and no hips, skin burnt almost black by the sun, her flesh juiceless and tight on her frame with a two piece bathing suit that looked as it had been made for a child. She had small glittering eyes under dyed yellow hair cut close to her head.

"So you went away from this place when you were a boy?" She made the question sound like an accusation.

"That is true," he said easily.

"But you came back. You came back before there was anything here like there is now... before the work began... before the island was even sold," she said in a hard flat voice with only a trace of a German accent.

"Yes, I came back to care for my father. I met someone on the mainland who had come over and he said my father was not a well man so I came home so that he would not be alone."

"Your father... he is not with you now?" she asked.

"No," replied Fidel, "he was old with the work...." He looked at the tiny woman with the glittering eyes and thought she had never known what it was like to struggle through each of the days that turned into years fighting with the sea, or working the land under the heat of the sun. "He died."

She nodded. "But you did not leave then... you stayed."

"Yes," said Fidel.

The woman smiled. "I heard you helped the developers to buy the island." She smiled again, but her eyes were cold in her face as she stared at him.

"That is right," Fidel said. He was beginning to remember how it had been with the rich. There were always some that had that cold streak of cruelty, born of the arrogance that comes with power and great wealth. He had learned how to play their game, to remain cool and never let them see you were afraid by their power. Sometimes they respected you because you were not cowed by them, although they never really liked you. He wondered if they ever liked anyone, even their own kind.

"So this island has been good to you... and I heard you are to have a house built for you, and," she paused and looked at Lyra, "your wife."

"Yes." Fidel nodded, "They have been generous to us." He smiled, his lips drawing back in the tooth-glistening smile. "I should thank you as well."

She frowned at him. "Why would you do that?" she asked, her voice suddenly bleak.

"Well," he said slowly, "if it were not for you," he spread his hands to take in the rest of them, "and your friends, I would not be here now and with such good fortune."

Her husband laughed loudly. "Well said, Fidel. You have your answer, Elsa." He touched Fidel's arm. "What will you and your lady have to drink?"

"Have you drunk the wine of the island?" asked Fidel.

Schultz frowned. "I did not know there was any wine here."

"Yes, there is wine. We grew the grapes up there on the far slopes of the mountain." He shook his head. "I think the vines will all go when the machines rip up the earth." He smiled at Schultz. "I brought a couple of bottles with me... it is not as refined as what you have here, but it has a taste that is all its own." He stood up. "I will fetch it from the truck."

When he returned with the wine he saw that Lyra was the centre of attention, especially the men. *They have never seen anything like her*, he thought. *All their manicured and pampered women have nothing like the raw power and beauty that she has.*

Schultz produced glasses and Fidel poured the wine. "Treat it gently," he said. "It has much force in it."

Schultz smiled. "Don't worry," he said. "We have drunk wine from all over the world."

He lifted his glass and looked closely at it, holding it up the light. "It has no sparkle." It was true, the wine was dull black and reflected no light.

Schultz drained the glass and waited a moment, then he looked round at the others and shuddered. "Mother of God! What is this?" He shook his head. "It tastes like... almost like a malt whisky with something I can't place... something that burns like fire...." He looked at the others. "Drink," he urged them. "Drink and tell me what it is."

Fidel watched as they drank, exclaiming to each other over the potency of the wine. He thought of how the men of the island would drink after a day of work, standing in the inn and using the wine as if it were their lifeblood.

"It is good?" he asked.

One of them coughed and pretended to stagger. "God!" he said. "I don't think I tasted anything like that in my life. Where did you say it is grown?"

Fidel turned and pointed up at the huge dark mass of the mountain. "Over behind that... on the slopes... the earth is warmer up there than anywhere else on the island; maybe because it is closer to the sun... they say that is why the wine is so strong."

The man nodded. "I won't argue with that. Christ! It's raw." He looked at the mountain. "Up there, eh. Seems a shame that we couldn't keep the vines; maybe hire people to tend them. We'd have our own wine then." He held up his glass and swirled the dark liquid round. "It's really something." He looked at Schultz. "How about it, Ernst? Wouldn't it worth it to be able to keep this stuff here," he swirled the wine round in his glass, "and always ready when we wanted it?"

Schultz turned to Fidel. "Would that be possible; could we get people to do the work up there?"

His wife broke in. "Of course you can... you can hire those people over on the mainland for almost nothing." She smiled at Fidel, her lips slashed together. "I am right, yes?"

He nodded. "It is true that they do not need so much to live on," he smiled back at her, the tooth-glistening smile, "as perhaps you do to live here."

Her eyes glittered furiously at him, but Schultz interrupted. "It is something we will have to consider." He took Fidel by the arm. "Let me introduce you," he laughed, "not that I know anyone very well yet... we are all new to this place."

He steered Fidel to the group sitting at the poolside. Fidel listened as names were put to faces.

The big man with the silver hair and booming laugh was Jack Erin who was something in merchant banking, Schultz told him. Then there was his wife, Dolly, whose tight skin on her face spoke of the surgeon's knife.

John Sloan, Schultz laughed, no one knew what he was, except that he had been the second one to buy a home on the island; and finally there was Tom Harper who made money work for him as he moved it all round the world, without leaving the comfort of his home. He winked and said that if Fidel had capital that he wanted to increase then he could do that for him.

As he went round to them all, shaking hands or nodding, and listening to the easy remarks that passed for conversation, looking at their well fed, oiled bodies that spoke of soft living and greed, he felt he knew them so well, almost as if he had never been away from their company; he despised them with a cold contempt as he smiled back at them.

"Did you bring costumes to swim?" Schultz indicated the huge pool. "We have spare ones inside if you like."

Fidel looked at Lyra. "You wish to swim?"

She smiled. "Yes." And looked at the pool. "It is almost as big as the sea."

"Do you swim in the sea over where you live?" asked Jack Erin.

"Yes," said Fidel. "It is almost at our door."

Dolly Erin shuddered. "That would frighten me. I don't like the waves."

Lyra laughed, a rich full sound that turned all eyes to her. "The waves are good. They have strength that you can use."

"Not me," said Dolly emphatically. "I stay about ten feet from the shore at all times." She shuddered. "If I put my feet down I want to feel the ground under them."

Scultz stood. "Come with me," he said to Fidel. "I will find you something to wear." He nodded to his wife. "You get Lyra a costume, dear."

He led Fidel through the big double doors that opened out onto the pool area, and through a room that he called his den that had a bar with rows of bottles and gleaming glasses; and walls panelled with beautiful light wood that supported shelving packed with books, and record albums and tightly stacked CDs. Just off that was a small dressing room where he rummaged in a closet and pulled out two costumes that he handed to Fidel.

"Use whatever you like."

Fidel chose the dark red one and slipping off his shirt and pants drew the tight fitting trunks on. Schultz looked at him appraisingly. "You're in damn fine shape." He patted his paunch and laughed. "Guess I need to lose a few pounds."

When they returned to the pool Lyra was already there waiting for him. Elsa Schultz turned. "You like?" she asked, waving her hand at Lyra, her glittering eyes intent on him. Fidel looked at the tiny two piece white costume that struggled to contain Lyra's full body; the scrap of material that left the big breasts almost bare, just covering the nipples that jutted through the sheer material, the triangle at her crotch that showed her pubic hair, and the string of cloth that had vanished up between her buttocks.

"Well," Elsa asked again, "you like her now?"

Fidel smiled at her. *You bitch*, he thought. *You twisted rich bitch. You want to make the island woman look foolish by parading her nearly naked, so your friends can look at her and think how stupid she is.* He nodded. "You chose well, Elsa," he said, his voice lingering over her name, and smiling the tooth-glistening smile right in her face.

She blinked and stared at him, the glittering eyes full of scarcely controlled spite.

Schultz broke in, looking quickly at his wife, then back to them. "I think you would both swim well," he asked, "You have grown up with the sea."

"Lyra is better than me," said Fidel, "far better." He laughed. "Sometimes when she is in the sea I think she is a dolphin."

"She is fast… really quick?" asked Schultz.

Fidel nodded. "I can never keep up with her when she really tries; she just leaves me."

"So, we have a champion here," said Elsa. She turned her head and called to someone down at the far end of the pool. "Martin, come here." She looked back to Fidel and smiled, her eyes glittering like diamonds in the tiny face. "We have a real swimmer here," she said.

Fidel looked at the man who had walked up to them. He was dark-haired with an open face, tall with broad shoulders and long powerful arms and legs and looked to be in his thirties.

"What is it?" he asked.

The little woman looked up into his face, then pointed at Lyra. "Martin, I want you to race her in the pool."

"No, Elsa," protested Schultz, "this would not be right." He turned to Fidel. "Martin used to be a champion swimmer… it would not be a fair match."

"He said she is as fast as a fish!" shrilled Elsa. "Now we see if he spoke the truth."

She took hold of Martin by the arm and shook him. "You will do this for me," she said.

He looked at Schultz who shrugged resignedly and looked at Martin. "Just one length, just for fun."

"No," Elsa said, "it has to be a proper race... maybe four lengths... yes, that would do... four lengths." She smiled the glittering-eyed smile at Fidel. "Enough to see her be like a fish."

Fidel smiled at Lyra who had listened, but not fully understood what was said. "They want you to show how fast you can swim."

She frowned. "Why?"

"Because he said you were so fast in the water," said Elsa. She smiled up at Lyra, the restless eyes probing. "Now we shall see if he spoke the truth."

"What does it matter if I swim fast or slow... it means nothing to me." Lyra appealed to Fidel. "What is this race thing? How is it done?"

Fidel realised suddenly that she had lived all her childhood far away from the other island children and had no idea what a race was. He smiled at her.

"All you have to do is go quicker up the pool and back down. The one who is first wins."

Lyra nodded slowly. "This you would have me do?"

"Only if you wish to." He indicated Martin. "He would try to be quicker than you... to see if he could be first."

She smiled and nodded. "Yes, I will do it."

Fidel held up his hand. "Wait. I must tell you that he is a champion swimmer."

Lyra shook her head uncomprehendingly. "What is that... what does it mean?"

"It is that he is a great swimmer... faster that anyone else... maybe faster than you."

She looked at Martin. "I do not mind... I will go hard."

Elsa walked to the edge of the pool and beckoned to them. "Start from here and do four lengths." She held up her hand and counted off four fingers to Lyra. "You understand? Make her know what it is she has to do," she said to Fidel. He stared at her thinking how easily she inspired dislike, and probably even hate.

He stood beside Lyra and looked down at the water. "Four times, you go up there," he pointed to the far end of the pool, "then you come back here," he tapped his foot against the pool tiles. "Then you do it again, up and back, very fast."

Lyra nodded. "I have it, Bardi."

Elsa clapped her hands together. "All of you listen. There is going to be a race. Martin will swim for us, and she swims for the island people," she smiled, the tight-lipped gash, "or what is left of them." Then she turned and looked at Fidel. "Do you wish to make a bet on your woman?"

Fidel smiled and shook his head. "I did not bring money with me; I did not think it would be needed."

She looked at her husband. "Lend him money... so he can bet."

"It's all right," Fidel said to him. "You don't have to."

"Yes," shrilled Elsa, "he must make the wager... lend him money." She stabbed her finger in Schultz's chest. "Do it... give him money. You can't lose; Martin will win easily."

Schultz looked hesitantly at Fidel. "I do not mind... if you wish to make a fun bet... maybe a small one." He paused. "A sum that would not be hard to repay." He nodded at Martin waiting by the edge of the pool. "I have seen him in the sea... he is very strong."

"No, it must be a proper bet." She turned the glittering eyes full on Fidel. "Are you afraid to lose money?" Her lips curled contemptuously. "Even if he," she nodded at Schultz, "lends you it?"

"No, I do not mind," Fidel said slowly. "I have money to pay if I lose."

"Good, good," the little woman said. She turned to the rest of them. "We must do this right. Someone must go to that end and see that they both touch the wall before turning." She looked them over, and then pointed her finger. "You, George, you will be the one that sees they touch the wall."

They watched as he walked off down to the far end and stood right on the edge of the pool.

"We will be here to watch this end," Elsa said. "Ernst, you will time Martin and see how fast he is." She stared at Fidel. "There will be no need to do that with her; she will be so far behind."

The big man, Jack Erin, stepped forward. "Did I hear you people say there was money being laid on this thing?" he asked.

"Yes," said Ernst. "Only a small sum." He shrugged. "It would not be fair; we all know Martin is a wonderful swimmer." He paused. "I do not see how he can be beaten."

Erin pulled out his wallet and looked at Fidel. "Do you want to back your lady?"

Sloan and Harper and several others joined them. Fidel listened as they discussed the wager with Schultz, who tried to keep it as low as he could. Finally, he turned to Fidel and said. "Look, you don't have to do this. Why don't we just let them race for the sport?"

Elsa pushed in front of him. "No, he has to make a bet."

Fidel looked at Schultz who was shaking his head at her. "It's all right, I will do it." He nodded at Schultz. "How much will you let me have?"

"Give him a lot, Ernst," she said. "Make it enough so he can cover the others."

"How about five hundred dollars?" asked Schultz.

"No, no, make it more... much more," shrilled Elsa.

Schultz's face hardened and he stared at her. "No. Five hundred will be enough." He looked at the others. "I will stake him to five hundred. You make your bets to that sum."

"Thank you," said Fidel.

Schultz shook his head. "You should not be doing this. He is too good."

They crowded round Fidel, wanting to place their bets and asking Schultz to look after the money.

When they had finished, Fidel went over to Lyra and held her arm. "How do you feel?" he asked.

She laughed. "I feel good. It is only a swim, Bardi. Why do you look like so serious?"

"I don't want the woman, Elsa, to see you if you do not come first." His mouth tightened. "She looks on us with disgust because we are people of the island."

Lyra stared at him. "Is this why I am here, Bardi?" She indicated the pool. "So that I can be made a fool of?" She looked round at the others lining up at the poolside. "For them all to see?"

"Yes," he said slowly, "that is what the bitch wants... to watch you made small to them."

Her eyes flashed and her mouth tightened in anger. "We will see, Bardi. I had thought to enjoy this... but now I see it is more... much more."

Just then Elsa called out. "Are you ready?"

Lyra moved forward and curled her toes over the edge of the tiles. She looked down at the water, then across to Elsa. "I am ready."

The little woman pushed Martin in the back. "Go on, get over there with her," she said.

He looked at Lyra. "Would you like a start... maybe half a length?" he asked hesitantly. "It's just that I've had a lot of races and maybe it would be fairer to—."

Elsa cut him off. "No, no," she shrilled, "you must both start together... we will see then how good she is." She raised her arms and called out. "Be quiet, everyone." Then she walked to the edge of the pool. "I will count to three, then you go." She waited till there was total silence. Then she counted, "One... two... three!"

The two bodies hit the water as one and the people began to move along the side of the pool keeping pace with the swimmers. Fidel watched as Martin began to draw ahead, moving easily and fast through the water, and he heard the comments from the crowd. "She won't have a chance... he was a champion."

Elsa was almost running, chanting as she went, "Easy, it is so easy... look, I said he would win... she cannot keep up."

Fidel moved with the rest, watching Lyra as she trailed six lengths behind. Martin came to the end of the second length, touched the wall and turned into the third, passing Lyra as she went past him to touch the wall.

Jack Erin shook his head. "She's a good swimmer, but it's no contest, she just doesn't have...." He stopped. "Christ!" he said. "What the hell?"

Lyra had touched the wall, gone under and stayed under, and was moving through the water at a tremendous speed, weaving her body from side to side, almost turning right over as she rolled, her feet making short stabbing movements and her arms criss-crossing her body as she moved the water.

Suddenly, she exploded up, snatched a mouthful of air and plunged down again to resume the weaving gliding motion. She caught Martin before he reached the wall, touched it, went back down under and surged forward, rising out of the water taking air, down again and driving on. When she touched the wall at the end and stopped, treading water, Martin was still the length of the pool behind.

Lyra put her hands on the edge of the pool and sprung out of the water and slicked her hair back tight to her head. They crowded forward, congratulating her. Schultz gave her a towel and she wiped the water from her body.

"My God, where did you learn to swim like that?" asked Erin. Lyra smiled at him.

"Where all the people did... in the sea.."

Schultz put his hand down as Martin came to the wall and helped him out. He stood and wiped the water from his face, then extended his hand to Lyra, shaking his head in amazement.

"How did you do it? When I passed you as I went into the third you had no chance, there was no way you could win... but I never saw you pass me... how did you do it?"

"She was under the water," said Schultz. "She swam almost all the way under the water. I have never seen anything like it." He looked round at the others. "She was like a fish."

"That's what it was," said Sloan. "She looked like a fish… you know the way they move through the water—kind of glide. Is that what it was? A kind of fish stroke?" he asked Lyra.

She nodded. "Have you seen the big dolphins swim when they wish to move at speed?"

"Only from a boat," said Sloan, "but I know what you mean… that's right… they did the same thing you did… that glide, and then they stay under like that."

"How did you get near enough to learn from them?" asked Erin.

"You have to be in the sea with them, so close you can feel them as they move," said Lyra.

"Isn't it dangerous to be so close? They are wild creatures and unpredictable," said Sloan.

Lyra shook her head. "They know who harms them and who is a friend." She handed the towel to Fidel. "I am hungry, Bardi; is there food?"

"Of course," said Schultz, "we have fish and meat on the barbeque. I will fetch you something." He turned and looked at his wife. "But first, Elsa, you must congratulate the winner."

The little woman looked at Lyra. "You won." She turned to Fidel, her eyes glittering in her head. "You won because you are island people." Her lips twisted in a sneer. "I suppose there was nothing else to do on this rock when you were growing up."

Fidel smiled the tooth-glistening smile at her. "That is right, Elsa. When we had finished working the land, and fighting the sea for the food to live, we would play in the water."

The little woman's lips tightened and she glared at him, but remained silent. He could feel the anger coming off her like body heat and he wondered why she was possessed by such bitterness. If Schultz could buy a home on this island he had to be one of the truly rich people. She could have anything she liked. Even buy herself a man for her pleasure. He remembered how she behaved with her husband and thought Schultz probably wouldn't care if she did have lovers.

Just then Schultz called out to everyone. "Come… eat," he indicated the barbeque area round the corner at the end of the pool.

Fidel noticed the men eyeing Lyra as she moved, her lush body gleaming. She had not bothered to adjust the skimpy top that had come free with the exertions of the race. It was simply hanging loose from her shoulders, completely exposing the big breasts that bounced on her chest as she walked.

The bottom of the costume was even tighter now, the triangle having been pushed down into her crotch by the pressure of the water as she swam, and was now forced right up into the lips of her sex. *She knows they are watching her*, he thought, *and she doesn't care.*

He spoke softly to her. "Wait, let them go on." He watched them moving up the poolside and round the corner. "The men... they look at you."

She nodded and smiled. "I know, Bardi." Putting her hands under her breasts she lifted them to him. "You told me that the women from the mainland swim with nothing to cover these," she stroked her hand down over her belly and into her crotch, "and nothing here." She gestured over her shoulder at the sound coming from the barbecue area. "So, if their women hide nothing, then I will be the same." She looked at him enquiringly. "You would have no anger if they saw me like that?"

Fidel felt his cock stir in his trunks as he thought of the men staring at the lushness of Lyra's naked body. "No, I would not be angry; and you... you would not mind them looking?" he asked.

She smiled and shook her head. "No, it gives me pleasure to see them look, those men of such money, able to buy all the island, and looking at me like dogs in heat." She pulled the triangle away from her sex. "This is what they want—to lay with me and make the madness."

Fidel looked at her, his mouth suddenly dry and feeling his cock stir in the trunks. "You do not mind them wanting?" he asked.

She shook her head. "No... all them with so much power, and I have this," she ran her hand down her belly and into her crotch, "and not one of them can get it." She looked closely at him, then laughed. "And you, Bardi," she glanced down at his crotch, "you want me as well, I think," and she reached out and quickly squeezed his cock through the trunks. She opened her eyes wide as he began to erect. "I am right... you are ready for me." She squeezed harder and his cock stiffened to its full length under her hand.

"Stop, woman," he said, pushing her hand away. "This is not the place for us to lay."

Lyra laughed again. "But you want it now... tell me... speak the truth."

He nodded. "Yes, I want you," he said. "If we were alone I would fill you, but," he looked around, seeing that the rest of them had gone ahead, "now we can only do this." He pulled her to him, pushed her top right down, crushing her breasts against him, and forcing his cock into her crotch. She kissed him, mouth wide and tongue seeking his, her hands squeezing his buttocks tight.

Fidel stayed hard against her, then suddenly stepped back, shaking his head. "No, we must go with them now."

The shrill voice sliced through the air. "We are eating now, and...." Elsa stopped and looked hard at them, her face tightening. "So," she said slowly to Lyra, "you are celebrating winning the race, I think." The little woman's eyes crawled over Lyra's body, gazing at the naked breasts, the nipples fully erect now and the triangle of cloth at her crotch pulled down exposing her sex. She turned her head and looked down at Fidel's trunks, his cock standing out rigidly under them. "Yes," she breathed, her voice suddenly hoarse, "it is good to celebrate," she nodded at Fidel's crotch, "with that." Then she took a long breath and smiled at them. "Come now, you must eat." She stepped forward, saying, "You permit me," and without waiting for an answer, pulled Lyra's top up, and pushed her breasts back into it; then reached down and drew the triangle up and pressed it hard into her crotch. She smiled again, her eyes glowing. "That is better; now the men will not be too big in their costumes." She looked at Fidel's crotch again and laughed. "Not like you."

As they ate and talked at the barbeque Fidel wondered at the abrupt change in Elsa's attitude to them. Now she included them in the conversation and refilled their plates and glasses continuously. When Schultz spoke of the island's wine again she said she would try it, and see if it was as good as they all said. She filled a glass to the brim and began to drink. Schultz touched her arm gently. "Slowly, Elsa, this is not like the wine we have here. You must be cautious with it."

Elsa stopped drinking and smiled. "Do not fuss, Ernst." She nodded at Fidel. "They were right, it is different," she frowned, "maybe like some of the Hungarian red, only stronger," she blinked and laughed, "much stronger." Then she lifted the glass and drained it and held it out to Schultz to fill again.

"No, Elsa," he protested. "Let one be enough... try something else."

The little woman's face darkened and she thrust the glass at him. "Fill it!" she shrilled.

He shook his head, then shrugged and slowly refilled her glass.

She smiled and patted his cheek. "Thank you, Ernst. It is so good when you do as I say."

Fidel watched Schultz's jaw harden for a fraction of a moment, before he turned away to talk to the big man, Erin.

As he listened to the conversation he thought, *It is always the same with the rich, whenever they meet they talk money. It is as if they have a need. Like the money flowed in their veins instead of blood and they had to keep it moving with talk of how to get it, make it grow; and which company was weak and ready to plunder, and who was strong and could make them more money; and where to hide money when you didn't want it to be seen. And who could be a friend because they had huge money, and who might be an enemy because they wanted your money.*

The night air was filled with the aroma of fine cigars and expensive wines and the steaks cooking on the barbeque, as the swift-moving, never-ending, flow of talk of the having, and the getting of money, continued. Deals were proposed and discussed. Percentages checked and analysed. Huge figures of profit and loss were calculated in seconds by minds honed to understand the complexities of the world of mega money.

Fidel looked across at Lyra who was talking with the women. As he watched, she threw back her head and laughed, the vibrant sound momentarily suddenly stilling the money talk, and drawing the men's eyes to her.

He thought how much she had changed from the bitter, frustrated woman that had lived with Mora, to be here talking with women that she could never have anything in common with, women that lived only to spend the money that their men made and often gave their lives for. Now she stood among them, stunning in her raw, earthy beauty, commanding their attention.

He poured half a glass of the island wine and moved over to the low wall bordering the area and sat down on it, looking out across the sea. He suddenly wondered where the islanders were now. *Probably scattered over the mainland*, he thought. He had overheard some of the security men talking one day about them and it had been their opinion that the people would be lost throughout the country. One of the men had said that once they split from the others they would probably live by any work they might pick up as they wandered, and by begging from tourists.

Fidel smiled as he remembered the plans they had made when they all thought they would have money, the lives they had intended to live, buying new boats, and sitting on them out in the ocean, drinking themselves into a stupor under the heat of the sun. "Never to work again," they had told him. "You were right, Bardi," they said, "to leave when you were a boy; there is nothing on this rock, but work and death. And you came back to care for your father, when you might have stayed away, and let him struggle through the rest of his days."

They had clasped him drunkenly in their arms and said that was the act of a real son. When the wine took them further into stupidity they said he would be welcome always in their new homes. They insisted that he look upon their home as his. Because, after all, he had made the miracle happen. "Him and the Turk," they said, laughing uproariously, because the Turk had made the rich ones that wanted their island pay so much more than they need have done for it. Yes, they said, some with tears of gratitude, Bardi was delivering them from a life of toil; it was all because of him, and one spoke up to say how strange it was that because Bardi had left all those years ago, he had learnt the things that had made him the one to talk to the rich ones, and to see that they were not cheated by them.

Suddenly, the face of Saur came into his mind, the narrow eyes filled with hate, the thin, powerful body, that always seemed about to explode into violence. He looked around as if fearful that Saur might suddenly appear, and thought it might have been safer to have asked Lannon to let them live over this side of the island, where they would have been amongst people, and not remote from help if Saur came back for him. *Not if*, he thought bleakly, *but when*.

There was a tug at his arm that jolted him out of his thoughts and he looked up to see Elsa staring at him and clutching a glass of the island wine.

"You do not care to join the men, Bardi?" she said, her eyes flickering over him.

He shook his head. "No, I mean no disrespect, but I have no mind to what they speak of."

Elsa smiled, her mouth relaxing for the first time since Fidel had met her.

"You are right. They speak of money, money and more money." She swayed slightly and he wondered how much of the potent wine she had drunk.

"Will you sit?" he asked, indicating the wall.

She nodded. "I will... your wine... it is good... better that all that over there that we paid much for." She leaned towards him. "How is it in the morning...? Is there pain then?"

Fidel shook his head. "I cannot speak for others, but it has never hurt me."

She nodded. "Good... I do not like that pain." She smiled, her lips twisting and her eyes glittered. "There are other times when pain is good." She leaned over and touched his chest. "You understand me?"

Fidel smiled back at her, understanding her completely. "I do, Elsa."

The little woman leaned closer, her head tilted up to him, eyes glowing in the half light as she studied him. "Yes, Bardi, I think you really do." She touched his chest again, her hand lingering this time, and brushing lightly down across his belly.

Fidel felt the wine move in his head and a tightening in his crotch. *Careful, he thought, this is the woman of a very powerful man who lives on the island. If she makes trouble for me I have nowhere to go.*

"Your woman," she pointed at Lyra, "she knows about pain." Her eyes narrowed into slits, as she leaned even closer until her face was almost touching his. "The pain that brings the pleasure when you put that," her eyes opened wide and glanced down at his crotch, "to her."

The little woman gave off such sexual heat that it was almost impossible not to respond. He looked at the tiny breasts under the top, and the flat belly and small bulge over her crotch. Despite himself he felt his cock hardening.

Elsa looked at him and smiled slowly, knowingly, her eyes struggling to focus as the wine took effect. "You are a man that likes to enjoy a woman, I think, Bardi, and…" her voice thickened, "a woman would enjoy you."

She swayed and would have fallen over the wall had not Fidel reached out and caught her under the arm. He went to take the glass from her, but she shook her head.

"No, wait," she said and drained it, then threw it from her down into the shrubs below. "Leave it," she said. "We pay people to take care of that."

She leaned forward again, and as she started to speak her husband came over to them.

"Fidel," he said, "we want you to tell us about this stretch of the sea they call the dark water."

Fidel stood up, thankful to escape. "How did you hear of the water?"

"Tom wants to take his boat out tomorrow," said Shultz. "Perhaps some fishing. The security man, Lannon, gave us a map of the area this water is in." He shrugged. "But it is not clear and I told him this." He smiled and nodded at Fidel. "He said to ask you… that you would know."

"He is right," said Fidel.

Schultz took him by the arm. "Come and talk to the others; tell them what you know." He steered Fidel into the group and raised his arm and called for silence. "Here is the man to tell us about the water."

"What the hell is this stuff?" asked Jack Erin. "Christ! I've sailed all over the world… through some of the worst storms and never lost a boat. What's so different about this place?"

"It is not a storm that they fear," said Fidel. "They have been in the sea when it was a mad place and no one was lost. A storm we knew how to live with." He shook his head grimly. "But the dark water is a place that you never come out of; once it has the boat, you are lost."

"I'm sorry," said Sloan stubbornly, "I don't believe it. I had my boat fitted by a German firm that specialises in the best marine engines you can get. That thing could tow a tanker." He stared at Fidel and shrugged. "I'm not calling you a liar, but I don't think you have had much experience with ocean sailing. What you have here is almost certainly a riptide that the little boats your people had couldn't cope with."

"I can only tell you what I know to be true," Fidel said quietly, "and I know this; if you put your boat into the dark water it will take you down, and you will not return to the land."

"Listen," Erin said, "why don't we go out tomorrow and take look at this water… we can see for ourselves."

"Suits me," said Sloan, "though I think it's a waste of good sailing time." He looked at Fidel. "Would you come and show us just where this place is?" He grinned at the others. "You could see what a real boat can do."

Fidel shook his head. "No, I will not go if you think to test your boat against the dark water."

Sloan laughed easily. "Well, if you're nervous.…"

Fidel cut him short. "I am not nervous, I am afraid and I would ask you not to do this."

Sloan studied him for a moment. "You're serious about this, aren't you… you really don't think a boat with more power than you could dream of can't handle a local riptide."

"I have told you what I know," repeated Fidel patiently. "If you go, you will die."

"Maybe we should listen to him," said Schultz. "After all, he was born here and has worked this sea, John."

Sloan's face tightened, and Fidel thought, *He is like all the powerful; they can't stand to be wrong.*

"I'm going," Sloan said flatly. He looked at the rest of them. "Anyone care to join me?"

"Sure, I'll go out with you," said Erin. "We can make a day of it, take a look at this…" he smiled broadly at Fidel, "*dark water* place; and if we don't drown there, we can head out to sea and fish."

"What time are you starting?" asked Tom Harper. "I have a call that I have to take at ten, but after that we'd love to come."

Erin glanced at Schultz. "How about you, Ernst?"

"I am not sure," Schultz replied, looking doubtfully at Fidel. "I just think we should listen to what he says."

"I listened to that stuff about boats being taken down," said Erin, speaking with a heavy authority, "and," he nodded at Sloan, "frankly, what John says is right. I've seen the motor on his boat, and it's of the strongest you can buy anywhere in the world."

"Well, at least come and tell us when we are near the danger area," Schultz said to Fidel.

"Would you stop when I said to stop?" Fidel said to Sloan.

He laughed. "Wouldn't be much of a trial to pull out the first time the sea got rough." He shook his head. "No, I guess I'll just have to show you."

"You're sure you won't come?" Schultz asked Fidel.

Fidel looked at him, then round at the rest of them. *I have to live on this island*, he thought. *If these fools die in the dark water then those that are left will blame me. They will say that I knew the danger and that I should have stopped them. Then they will make trouble for me, maybe even try to make me leave.*

"This I will do," he said slowly. "I have a small boat and, if you agree, I will go in it and you can follow me."

"Where the hell to?" asked Erin.

Fidel pointed at the sea. "Far out there where the Run...." He stopped, seeing the incomprehension in their faces. "The Run is what we call the beginning of the dark water, where the Run begins. Then you will feel the power in the sea." He stopped for a moment looking at their faces. "If you go on into the Run I will not go with you. All I can do is try to stay outside the Run and pick you up when you leave the boat."

"What do you mean," asked Schultz, frowning at him, "leave the boat?"

"When you see that the boat has no chance against the Run and you jump into the sea to escape." He laughed bleakly. "It will be a miracle if I find you because by then you will be in the Run." He sliced his hand through the air. "Finish."

There was a moment's silence, then Sloan looked at the others and shrugged. "Sorry, I don't buy this stuff, and tomorrow, I'll prove it."

"You have people to sail your boat?" asked Fidel.

Sloan frowned. "Sure, and they're a damned fine crew," he said bluntly. "They won't be afraid of a little rough water."

"Will you tell them of the Run and the dark water?" Fidel asked.

"They're professional people at their business," said Sloan tightly, "real sailors that have shipped all over the world, not local fishermen that wouldn't last a day racing out in the big seas." He stared at Fidel. "Anyway, I'm not letting them on the boat tomorrow." He looked at the others. "I'll handle the thing myself; that way no one can say I was afraid of a little rough water."

Fidel thought it was useless to argue with them. They had bought the best and the most luxurious boats that money could buy, beautiful, sleek state of the art machines, designed to travel at speed and in comfort, equipped with the most sophisticated technology to guide them anywhere in the world. How could they see that once in the grip of the Run all boats were the same?

He turned to Schultz. "Do you wish this… that I bring my boat out tomorrow? I will if you want it."

Schultz looked at John Sloan's set face and shrugged resignedly. "Yes, bring your boat and show us where to go." His voice hardened as he spoke to Sloan. "Just promise me, John, that when you feel this water pulling the boat you will come out of it immediately."

Sloan threw his up his hands. "All right, all right, for Christ's sake! If it looks bad I'll back off!" he said disgustedly.

"What is all this noise here?" a voice shrilled. Elsa had joined the group and was pulling at Schultz's arm. "What are you making such a fuss of a boat trip for?"

"It is not just a boat trip, Elsa," explained Schultz. "We are going to see this place that could be dangerous to take a boat into." He nodded at Fidel. "He knows where it is and will show us tomorrow."

The little woman raised her eyebrows at Fidel. "There is a danger in this trip?"

He nodded. "Yes, if the boat gets too close to the Run of the water then they could all die."

"Why not you?" she asked.

"He is taking his own boat," said Schultz. "That way he says he won't get too close."

Elsa shook her head at him. "Why do you have to go and see this thing? Why can't you all believe what he says? He was born here, so he should know where it is not safe to go."

"He does and that is why you should not go to the dark water," Lyra said. She looked around at them all and raised her voice. "I heard you speak of this and you must see that it is a place of death." She turned to Fidel. "Tell them, Bardi."

"I have said all that I can," said Fidel. "If they do not believe me, then I cannot stop them going to see the water."

"You will not go with them?" asked Lyra. "You would not do that?"

He shrugged. "I said I would take my own boat and take them to where the Run begins."

Her eyes widened in alarm. "You must not do this, Bardi... you will be pulled into the Run... you will die!"

He shook his head. "Have no fear for me. I will stop away from where the water goes from blue to the dark."

"Others have thought to do as you say and they have died," she said. She turned to them. "Those that have gone into the dark water have never been found. They are gone for all time."

"Christ!" Sloan said exasperatedly. "Look, if it's going to be such a damned hassle I'll go on my own and look at this place."

"No, no," shrilled Elsa. "No, we must all go... it will be something different to do," she said slowly, staring at Fidel. She smiled glittering-eyes at them all. "Then, after we have seen this wonder we can eat and drink and swim in the sea."

"Have you not heard what has been said?" asked Lyra urgently. "Bardi and I are the only people here that know what that place in the water can do. Why do you all not believe us?"

"It's not that I doubt that you believe what you say," said Sloan. He smiled at Lyra indulgently. "But you have to see that I am talking about a modern boat that is so different to anything that you could imagine. The power in the thing is enormous," he shrugged. "Christ! I've never even had it open to its max speed."

Elsa clapped her hands. "Yes, we will go tomorrow," she shrilled. "How many will come with us?"

"Count me in," grunted Jack Erin. "Let's just do it and see what all the fuss is about. You want to take your boat, or mine, John?"

"Take mine," said Sloan. "I was going out tomorrow, anyway." He stretched and yawned and turned to his wife. "Are you ready to leave, Gina?"

"That will be six with Ernst and me," said Elsa. "We need more people to see the bad place!"

She pulled at the arm of Tom Harper. "You will go, you and Jean, you will come with us."

Harper hesitated. "We were going over to the mainland tomorrow."

Elsa clapped her hands together. "Oh, you can do that anytime, Tom. You must come with us... it will be fun to show these people," she indicated Fidel and Lyra, "what a proper boat is like. One that has all comforts and does not sink when the sea is a little rough."

Harper looked at his wife enquiringly. "What do you think, Jean; you want to go?"

"Yes, yes," shrilled Elsa. "Say yes, Jean!"

"Oh, I suppose so," said the slim, dark-haired woman. "We can go over the next day."

"Good, good," crowed Elsa. "That will be eight of us. We can all go on John's boat." She looked at Fidel. "You will come with us?"

"No," he said, "I have told you what I will do. I will go in my boat and show you the way."

Elsa frowned at him. "But you will not see Tom's beautiful boat if you do not come with us." Her mouth twisted in a sneer. "It is not like your little fishing boats."

Fidel shrugged. "I have seen all kinds of boats; it will not worry me if I do not see one more."

"Okay," said Sloan, "I'm for bed." He stood up and looked at them all. "See you at the harbour at... say eleven?" He looked at Harper. "You said you had a call coming in at ten; will eleven be all right for you?"

Harper nodded. "It's just a progress report, shouldn't take long. Eleven will be fine."

As the truck bounced along the track to the little house in the rocks, Lyra turned to Fidel and held his arm. "Do not do this thing, Bardi." When he made no answer she shook him angrily. "Why do you not speak? Are you so stupid that you think you will cheat the death out there?"

"Do you not see... how can I not go?" he asked. "If they are taken and I am not there people will say that I knew what the Run would do... and that I should have tried to stop them from going."

"But you did," said Lyra hotly. "I heard you tell them not to go. If they do not listen it is not your fault." She gestured angrily. "Let the fools go... let them know the power in the Run... I do not care if they die!"

Fidel held the wheel tighter as the truck bounced out of the ruts in the track. "You are right but I must go... it must be known that I went."

Lyra was silent for a moment, staring out through the windscreen at the darkness. "I will go with you," she said.

"No," Fidel said, "you will not."

She turned to him in the seat. "I have to be with you. I cannot wait back here and not know if the sea has taken you." She paused. "If there is trouble, then I can help. I know the water better than you and I am stronger in the sea than anyone on the island." She nodded firmly. "Enough."

Chapter Twenty-Six

As the morning sun beat into the land Fidel stood on the rocks by the sea; and using the field telephone, rang through to the security block and asked to speak to Lannon. He waited as they tried to connect him to the security boss, who was already down at the harbour checking a supply boat. Then the phone crackled and Lannon's voice came through. Fidel told him that Sloan and the others were going to the danger area, to test their boat against the Run. He said that if they did this and got too close they would die.

Lannon asked if he was sure of this and Fidel said that he had tried to stop them, but they would not listen. The security chief said he would ring Sloan and see if he could persuade him to change his mind, and that he would contact Fidel as soon as he could.

Fidel took food and drinks down to his boat and lashed ten thirty-metre lengths of line with small plastic rings on the ends to the rails on either side. The phone rang as he finished, and Lannon said Sloan was determined to go ahead, and demanded to know who had told him about the trip.

Lannon said that Fidel had only been concerned for their safety, but Sloan said there should be no interference from anyone, and that was the end of the matter.

Fidel asked if there was nothing more he could do. There was a short silence, then Lannon lowered his voice and spoke quietly into the phone. "Listen to me, Bardi, and I will tell you how things are with these people. When you deal with them you are not talking with people such as you and I. The man Sloan inherited a personal fortune of two hundred million dollars when his father died. He took over the company. He is in electronics that supply the computer industry and his dealings are worldwide. It is said that his accountants talk in billions."

"All his money will not save him if he puts his boat into the Run," said Fidel flatly. "The water has no respect for rich or poor."

"You cannot talk to them, Bardi. They make their own laws and go their own way," Lannon said. "I have done what I said I would do. If they choose not to listen, then so be it."

"Then if they die, how will that be for the island? What will your people say? It will not be good to have a place to live where death is in the sea," asked Fidel.

"Listen, Bardi," said Lannon, "I have spoken to them today after you told me what Sloan and his people were going to do; and they said I was to warn them of the danger but not to cross them in any circumstances, and never to interfere with them." He paused. "Now you see how things are... there is no more I can do."

"I hear what you say," said Fidel slowly, "but I will go out in my boat and watch them, and it may be that when they touch the beginning of the Run they will be satisfied and leave that place."

"I wish you well of them," said Lannon. There was a sharp click as he switched off the phone.

Fidel stood for a moment, then shook his head and went back to the house.

Lyra looked at his face as he came in. "The man... Lannon, he could do nothing then?"

Fidel shook his head. "He tried, but they will not listen." He laughed harshly. "They think their money will take care of them."

"It will not be you to blame, Bardi; you have done what you can."

"No," he said, "you do not see. If there is trouble they may try to make me leave the island."

"Why would they do that?" she asked. "You are trying to stop them; it will be their own fault if they die."

Fidel was silent, suddenly thinking of all the blood he had spilled to get here, to be in a place safe from the outside world and with money to ensure a good life. Now all that could be changed in one day, because the rich ones wanted to show that the boat their wealth had bought could subdue the sea.

He picked up the basket of food and drink and looked at Lyra. "I ask you for the last time to stay here."

She shook her head. "No, I go with you."

Fidel shrugged. "So be it."

He swung the motor launch out from the rocks and they cruised round to the other side of the island where the big boats were moored in the new harbour. As he eased in beside the jetty and tied up he remembered all the times, years ago, when he had returned every night exhausted from the heat and the backbreaking hauling of the nets, to pull the little boats up on the shore. Now it was a place for the rich to live. *Maybe a few less after today*, he thought grimly.

He stepped onto the jetty and looked over to where Sloan's huge white yacht of lay in the water, moving gently with the swell. As he waited for Lyra to join him Sloan appeared on deck and, seeing Fidel, motioned him to come over.

"Wait here," he said to Lyra.

He made his way along the jetty, watching as Sloan stood there, hands on his hips, waiting. *He does not look a happy man*, he thought. As he walked up the gangplank and stepped down onto the deck Sloan was already speaking.

"What the hell did you have to talk to Lannon for?" he said. "I had the guy ringing me first thing with some damn fool talk about how he didn't think it was a good idea for me to go and look at this place." His face flushed with anger. "When I want the opinion of some human burglar alarm I'll ask for it." He glared at Fidel. "He said you told him we would be in danger."

"That is right..." Fidel began.

Sloan cut him off. "I'm not interested in what you think." He stepped forward and looked directly into Fidel's eyes. "When I make decisions I'm not accustomed to having them questioned." He waved his hand around him at the yacht and smiled tightly at Fidel. "This is what you get for being right in life." He nodded abruptly, as if dismissing Fidel. "Get back to your boat now and wait until we're ready to leave, then you can go ahead and show us the way." He smiled coldly. "I'll try not to run you down out there."

Fidel turned without answering and walked back to his boat. It had been a long time since he had felt the sting of contempt from someone like Sloan and he struggled to control his anger.

Lyra looked at his face as he stepped down in to the boat. "What happened?" she asked.

"That is a man who is sure he can cheat death," Fidel said harshly.

"He would not listen?" she asked.

Fidel shook his head. "That one is never wrong." He looked up at the mountain brooding huge against the sky at the end of the island. "Maybe after today he will never be so sure again."

"You would not let him go too far into the Run, Bardi?" Lyra said. "You would not do that?"

Fidel shook his head. "No, I would not do that, but," he gestured at Sloan's boat, "you saw how they are... suppose they will not heed the word of an islander; what then?"

"When he feels the sea begin to pull his boat he will stop," said Lyra.

"I hope you are right," Fidel said grimly, "but I think he will want to show them all that his money has bought him a boat that is better than the sea."

"What will you do if he does not listen when you tell him to stop?" she asked.

"What can I do?" said Fidel. "I will give him a warning, but if he goes in and the boat does not answer to him, then," he pointed to the ropes lashed to the rails, "I will throw these to anyone that is in the water."

"You will not go close to the Run. Promise me."

Fidel nodded. "You have my word," he said coldly. *Let the fool know the terror*, he thought. It would be something to see him then.

He turned round as the sound of a V8 engine sounded on the morning heat. A big off-roader swung into the parking area and stopped at the harbour wall. Elsa Schultz jumped out, followed by Jack and Dolly Erin.

Erin lifted the tailgate and pulled out a big hamper and hoisted it on his shoulder. "Come on," he boomed. "Let's go see this bad water."

Schultz locked the car and they all walked along the jetty and, as they passed Fidel and Lyra, Erin looked down and at the little boat and laughed.

"Sure you're going to be safe in that?" He walked on, his huge laugh resounding out over the water.

Elsa stared at them, then smiled. "You are sure you won't come with us on John's boat?" The smile twisted. "When we get out to sea we can do whatever we like... really enjoy ourselves." She nodded at Lyra, knowingly. "You would like that, yes?"

Lyra shook her head. "No, I go with Bardi."

The little woman shrugged. "As you will... maybe later." At that moment she caught sight of the Mercedes estate car of Tom Harper and she shrilled out to them. "Over here... we are ready to go!"

The Harpers had brought Martin with them and they hurried along the jetty to the yacht, nodding to Fidel as they passed. As Fidel watched he saw Sloan clamber down off his boat and walk along to them. They exchanged greetings, then he continued up to Fidel. "Here," he reached down and passed Fidel a portable phone. "I've set it open," he explained. "When I speak to you don't do anything to it; just speak into it to answer me." He looked closely at Fidel. "You understand me. Don't touch any of the controls... any of them; just speak directly into it." He turned to go, then stopped and pointed his finger at Fidel. "And for Christ's sake, don't lose it over the side!"

Fidel put the phone on the shelf. Lyra watched Sloan as he went back to his boat. "He is not a man to care for," she said coldly.

Fidel nodded. "It is as I said... one of the rich."

Suddenly air horns splintered the air and Fidel saw Sloan waving at him and, pointing out into the ocean he waved back, and started his engine, and the boat throbbed slightly as they moved away from the jetty and out into the harbour. He waited as the huge gleaming white yacht slid through the water and towered above them.

Sloan looked down at them. "All right," he called, "you go on. I'll stay back to avoid swamping you."

Fidel nodded and Sloan shouted down, "Use the phone; that's what it's for."

Fidel stared up at him, then nodded again, put the engine in gear and pulled away, heading in a direct line out to sea.

After about five minutes Sloan's voice crashed through the phone. "Where the hell are we going? I thought this water was close to the shore? Why are we moving out to sea?"

Fidel picked up the phone and spoke slowly and clearly. "We have to go out where the Run begins; if you move into it where it is strong you will be gone."

"This is crazy, Bardi." His voice faded and Fidel heard him talking to the others. "The guy's too scared to go closer to this Run thing so we'll have to wait on him." His voice came back to Fidel. "Okay, just don't be all day."

Fidel put the phone down and looked back at the yacht that was about five hundred metres behind them, with the island slowly fading from sight in the shimmering haze. Fidel went on a way, then looked back, past Sloan's yacht. The island was no longer visible and he slowed right down and turned the boat cautiously to meet the incoming sea, just using enough power to move it through the water.

"Be careful, Bardi," said Lyra. "We are near."

Fidel looked at the sea intently, waiting for the water to turn from blue to the dark of the Run.

Suddenly he felt the little boat move faster, and Lyra called out, "Look, there!" She pointed and Fidel saw the water tinged with a dark shade. "We are on the edge, Bardi," she cried. "Pull back!"

Fidel slammed the throttle into reverse and, as the boat slowed, he turned and waved his arm in the air to Sloan, indicating to him to stop. A second later the phone crackled and Sloan's voice exploded through it.

"What the hell's wrong now?" he shouted.

"We are at the Run!" said Fidel urgently. "You must stop now—do not go any further!"

There was a moment of silence, then the big yacht was almost on them and Sloan spoke again. "For Christ's sake, man, the sea's like glass! There's no danger out here!"

As he spoke the yacht slid past them, powering through the water and almost swamping their boat and continued on.

"No," shouted Fidel desperately into the phone, "come back before it's too late!" He heard Sloan's phone being slammed down as the yacht went on. He turned to Lyra. "He won't listen," he said.

"Do not go after him," she said, looking down at the sea. "Stay at the edge and watch him."

He swung the boat round and held it almost still as he looked at the big yacht. He could see Sloan at the wheel holding a drink and talking to Jack Erin standing beside him. Suddenly Erin looked back and waved to him.

Fidel picked up the phone and shouted into it. "You're right in the Run now. Bring the boat round and come out before it is too late!"

As he watched, the big yacht slewed to one side and Sloan shouted into the phone. "Hey, this is really strong out here!" He handed his glass to Erin and gripped the wheel with both hands. "That's better," he said as the yacht started to come back round.

Erin looked over the side and frowned. "Look at the water, Tom," he said urgently. "It's darker here now, almost black."

Elsa came up on deck followed by Dolly Erin and Tom Harper. "What are you doing, John?" she scolded. "All the drinks came off the top... there is mess all over down there."

Harper looked at Sloan who had his feet braced on the deck and was straining to hold the wheel. "What's wrong, John?" he asked.

"Nothing," Sloan replied. "It's all right... we're just caught in a cross current. It'll be okay in a minute. When she comes round I'll open up on full power and take us out."

Harper nodded, then looked over at Fidel and Lyra who were waving frantically at them. "What's wrong with them?" he said.

Sloan took a fresh grip on the wheel as the yacht began to slew round again. Erin moved over to him. "Can't you hold her... do you want a hand?" Sloan nodded and Erin reached down and gripped two of the lower spokes and heaved his bulk against the movement of the yacht.

"That's it," panted Sloan. "She's coming now."

Erin grunted with exertion. "Open her up, John, let's get out of here."

Harper looked down at the sea and frowned. "There's something wrong," he said, pointing down at the water. "Look at the sea... it's moving like hell... almost in a straight line!" He looked at them struggling with the wheel. "What's going on?" he demanded.

"It's all right," Sloan shouted. "It's just a freak stretch of water. If we hold her she'll pull out."

Suddenly, the yacht dipped right down in the sea, then came lunging back up, sending Harper sprawling across the deck. There was a scream from below, and Erin looked at Sloan, then shouted to Harper, "Get everyone up here now, Tom; we're in trouble!"

Harper lurched across to the entrance to the big cabin and called, "Come up, come on!"

Erin stretched out one hand from the wheel and took the phone off its pad. "What's happening?" he shouted into it.

Fidel's voice came through clear. "You must leave the boat... it's your only chance... jump now before it goes down!" He held up a line and waved it in the air. "We have these... you can catch them... you must do it now!"

"Why can't you do something?" Elsa screamed at Sloan. "What is wrong?" Sloan did not answer, remaining locked onto the wheel. Schultz came up followed by the rest of them, except Martin, and they clung to the side rails as the yacht pitched and slewed, always moving now back to the island.

Erin looked up and shouted, "Look, there's the mountain!" He let go of the wheel and came down from the bridge, onto the deck. "We have to get off." He pointed at the huge out flung arm of the mountain. "If we wait, we'll go down!" He took hold of Dolly's arm and pulled her to the side. "When I say go," he shouted, "you jump!" He waved at Fidel, shook Dolly's arm and shouted, "Go!"

They plunged over the side and were swept along in the fast-running water. Fidel rammed the throttle open and raced down the edge of the Run to get ahead of them, then Lyra threw the two lines far out across their path.

Jack lunged at his, caught it and swung round as Dolly came past, catching her with his free hand, and taking the strain as the water tore at him.

Schultz took hold of Elsa's hand. "We have to go!" he cried.

Elsa pulled back and screamed at him. "No, no, we will die!"

She lashed out and struck his face, but he dragged her to the side and up on the rail, as she struggled frantically, hitting at him and screaming. Suddenly, Schultz scooped her up in his arms and they both fell over the side.

"I can't see them," Fidel shouted. "Where are they?"

"There! There!" cried Lyra pointing to where Elsa had come to the surface and was kicking and struggling in the water. Then Ernst appeared behind her, waving his arms and trying to stay afloat.

Fidel throttled back to adjust to their speed as they came past him, then accelerated and stayed in front as Lyra threw the lines. Schultz took hold of his and looked round for Elsa just as she was picked up by the water and flung into the air, landing almost beside Fidel's boat. Lyra leaned over and threw a line right at her. Elsa grabbed at it and wrapped it round one arm, and paddled furiously with the other one.

Fidel looked back to the land and saw the shape of the mountain looming larger now. "We are getting close to the mountain," he shouted to Lyra. "They have to jump now!"

As Sloan kept the engine revved to its maximum the stench of hot oil filled the air.

Martin came up from below holding his head. "What's happening?" he asked. "What's wrong with the boat?"

He looked up at Sloan on the bridge, spread eagled on the wheel, his face red with strain as he tried to turn the yacht out of the Run. "Christ!" Martin said, and leaped up beside Sloan and gripped the wheel, heaving with all his strength to force it round. After a moment he straightened up and took Sloan by the arm and shook him hard. "John! John!" he shouted. "Look!" He pointed to the arm of the mountain, now suddenly huge in the fading haze of the morning. "It's no use, John! We have to get off before we hit that!"

Sloan shook his head, then pushed Martin away from him. "Jump if you want!" he cried. The veins in his forehead stood out with strain and his eyes were bulging. "Go on!" he screamed. "Jump! I'll bring her out... she will come."

The yacht slewed again and the wheel spun wildly, jerking Sloan's body with it. Martin was pitched off the bridge and landed on his back on the deck. He struggled up, helped by Tom Harper. "We have to jump, Martin," said Harper. "Now!" He pointed at Fidel who was still keeping pace with them, with Lyra waving frantically and gesturing at the mountain.

Jean took her husband's arm, her face tight with fear. "Tom!" she said, her voice trembling. "It's all right," he said. "They'll get us." He looked at Martin. "Get Gina!" He nodded at Sloan. "He's crazy... save yourself!" He pulled his wife to the side, waved to Fidel and pointed down at the sea, then lunged out and down taking Jean with him.

Fidel watched as they hit the water and went under. Jean came up first, struggling and trying to stay up, then went under again. Lyra snatched up one of the rings, wrapped it round her upper arm and dived over the side. She went under, came up and swam in a slanting line across the Run in the powerful, weaving style that propelled her through the water. As she did, Jean surfaced just ahead of her and fell back on the surface, not moving her body at all. As she reached her, Lyra took the ring and thrust Jean's arm through it and waved to Fidel.

Tom Harper came up on the other side of Fidel's boat, thrown clear out of the Run. He swam over and clung to the side of the little boat.

"Where's Jean?" he shouted.

Fidel pointed. "Lyra has her."

Just then Fidel heard the scream of engines and looked round to see two black and orange security launches closing on them, and then circling to pick up those hanging on the rings.

He shouted out to them, "Keep out of the Run!" He pointed down at the dark water and swung his boat right over so that the security men could get to them safely. He looked back at the yacht where Sloan was still on the bridge, convulsed over the wheel. Fidel could see Gina Sloan shouting at her husband and Martin trying to pull her to the side.

Suddenly, the yacht shuddered. Then there was a muffled roar as the engine exploded and a cloud of thick oily smoke belched up from below. As it cleared he saw Martin on the rail holding Gina by the arm, then both dropped into the sea. When they surfaced Martin struck out and caught Gina by the shoulders, turned onto his back and kicked out strongly trying to force his way out of the Run. Fidel threw the ropes high and they landed in the water almost in front of Martin, who held onto Gina with one hand and grabbed a rope with the other.

"Where's John?" shouted Erin. "Where the hell is he?" He clutched the rail and leaned out over the side. "He's got to get off before it goes down or he's finished!" The yacht began to sit lower in the water, thrashing from side to side, and they could hear the crashing sound of the interior fittings being torn loose.

Erin gripped Fidel by the shoulder. "What can we do?" he asked.

Fidel shook his head. "Nothing now; he has to jump or die!" He thought that even if Sloan went into the water now he would have no chance; the Run was moving faster as it got closer to the land and in minutes the yacht would be at the mountain wall and smashed against it, then flung under the water and battered to destruction as it was hurled along the great trench and out to sea.

Then, suddenly, shockingly, the yacht was gone, as if it had been sucked under, no disturbance on the surface, nothing to indicate that it had ever existed, just the swift-running water that raced in to the sheer wall of the mountain.

Erin turned to Fidel, stunned as he stared at the sea. "Christ... he's gone." He pointed at the dark water. "He's gone!"

Fidel nodded slowly. "Yes," he said, "there was no hope for him."

Erin slumped back in his seat as if all his strength had left him. "Christ!" he muttered over and over again. After a moment he looked up at Fidel. "Will they find the boat?" he hesitated. "Or him?"

Fidel shook his head. "They never find anything... whatever the Run takes into the mountain," he made a sweeping gesture with his hand, "it takes miles back out to sea."

Erin looked out over the water. "Why the hell didn't we listen to you?" he moaned. "Jesus, why the hell didn't we listen to you?"

Fidel was silent. Now was not the time to remind Erin that the arrogance of one man had almost cost them their lives, had indeed taken that one man's life. *No*, he thought, now he had to ease the blame away from Sloan, and make it appear that it was not wholly his fault.

He patted Erin on the shoulder. "Listen," he said slowly, "he had a wonderful boat... one that you could sail the world in." Erin nodded. "And," Fidel went on, "something like that, so fine and strong... who could know that a place like this could destroy it?"

A loudhailer sounded clear in the air. "Are you all right?"

Fidel waved his arm to them. "Yes, we are coming in." He drove his boat along the edge of the Run slowly, as if looking for any sign of Sloan, knowing that there was no chance, short of a miracle, that the man was alive. *Indeed*, he thought grimly, what was left of Sloan was probably hurtling back along the trench hundreds of feet beneath them right at this moment.

When they drew up at the jetty the waiting ambulance took them up to the small medical centre behind the security block where they were treated for shock and bruising and exposure.

The following day private medical teams flew into Kalamata on Crete and were taken by the helicopters of the survivors to the island where they administered to their clients.

Four days later Lannon rang Fidel to tell him that the developers had instructed him to hold an enquiry into the accident. It was, he stressed, completely unofficial as they had no legal standing, but his employers felt that for the sake of appearances there should be some form of report into the tragedy.

Fidel asked if the law from outside the island, either from Greece or Turkey, would wish to be present.

Lannon said no, the island came under no legal jurisdiction or governing body but its own. Anyway, he said, most of the people that had chosen to own homes on the island almost certainly had armies of legal people in the companies they ran, but he was sure there would be just the people involved in the accident. Lannon lowered his voice, and said the feeling among them was that they had totally disregarded Bardi's warning, the same one that he had voiced to him, and that he had passed it on to his employers who, in turn, had told him not to obstruct them—just pass on the warning and let them make their own minds up.

Chapter Twenty-Seven

The enquiry was held one week later in the small main hall of the security block. Lannon sat at a table and opened the proceedings by checking that all those involved were present. He then calmly led them through the morning of the trip, simply letting it be recorded that the engine on the yacht had failed for some reason that they would never know, and that the yacht had then been caught in a treacherous stretch of water.

This was in no way the fault of John Sloan, the owner of the yacht. When the engine had caught fire Sloan had tried desperately to control the yacht, staying at the controls, whilst urging the others to jump overboard and swim to safety. "This," he said, looking calmly at Fidel, "brought them to the man and woman Fidel and Lyra Bardi, who had been in the area and, seeing the yacht in trouble, had immediately come to their aid."

He had been instructed to pass on their sincere and heartfelt thanks to them both for their courageous actions in preventing what could have been a far greater tragedy, especially to Lyra Bardi, who had leapt into the sea to rescue people who otherwise would have surely drowned.

The entire business was over in just one hour. Lannon collected signatures from all those concerned in the incident, corroborating that everything written into the record was the truth. Fidel was the last to sign and Lannon told him quietly to stay behind after the others had gone. When they were alone he took Fidel into his office, and they stood by the window for a moment, watching the gleaming cars and four wheel drive machines depart and climb up the road to the high ground and then on to Jack Erin's house.

Lannon smiled grimly at Fidel. "Well, Bardi, what did you think of it?"

Fidel frowned at him. "I think I must have been somewhere else when it happened." He looked quizzically at the security chief. "Is that what your people wanted—to make it look like as you said… and what they put their names to?"

Lannon opened a drawer in his desk and took out a bottle of whisky. He reached two glasses from the shelf over his filing cabinet and looked at Fidel. "You will join me?"

Fidel nodded, and watched him as he poured a generous measure in each glass. He pushed one across the desk to Fidel and raised his own. "I give you a toast," he smiled tightly. "To truth."

Fidel nodded and took a drink.

"Sit down, Bardi," Lannon said. "I have to thank you for agreeing with all that you heard in there today."

Fidel shrugged. "I saw no reason to interfere with it," he said slowly. He leaned back in his chair, savouring the drink. "Would it have made a difference if I had?"

"It would have made it a little awkward," Lannon said, "but the report would have been the same."

He stroked his small moustache and eyed Fidel reflectively. "I told you, Bardi, they are not like us, the rich ones. Even if there had been legal people here." He paused. "Say this island came under legal jurisdiction from another country… Turkey or Greece, and they had sent an enquiry team to seek the real truth as you and I know it… if that had happened, these people here would have made phone calls. In one or two days their own legal teams would have been here," he pointed his finger at Fidel, "people that are paid millions to keep their clients safe from all trouble or scandal." He drained his glass, refilled it and held out the bottle to Fidel, who nodded and pushed his glass across the table.

"Shall I tell you what really happened, Bardi, what happened out there in the sea?" He smiled at Fidel. "I was not there, but I know what these people are like, so I know what happened."

He cocked his head enquiringly, and Fidel nodded. "Go on, tell me."

Lannon settled himself in the chair. "You all met at the harbour. I saw you from here and they told you what to do… you were to take them out to look at this water that was dangerous and that Sloan thought was nothing." He looked at Fidel. "Am I right?"

Fidel nodded. "That is what happened, yes."

Lannon went on. "So, Sloan went first and you followed him out to sea where you were to lead him to the place where he could show all his friends what a wonderful sailor he was." He stopped suddenly and grinned at Fidel. "Did he give you a phone so that he could shout at you?"

Fidel nodded again.

Lannon continued. "He wanted to give me one as well, but I told him it was forbidden by the company that I carry anyone's private phone." Lannon leaned back and smiled sardonically. "Then you came to the place, you told me you would go to, what you call the Run, and you would stop and let him feel the pull of the water. Then you thought he would be happy and go off and enjoy the rest of the day."

"You knew that would not happen, I think," said Fidel.

Lannon nodded. "Right. I knew that he would try to master the sea. Look at his boat... they say it cost twelve million dollars... how could a thing like that be beaten by a little island water?"

"That little water has taken down bigger boats than that," said Fidel.

"I believe you," said Lannon. He leaned forward and looked hard at Fidel. "When the water took hold of him he fought it, yes?"

"You are right. He thought he could take his boat out of it," said Fidel.

"But tell me this, Bardi," Lannon said, staring at him intently, "there was a little time when the water was not so strong... when a man could have taken the boat out of danger... perhaps not much time, but enough."

"Yes," said Fidel slowly. "I called to him on his phone and told him to come away before it was too late."

"He didn't listen," said Lannon. "He wanted to show all his friends that he was in control." He nodded at Fidel. "They all have to be in control, you see, it is like a sickness with them." He laughed harshly. "A sickness that killed him!" His face hardened. "And then, Bardi, when he realised that he was caught—that after all that his millions had bought him, that floating marvel was simply being overpowered by the strength of the sea, even then he would not give up and save himself."

"You tell it as if you were there," said Fidel.

"I know them, Bardi." He stretched his stocky body in the chair. "I have been working among people like these for a long time now." He turned his head and looked out of the window at the harbour. "My contract has two more years to run, then if I wish they will renew it." He looked down at the whisky. "I am good at what I do, Bardi. They value my work, but I do not think I will stay with them."

Fidel remained silent.

Lannon continued. "So they jumped off the boat, Bardi, and you had the ropes and the rings ready for them." He nodded at Fidel's surprise. "Yes, I watched you from here before you left… I saw you through the glasses… you had ropes with rings at the ends, lashed to the rails." He nodded approvingly. "You were ready for the disaster. Who jumped first?"

Fidel thought for a moment. "It was the big man, Erin; he jumped with his wife."

"Did you tell them to jump?" asked Lannon.

"Yes," said Fidel, "I shouted to them."

"And the others… they also jumped after that?"

Fidel realised he was being questioned by the security chief, regardless that they were both drinking Lannon's whisky. The man was still working, still stockpiling facts away in his mind, eager to know the truth, and then manipulating it to serve his employers' best interests.

"Yes," he said, "I think when they saw Erin and his woman go over the side they knew it was not good to stay."

Lannon looked at him through half closed eyes. "Did any of them want to remain with the boat?"

Fidel was silent for a moment. Then he thought it would do no harm to tell him the truth. After what had been said and recorded today the truth would be of no more consequence than the lies. "The woman… Schultz," he said slowly. "She gave her man, Schultz, much trouble before he got her off."

Lannon nodded thoughtfully. "You mean Elsa," he said. "She would be the one to do that." He paused and swirled the whisky round in his glass. "I will tell you something now, Bardi, that you do not speak of to anyone on this island." He eyed Fidel sternly. "You have seen how she is." He made an up and down motion with his hands. "Like a stick; nothing on her to excite a man. But people that I trust to be right in these matters say that she has a large appetite for the taste of a man." He closed one eye in a conspiratorial wink at Fidel.

"That is the truth," asked Fidel, remembering how she had acted towards him at the barbeque, the raw sexuality that had radiated from her. "She does not look like a woman that is that way."

Lannon nodded. "That is right, but you forget she is one of the rich; they can buy anything, even that when they want it." He grinned. "It is said that she gives Schultz no peace and that because of this he lets her have whatever she wants." He took a pull at the whisky. "Imagine, a man that commands all the committees that run his empire and he is at the mercy of a stick insect." He put his head back and laughed. "There is something to think on, eh, Bardi?"

Fidel nodded. "As you say," he agreed. "And now, what happens now to all this business with the yacht going down… is this the end of it?"

"All over," said Lannon. "My report," he tapped the thin plastic file containing the four sheets of paper, "will go to my employers so they will have a complete and full record of what happened." He smiled at Fidel. "One that would stand up in any court if it had to." He smiled tightly. "There will only be the memorial service for Sloan and they will not hold that here; they'll go back to America where he came from."

"Will all those that were on the yacht with him go as well?" asked Fidel.

Lannon nodded. "Yes, they will go." He smiled coldly. "They may not want to go, but they will because they have to back up the lie that Sloan gave his life saving them from the sea." He looked down at the report. "It's all in here, what a brave man he was, and how they all owe their lives to him." He stood up and went over to the big window that looked down over the harbour. "And his family will put up a big stone, the biggest and most expensive their money can buy, and it will say what a hero he was; and only all the people that were on the boat with him will know the real truth." He turned to Fidel. "And you, Bardi, you will know the truth, you and your woman."

"How will they be with me now—the people that know the real truth?" asked Fidel. "Will they not find it hard that I know what happened out there?"

"I can't give you an answer," Lannon said slowly, "but take care. You saw them when they were frightened because they thought they were going to die." He shook his head warningly at Fidel. "They are not the kind of people that like to be seen like that. They lost their control and you were there to see it. I would say to you, be careful. Do not speak of what happened unless they do and then make no criticisms of Sloan, or any of them."

"You are right," said Fidel. "I will do as you say. Thank you."

He shook hands with Lannon and went outside and over to where Lyra was sitting on the low harbour wall.

She looked round as he approached. "Did he ask you to agree with all the lies?" she asked.

Fidel nodded. "Yes, and I did."

She shook her head in anger. "Why did you not tell him what a fool the man Sloan was? Why did you not say how he was so stupid that he tried to fight the Run?"

He sat down beside her on the wall. "Listen," he said evenly, "and try to understand. We have to live on this island with these people. People that are so powerful they can do anything they like." He pointed out to sea. "You have been to the mainland; do you wish to live over there?"

She frowned at him. "I would never live there… you know that!" she said vehemently.

Fidel nodded. "Then listen to what I say," he said slowly, "when the man Sloan's boat went down, we saw the people with all the money and power frightened because they thought they were going to die.…"

Lyra broke in. "But we saved them…!"

"Yes, we saved them, and we saw them screaming with fear and they do not like to be seen like that." He shrugged. "It is not good for them to be known as other people. And there is one more thing. They all knew that I had told Sloan to stay out of the Run, and they thought it was a thing to laugh about." He watched as Lannon came out of the security block, got in his truck and drove off up to the high ground. "You heard him when I spoke to him on his phone, how he was then, speaking as if I were a fool from the island that knew nothing. And the people with him acted the same until they felt the Run."

"I still don't see why they could not tell the truth," she persisted.

"Because then Lannon would have a record for his people that told of Sloan's stupidity and his friends' fear… of how they all behaved like fools and almost died because of it. And how they were saved because two people from the island knew better than all the clever machines on a twelve million dollar boat."

Lyra was silent, staring at the water.

Fidel went on. "So, that is why the lies were written in the book—so that no one looks like a fool or a coward. And why we must not speak of what happened, unless they talk of it first." He looked into her face. "It's very simple. We don't ever let them see that we saw them afraid and stupid with fear. As long as they don't have to think too much about what happened out there," he gestured out to sea, "then they will have no reason to make us leave the island." He stood up, suddenly impatient of trying to explain. "Come on, let's go home," he said.

Lannon drove along the smooth tarmac road and thought about Fidel Bardi. It had been good that he had corroborated the smooth lies that had formed the basis of the inquiry into the American's death. Lannon knew that he could have made it acceptable without Bardi's testimony and signature, but the inclusion of a man that had been present at the tragedy; a man moreover that came from the island, and was aware of the treacherous water, added an authentic touch to the final report.

Lannon had wondered about Bardi from the first time he had appeared on the shore and asked to be given shelter. He had made some perfunctory enquiries as to why Bardi should be given special treatment, and why those orders came from the highest people in the company.

When he had come up against a wall of total silence concerning Bardi his professional curiosity had been awakened. Lannon had people in various places that were able to supply him with different aspects of Bardi's position in relation to the company. Gradually, Lannon had assembled all the bits he needed to realise why a man of the island—a man with only the most basic learning skills and no influence in the outside world, a nothing factor in the business of immense money—should be given a free home on the most exclusive place on earth to live.

When Lannon had looked at the picture when it was properly assembled it was so simple to understand. Bardi had literally given the island to the developers. He had used the islanders' inbred greed and stupidity, and turned it against them to such effect that their homes had been legally stolen from them. And, from a faint whisper from a source in the accounts section, Lannon had deduced that Bardi had not only been given a home on the island, but a very large sum of money as well.

None of this bothered the security chief at all. He saw nothing wrong in what Bardi had done. Not when you stacked it up against the savage deals that the rich grew fat from. Entire peoples made to live in poverty, struggling to exist on the starvation wages that forced them to strip continents of their natural wealth, so that the ones with the money could continue with their way of life. Lannon thought it was just how things were. You rose above the poor and suffering and you stayed above them.

The one thing about Bardi that had not settled easily in Lannon's mind was that it had been said that he had come back to the island to care for his ailing father. Lannon had started to wonder about this when he realised that Bardi had come back to the island a long time before the company had expressed an interest in the place. Nothing wrong with that. A man might return to tend to a sick parent. *But,* Lannon wondered, *would a man capable of lying to the total population of an island, and helping the company to steal their homes and the island from them, be the kind of man to look after a sick man, on a hellhole, set in the middle of nowhere?*

Lannon had served as a mercenary soldier before he joined the company, and he had no illusions about what his fellow man would do for money and power. He had been a capable soldier, one with a talent for intelligence work, as well as killing. The former talent had served him well in his service to the company. The killing aspect of his nature shaped the ruthless decisions that he sometimes made and saw carried out to the letter. He had risen to the top of his field in the company and, when the island project had been first mooted, his name had automatically been written in to guarantee the secrecy and security of the work.

So, the question mark that he had hung over Bardi had been one that he could not resolve without words from the outside world. Almost casually, when he had a moment away from the work—because it had no real bearing on any of the work involved in turning a scorching rock in the middle of the sea into a paradise, for the rich to take their leisure on—he would make enquiries to those on the mainland. People that would never know each other, and could only ever answer one question from Lannon, therefore never gaining the whole picture.

He had not hurried with it. In a way it was a small relaxation from the pressure of the island to add another fragment of Bardi to the body of the man that he was creating. And the informat ion was slow in coming because Lannon had learned early on that Bardi had no record; he was on no police files in any country.

Then, a contact in Athens sent word that Bardi had friends in the city that he sometimes stayed with. It was believed that he mixed with the rich people that came in on the big yachts and lived in fine hotels. Bardi, it appeared, would supply these people with certain services, ones that required discretion and a total lack of morals. Also, the contact said, in the course of these services, things of an expensive nature would go missing, and so would Bardi.

The trail that he left was often difficult to follow and Lannon would wait patiently for the next fragment to arrive. When it did he would simply write it in the slim notebook he had opened on Bardi.

Then, abruptly, the trail went cold in Crete. The notebook remained unopened for several weeks, until Lannon pulled it out of the drawer and read it through from the start. He was satisfied that, up to Crete, Bardi had been a small time thief, who also gave the wealthy any kind of pleasure they wanted. So why had he apparently stopped his way of life in Crete, and what had made him return to the island when he had all the mainland to plunder?"

He wrote down the approximate date that Bardi had arrived back, and then underlined it.

The following day he rang a woman in Athens, and asked her to try to obtain and send him copies of newspapers covering the period just before Bardi's return. In three weeks, a bulky parcel addressed to Lannon arrived on the store boat.

That evening he settled down in his quarters and unwrapped the parcel to find papers covering one month of news before the estimated time of Bardi's homecoming. Lannon put the papers on the floor, took the first by date, and spread it out on his desk. Pouring a large whisky, he settled down to read each column.

When he had started to read the front page of the seventh paper he stopped. There, in the centre was a report of a double killing. A man, known to the police as a thief, had been found in an alley beside the body of a local priest. Both had been stabbed. At first it had been thought that the priest had been killed by the thief, but no knife had been found at the scene of the killings.

There had been an uproar at the death of the priest and the police had made an intensive search of the area as soon as the bodies were discovered.

The local criminal element had been brought in but, despite the severity of the questioning, no arrests were made. The ferries had all been checked, but in the tourist season hundreds travelled daily, and it proved a fruitless task. Gradually, interest waned and the story moved to the inside pages, then to the back, and then finally disappeared.

Lannon read the reports through again, a total certainty settling in his mind as he did. *This* was what he had been looking for. This was why a man that had never bothered about his father since he left him many years ago had come back. The island had been the only refuge left for him; who would think to look here? Indeed, many people never knew of its existence.

He wrote down dates and times in the notebook. He knew he had no real legal proof that Bardi was a killer, only a string of incidents and happenings, but Lannon had lived in a world of such events, and had grown to understand that the truth often lay just out of reach of the legal system. But if you had a few hard facts, you could often peel away the layers of time and look at the reality.

He also knew that Bardi was afraid to leave the island and he thought he knew why. When the people had been forcibly moved from their homes there had been the incident with the man, Saur. Lannon had instructed three of his men to accompany the ferry taking the people to the mainland and find out about him. Knowledge of a potential troublemaker was essential.

From their report it seemed that Saur was a man with a reputation for violence, someone to be feared, and the security people that had been on shore at the time Saur had escaped from the two men, had said that he had looked insane with rage as he'd turned back to the island and screamed out Bardi's name.

Lannon remembered that Bardi had questioned him regarding the security of the island. He had asked if they kept watches throughout the whole day and he had seemed pleased at Lannon's answer that they did.

So, Lannon was certain that he had all that he would ever have regarding Fidel Bardi. He went over it carefully in his head, making a written account of it as he did.

Bardi had killed two men. This irritated Lannon slightly as he did not know why the killings had taken place. Then Bardi ran to hide, but where? The outcry at the murder of a priest would be so great that it would be almost impossible to find a safe place to vanish. *Almost, but not quite*, thought Lannon.

Bardi had come back to the prehistoric hellhole where he had been born, and that he had left as a young man, not to care for his father, but to escape a legal death. Then he had sold out the whole population to the developers.

Finally, when he had enough money to go anywhere in the world and be comfortable, he remained on the island, trapped here by the threat of a man who wanted to kill him if he set foot on the mainland.

There was the one overriding factor in all this. Lannon knew that Bardi could never be brought to justice because he knew how the island had been stolen from the people, that the developers had ruthlessly tricked them out of their homes and land, and Bardi knew the whole circumstances of how it had happened. If he were ever brought to trial for the killings, it was inevitable that it would all come out and the resulting scandal would ruin the developers; maybe even lead to prison sentences for them.

No, Bardi was safe. There was no way he could ever be linked with the murders. Lannon allowed his mind to take in a little more of the events that shaped the life of Bardi. Lyra, the woman that he lived with; it had been said she had been the innkeeper's wife until the accident that had plunged his mule cart over the cliff and killed him.

Lannon had looked at her and seen the truly astonishing beauty, her natural grace and power, and when he had seen the darkness that lived in Bardi, he knew that the man would have killed to have her.

Again, nothing could be proved, just a few facts and instincts to go on, but it was enough for Lannon.

He had instructed one of his most trusted men to take an extra careful look at the place where Bardi lived when he made his daily inspection of that part of the island. The man was to report immediately to Lannon if he noticed anything out of the ordinary; if the house was closed or Bardi's boat gone from its moorings.

Chapter Twenty-Eight

A week later the people that had almost died with Sloan arrived back from America. There they had stood in the driving rain in the small, beautifully tended private cemetery in Washington and watched the family as they walked up the steps of the huge marble mausoleum. They saw them file through the wrought iron gates, and into the family vault, where Sloan's ancestors lay. Those that had come to the country at the birth of the new century to wrest the immense fortune, then hand it over to Sloan's father, who enlarged it enormously before dying, and leaving it to Sloan.

His two sons, not long having graduated from business school with high honours, carried a gold cross inscribed with their father's name and date of birth and an inscription that read "He gave his life so that others might live."

The cross was placed on a black marble slab beside the tombs of the Sloan dynasty.

Jack Erin wept, but only out of relief that he had not followed the stupid sonofabitch to the bottom of the sea. Gina Sloan held the arm of Teddy, Sloan's brother, who had flown in from the Bahamas where he lived all the year round after having sold Sloan his share of the business fifteen years ago—when he realised that there would only ever be one voice that ran the company, and that it would not be his.

Teddy had asked Erin in private whether the damn fool had got himself killed because he was too damned stubborn to back off. Erin had stared at Teddy, and stumbled for an answer, whereupon Teddy had said he thought as much; his brother never could see any other point of view, but his own.

Elsa Schultz had told Ernst he should bring a legal action against Sloan's estate for the distress and danger that he had caused them for not listening to

Bardi, who repeatedly warned him not to go further into the dangerous water.

She said it was their right to do so, and that someone should be made to pay. Schultz had had looked aghast at her, and said that they were here to pay their respects to Sloan's memory and could she not see how his widow, Gina, was destroyed by grief at the loss of her husband?

Elsa's eyes had glittered and she had laughed shrilly at Schultz. Was he so blind, she asked, that he did not know that the grieving widow had a lover in her late husband's organisation, who would soon be consoling her. And when they returned to the island, she said, he was not to give the man, Bardi, any money because he had been right about the water being dangerous and had not let them die. She said the security launch would have picked them up, even without Bardi's ropes to hang onto.

Lannon had watched through his glasses as the helicopter circled the Schultz house, and had focused in on the face of Elsa, as the machine hung in the air over the launch pad. *Now they are all back,* he thought, *the rich are once again in residence on their billion dollar island.*

Chapter Twenty-Nine

Saur sat in among the rocks and wolfed down his food hungrily. As he ate he looked out at the dark sea and thought again how he would kill Fidel Bardi. It was something he never tired of doing, contemplating the taking of Bardi's life. From the time, exhausted and raving with anger, that he had brought the little boat through the heavy seas, and finally reached the shores of Southern Crete, his life had only one purpose… to kill Bardi. He had lain all night on the warm sand under the cover of darkness, and when the morning sun had touched his face, jolted awake, cursing the name of Bardi.

When he had looked for his boat it had gone, drifted away on the tide. He knew he could not go back to the island yet; the men that had rounded up the people and herded them down to the shore would be there now looking after the rich ones that had robbed them all of their homes. He would have to wait until they had forgotten him. Then he could return and kill the man, Bardi.

For a long time, through many days that turned into months, he had lived like an animal, always on the edge of starvation and continually moving through Crete, stealing vegetables from the fields and sleeping in the olive groves up on the hillsides.

Sometimes he would get a day's work, picking fruit under the sun, or cleaning the boats when they were brought out of the sea to repair, or the labouring work on the many new buildings under construction all over the island. Always he would be cheated, mainly because he could not speak the language of the people, and because he was too frightened to protest at his exploitation for fear the police would take him away and put him somewhere where he would never find Bardi.

It was only his obsession that drove him to survive any pain or discomfort. To know that somewhere, back on the island, the man that had looked into his eyes, smiled and lied to him, was still living. Saur had no pity for those that had lost their homes as he had. They had all trusted Bardi, and he had betrayed them and now they would curse his name, but Saur knew that he was the one that would take Bardi's life from him. It was the prayer of hate that took him into sleep every night, and that brought him back into each day. His family and their fate when they had been put off the ferry over on the mainland, or one of the islands, did not concern him. They could not be allowed to turn him from Bardi, so for him they did not exist.

Saur had almost ceased to be human, the frenzy that dominated his every waking moment, and beat relentlessly in his head, was dedicated to the execution of one man.

As the moon began to wane, Saur moved across the island heading south. He had to try to find in what direction from Crete the island lay, and thought he should start from where he had landed. He had never been away from his own land and it was sheer chance that had brought him to Crete. He could just as easily have missed it and been lost in the huge sea.

In five days he had crossed the spine of the island, sometimes walking, or riding in the back of trucks, with people that picked the fruit and lived where they worked. Saur never spoke to them when they picked him up, save to grunt his thanks and then sat hunched and silent. His filthy clothes, matted beard and crazed eyes did not encourage conversation and they left him alone, only speaking to indicate to him where he was to get off. When he finally stood on the south shore and looked out to sea he felt a great exultation sweep through him, like a cleansing wind. Now he was finally here. All he had to do was steal a boat, return to the island and find Fidel Bardi.

When he finished the food he stood up and walked slowly among the rocks, gradually moving down to where a few small boats were moored along the rough concrete jetty. He looked all round as he walked, sensing the air like an animal, alive to every sound. The thin moon cast a soft half light, and every few minutes the heavy clouds rolled across the sky plunging the land into darkness.

When Saur reached the boats he stopped. This was the place where he had first landed on Crete, and where his time of waiting had begun. He walked out to the end of the jetty, looking closely at the small craft. He knew he had come a long way from the island, farther than he had ever sailed before, and he had to be sure that he chose a boat that would take him back. He thought they might have men guarding the island, and that he would have to wait out at sea until nightfall before he tried to land. Even then it would not be easy; the rocks ringed the land all round the island and he might have to leave the boat and swim the last distance. And there was the Run to think on. If he could see the mountain he could keep out of the death that ran below.

As he walked back to the shore he saw that all the boats, bar one, had the engines that he did not understand. He had seen how the men gave them life with a cord that they pulled in a certain way, sometimes two or three times, cursing when the engine did not speak, then settling back in the seat as the phut phut sound drove the boat forward. Saur knew that they were not for him even if he made the engine work. Suppose he was out in the big sea and the engine fell silent, what would he do, just drift with the swell until he died? With a sail he would know the wind, and feel the water under the keel, and the boat would answer to his hands.

He walked back down the jetty to the boat with the sails, and sat down on the concrete, then stepped into the boat, taking care not make a sound. He put his big plastic water bottle under the seat and untied the mooring ropes, put his foot against the jetty wall and pushed off. The boat moved sideways, rocking gently as it slid out into the water. Saur rigged the sails, working swiftly, then sat back on the crude seat and held the tiller as the canvas filled and he began to move past the other boats and out into the sea.

For the first time since he had landed in this cursed place he felt strong, the wind against his face, the little boat picking up speed as it glided out into the open water.

Saur looked up at the stars and set his course to the east. There was no compass in the boat and he would not have known how to use one if there had been. Only a lifetime of living with the sea would be his strength now. He took a long drink from the bottle and settled back on the wooden seat, one arm draped over the tiller, his mind now free at last from the harsh existence of his time on Crete.

As he sailed on he thought of the prayers the island people would say as they went to the sea to search for fish; words, woven into incantations, that were almost songs, and that had come down through the years from the tongues of men long dead, who had known the same fear of the great waters. Saur had never believed in the words, he had seen too many taken down and lost to believe that anything said by men would stay fate's hand. But now, as the lights on the land of Crete slowly faded into the darkness, and he was suddenly alone in the huge dark world of water, he found himself trying to remember the pleas to the God of life.

Then, in a couple of hours, the wind died, and he began to drift, slowly at first, then almost stopping. A fear began to grow in him that he might never leave this sea, only lie out here in the vastness and wait to die. He got up and worked the sails and tried to close his mind to the stories that all sailors know well; of men becalmed in the great wastes of the sea, the sails desperate for a breath of the saving wind; the raging thirst, and the gradual descent into madness and death.

When he had struggled for an hour he realised it was no use; the sails hung lifeless and the boat refused to answer to the rudder. He sat down and looked all round into the darkness as the clouds rolled across the moon, taking the light with them. Saur held onto the tiller, his fear almost out of control, his lips mouthing half forgotten snatches of the ancient prayers for life.

Time moved as slowly as the sea, each minute an eternity to him, every second seeming to keep pace with the beat of his heart. He stared up at the sky that had darkened into a heavy mass; the thin moon obliterated now, the mass bearing down on him, almost threatening to crush the little craft where it lay helpless upon the sea. Slowly, he lay down in the bottom of the boat and closed his eyes, falling into a sleep that matched the ceaseless motion of the boat as it rocked gently to and fro, all the while never moving from that one place.

When he woke later nothing had changed. He struggled up, confused and afraid, and looked out at the sea that was so dark that it seemed part of the sky. It was as the world had died and he was the only living thing left. He lay down again and made himself think of Fidel Bardi. Where was Bardi, and what would he be doing now? Maybe he was eating a meal, or lying with the woman of Mora.

Saur knew that Bardi had killed Mora. He had thought about how Mora had died and it was clear to him what had happened. Bardi had wanted the woman and had killed to get her. The innkeeper had made the journey from the inn to the store down on the shore hundreds of times over the years; he would have known every rock and blade of rough grass in the track. The mules of the island were surefooted on the high ground. They would have never fallen over the edge of the cliff.

And there was something else that Saur had seen. The people had brought Mora up from the rocks and laid him in the inn and had left the smashed cart and the broken body of the mule where it had landed. Saur had gone among the rocks after everyone had left, and looked at the wreckage of the cart, and then the mule. The animal's spine had broken with the impact of the fall and the hind legs had been driven up, bursting the belly, spilling the contents of the stomach over the ground. Saur had finished looking and almost turned away when he had seen the two wounds in the animal's rump. Two small jagged rough holes about a hand span apart. He had looked closer and poked his finger as far as it would go into the wounds. Then he had known the truth. They were the same shape that Bardi's knife had made when he had stabbed the boy in the body, the same tearing of the flesh and torn skin on the withdrawal of the blade.

He thought how Bardi had ignored Lyra Mora when he was at the inn, almost as if he were oblivious to her, and he had wondered why, knowing that Bardi had no woman of his own. Now he knew. Bardi had been careful not to arouse suspicion by showing his want for her and had waited until he felt the time was right, then caught the innkeeper on the high ground and put him over the cliff.

Saur remembered how the islanders had praised Bardi when they thought they were going to be rich. They told him what a good friend he was to them, and the talk was all of what Bardi had done for his people. They had said that truly it was a great sorrow that his father, Frado Bardi, had died before he could see and enjoy the miracle his son had brought to them.

Saur sat up suddenly. Of course, the old man had died just before the Turk had come to take the pictures and collect the marks of the people that owned the houses. Fidel Bardi had no house. He was a man without property, so he could not share in the people's good fortune, and then his father had died just in time for the son to inherit the home.

Saur smiled grimly. That had been the way of it. Bardi must have killed the old man just in time. He remembered how the boy had acted when Bardi had put his father in the ground. That he had stood by the coffin and laid his hand on it and spoken to Bardi, and that he had seemed almost mad with something that only he could see; and that Bardi had raised his voice so that all might hear and said that the boy was a fool.

But now Saur thought of all the times the boy had known things that they could not see, and he had always been right, and that he had truly possessed the gift of sight. And he remembered what the boy had called Bardi just before they killed him… Abbadon. The man that had tried to teach them to worship someone called Jesus, who he said was a god to all the people on the earth, had also said there was another being called Abbadon, the Dark Angel, the destroyer of men.

Bardi had said it was just foolish talk, and that the people that spoke of it were often mad themselves. But Saur thought the boy had not been mad until Bardi came back to the island. It was then that he had begun to wander the high ground for days, refusing to share their homes or food, and with the terror in him for all to see.

Saur shook his head, raised up and spat into the darkness. He did not care what any of it meant; he was the one that would kill Bardi, that much he did know. He lay back, his mind turning over the things that he had thought of until he drifted into a fitful sleep; his body turning first one way, then the other, almost as if he were trying to force the boat through the water.

He slept all through the night and only woke when the heat of the sun was burning down on his face. He looked up at the sky, and winced as the glare struck his eyes, then he felt the little boat moving, turning and slewing round without guidance from sail or rudder. He stood up cursing his stiffness, and reached for the sail rope and the tiller. The boat steadied as he looked at the position of the sun, then chose his course.

He drank from the bottle and settled back on the seat, feeling the tug of the wind in the sails. There was no shade now for him, and the sky was on fire with heat so strong it made the air hot in his lungs. Saur did not care. He was moving again. The little boat rode the sea all through the long day, moving steadily under Saur's hands as he guided it by the set of the sun in the white sky.

As the hours passed and the sun began to fall slowly towards the sea, Saur ate the last of his food, bread, cheese and tomatoes, and drank the water. Soon the sky began to lose its light and he wondered how much further he had to go, and if he would find the island at all. The certainty that had sustained him for so long began to waver now. He knew that if he were lost out here he would never be found alive.

When the darkness came he sat rigidly at the tiller, eyes constantly searching the sky and checking the set of the stars. Through the long night he stayed in the one position, as if he were part of the boat itself. When the sun's first light appeared and spread its long line along the horizon, Saur relaxed and stretched his thin frame, grunting with fatigue and nervous exhaustion. He knew he would not have to endure another night. When he had left the island it had only taken a day and a night to reach Crete, though he had run before a strong wind then and that could have taken hours off the journey.

He picked up the bottle and looked at it; there were only two or three mouthfuls left now. He drank, careful not to spill a drop. The wind freshened and the little boat skimmed across the surface of the sea.

As he watched the birds wheeling and diving for fish, Saur thought how he would get onto the island. He wondered if there would be people guarding the rich ones, and tried to remember what had been said when the islanders had talked of the great change that would come to them. Amid the frenzy of babble at the inn he was sure that Bardi had said the new homes would be so fine that men would be paid to guard them. Did he mean only when they were being built, or would there always be men on the island caring for the safety of the rich? He decided that he must take no risks in landing. If he were seen, then his chances of finding Bardi were gone.

The sun moved to its highest point, and still Saur had not found land. It was as if the whole world had turned into this limitless sea. He felt a great anger blaze up in him. Surely he could not have endured so much, and come so far, to die out here alone; to fail after all this time, never to feel Bardi under his hands as he took the life from him.

He lurched up from the seat and looked out across the sea. "I am Saur!" he screamed wildly. "I cannot die!" He clutched the side of the boat. "I have come to find Fidel Bardi... he must be punished!" He lurched as the swell flung the boat down then cast it up. "I have to punish him!"

This time the boat rolled so strongly that it flung him backwards and he struck his head on the seat as he fell. He struggled up, cursing vilely, gripped the tiller and looked, stunned into silence, at the unmistakeable sight of the huge out flung arm of the mountain, shimmering through the heat haze on the horizon. He remained motionless, staring and struggling to think as the island began to take on shape and form. Then he rammed the tiller over and swung the boat round and back out to sea; before collapsing on the seat, clutching the side of the boat, still staring at the island, trying to accept that he had found it again.

Gradually, as the boat rolled gently across the sea he realised what he had to do. He must wait until nightfall, then get onto the island. If he went now they would see him and he would be taken.

Through the long hours Saur steered the boat back and forth, far enough out from the land to avoid being seen. He drank the last of the water and threw the bottle over the side.

When the darkness had almost taken the light from the sky, Saur turned and headed in. It was a risk he must take, to see the mountain and to know where the Run was. A mistake now would cost him his life. As he drew nearer to the huge bulk of the arm he felt the little boat begin to move faster and he knew it was not the sails pulling him to the land, he was at the edge of the Run.

Saur swung the tiller over and strained to hold it fast, as for one awful moment the boat resisted and he thought he was lost to the power in the water. Then the boat lurched forward, almost as if slipping free from some great force, and slid into calmer water. Saur, trembling, whispered thanks into the night sky and brought the boat round to face the land.

Now was the most terrifying part of the journey. He knew he could not put the boat on the island. Even if he got it in on the rocks it would be found the following day and they would know someone had landed. The boat had to be sunk far enough out to sea so that it would not be washed ashore, then he had to swim to the land.

He took the heavy broad-bladed knife from his belt and ran his hand over the decking, feeling for any hollow, or split in the timber. When his fingers felt a long shallow crack where the caulking had come loose, he looked under the seat to see if there was anything he could use as a hammer. Amongst the stinking rags and beer cans there was a short iron bar with a cloth wrapped round one end. Saur pulled it out and placed his knife blade in the crack and struck it with the bar. He looked back to the island in alarm at the noise the blow made, then rolled a piece of the rag over the handle of his knife to muffle the sound. He set himself firmly on the deck and began hammering at the knife, driving it deeper into the wood.

After a while he saw water pooling up round the blade and he worked faster, enlarging the hole. When the water began to enter the boat in a steady stream, Saur sat back, struggling to control his fear. It was done now, he told himself, *you must go on.* The water was around his feet now; the boat felt heavy, and when he tried to bring it round it would not respond to the tiller. Saur put his knife back in his belt, ramming it down tight, and swung his legs over the side, sitting there for a moment to try to see the island. Then he looked down at the deck. The water was rushing in and the boat began to sit lower in the sea. Saur waited, wanting to be sure that it would sink and not just drift in to the land.

Suddenly, it tilted and Saur pitched forward into the sea. He went down under the water, then kicked frantically to the surface, crying out in terror. He glimpsed the boat as it keeled over; the sails flat on the surface, then dipping under. Saur struck out away from it, before it could pull him down as well. He shook his head to clear his eyes and settled into a long powerful stroke that eased him through the water.

As he swam he repeated the name of Bardi over and over in his head. He swam on and on for a long time, before he began to be very afraid. He wondered if he had missed the island and was just swimming out to sea to drown when he became too tired to go on.

The water was so cold now, it was becoming harder to move his arms and legs, and he was tired, more tired than he could ever remember. He thought it would be so easy to just let go and sink under the water, to end his great struggle to find Fidel Bardi.

The face of Bardi flashed before him, smiling that tooth-glistening smile that had fooled the islanders and that Saur had always hated. He felt the anger pour through him like a flame that purged the tiredness from his body and he struck out strongly, swimming now with a kind of rhythmical frenzy. He would find Bardi; it was his right; nothing could deny him that, not the sea, or the men on the island that were there to keep him out.

He raged, as he swam, to think that the place where he, and his people and their people, further back than memory could span, was now closed to him; because one man, who was not even a real islander because he had left long ago, had destroyed them all with his lying tongue—which Saur vowed to cut from his mouth.

Suddenly, the sound of waves breaking on rocks drew Saur's head up from the water and he saw the huge bulk of land before him. It was the island. He had done it; the relief flooded through him and he stopped and trod water, trying to get his bearings and to see where he could go in. There was no mountain here and he knew he was safe from the Run. He lay out, spread eagled on the water, tired now, the enormous fatigue trying to pull him down. He struggled forward and felt the wave begin to carry him in. As he worked his arms and legs he looked at the rocks as the water pushed him in to them. The sea was too strong now for him to do anything but go with it and suddenly, terrifyingly, the rocks were rushing towards him.

Saur felt himself flung into the air as the wave carrying him smashed into the jagged shoreline, hurling him bodily with a sickening crash against the rocks.

He fell back down into the sea, stunned and choking, and then worked his arms frantically to stay afloat as the next wave picked him up, and, holding him at the very tip of the mass of water, slung him as if he were ejected from a slingshot, higher up the rock face this time.

Saur hit the rock and clung to it desperately, digging his fingers hard into the slimy surface and willing himself not to fall. The next wave broke over him and he reached up for a fresh hold, then another, forcing himself on and up, until he was almost at the top. He hung on for a moment, then eased himself over. He fell all the way down into the jumble of smaller rocks, with their pools of seawater that stretched on up to where the scrubby tree line began. Saur lay, spent, then got to his knees, hunched over and vomited. When he finished he stood up, clutching the rocks for support and looked up to the high ground, trying vainly to see where he had landed, but unable to in the darkness.

Finally, he moved higher and found a gap in the rocks that would hide him and crawled into it, flattening himself against the smooth stones to try to draw some of the sun's heat from them.

He slept the sleep of total exhaustion, not waking until first light and the sound of the birds overhead searching the shoreline for food roused him.

He stretched, feeling the protesting muscles and joints reluctantly returning to life, then very slowly inched his way to the edge of the rock and looked out. He knew immediately where he was. When he had sunk the little boat and struck out for the shore he had drifted away from his first sight of the island and landed almost at the most narrow point of the land. Now he had to find Fidel Bardi and he had no idea where to look.

But first, if those men that were paid to look after the rich were on the island, then he must remain hidden from them. Saur knew every stone and tree and could move under the cover of darkness as well as a man might move in daylight; but he had to get food and drink and soon. The journey, and his time on Crete, were taking their toll on him, and he wondered if it would be wise to steal food and lie hidden somewhere until his strength returned.

The sun was climbing in the sky and he could feel the heat warming his body and taking the chill from him. He felt desperately hungry and wondered if he could catch one of the seabirds that waddled among the rocks, looking in the pools for trapped fish.

Now that he was finally here the reality of his situation struck into Saur. He had no idea where Bardi was, or even if he were here at all. For the very first time, Saur began to see that taking Bardi's life would not be as simple as he had thought.

He looked all round to see that there was no one near, and then began walking up through the trees, moving in short stretches, pausing at every third or fourth tree and checking the landscape again. He was almost at the top of the high ground when he tripped over a root and sprawled full length on the ground.

Cursing, he began to rise when the sound of voices made him flatten out on the dusty soil. Two men, dressed in the dark green shirt and pants that Saur remembered from the day of the island clearing, were walking on the track just below him. He forced his body harder into the earth, scarcely breathing, and watched as they passed, noticing that they looked all round as they walked, really checking the area.

When they had gone he sat up and looked up at the sky. *They are here just after the land begins to feel the sun.* He thought it was good to know the time that the men walked the path. Slowly, he moved up and over the high ground, going down through the scrub and towards the village. He crossed over a track that was wide and black and very smooth, like the ones he had seen on Crete that the machines with people in them moved along. He wondered why there were no goats or mules feeding on the land, and wondered if the rich people had put them off the island.

Now the sun was starting to burn down on him and he knew he had to find water; he wondered if he could get to the well without being seen. There was a noise now that he couldn't recognise; a dull pounding sound that grew louder as he got closer to the village. Then he scrambled awkwardly up the ridge just before the track to the village and stopped in shocked confusion, staring in amazement.

The village had gone. All the little houses with the stone roofs and walls, that had clustered together in a sprawling mass, and clung on the steep side of the hill that rose up from the harbour, with the thin tracing of the track that he had walked up thousands of times from the shore, weary after the work was done, were gone.

Saur lay in the scrubby grass and shaded his eyes from the glare of the sun, trying to find something of his life down there that he could recognise. There were three houses, set well apart from each other, unlike any he had seen on Crete. They were made of white and pink marble that gleamed in the morning light, with ground all round them, set with trees and flowers and winding paths to link the houses to the gardens. He could see water glinting from the big pools in the gardens, and chairs and tables set outside. There were iron gates at the end of the smooth tracks that led to the buildings, and way up behind each house was a big round concrete slab that he did not understand.

He looked down to the shore where the little boats had always been beached. Now there was a big clearing and a wall had been built, and the sea was held inside the wall; and there were boats like the ones he had seen on Crete, only bigger; and there was a concrete path out into the sea to get to the boats. Otem's store had gone, and a big square building with flat metal dishes fastened to metal poles on the roof stood in its place. Saur could see men moving in the building and he flattened closer to the earth. The noise he had heard was the sound of pilings being driven into the rock down in the harbour.

Slowly, he eased back through the grass and down the ridge, then moved up to the high ground again. He felt safer up here. He could see all around him and, if he were careful, he thought he would remain unseen. He moved bent over, almost hugging the ground and looking for the squat cacti that grew out of the black soil. When he found a clump of them he drew the big knife, dug up three and put them inside his shirt.

As the sun rose higher he looked for shade and found it in a patch of scrub that he crawled right into, and then pulled the tough thin branches down almost to the ground to hide him.

He took the cacti out of his shirt and chopped off the long edible root, and scraped off the hard skin, exposing the soft pulpy flesh. He took a bite, wincing at the bitter taste, and chewed it slowly before swallowing it. It would provide him with food and drink until he could find water. He ate all three and lay stretched out on the ground, listening and trying to think what to do. It had been dark when he came ashore, and he had no idea how many more of these big houses there were or how many men would be walking the island looking after the houses of the rich. Truly, now, he realised that he no longer had any place that he could call his home. The island that his people had known since further back than memory could see was gone. He cursed Fidel Bardi silently and viciously for what he had done.

Chapter Thirty

Lannon had taken the call from the men on the south shore at ten-thirty in the morning. They reported finding a broken mast with a scrap of sail hanging from it wedged between the rocks. He told them to stay with it until he arrived. As he drove he wondered if it would be the usual remnant of a wreck that ended up on a shoreline somewhere in the world. When he rounded the bend in the road, he saw the two men standing by the jagged rocks that faced out to sea like broken teeth.

He climbed out of the vehicle and returned their salute. "Have you touched anything?" he asked.

They shook their heads. "No, Chief," said the taller one. "It is as you see it."

Lannon walked down to the rocks and looked at the wreckage. He noticed instantly that where the mast had snapped the break was fresh and the sail cloth was dirty, but not faded by prolonged exposure to seawater. He turned to them.

"You both did this patrol yesterday?" he asked. They nodded.

He took out his notebook and checked the names of the men that had the night watch on this stretch. He would question them later, but it seemed certain that the wreckage had come in during the night.

"All right, leave this where it is." He looked up at the high ground. "Listen," he said, "be extra careful in your work. Look for any signs that there is anyone on the island that has no right to be here." He spread the fingers on one hand and tapped them as he spoke. "Look for food on the ground… discarded clothing… broken branches on trees that indicate someone might have passed that way; the remnants of a fire, though I don't think that's likely… human shit… anything." He looked at their suddenly attentive faces and raised his hand. "Make your reports with extra care; overlook nothing," he said, warningly. Then he paused, and gestured at the wreckage. "This is probably nothing, but until I am sure then you do as I say."

Lannon drove along the high ground road until he came to the harbour, and then pulled in to the side and sat, looking out over the sea, thinking of what he had just seen at the rocks. The wreckage was fresh. He had seen enough timber taken from the sea to know that the mast had only just been broken. What would a small boat have been doing so close to a private island at night? No one but a fool would sail those waters in darkness. *Or a madman*, he thought grimly, remembering what Fidel Bardi had said about the man, Saur, "He has great strength, and the face of a man born for anger."

When he had first come to the island, Lannon had walked the patrol routes himself, so that he would know exactly what his men had to contend with. He had seen the great sea in the darkness, and now he wondered what kind of a man would try to bring a small boat into the rocks at night. His mind clicked a fact into place… if it were, then he would know the island was guarded and that he could never land without being detected. So, had he sunk the boat at sea, then swum in? Lannon had a mental picture of a man deliberately sinking a boat in the darkness; then plunging into the water, and swimming through the sea for the shore. He shook his head—that would be insane, yet the vision would not go away. If it were true, then they had a madman on the island.

He thought how carefully the recent tragedy had been handled. If Saur was among them now then he had to be caught and quickly before the rich ones found out about it. Lannon did not care if Saur killed Fidel Bardi, or if they killed each other. The bodies could always be disposed of if they were found in time. The problem was to keep it quiet. A murder would almost certainly bring someone from the Greek or Turkish side over to the island. Although neither had legal jurisdiction, the whole business would be out in the open with all the resulting publicity. *Just*, he thought grimly, *what the developers pay me to keep from happening.*

He unhooked the phone from the dashboard and rang the men that had been on patrol last night. He spoke to them both and they said that they had seen nor heard anything unusual, and that their reports were in his office. He hung up and lit a cigarette and thought over the events of the last hour.

He did not doubt the men's word. They were both good handpicked operatives; if there had been a boat coming in they would have seen it. *No*, he thought, *either it was nothing, or it was something very serious.*

He drove up to the security block, parked the vehicle and went up to his office. From a cabinet he took a sheet of blank paper, sat at his desk and drew as near a likeness as he could remember of what Fidel Bardi had told him of Saur's image. When he finished he looked at the unshaven, frowning, tight-eyed face staring back up at him.

He put it through the copier machine and printed copies for the men that patrolled the island. At least they would have some idea of whom they were looking for. He wondered whether to issue side arms to them, then thought it best to wait until firm proof was shown that someone was on the island. He went downstairs and left the drawings in the front office, with instructions to hand them out to the patrols when they signed in for duty.

Chapter Thirty-One

Saur moved carefully through the scrub, heading for the mountain at the end of the island. It was the only place he could think of to hide from the patrolling men. However careful he was, he knew it would only be a question of time before they saw him if he kept moving about. The arm of the mountain was the one place where he thought they would not patrol. They would have no reason to climb up the rocky slope, and then struggle the rest of the way to stand at the tip, and look down at the hell of the Run.

He dug more of the cacti out of the ground as he went, keeping them for later when he found a place to stop.

The sun climbed to its highest point, blazing into Saur as he walked, half bent over, almost hugging the ground. Finally he came to the foot of the mountain and looked up at the huge arm that soared out over the sheer drop.

In his lifetime he had seen two men beaten with clubs until their bones were broken, then hurled down from the arm into the boiling mass of sea that smashed into the rocks. The men had raped a woman whose man had died at sea. When they had finished with her, they had fled to the high ground, desperate to evade the retribution they knew would follow.

Saur had joined in the hunt with the men of the island, combing through scrub country as others searched the shore. The two had been found trying to launch a wrecked boat that had drifted in among the rocks. They had been taken back to the village and made to face the woman as the islanders watched. When she accused them, they denied her and said she had invited them in to her home, then forced herself on them.

One of the elder people had stepped forward, taken hold of the woman's head, and lifted the heavy mass of black hair, revealing the purple bruise under her ear. "How," he had asked, "had she come by this?"

The men had fallen silent; then one had dropped to his knees and cried out that the older man had made him do it; he had not wanted to harm her, but once they had started he could not stop. There was a short silence, then the elder had stepped back and said to take them to the high place. The men had screamed out at this and struggled madly as the woman's relatives dragged them along the track, beating them with clubs about the head and body as they went. When they fell down they were dragged along the ground, still being beaten, all the way to the tip of the arm. There, bloodied and broken, screaming and babbling with terror, they were picked up and slung out over the edge and down into the death that waited below.

Saur climbed into the uplands of the mountain, looking for a place to hide, anywhere away from the guards, somewhere to rest until he found Fidel Bardi. And if he did not find him right away; then a place to return to. Finally, he stood almost at the tip of the arm, listening to the thunder of sound that came from the sea. He chose a huge rock, embedded in the earth, shaped in a half circle that faced the tip and could not be seen from the rest of the island. He crouched behind it and dug a long shallow trench in the black soil, just wide and low enough for him to lie in, throwing the earth as he dug over the edge of the mountain.

When he was done he moved out from behind the rock, very slowly and almost crawling on all fours, gathering strands of the coarse grass that clung to the soil. He did this until he had enough to cover him when he lay in the trench. He thought if the men came this high, then he would be hidden from them if they did not come right to the tip. Exhausted, he lay back against the rock and rested, dozing fitfully.

Suddenly, the touch of something on his arm exploded him into consciousness, and he stumbled forward, falling onto the body of a large black dog that had nuzzled his arm. The dog leapt away, startled, and sank to the ground, whining and wagging its tail. Saur stared at it, confused for a few seconds, then gathered his senses. He had seen dogs like this on Crete, animals that people fed and kept in their homes. Unlike the animals that had lived on the island and that had scavenged for every scrap to stay alive, sometimes even killing each other for food.

This was a plump animal with alert eyes and a shining coat. There was a leather collar round its neck, inlaid with a brass design and a small plate with a sign on it that Saur could not read. The dog whined again and scratched the ground with its paw. As he looked at it he realised that it must belong to one of the rich people, and must have somehow got loose and wandered all the way to the end of the island, up onto the mountain.

Very slowly he drew the heavy-bladed knife from his belt and got to his knees, talking softly to the dog all the time. He wondered if anyone was on the mountain at this moment looking for the dog, but knew that was a risk he had to take. He extended his hand, still crooning, and the dog crept forward, its tail wagging furiously now. When it was close enough he stroked its head and neck as it wriggled delightedly and pressed its wriggling body against his chest, reaching up to lick his face. Saur slid his hand under its front legs and rubbed its belly, then in one movement reached up and clamped his hand over the dog's jaws, crushing them tight together, then slammed the knife into its throat, tearing and slicing the flesh as the dog struggled frantically in his grip.

Saur held it away from him as the blood gushed out and seeped into the earth, and the animal jerked spasmodically for a few moments before hanging lifeless in his hand.

Saur shook it twice, then let it fall to the ground. He watched as the body twitched for a few moments, then lay quite still. He crawled to the edge of the rock and peered round. The island lay before him, gasping in the merciless heat, and there was no one to be seen. He went back to the dog, picked it up and working swiftly, skinned it and threw the coat and the severed head over the edge. Then he stripped the still warm flesh from the carcass and ate some of it.

Saur had eaten enough raw fish when he had been out on the sea catching them not to have any qualms about eating a dog. Flesh was food, and that flesh was life, and he had to have strength to find and kill Fidel Bardi. He sucked the blood out of the flesh and swallowed that as well. Nothing could be wasted.

When he had finished he wrapped the remaining flesh in a few handfuls of scrubby grass and put it in a corner of the trench. He threw the bones over the edge, wiped the blood from his mouth and sat back against the rock to wait until nightfall when he could continue his search for Fidel Bardi.

Chapter Thirty-Two

When one of the shore patrols rang in and said they had just found what looked like human excrement under trees, just up from where the wreckage of the mast and sail had been discovered, Lannon knew he had been right. It had to be Saur. Anyone involved in a genuine sinking would have contacted someone for help as soon as they got ashore.

Lannon had no choice now. He woke the sleeping night patrols and told them to report to his office right away. He unlocked the steel gun-cupboard on the wall of his office and drew the sets of automatic pistols, fitted them with silencers and laid them on his desk with the clips of shells beside them. When the men arrived he told them that evidence had been discovered that showed that the man they had thought might be on the island was in fact here now. If he were seen he was to be apprehended.

Lannon said he thought the man was probably armed with a knife, but they were to take no chances with him; he was known to be dangerous. Any contact with him that resulted in his being wounded, or killed, was to be handled with the utmost secrecy. Lannon was to be informed directly the man was seen. The owners of the homes were not to know of the situation at all. If the man was seen in the vicinity of a home, the men were to simply observe him. Lastly, all the weapons would be worn in the shoulder holsters provided, with shirts over the top to hide them. He did not want to have to answer questions from anyone as to why his men were armed.

He wondered whether to tell Fidel Bardi that it was almost certain that Saur was on the island, then decided against it. He would leave it for a couple of days. There was a chance that if the man found Bardi one of them would kill the other, even that both of them might die. Lannon thought that would be the best thing that could happen. If the deaths were unseen by anyone other than his men, he could have the bodies put into the Run and lost forever.

Later that night, just before he went off his shift and back to his small apartment at the rear of the security block, Lannon sat at his desk and looked out of his window at the island. There were the huge lights suspended high in the air over the sites where the men worked through the night; the heavy machines crawling over the earth, the constant development of each section of the work. It was a thing he had seen many times over the years of his employment with the company. But never, he thought, quite like the circumstances that had sprung up on this rock.

He smiled coldly to himself at the thought of the wealthy in their island paradise, surrounded by the latest and most sophisticated surveillance that money could buy. And totally unaware that a madman had sailed a boat from God knows where, and sunk it at night, and then swum to the island undetected; and was even now probably roaming the darkness looking for Fidel Bardi, the man that had been responsible for the sale of the island, in order to kill him.

He thought he might take a motor and drive all round the island before he went off duty. He was confident in his men; they were capable operatives, but the man, Saur, had to be something special to have come back against all the odds, and he had one advantage over them. He knew the island in a way that they never would, and Lannon was sure that Saur could easily evade them at night. The one thing that would slow him was that he didn't know where Bardi was living, although it wouldn't take him long to realise that Bardi would not be among the luxury homes; that he would be somewhere off on his own. That would still leave a very big area for him to search, and if he only looked at night then it could be a long process.

He suddenly stopped and slapped his hand sharply on the table. Saur had been born on the island, he would know about every dwelling and Bardi's house had belonged to the mother of Lyra Mora, the wife of the innkeeper. Then the innkeeper had met with an accident, Lannon smiled bleakly, and now she was living there with Bardi. Maybe this business might be over sooner than he had anticipated.

He opened his desk drawer and took out an automatic pistol, fitted the silencer, closed the drawer and went downstairs. He took the keys to one of the vehicles, signed for it and told the man at the intercom what route he would be on, and that he was to be told immediately if the man were sighted.

As he drove along the high ground he looked out at the huge sea, and shook his head at the insane hatred that had driven Saur to pit his life against such terrible odds to get to a man to kill him. In the past Lannon had killed for money; that he could understand, if you had to have reason for killing, that at least made sense to him and you were always acting under the instructions of superior officers in some foreign army. But this—to almost certainly throw away his life? Because once he had killed Bardi there would be no way off the island for him, no small boat to take him out to the open sea and freedom. Lannon had issued orders that all motor launches were to be locked to the jetty with heavy duty steel cable and a two-man guard posted within sight of them.

He knew Saur would never touch one of the big yachts; they would be a mystery to him. Also, Lannon realised grimly, Saur probably wouldn't care what happened to him after he killed Bardi, and might just go on a slaughtering rampage.

He suddenly thought they had better find Saur quickly. He came to the end of the island and stopped the motor. He took a torch from the dash, got out and picked his way carefully over the stony ground till he came to the edge of the cliff. He shone the torch and looked over at the spray rising up from the sea as it smashed in on the rocks far below.

Lannon had never been right at the place where the mountain and the sea created the Run and now, standing alone in the darkness, feeling the impact vibrating up through the earth, he remembered Fidel Bardi's words; that no boat could withstand its power. He thought, coldly, that John Sloan should have come and stood here before he went on his voyage of discovery.

He shone the torch all round the area, then up at the out flung arm of the mountain, its immense bulk standing stark against the night sky. He shivered in spite of the thick heat, and thought what an awful place this was.

Saur lay motionless behind the rock, his hand clasped round the broad-bladed knife, listening to the sound of someone struggling through the scrub, coming closer to the top of the arm of the mountain. He gathered his feet under him in readiness to spring out at whoever was approaching. Then he heard a curse and the sound of someone falling to the ground. The light from the torch went out and Saur heard someone groping around on the ground. After a moment the light came back on, and the footsteps sounded fainter as they retreated back down the mountain.

Lannon climbed back in the motor and sat rubbing his shin for a while, then drove all the way round the other side of the isl and, criss-crossing some of the roads into the remote areas twice to check that the patrols were alert.

When he arrived back at the security block he was sure that all that could be done to find Saur was being done, but he still knew that the chances of catching him were remote. He wondered if something would happen to break the situation.

Sometimes, over the years when he had faced a crisis in his work, it had only taken the smallest incident to jolt the action. Though, as he considered the facts: that a madman that would have no trouble evading his men was probably moving right now in the darkness, maybe only a short distance from the patrols, yet easily able to pass them unseen; he did not see what could possibly happen to trigger this into a situation where they might take Saur.

He made one last call on the hand phones to all the men in the field, then went below to his quarters and turned in. He had done all that he could. Now it was up to the patrols.

Chapter Thirty-Three

Saur sat against the rock and looked up at the heavy clouds moving across the face of the moon. He nodded to himself; the night was good to him, just enough light to let him move over the ground and deep shadow to hide him. He stood up, leaning against the rock, wincing at the pain in his back and legs. He had lain in the trench all through the heat of the sun, and there had been no shade that high up on the mountain until the fireball had dropped almost over the other side of the island.

He moved to the edge of the rock and peered round it. Far below he could see the lights bobbing in the darkness, always two lights together, and he knew they were carried by the men who would be looking for him now. Saur had realised that the boat would probably come in on the rocks and be caught fast there; the sea was too strong for it to drift out and, once ashore, it would be seen by the men. He stepped out, bent over, from the shadow of the rock and began a crouching run down through the scrub.

When he reached the little straggle of trees he stopped and crouched down among them, straining his ears to listen for the men. He made himself concentrate on Fidel Bardi, trying to imagine where he lived now. He did not think he would be living among the rich ones that had bought the island. They would not want Bardi beside them. So where would that leave him?

Saur knew the island as well as any of his people; all the high places and the rock-toothed shoreline. He shook his head and cursed Bardi silently. Ever since he had come back to the island the gods had smiled on him. First he had won the people's trust with his smiling lies, then sold their homes out from under them; and Saur knew that the ones that had bought the island had made Bardi a rich man.

And then the innkeeper had died when his mule had run amok, and bolted over the cliff—*With the help of Bardi's blade in its rump*, he thought. Then there had been the whisper that the woman of the dead Mora had been seen at night with Bardi. No one dared speak openly of it—after all it was known that Lyra Mora had a way with her that did not allow any kind of rebuke in any form. And it was true that now, as she was no longer the wife of Mora, she was free to do as she chose.

Saur began to move through the scrub again when he stopped and sank to the ground. His mind closed on one single thought; Lyra Mora and her mother, the old woman who was thought to be mad and who lived over on the far side of the island in a ruin of a dwelling. And that, he thought with a growing certainty, was where Bardi could be right now.

He calculated the time it would take him to move across the island to the hovel by the sea. The journey would have to made under the cover of darkness, evading those who would be searching for him, and that would make him slower. There would be no trench up behind the high rock to lie up in during the day. He would have to hide wherever he could and there would be very little food or water that he could safely get. Maybe none at all. Water would be his main worry, the heat of the sun always carried over into the night, making the air hot and heavy with almost no respite from the day.

He pushed everything from his mind and thought only of the moment when he would find Bardi and take the smile from his face forever. He went back up the mountain and picked up the bundle of coarse grass containing the flesh of the dog and put it into his shirt. He checked the land below the mountain again, then moved out as the clouds took the light from the sky, travelling west, keeping just below the spine of the high ground. Several times he saw the handlights of the patrolling men, but he always found cover and remained motionless until they passed.

When the first fire of the sun arced into the sky Saur looked for a place to hide. At the bottom of a dried water gulley the earth had formed a deep depression almost hidden from the path. Saur tore some grass from the earth and curled up in the ground, spreading the grass over himself. Through the long scorching day Saur lay fighting the thirst that raged through his body, almost driving him mad.

He heard the patrols very close sometimes and he forced his body deeper into the ground as they moved high above him. Sometimes they would be talking, but he did not know enough of their language to understand what they said. One thing he did know, they were not careless people. They really walked all the tracks and paths, constantly checking behind them and to the sides of the tracks. Saur thought if he made one mistake they would have him.

When night finally came he rolled groaning softly out of the hole, and tried to straighten his body. Finally, he moved up to the high ground and looked for the lights of the patrols. He took his bearings from the stars and made his way down to the middle ground. Saur had noticed that the men always seemed to be more regular on the high ground and down by the seashore. He thought if that were true then he would have a better chance to avoid them by keeping to the ground in between, also, the deep shadow favoured this part of the island.

Saur knew that he had to find water. The roots that he dug up and sucked were not enough to sustain him. He tried desperately to remember where there was water on the island. When the goats had wandered free they had always found drink, but Saur had seen neither goat nor mule since his arrival. When, at the end of the second night, almost crazed with thirst, he had almost fallen into a stagnant pool, he had laid head and shoulders in the foul water drinking frantically.

Finally, he fell back and lay, chest heaving, looking up at the heavy clouds that hardly moved in the huge sky. Suddenly, the images of his children seared into his mind and he turned over on his face and wept bitter tears into the earth. Then as quick as they had come they were gone, and the face of Fidel Bardi looked back at him, smiling the tooth-glistening smile. Saur snarled deep in his throat and beat his clenched fists on the ground.

He waited all through the day by the little pool, forcing his body half under a small mass of rocks and willing himself to remain still, despite the pains in his body, as the patrols moved past him. Then, at then end of the third night, exhausted, and frantic with the voices in his head, he found the house by the sea. He staggered up the rise in the ground, stopped and sank to his knees. He stared at the building that at first he could not recognise as the old woman's house, which he remembered from so long ago; where he had seen the woman of Mora naked among the rocks.

He lay still for a while, then as the sun began to climb out of the sea, he knew the men would soon be walking this way and that he must hide. He looked around quickly and saw there was no cover here at all. He had to get high up among the rock face where he could look down on the house, and watch to see if Bardi were really here.

Spurred on by the fear of discovery he turned and went back down the rise and moved off to the left, always keeping below the ridge.

When he came to where the rocks formed a wall against the sea, he climbed up among them and settled into an angled fissure. This not only concealed him from the land if he laid back from it, but gave him a clear view of the house and the track to it from the high ground.

He eased his body into the opening and settled down to wait. He saw how the track approached the house up a small rise in the ground so that anyone coming from the road would not see the house until they had cleared the ridge.

He thought that was good in case he had to act quickly out in the open, at least he would have a chance to escape unseen. Then he slumped back into the fissure, as he realised that he would never leave the island once he had killed Bardi.

All the boats he had seen here were either huge like those in Crete or the small ones with the noise that moved them through the water. Saur was sure that he would never find a boat with sail that he could handle and, even if he did, once Bardi was dead the hunt for him would be so intense that there would be no time to search for a craft.

He wondered about the woman, Lyra Mora. Would she be with Bardi now, out here in the house? And would he have to kill her as well? He remembered the time, so long ago, when she had been naked in the sea, her body wetly gleaming and the want of her choking him. Even now, when he knew she must be with Bardi, he was not sure how he would deal with her.

He lay back, cradling his body into the fissure and drifted into a trance-like sleep. It was only when he heard voices that he jerked back to consciousness, and then froze as he recognised the sound of Fidel Bardi. He inclined his head ever so slowly forward and looked out to see the figure of the man he hated walking down on the seashore, talking with Lyra Mora.

Saur felt the flame of hate burn through him as he watched Bardi. He fought the savage impulse to leap from the rocks and slaughter him there and then. As he struggled with his rage he knew that now was not the time for the killing to happen. He must be sure that there were no patrols close by. Then, he would have a tiny chance to get away before the body of Bardi was found.

He watched, unable to turn away from the man that he had hunted for so long, as the couple walked slowly along the shore, pausing and talking, then moving on. Saur watched intently, noting every footstep, burning it all into his mind, feeling the need to know everything he could about the man he would kill. To know him so well that he would practically own him before he stopped his lying mouth and easy smile.

Saur watched the two men standing on the high ground above the house. He had watched them for hours until he was sure they had been put there for a purpose, to watch over Fidel Bardi. As the sun slowly scorched the land Saur remained still, enduring the heat and totally focused on the little house by the sea. He saw two more men, dressed like the others, arrive as the sun blazed at the top of the sky. The first men spoke to them briefly, then left.

It was then that Saur realised that it was not going to be easy to kill Bardi. The men changed with their replacements every few hours and checked the area, looking all round the beach, then up on the high ground. Several times they came to the cliff edge and looked over. Saur had shrunk back into the fissure and hardly breathed as he listened to them talking. When night finally came, he climbed down from the fissure and half fell into the rocks at the sea edge. He ate the last of the dog meat and then sat for a while wondering what to do.

He knew he would never get to Bardi here. The men on guard were too alert to miss any attempt to get into the house. Saur thought he would have to move away from the house and try to take Bardi somewhere else, and it would have to be quickly because he had no food and there would be little chance of getting any more.

He looked at the truck standing by the house, and wondered if Bardi used it to go over to the other side of the island to collect his food from the buildings by the harbour. If he could find a way to stop the truck when Bardi was in it he would have him. *Where to do it?*

He moved slowly out of the rocks and began to climb up the rock face. Once at the top he lay still for a while, looking all round him. As he watched he saw the lights bobbing in the hands of the patrols. He waited till the clouds hid the moon, then crawled over the ground and into the scrubby trees. Then he moved keeping parallel to the road and looking for a place where he could stop the truck of Bardi. When he came to a bend in the road that twisted down, then went on up an incline; he knew this could be the place. Bardi would have to slow the machine here and that would give him the chance to attack.

All he could do now was hide and wait. As he looked for a place of concealment he saw a big twisted dead branch on the ground under the trees. He picked it up and laid it by the edge of the roadside. Then he went back and struggled into the thick scrub, positioning himself so that he could watch the road from the direction that Bardi would have to take from his house.

He never slept properly, only drifting into a state of semi-consciousness, then jolting back out as the lights from the patrols swept across the ground, freezing him into immobility. Twice he heard the sound of an engine and lifted his head to see the big machine of the man that had come to the end of the island and that had fallen in the darkness.

Saur had watched as the red lights on the back of the machine flared as the man slowed. Saur thought that was good because Bardi would have to do the same. The cold rage filled him at the thought of Bardi in his hands and drove all the hunger and thirst out of him.

When the night finally died as the sun began its relentless attack on the land he stretched out on the ground, flexing every muscle in his body in anticipation of what was to come. He waited through the heat of the morning. Several times trucks came along the road and Saur watched as they all slowed at the same place. He nodded over and over to himself at the thought that this was the chosen place where Fidel Bardi would meet the vengeance he so richly deserved, and that only Saur had been chosen to carry out.

He had been in the scrub almost three hours when he saw the red truck moving along the road up on the high ground. He scrambled up, almost falling in his haste and stumbled down to the road. The sound of the engine grew louder as he picked up the branch and threw it high into the air, watching as it hit the ground and bounced once, then slewed across the road. Saur crouched down and drew the heavy-bladed knife from his belt and waited.

Fidel braked gently as he started the descent into the bend, slowing the truck down and keeping to the edge of the road. As he rounded the corner he saw the branch lying in front of him and he applied pressure to the brakes and brought the truck to a halt. He sat for a moment staring through the windscreen, then turned to Lyra.

"That was not there yesterday," he said slowly.

"Maybe the wind brought it down from a tree," Lyra said.

Fidel shook his head. "There was no wind in the night." He turned off the ignition and opened the door. "Wait here," he said. He looked all round at the scrub on either side of the road, then walked up to the branch and bent down to pick it up.

Then Lyra screamed. "No!"

He looked up and saw a tall figure, dressed in rags, bearded face with glittering eyes that raged at him as he came out of the scrub and hurled himself down onto the road, shrieking his name, "Bardi!" and Fidel realised with a convulsive horror that it was the man that had obsessed him ever since he had returned to the island.

Fidel dropped the branch and tried to lunge to one side as Saur smashed into him. They sprawled out in the road, Saur on top, lunging at him with the knife as Fidel rolled from side to side, frantically trying to avoid the heavy blade that slashed at him. Saur gripped him by the throat, his face inches away, so close that Fidel could almost taste the foul stench of his body.

Suddenly Lyra was on Saur's back, her arm round his neck as she tried to pull him off Fidel. Saur jerked his head down as she clawed at his eyes with her fingers. He released his grip on Fidel's neck, swung his arm round and struck her savagely across the face, sending her sprawling in the road. Fidel rolled to one side and lunged up onto his feet, ripping the knife under his arm out of its sheath.

Saur stopped short at the sight of Fidel's blade, then crouched and weaved from side to side, holding his own knife high in the air. He looked at Fidel, his eyes glowing in the haunted face and then, moving unbelievably fast, he came forward and slashed at Fidel's body. The heavy knife cut the shirt across Fidel's stomach and Saur stepped back and stared at the blood staining the shirt.

"Yes," he breathed. "Yes, Bardi, now it is your time to die!" Fidel felt the warm blood coursing down his body and into his groin. He moved back fast, putting distance between them. They circled each other, moving just out of range of the knives.

Then Lyra came forward again holding the branch in her hands. She pushed Fidel's arm. "Go round him!" she screamed.

Fidel began to move to one side of Saur as Lyra went the other way. Saur grunted and backed away, turning his head and trying to watch them both at the same time.

Suddenly Lyra slid forward and raised the branch over her head and lashed it down on Saur's shoulder. He cried out in pain and reeled back, his knife arm dropping to his side.

"Now!" Lyra screamed. "Now, Bardi!"

Fidel threw himself forward and caught Saur by the shirt and jerked him close onto his blade that slammed into his body just above his belt. Saur stiffened upright as Fidel ripped his knife out of his body and stepped back.

Saur shook his head as if to deny the pain, then stared at Fidel, his eyes slitted and burning with hatred. "No," he said. He held out his hand, almost in supplication. "You have to die." He swayed, then recovered and pressed his hand over the wound in his stomach.

Fidel watched as the blood slid out over Saur's fingers and dripped down onto the filth-stained pants. He moved back and held up his hand to restrain Lyra who was coming forward with the branch again. "Wait," he said.

She stopped and looked at Saur. "You have hurt him, Bardi," she said. "Look at him."

As she spoke Saur let the hand holding the knife fall to his side as the blood continued to pulse from his stomach. "Finish it, Bardi!" Lyra said urgently. "Do it now." She stepped away from Fidel and stood staring at Saur. "We must do it, there has to be an end to this."

Fidel nodded slowly, still watching Saur intently. The tall man was breathing faster now and the colour had begun to drain from his face. He swayed back on his heels, then slumped down on one knee, his eyes still locked into Fidel's. His mouth opened in a twisted grimace of pain as he repeated the same words over and over again. "You have to die, Bardi... you have to die!"

Lyra raised the branch over her head and turned to Fidel. "Why do you wait, Bardi?" she spat out angrily. "Look at him... he has no strength now."

Then she smashed the branch down over Saur's head. As the blood began to pour down his face Saur started to fall over onto his back. His knife arm rose in the air, the blade still pointing at Fidel, his lips struggling to repeat the litany of hate that had kept him alive for so long, his voice growing fainter.

"Bardi," Lyra said.

He nodded. "All right." He stepped forward, bent down to Saur and reached out and took the heavy bladed knife, wrenching it from the bloodstained fingers.

Saur's face contorted with hate as he breathed the words into Fidel's face, a sound almost too weak to hear. "You have to...." He stopped as Fidel bent closer and gripped the matted beard, forcing the head back.

Saur's eyes widened in horror as Fidel held him and brought his knife to rest against his throat. He made one last agonised attempt to speak as Fidel drew the blade over the skin, hacking it deep into his carotid artery and severing the windpipe. He lunged up, staring frantically into Fidel's eyes; then as Fidel pushed him away he fell back onto the road, the blood gushing out from the obscene mouth that gaped across his throat. His body convulsed twice, the legs drawing up, then straightening out and were finally still.

Lyra gripped Fidel's shoulder and shook him hard. "It is done, Bardi, now we must put this," she kicked Saur's legs, "into the dark water."

Fidel turned his head away from the carnage on the road and nodded to her.

"Yes. It must be quick before any of them see." He took hold of one of Saur's arms. "Lift him into the truck." They dragged the body over to the truck and heaved it up into the back. Fidel closed the tailgate and motioned Lyra to get in. He made a U-turn and gunned the motor back up the road.

When they came to the track that led up to the arm of the mountain, Fidel stopped and got out of the cab and looked all round. When he was sure that there were none of the patrols in the area he turned to Lyra. "We must be quick now," he said. "They will be here soon."

She nodded. "Hurry then, Bardi."

Fidel got back in the truck and began the ascent to the tip of the arm. When he reached the place where the track ended he stopped the truck. "This will do," he said.

He pulled the body from the truck and let it drop to the ground. "Take him by the leg," he said.

They dragged Saur over the rough ground, catching his clothing in the spiny undergrowth and tearing him free, then carrying on until they stood at the edge of the cliff and looked down at the raging waters.

Fidel nodded. "This is where he belongs."

They took hold of the body and swung it out and let go. As they watched, it smashed into the sheer wall of rock, and then plunged on down; turning over and over before vanishing into the rising wall of spray.

They stood for a moment, caught by the awesome power below them, then Lyra stepped back.

"Come Bardi, we must move now as if this has not happened," she said.

They went back to the truck and Fidel looked all round again for the patrols then, satisfied that they had not been seen, he continued the journey over to the harbour side of the island.

Chapter Thirty-Four

The two-man patrol that discovered the blood on the road immediately rang Lannon who told them to wait there for him. When he arrived, he looked at the blood.

"Have you found anything that connects with this?" he asked them.

They shook their heads. "No, Chief," said one. "We went both sides of the road and," he pointed down to the lower ground, "all down to the other track."

He looked at his companion, who nodded. "Nothing."

Lannon's lips tightened. "All right. Carry on with your work." He looked at them warningly. "No one must hear of this."

When they had gone he sat in the truck staring at the vivid stain on the road. *So,* he thought, *Saur has finally found the man he had hated with such an insane fury that it has killed him. But what has Bardi done with the body?*

He let his mind range over the facts; over everything that was in any way connected with Saur and Bardi and the ground where they had fought each other to the bloody end.

Suddenly he jolted upright. *Of course,* he thought, as the sequence of events slotted into place with such clarity, *the water that had taken down Sloan's boat.* The dark water where nothing that ever went into it was ever found, Bardi had told him.

He started the motor and drove along the road until he came to the track that led up to the arm of the mountain. He stopped the truck and got out and began walking slowly among the scrub, moving higher, head down, scanning the ground.

Suddenly he stopped and bent down, putting his hand on the dusty earth, then lifting it and staring at the dark blood on his fingers. *Yes,* he thought.

This was how it was done. He moved on, constantly checking the ground. *The woman must have been with Bardi,* he thought. It would have been impossible for him to have carried Saur on his own all this way, and there was no sign of the ground being disturbed as if anything had been dragged over it.

He remembered how strong Lyra Mora was, her physical power and the strength in her face and bearing. She would have certainly helped Bardi.

He silently acknowledged the implacable logic of the act. First the killing. Then the disposal of the body.

At the same time he felt a detached irritation that a killing had taken place on territory that he was responsible for; a crime that could never be brought to light because of a sea that totally claimed everything that went into it, and because of his employers, who were bound to Bardi because he alone knew the truth of how they had come to own the island.

He thought it through again, then shrugged and tried to put his mind back to the daily routine of keeping the island safe for the mega-rich. But the nagging sense of his work being denied stayed with him.

That night Lannon sat in his office and listened while the two men went over their account for a second time of what they had seen at the tip of the arm of the mountain. As they spoke he made notes, detailing the killing of the man known as Saur. When they finished he told them to tell no one of what they had seen.

After they had gone he poured a generous measure of whisky, sat back in his chair and thought about Fidel Bardi and Lyra Mora.

He reflected on the fact that they had committed murder and then disposed of the body in such a way that it would never be found. One part of his mind admired the way they had handled the situation, though he knew that in his official capacity he should not harbour them on the island. He took another pull at the whisky and wondered dryly what his employers would say if he were to inform them of what had happened on their island. He smiled tightly at the thought. He knew that they would want no part in it.

Saur was gone, and Bardi, the man who knew the way the island had been stolen from its people, was alive and would continue to be under their protection as long as he remained here.

Two days later Lannon drove over to the little house by the sea and parked the truck at the top of the high ground. He sat for a moment, then climbed out and walked slowly down the track, reached the house and knocked hard on the door. After a few seconds it opened and Fidel stood looking at him.

"I'd like to speak to you, Bardi," Lannon said.

Fidel stood to one side and motioned him in.

Lannon shook his head. "No, Bardi." He pointed up to the high ground. "Up there."

Fidel shrugged. "As you wish."

When they were standing looking down on the house Lannon turned to face Fidel and stared at his shoulder. He spoke clearly and slowly. "You are bleeding under your shirt, Bardi." Fidel looked down at the dark stain spreading under his shirt.

"Yes," he said easily, "you are right." He touched the stain gently. "I fell while I was holding a knife and cut myself."

Lannon let the silence build as he stared into the dark eyes. Then he smiled bleakly. "You killed him," he said coldly. "You killed Saur and you and the woman put him into that water... the same water that took Sloan's boat down."

Fidel shook his head and smiled the tooth-glistening smile at Lannon. "No, you are wrong. I did it with a knife."

Lannon took a step back. "Would that be the one that you carry under your arm?" he asked. "The one that you never leave from your body?"

Fidel shrugged, then winced painfully. "I must remember not to do that," he said. "The wound is still fresh and needs time to heal."

"How fresh, Bardi?" Lannon asked. "When did you..." he paused and raised his eyebrows, "have your accident?"

Fidel smiled again. "I think it was three days ago." He nodded. "Yes, three days ago."

Lannon's face darkened. "You and your woman killed him on the road where it bends before it goes past the top of the mountain." He turned and pointed up at the high ground. "Up there. You killed him and then you put him in the back of your truck and put him up there."

Fidel stared at him silently.

Lannon waited, then went on. "When you got there you and the woman carried him so there wouldn't be any blood on the ground to show what had happened." He shook his head slowly. "There was blood on the ground, Bardi. It was on the ground and the scrub grass. Anyone could see it."

There was a long silence as both men stared at each other. Then Fidel smiled warmly. "You are right. Everything happened just as you said." He touched his body. "Saur gave me this."

His eyes darkened until they were almost red and Lannon took another step back.

"He waited on the road, just as you said, at the bend," Fidel went on. "He had laid a branch in the way so we had to stop." His mouth tightened. "He had the face of a madman. No one could have reasoned with him." He touched his body again. "So he had to be killed." The redness had completely filled the dark eyes now. "I cut his throat while he was on the ground." He smiled, a swift drawing back of the lips that bared his teeth. "I put the blade to his throat and opened it wide." His eyes held the other man's with such a terrible power that Lannon could not look away. Fidel pointed down at the ground. "You saw the blood on the road. He bled like butchered goat." He nodded at Lannon. "I knew your people would see it and tell you and then you would know what had happened."

The redness began to leave his eyes and he smiled at Lannon. "Then we put him in the Run," he shrugged, "and he was gone." He laughed—a short explosive sound. "You can do nothing, Lannon. You have no body and no proof, only some dried blood on the road that will be gone with the first rain."

Lannon was silent before the horrific enormity of Fidel's words. Then he spoke slowly. "You are truly an evil man, Bardi."

Fidel smiled the tooth-glistening smile and for one charged moment Lannon fought with the almost overwhelming urge to smash his face into the other man's face.

"You are wrong, Lannon," Fidel said calmly. "I only did what I had to do." He made a slicing gesture in the air with his hand. "Saur left me no choice. It was my life or his."

Lannon shook his head. "And the priest on Crete… and the man who died with the priest?" He opened his hands. "Did they deserve to die?"

Fidel stared at him, the dark eyes probing, then the smile again. "Yes." He nodded slowly. "They were in my way." He made the slicing gesture again. "They tried to hold me. " He looked at Lannon, his face expressionless.

Lannon nodded. "So you came back to this place to hide." He looked around at the bleak landscape. "This was the perfect place for you." He smiled thinly. "Then you cheated your own people out of their homes, the land they had been born into for centuries. You sold them out so that you would always have a place to hide and all the money to keep you comfortable for the rest of your life."

Fidel nodded. "They were nothing; less than the goats that grazed the high ground," he said coldly.

"And you knew you could never be touched while you remained on this island," Lannon said tightly. "They paid you well, my people... they saw that you would never be poor again."

"You are right," said Fidel. "You know all there is to know." He opened his hands in a parody of Lannon's gesture a few moments ago. "So, now that you have all this knowledge, what can you do with it?" He smiled contemptuously at Lannon. "As I said you can do nothing. Your people will never let you touch me." He gestured around at the land. "All this is too precious for them to lose. And I hold the secret of how they bought this island." He smiled the tooth-glistening smile at Lannon. "I am too valuable for them to let you make trouble."

Lannon stared at him, seeing the man and hearing the truth he spoke. Bardi was right. While he stayed on the island he was untouchable.

Finally, he spoke. "Be very careful, Bardi. This island is a private place and I am the law here." He held out out his hand and turned it palm down. "There is room for you in the water as well!"

Fidel's eyes hardened and he shook his head slowly. "Do not threaten me with your words, Lannon." He stepped forward until his body was almost touching the other man's. Lannon stood his ground, looking into the eyes that burned with the redness again. They stood like this for a moment, then Fidel relaxed and stepped back. He smiled warmly.

"This is foolish." He put out his hand and patted Lannon gently on the shoulder. "We should not be enemies because a man that was sick in the head was killed." He nodded. "After all, Lannon, you had your people looking all over the island for him." He raised his eyebrows amusedly. "If you had caught him what would you have done? Put him off the island so that he could have come back again?"

He stopped and suddenly grinned at Lannon. "Or maybe you would have put him in the Run." He pointed up at the great arm of the mountain at the end of the island. "That would have been perfect... then you would have thought as I did... to lose him forever!"

He waited for some response from the other man but Lannon remained silent. Fidel's tone changed and he spoke harshly. "Know this, man who keeps the law on this hellhole. I have put papers with certain people telling how this island was stolen. If I die suddenly then those papers will go to the authorities on the Greek and the Turkish sides." He nodded at Lannon. "Yes, my friend. You see I am not the fool you took me for. I am sure that someone would want to know the truth of what really happened." He tapped Lannon on the chest. "Especially some of the others that make places for the rich to live. I think they would be very happy to see your people in trouble." He shook his head gently. "You must see that there is nothing you can do to me… just leave me alone." He spread his arms wide. "After all, now that Saur is gone I do not have to stay here anymore." He smiled the tooth-glistening smile. "As you said I have the money to be comfortable so why should I stay here and suffer when the world is out there?"

He looked very closely at Lannon for a long moment, then smiled. "Ah, I see. You do not want me to go from this place." He nodded. "You think that if I stay you can wait, and then punish me for my sins. You think that if I go you will never find me again, and you will have to live it in your head that I escaped your law and," he smiled savagely, "got rich through what you call my crimes."

Lannon shook his head. "It will be better for you to leave this place, Bardi." His mouth twisted bitterly. "I do not think that I believe you when you say that you have put papers with people telling how the island was bought. I think you only say that because you are afraid now."

"There is only one way for you to find out," said Fidel. He laughed shortly. "Are you ready to ruin the people that pay your wages because you want to kill me?" He looked closely at Lannon and smiled tenderly. "Have you not thought, my friend, how close we have become?"

Lannon stared at him. "You talk like a fool," he grated. "You are a murdering scum that does not deserve to live. We are nothing to each other."

Fidel shook his head. "No," he said firmly, "we are much the same. You want to kill me now. You feel the same way as I felt about Saur." He grinned at Lannon. "How does it feel to want to take the life of another man?"

Lannon's face darkened and he struggled to control himself. "Be careful, Bardi," he said. "Be very careful." He looked closely into the other man's eyes one more time, and then turned away and walked back up to the truck on the high ground.

Fidel stood and watched and raised his arm in farewell as Lannon swung the truck round, slamming the tyres into the loose soil and roared off up to the road on the high ground.

CHAPTER THIRTY-FIVE

When morning came, the island remained in the night, the sky a sullen blackness, sealing the land in darkness. The rich rang Lannon to ask what the hell was happening and why was there no light… was it some kind of freak electrical storm?

Lannon said he would ring the mainland to find out if they knew anything. When he got through to his people they had no idea what he was talking about. Everything was normal on their side; the sky was clear and it was just another hot day. Lannon put the phone down and looked out at the huge blanket of cloud that was sealing the island all the way to the horizon, and felt a sudden chill that he could not explain.

He rang the men on patrol and instructed them to notify him immediately if they saw anything out of the ordinary, any change in the sky or the sea. Then he walked down to the harbour and went into the small building that housed the satellite weather forecasting system.

The man that was sat before it looked up as he came in. "Something's either wrong with this," he tapped the big screen with his finger, "or that," he pointed out of the window at the sky, "isn't happening."

Lannon moved closer and looked at the screen. At the top it displayed the date and time of day, then the total forecast for the next twenty-four hours. The information it gave out was for a bright sunny day, with temperatures hovering in the nineties and no wind at all.

Lannon frowned. "What the hell's going on, Rice?" he asked. "Can't this damned thing see out there?"

Rice shrugged. "Don't ask me, Chief," he answered. "I've checked it four times already. It gives perfect forecasts for any place in the world except here." He nodded out at the sky. "Maybe it's interference from some kind of probe way up in the system that someone forgot about." He frowned and looked at Lannon. "Shouldn't make any difference to this." He tapped the screen again. "With the tracking gear installed in here there isn't anything anywhere in the world that could throw this out." He shook his head. "This is the best system I've ever worked with. There's no way it can be doing this… completely missing out on something so huge." He clicked his tongue disgustedly. "Christ, it can pick up a ripple on a pond on the other side of the world." He put his arms behind his head and leaned back in his chair. "So what the hell is going on?"

"Have you asked anyone for help with this?" said Lannon.

Rice nodded. "Sure, I rang the guys in the meteorological department in Washington." He nodded at Lannon. "You can't get in there without some kind of identification check, but you know I worked there for two years." Lannon nodded. "So I got onto a guy I knew was still there and asked him for a report on this particular area." He shook his head and grimaced. "He said what everyone else is saying; that we have clear skies and great weather here."

Lannon gestured at the bright screen with disgust. "All the money this thing cost and it can't see out the damned window?" He tapped Rice on the shoulder. "Let me know the moment this thing tells you something accurate." He leaned forward and looked Rice directly in the face. "I mean right on the second you know, Rice."

Rice nodded. "Okay, you got it." He sat forward and stared at the screen. "I'll try to raise other people that I think might help."

Chapter Thirty-Six

Fidel had sat up on the high ground all through the long night looking at the huge black clouds as they moved over the island and settled like a dark shroud over the land.

When Lyra had walked up to call him in to eat, he had refused to come down saying that he was not hungry. She had asked if he was angry with her, was that why he refused?

Fidel had told her no, there was something he had to see and he must wait in this place.

Lyra had said she would wait with him, and if he liked she would bring him food. He had refused the food, but said she could stay if she were quiet because this thing that he had to know would appear to him and he had to be ready.

Lyra asked if he had drunk much wine because he made no sense. Fidel had rounded on her angrily and told her to go if she could not do as he asked.

Lyra had stared at him coldly, then sat a short distance away from him and looked out at the dark mass of the sea.

As the hours passed and the sky remained the same, Fidel felt a sense of foreboding filling him. When the time of the dawn came and there was no light he stood up and looked all round at the dark silent land. *Even the birds have no song, and there is no morning wind*, he thought. *It is as if the earth has died.*

After an hour had passed, he used the island phone to contact the patrol at the harbour to ask them if they knew what was happening to make the darkness.

They could not tell him why, and said they thought it might be some kind of shift in the wind that would not allow the clouds to pass from the island. Fidel asked, what wind—could they not see there was no wind anywhere?

They repeated that they had no answer for him, and would he get off the line, as they had to take calls from the residents.

Fidel slammed the phone down onto the ground and stood up. He began to pace along the rocks, and then stopped and turned to look up at the arm of the mountain.

Lyra came and stood beside him. "What is it, Bardi?" she asked. "Why are you like this?"

Fidel held up his hand to silence her. "Enough," he said. "You must be silent or you cannot stay with me."

Lyra frowned at him, but said nothing.

He remained staring at the mountain, his eyes tight with concentration. Then he turned to her and spoke. "I have to go up there."

Lyra shook her head at him. "What is it, what is wrong with you? You are like a man gone mad!"

Fidel caught her by the arm and drew her close to him. "Do not ask me things I have no answer for." His eyes glittered and she pulled back from him, suddenly afraid. Then he let go and pushed her away so hard that she almost fell. He turned and began walking quickly up the track to the high ground. Lyra called after him to wait for her.

As they climbed higher Fidel felt his earlier foreboding turning to a great fear, but kept moving upwards, sometimes falling on the broken ground, and cursing, but always keeping going higher and higher. Lyra struggled after him, sometimes calling out to him to slow down, but he refused to stop or answer.

When he reached the place where the track began that led up the arm to the top of the mountain Fidel halted. He looked up at the sky and spoke.

"This is where I will know."

Lyra came up to him, gasping for breath. "What is it you will know, Bardi?" she panted. "What has made you mad like this?"

Fidel ignored her, intent on the sky over the top of the mountain. He breathed in, drawing the air deep into his body. "Yes," he said, "it has to be here; this is where I will know."

Lyra stared at him. "What are you saying? What is it you must know… and why are we here?" she asked.

"Be quiet, woman," Fidel snarled at her. "I told you to be silent."

She took a few steps away from him and stood very still.

Fidel remained in the same attitude, head up, staring at the sky above the top of the mountain. He remained like that as the time passed in the great darkness. Lyra listened as he seemed to be talking agitatedly to someone. When she called out to him in fear he ignored her completely, and went on with the fractured speech that made no sense to her.

Finally, she could stand it no longer and scrambled to her feet and went to him. She put her hand on his arm.

"What is it, Bardi?" she began, then stopped as he turned round.

His eyes were completely red and almost gone up into his head and his lips were drawn back over his teeth. Lyra stepped back in fear from him, stumbling and falling on the broken ground. When she looked at him again she saw he had fallen to his knees, with his head still back, eyes staring blindly. Suddenly, he began to scream, the sound wrenched from his body as if by some force beyond his control.

She heard the one word over and over again. "No! No! No!" It went on and on, and then when she thought he must really have gone mad she heard a low rumble, and felt the earth shudder beneath her feet, almost throwing her to the ground.

"Bardi!" she screamed. "The earth is moving!"

Fidel opened his arms wide, almost in a gesture of supplication, then got to his feet and turned to her. His face was contorted in terror and he cried out to her. "It is here… the sign!"

He pointed up to the top of the mountain. "There… can you not hear? It has come for me!" he screamed.

Then they heard the sound again, stronger this time, and seconds later the earth moved, splitting open in long thin fissures with jets of steam hissing out of them.

Lyra screamed out in fear and ran to Fidel and clutched his arm. "Run, Bardi!" she cried frantically. "Run!"

She began to drag him down the mountain, pulling at him desperately, forcing him to move, stumbling as the ground splintered open around them and steam came slicing out.

Then Lyra crashed heavily to the ground, crying out in pain, and as Fidel was pulling her up the earth shook violently; there was a colossal roar and the top of the mountain exploded, shooting a huge plume of fire into the air. It was followed by molten lava that poured out of the immense crater and began cascading down the sides of the mountain.

Fidel stood transfixed, staring at the spectacle until Lyra smashed her hand across his face. "Run, Bardi!" she screamed. "Now... run!"

Fidel turned to her, his eyes wide with fear. "Yes!" he cried out, and holding her round her waist they began to run down over the scrub ground. Already the air was beginning to fill with the ash from burning trees and scrub and they could feel the heat all around them.

Suddenly Lyra fell again, tried to get up and fell back, crying out in agony. She stretched out her hand to Fidel.

"Help me, Bardi!" she cried, looking behind her at the lava that was spreading out as it advanced, incinerating the trees and scrub in seconds.

He gripped her hand and tried to pull her upright, but she screamed and fell back.

"My leg!" she gasped, "My leg is broken!" She put her hands on the ground and levered herself up on her knees. "You must carry me, Bardi."

Fidel stood motionless, staring at the molten sea of lava that was spewing out of the crater. He spat out a mouthful of the black dust that was swirling all round them, and then reached down and gripped her round her waist and tried to pull her to her feet. When she was upright they began to scramble down the scrubland, with Lyra moaning in pain and trying to keep her weight off her injured leg.

When they were almost through the scrub, Lyra suddenly cried out and fell hitting the ground hard with her leg twisted under her body. She convulsed in agony and rolled over onto her back.

Fidel looked at the sea of molten fire, moving faster now with a relentless speed and power that destroyed everything in its path. For one moment he looked into her eyes, then back at the burning land.

"Bardi," she pleaded, "Please!"

He took a step back from her. "No, Bardi, please!" she implored. She twisted round, crying out in pain and saw the hell rolling down at them, then turned back and lunged forward catching hold of his arm. "Don't leave me!" she screamed desperately. "Please, Bardi, please!"

Fidel wrenched his arm back but she held on, her fingers biting into his flesh. He thrust her away savagely and tore his arm from her grasp. The heat from the lava was almost unbearable now and the black choking dust in the air made breathing almost impossible.

Lyra tried to reach him, her face contorted in terror. "Please, please," she moaned, "Don't leave me!"

Fidel looked down at her, seeing the abject fear. Suddenly he felt a great sense of power sweep into him. He shook his head. "No," he grated.

She tried to reach him, but he stepped back and she slumped to the ground. Fidel turned and began to run down the hill, his lungs struggling to draw in air from the thick clouds swirling round him.

Suddenly he heard his name screamed, one clear sound among the roar of the burning land. He turned and saw Lyra raised up on her knees, her arm stretched out to him. Then the lava hit her, engulfing her body in a grotesque figure of fire and she was gone.

Fidel began to run faster forcing his way through the dense scrub. As he got nearer the sea he heard the hissing explosions as the lava poured down the sheer side of the mountain and plunged into the dark water, turning the sea into a boiling mass.

Fidel reached the rise beyond his house and raced on down the slope, lungs pumping, never once turning to look back. When he got to his boat he flung himself in, fired the engine and began to move out with the lava piling into the sea behind him. He put his hand to his face to shield it from the scorching heat. Then he opened the throttle and raced the little boat out into the open water, and as he did he felt the same great power that had filled him when Lyra had begged him to stay with her. He looked back at the island.

The lava was moving like a great blanket of raging fire and he could see the huge area that had already been destroyed. He slowed the boat and shifted round in a half circle and held it there as he watched. He wondered how long it would take the lava to reach the harbour side of the island, and thought that Lannon would be getting the rich people out of their homes and onto the big yachts to escape.

He began to move out further from the shore and, as he looked at the colossal inferno that was destroying the island, he felt the surge of power again. His mind raced furiously with the emotion and he let go of the wheel and raised his arms over his head.

"I am Fidel Bardi!" he screamed at the flame red sky. "This hellhole couldn't kill me!"

He felt the blood pounding in his head, almost as if he were drunk on the island's bitter wine. He laughed, a harsh snarl that was lost in the roar of the destruction on the land.

When the boat slewed gently to one side, Fidel let it go unchecked, gripped by the awesome fury of the spectacle before him. Then the prow dipped sharply sending him pitching to his knees. He scrambled up and reached for the throttle, opened it and tried to pull the wheel over to right his course. When it refused to move he gripped it harder and heaved on it. Still he couldn't shift it, and then he looked over the side at the water lit by the flames. He felt the panic flare in him as he saw the sea moving faster and stronger, taking the boat out of his control.

He tried to see through the swirling smoke and clouds of acrid black ash that were drifting down from the high ground. Then, suddenly, the wind shifted and Fidel looked up at the great arm of the mountain that was lit by the flames of the burning lava looming high above him. He threw himself on the wheel, fighting to turn the boat round, but it remained locked in the relentless grip of the water.

As the boat surged closer to the huge jagged rocks at the foot of the mountain Fidel stood transfixed, feeling an icy numbness throughout his body. He tried to call out, to speak, to make any sound, but he was mute, his mouth working spasmodically, eyes wide and staring at the great wall of the mountain looming huge before him.

In the final moment of life left to him, and as the dark sea engulfed the little boat and took it down into the immense undercurrents, Fidel was hurled high into the air; and, arms opened wide, he smashed into the rock wall, then fell back and plunged down into the hell of the savage roaring water and was gone.

Chapter Thirty-Seven

The destruction of the island took one day. As the boiling lava continued to pour out of the huge crater and slide down the high ground, great areas of land were ripped apart by the enormous pressure exerted from below.

At the first sound of the eruption Lannon had rung the harbour patrol and told them to tell the crews on the big yachts to be ready to cast off directly their employers came on board. Then he sent two men to the high ground directly over the harbour to watch the volcano, and to ring him every ten minutes with reports on how close the lava was approaching.

He knew that if it got to the harbour before the yachts put out to sea they would be engulfed in seconds with everyone on board. He put three men to ring the residents to tell them to leave everything and get to the harbour now. There was no time left... the island was breaking apart.

When the lights went out all over the island he knew the power lines had gone. Then the big emergency generator kicked in and they came back on for five minutes, then went off.

Lannon looked out of his window and saw the building that had housed the generator had gone, crumbled to the ground. He grabbed a hard hat and a torch and ran down the stairs.

"Everyone get out!" he shouted. "Don't wait... there's no power now. Take torches and go to the harbour. Do what you can to get people on the boats when they get here!"

He went outside and stood stunned for a moment at the sight and sound of the devastation, the roar of the fire and the explosions as the ground tore open and the boiling hiss as the lava rolled into the sea.

He climbed into one of the trucks and started up the road to the high ground, turned the first corner, and then braked hard as he saw the lava moving steadily down the road towards him. He slammed the truck into reverse and began to move forward, then stopped again as one of the men from the patrols staggered out of the scrub ground and fell against the side of the truck.

Lannon got out and helped the man to his feet. "Are you hurt?" he said.

The man shook his head. "No." He looked behind him. "Christ!" he gasped. "Jesus Christ!"

Lannon shook him by the shoulder. "Where's Pardoe?" He shook him again, harder this time. "Come on, File, where is he?"

File pointed back at the inferno. "He didn't make it, Chief." He scrubbed his hand across his face. "He was behind me, way back when it blew." He shuddered. "It caught him, he never had a chance… he just burned in a second!"

Lannon looked at the lava that was now less than fifty feet away; the heat almost unbearable. "Get in, File!" he shouted.

He raced the truck back down to the harbour where he saw the big station wagons and cars of the people from the homes closest to the harbour. He got out and saw the crews from the yachts carrying supplies to the boats.

"For Christ's sake," he roared, "leave all that!" He turned and pointed up the hill. "Are you blind? That will be here in minutes… the bloody lot will go up… there won't be time for anything. Get on the boats and get out to sea before the harbour gets hit!"

As he spoke a huge section of ground behind the security office erupted into the air showering them with rocks and debris and the crews dropped everything and raced for the yachts.

Lannon ran to the shore office, went in and seized a loudhailer, went back outside and stood on the harbour wall. He switched the loudhailer on and shouted into it. "Start moving these boats out to sea now!"

He waited as the engines roared into life, then turned and spoke to one of the patrolmen. "How many of the residents got here?"

The man shook his head. "About ten I'd say, Chief." He looked up at the high ground. "Anyone over the far side wouldn't have a chance… one of our people said that the lava cut them off from us completely. "

"Not even if they'd run as soon as it blew?" asked Lannon. The man stared at him, then shook his head again.

"They're all that made it, Chief," he said, pointing at the yachts that were heading out of the harbour.

"All right," Lannon said. "Did anyone get a message to the mainland?"

The man nodded. "Right after it happened. Fowler got onto the Greek and the Turk side. They are sending help as soon as they can."

"Get into a launch," Lannon said. "Get out of the harbour. Stay well out to sea because when that stuff hits down here the water will boil."

The man hesitated. "What about you, Chief?" He gestured at the advancing lava. "Not much time now."

"I'll be all right," said Lannon. "Just make sure there's someone here to pick me up when I'm ready."

He turned away and ran back up the short slope to his office. Then he went inside and up the stairs to his room. He unlocked the safe and took out all his private papers that contained the information on the residents, and the thin file he had put together on Fidel Bardi. He thrust them all into a bag and ran back downstairs. As he went out of the door the ground burst open at the dockside with a tremendous roar and the harbour wall collapsed, letting the sea pour in.

Lannon stood for a second, watching the onrushing water, then leaped for the wall that flanked the office, scrambled up and threw himself over. He heard the water sweeping past on the other side and then saw the wall begin to crack open as the ground beneath it erupted.

He raced up the slope as far as he could, coming to a halt as he saw the fire spreading swiftly across his path. He looked around desperately, then saw a track that went up to the cliffs behind what was left of the harbour. He ran, lungs pumping for air in the acrid heat, to the top of the cliff and stood, heart pounding and struggling for breath, at the edge, looking down at the sea. He turned and saw the hellish spectacle of the island in flames and tearing itself apart, with huge chunks of ground vanishing down from sight into the water.

Suddenly he heard a voice and turned to see one of the security launches coming towards him with a man standing up and shouting through a loudhailer.

"Jump! Jump now!" The man waved, indicating to him to leap into the sea.

Lannon looked over the edge at the rocks that lined the shoreline, then looked back again at the advancing fire. He was trapped now; there was no way out for him except the sea. He waved to the man in the launch and pointed down. The man waved back and brought the launch further in and throttled back, holding the little craft almost still in the water.

Lannon walked back twenty paces, stopped and drew a deep breath, then hurled himself forward, out and over the edge. He just missed the rocks and hit the water hard, going deep down under the sea, thrashed his arms and legs frantically to propel himself to the surface.

As he did the launch drew up beside him and two of the security men leaned over and hauled him into the boat where he lay gulping in air and struggling to speak. Finally he got to his knees and looked out at the island. Almost all the land had gone, ripped apart and crashing into the sea amid the steaming lava.

Lannon turned to the man at the wheel. "Get out to sea!" he shouted. "When the rest of the island goes down there will be a suction that will take us with it!"

The man spun the wheel and raced the launch out into the open water.

Lannon held up his hand. "This will do," he said. "We're out of danger here."

They stared silently at the terrible final moments at the death of the island. Then one of the men lifted his arm and pointed. "Look," he said. "Up there! Christ!"

The great arm of the mountain was on fire, burning with a ferocity so intense that the flames lit the dark sky that had covered the island completely. As they watched, they were suddenly stunned by a great roaring sound that went on and on. Then, as the mountain tore itself apart, the huge arm began to move, almost in slow motion, tilting at first, as if able to defy gravity and remain where it had stood for millions of years. Then it seemed to launch itself out into the sky, and hang like a great arc of fire before thundering down and crashing into the water where Fidel Bardi had died.

Chapter Thirty-Eight

The fishermen had been out in the heat of the sun all day and were hauling in the long nets, preparing to head for home. One wiped the sweat from his face and looked up at the sky.

"I should have followed my father and worked the land," he grunted. "He loved the sun on his vines."

The man pulling on the net beside him grimaced. "You are wrong, Andoni." He straightened up and rubbed his back. "I have walked behind a plough and eaten dust from first light to the darkness." He bent back to the net. "A man is no more than a beast in that life."

Four men heaved in the nets to the side of the boat where they were winched up and swung over the deck, and two more of the crew loosed the drawstring and let the slippery mass cascade to the deck, where they sorted out the unwanted fish and threw them back over the side.

They were working the last of the nets in, slower now; the strain of the day telling on them, when one of them gasped and pointed to the half-submerged net. "Mother of God! What is that?"

The others crowded close to the side to look, taking hold of the net to help pull it in.

As it rose heavily out of the water they could see a human body almost hidden among the fish. They reached out as the winch picked the net up and, taking hold of it, dragged it over the side and let the contents out. As the body fell free they saw it was a man, naked except for a thin cord slung over one shoulder that held a sheath under his left arm. The body was clean and almost unmarked by the sea. Andoni bent down and gingerly tilted the body over onto its back.

The captain of the boat, Nico Dukakis, came forward and knelt by the body.

"Do you think he fell off one of the big cruise boats?" asked Andoni.

"It makes no matter," Dukakis replied. "If he did, he won't be taking any more trips." He looked at the men grouped round the body. "We should report this," he said slowly.

The men were silent. To do so would almost certainly mean losing at least a day's fishing, maybe two, while questions were asked and papers filled in by the authorities who seemed to enjoy keeping them on the dockside instead of out at sea earning a living.

Dukakis straightened up and stared at them. "If we do they will hold us for their damned questions," he said flatly.

One of them nodded. "That is right," he said vehemently. "I was on a boat last year that picked a woman from the sea." He shook his head disgustedly. "They kept us tied to the harbour wall for three days while they made tests." He crossed himself. "No disrespect, but how long did it take for them to know that death had taken her?"

Dukakis leaned back against the side of the boat and rubbed his hand over his stubbled jaw. "Then we are agreed?" he asked slowly. He jerked his head at the body. "We lose this to the sea?"

The men looked at each other, then all of them either nodded, or murmured their assent.

"Then do it," said Dukakis.

As they moved forward Andoni held up his hand. "Wait," he said. He reached down to the body and pulled the cord holding the blade over the head. He shrugged awkwardly. "It would be a sin to waste it." He drew the blade from its sheath and as he held it up the sun glinted off the steel. "Look," he said, "the water has not even touched the blade." He slid it back into the sheath and thrust it into his belt.

The men lifted the body up onto the side of the boat.

"Wait," said Dukakis. "There should be something said for him... there will not be another time now."

They bent their heads as he murmured a prayer for forgiveness and acceptance. When Dukakis nodded, they lowered the body into the water. As they watched it remained almost in an upright position, then the head went back and the men saw that the eyes were wide open and looking at them.

Then one of them gasped. "Look! Look at the hands... the feet!"

Then, they all saw, drifting up through the calm clear water, the blood from the jagged wounds in the hands and the feet. The arms opened wide, almost in a gesture of supplication, then the head bowed and the body slid slowly down into the vastness of the sea and was gone.

THE END...?

Printed in the United Kingdom
by Lightning Source UK Ltd.
117102UKS00001B/109